ABOUT THE AUTHORS

MARY BALOGH was born and raised in Swansea, South Wales. She moved to Saskatchewan, Canada, after graduating from college and taught high school English for twenty years before retiring to write full-time. She currently enjoys a stress-free life at home with her husband and the youngest of her three children, and with the family dog and her computer. She has won the *Romantic Times* award for Best New Regency Writer in 1985, four Waldenbook awards and a B. Dalton award for Bestselling Regencies, and a *Romantic Times* Lifetime Achievement Award in 1989. Her latest Regency is *A Precious Jewel*.

JO BEVERLEY has been critically heralded as an "extraordinary talent" and is the author of the critically acclaimed Regencies *Lord Wraybourne's Betrothed* and *The Stanforth Secrets*. Ms. Beverley, who lives with her family in Ottawa, Canada, is also the author of award-winning science fiction.

ANITA MILLS resides on a small acreage in rural Missouri with her husband, Larry, eight cats, and two dogs. A former teacher of history and English, she has turned a lifelong passion for both into a writing career. Her latest historical romance is *Falling Stars*.

PATRICIA RICE was born in Newburgh, New York, and attended the University of Kentucky. She now lives in Mayfield, Kentucky, with her husband and two children in a rambling Tudor house. Ms. Rice has a degree in accounting and her hobbies include history, travel, and antique collecting. Her latest historical romance is *Shelter from the Storm*.

MAURA SEGER, the critically acclaimed author of numerous contemporary and historical romances, has over 5 million books in print in 13 languages. She lives with her husband and two children in Connecticut. Ms. Seger recently contributed a devilish hero to the Super Regency *Rakes and Rogues*.

Moonlight Lovers

Mary Balogh

Jo Beverley

Anita Mills

Patricia Rice

Maura Seger

A SIGNET BOOK

SIGNET
Published by the Penguin Group
Penguin Books USA Inc., 375 Hudson Street,
New York, New York 10014, U.S.A.
Penguin Books Ltd, 27 Wrights Lane,
London W8 5TZ, England
Penguin Books Australia Ltd, Ringwood,
Victoria, Australia
Penguin Books Canada Ltd, 10 Alcorn Avenue,
Toronto, Ontario, Canada M4V 3B2
Penguin Books (N.Z.) Ltd, 182–190 Wairau Road,
Auckland 10, New Zealand

Penguin Books Ltd, Registered Offices:
Harmondsworth, Middlesex, England

First published by Signet,
an imprint of New American Library,
a division of Penguin Books USA Inc.

First Printing, September, 1993
10 9 8 7 6 5 4 3 2 1

Contents

The North Tower
by
Mary Balogh

IF IT WAS a moldering heap, she thought, peering from the carriage window as they approached it, it was certainly an impressive one. Uncle Cyrus had said it was moldering and was not at all the sort of place she would want to make her home. But it was hers. The only thing of any real value she had owned in her life. Her house, her home. Her castle. Roscoe Castle—all towers and battlements and massive, ivy-colored gray walls. Hers, though she had never set eyes on it before this moment—or on Baron Selborne, her maternal grandfather, who had recently died and left it to her.

It was magnificent, her new home. There was also something rather sinister about it. It seemed more a fortress than a home. Perched as it was on a rise of land and outlined against the darkening sky of late afternoon, it looked somewhat overpowering to a young lady of only twenty years and average height and slight build. Her grandfather had lived there alone for years and years, cut off from his only daughter, who had incurred his undying wrath by marrying unwisely, eloping when he had withheld his permission. The trees of the park had grown into something of a forest to the very foot of the rise about the castle, leaving very little space for lawns and gardens or for anything that would make it seem like a pleasant home. The sea was not far away. The land rose bleak and barren behind the castle until it fell away sheer to the sea and the rocks far below. Uncle Cyrus had described it to her. He had been there once with his brother, who had been intent on winning the hand of the baron's daughter.

"Impressive, is it not?" one of the other occupants of the carriage said. "It is not often that a woman is sole heiress to such a property, Miss Borland."

"And such a very young woman, too," the other occupant said.

Daphne Borland turned her attention from the approaching castle and looked at the thin, stern figure of Mr. Cecil Tweedsmuir, executor of her grandfather's will, and at the equally thin and stern figure of his sister, Miss Jemima Tweedsmuir, who had been appointed her chaperone for the journey and her companion for at least the first few weeks of her residence in her new home.

Until her marriage.

"But there is the condition," she said quietly.

"An easy one with which to comply, surely," Mr. Tweedsmuir said. "Most young ladies of limited means, about to take employment as a governess, would think it a dream come true to find themselves suddenly considerable heiresses with a castle for a home."

"And an earl for a husband," Miss Tweedsmuir said, completing her brother's thought and pursing her lips. "A young man, too, my dear Miss Borland, and reputed to be as handsome as Adonis."

"And wealthy enough to make you, even with your newfound inheritance, look like a pauper," Mr. Tweedsmuir added.

Yes, it *was* a dream come true, Daphne thought as

the carriage climbed the steep slope to the massive pointed stone archway that must lead through to a courtyard. There must once upon a time have been a moat at the foot of the slope, she supposed. It was a dream come true. She had lived most of her twenty years with her aunt and uncle, her father having died in debtors' prison when she was an infant and her mother having passed away three years later. Her aunt and uncle had been kind to her, but they were not wealthy and they had a large brood of their own for whom to provide. After refusing two offers of marriage—both from tenant farmers, one of whom she found dull and the other repulsive—she had decided to take employment. She had already been hired as a governess and was within three days of leaving home when Mr. Tweedsmuir had arrived at her uncle's door.

The only other known surviving relative of her grandfather's—also female—was a very distant connection, Mr. Tweedsmuir had explained. And she was believed to be living in America to boot. The baron had chosen to leave everything to his granddaughter, since nothing was entailed. But there was a condition. She must agree, within two months of inheriting, to marry the Earl of Everett, owner of Everett Park, eight miles distant from Roscoe Castle. The marriage must be solemnized within three months.

"But what if the Earl of Everett does not wish to marry *me*?" Daphne had asked, aghast.

It seemed that the earl, and his father before him, had been wanting to buy Roscoe Castle and all its land for some time past. But a bitter and longstanding feud between the two families had made negotiations difficult. On his deathbed the baron had finally agreed that the property might pass into the earl's possession if his lordship married the baron's granddaughter within three months of his death.

If either refused to marry the other, Mr. Tweedsmuir had gone on to explain, then the one remaining relative in America was to be the inheritor. Neither, it seemed, was to be allowed to escape from the arrangement by deliberately appearing disagreeable to the other.

And so, Daphne thought now as she was helped down from the carriage and looked about the large courtyard with eager curiosity, this was all to be hers for only a very short while. If she refused to marry the Earl of Everett, or if he refused to marry her, then she must look for another governess's post in three months' time. If she married him—but how could she marry a complete stranger even if he were as rich as Croesus and as handsome as Adonis?—then it would all belong to him.

Her grandfather, she decided, taking Mr. Tweedsmuir's offered arm, and stepping into the great hall, in addition to all his other faults, had been a tease.

Mrs. Bromley, the housekeeper, who greeted them in the great hall, did not seem quite to fit her surroundings, Daphne thought. She was plump and pleasant and smiling. It might have been more appropriate for her and Miss Tweedsmuir to change places. Miss Tweedsmuir, reed thin and with her severely styled dark hair and black dress—she and her brother wore mourning out of respect for the baron's memory, though Daphne had declined to wear black for a man she had never known and one who had always refused to acknowledge her—would have been a suitably sinister housekeeper for such a starkly medieval castle.

Especially it seemed so when Mrs. Bromley conducted them upstairs to their bedchambers and walked ahead of them with a candle held aloft. The candle would have been necessary even if it had not been five o'clock and fast getting dark outside, Daphne thought. The windows down one side of the long stone passageway were small and narrow. If Miss Tweedsmuir had been walking ahead, casting long shadows on the walls instead of the comfortably fat ones of Mrs. Bromley, one might almost have believed that ghosts lurked in dark recesses. And it was a good time of the year for them, too. It was almost the end of October. Daphne smiled, diverted by her flight of imagination.

Mrs. Bromley stopped finally and opened a heavy oak door into what she proclaimed to be Miss Borland's bedchamber. But Daphne hesitated for a moment before following her inside the room. Miss Tweedsmuir, like a silent shadow, stopped at her shoulder. Daphne frowned, looking at the blank stone wall ahead in the passageway. One did not expect a blank wall at the end of a castle passage. All passages led somewhere. The rounded door into the tower should be there, she thought, before catching herself in the thought and smiling outright. A rounded door? To the tower? What fanciful thought was she indulging in now? She shook her head.

"I can see that a fire is burning in your bedchamber," Miss Tweedsmuir said hopefully. "Shall we step inside, my dear Miss Borland?"

The passageway was indeed cold and drafty, Daphne thought, turning into her room only to find that the heat from the fire hardly carried across to the door. Castles, with their thick stone walls, were reputed always to be cold, even in summer. She was thankful that she still wore her heavy winter cloak.

"It is a delightful room," she said, feeling some enthusiasm despite the chill as she looked about her. It did not have any of the pretty coziness of her room at Uncle Cyrus's, but it had character, with its high ceiling and tapestry-lined walls and heavy canopied bed.

Mrs. Bromley looked dubious. "I am new here, madam," she said, "the old housekeeper having retired on his lordship's passing. I could wish that the place was warmer, but I have ordered fires kept constantly burning in all the rooms that will be in use. Perhaps a little light and warmth will dispel some of the rumors and make the maids less silly about moving from place to place unless there is a manservant with them."

"Rumors?" Daphne asked with interest.

Mrs. Bromley clucked her tongue. "Ghosts," she said. "It takes only one silly servant to claim there are ghosts, and pretty soon she has everyone believing in them and jumping at their own shadows. I have no patience with such nonsense."

Miss Tweedsmuir cleared her throat. "I hardly think such gossip suitable for the tender ears of a young lady," she said, her voice as chilly as the corridor beyond the door.

Daphne laughed. "Oh, but I am fascinated," she said. "I must hear the stories tomorrow when I have recovered from the journey. You need have no fear that I will awake screaming from nightmares in the middle of the night, Miss Tweedsmuir. I have not the smallest belief in ghosts."

"You are a sensible young lady," Miss Tweedsmuir said approvingly.

"Of course there are no ghosts," Mrs. Bromley said. "But I am sorry to have mentioned them, madam. Would you like me to have tea sent to the drawing room, late as it is? I am sure you and your lady companion and the gentleman must be chilled after the journey. A wicked raw day it is today, for sure."

"That would be lovely," Daphne said. "What is at the other side of the wall at the end of the passageway outside the room?"

Mrs. Bromley looked blank.

"One does not expect passageways to come to an abrupt end," Daphne said.

"Well, I suppose all of them must end somewhere, madam," the housekeeper said.

But there must be something the other side of the wall, if only space, Daphne thought. Mrs. Bromley was new to her job, though, and seemed not to have got her bearings sufficiently yet to answer detailed questions. She would have to wait for tomorrow and daylight, Daphne decided, and go exploring both inside and outside. The excitement of being the owner of a castle, complete with extinct moat and resident ghosts, grabbed at her again as it had at frequent intervals since she had first learned of her inheritance the week before—though she had not been told of the ghosts then.

And it was all hers, even if only for three months.

There was a massive round tower beyond the blank wall in the passageway outside Daphne's bedchamber. She discovered it the following morning when she

donned her half boots and drew on her cloak over a
wool dress and went striding off to explore the out-
doors, despite Miss Tweedsmuir's protests that it was
a cold, windy day and likely to rain at any moment.
It was clear that she had no wish to take to the out-
doors merely in order to chaperone a young lady who
was showing an alarming tendency to be curious and
energetic. But there was no need for her to exert herself, Daphne assured her. She was merely going to
explore the courtyard and the circumference of the
outside walls. She hardly needed a chaperone to ac-
company her. Miss Tweedsmuir did not argue the
point.

Her bedchamber was in the middle of the north wall
of the castle. When she arose from bed and gazed out
of her window, she found that she was looking down
into the courtyard. The arched entryway lay to the
left. What was perhaps a vast bed of flowers during
the summer was now dull brown earth. The view from
the window in the passageway outside her door con-
firmed her impression. She looked down the slope to
the no longer existent moat and inland over the tops
of trees into the distance. If she had been placed in a
room on the other side of the courtyard, perhaps she
would have been able to see the sea. Though perhaps
not. A fortress would have been built to be invisible
from the sea and invading ships.

Her explorations out of doors revealed a castle not
quite square in shape, with massive towers at each
corner, and one in the center of each of the northern
and southern walls. It was the northern one that was
next to her room. There was no entrance to it from
the outside. But of course, for defensive purposes, the
castle would have been built with only the one en-

trance. There was a rounded archway leading into the tower from the courtyard, but when Daphne peered eagerly inside, she found a stone wall where she had expected to see the beginning of a circular stone staircase. When she went inside to explore the lower passageway beneath hers, she discovered without surprise that it ended as hers did—with a stone wall.

There was a simple explanation, of course, as she discovered later from an elderly groom in the stables. The tower and the stairs had been deemed unsafe by a former baron—not his lordship who had just died—and had been walled up to put it beyond temptation's way. It was a shame, though, Daphne thought, absently smoothing her hand over the back of the horse the groom was brushing. When a castle was one's home, it should not be allowed to fall into ruin. She wondered if her fortune was large enough that she could restore the tower. She must ask Mr. Tweedsmuir. Of course, there were probably several other parts of the castle that needed restoring, too. Besides, whatever happened with the Earl of Everett, Roscoe Castle would be strictly hers for only three months. Less—a week had already passed.

"Of course," the groom was saying, "there are those who say that the tower was shut off because of the foul deeds done there."

Daphne brightened into instant alertness. "Oh?" she said. "What deeds, pray?"

"I don't know the rights of it, miss," he said. "But it's all nonsense if you was to ask me, just like all them stories about ghosts. I been here more than forty years, miss, and I never yet seen no ghosts. Murder most foul it was supposed to be."

Daphne was disappointed. No one she had yet spoken to at Roscoe Castle seemed to suffer in the least from curiosity. Most of the servants were as new as Mrs. Bromley. Even those who were not could only hint darkly at ghosts and murders. Did no one know any of the facts?

"Word has it," the groom said, "that that is what set the family here and the family at Everett Park at each other's throats all down the years. But I call it all nonsense, miss. Jealousy and greed is all that has ever been between them—both of 'em wanting the other's land. It don't do to have two men of influence living so close."

"But how splendid," Daphne said, "if the feud originated in 'murder most foul,' as you put it. I like that description. Would anyone know the details of the story?"

The groom scratched his unshaven chin. "Some of the old people in the village," he said. "And perhaps the Countess of Everett, miss. She always was keen on gathering local history, I have heard. She even writes it all down, some say. Doesn't have nothing else to do with her time, if you was to ask me."

The Countess of Everett. She must be the mother of her prospective bridegroom. Daphne's heart sank as she was reminded of what was coming within the next week or so. There was to be a temporary reprieve from the nasty business of meeting the earl and sizing him up while he did the same to her, both wondering whether they could bear the thought of spending the rest of their lives with each other. Mr. Tweedsmuir, who had sent early to Everett Park, had had a reply after breakfast informing him that his lordship was in London and would not return for a week, having assumed that it would take longer for Miss Borland to arrive.

Or because he wanted one more week of glorious freedom, Daphne thought. But in the process, of course, he was granting her one more week of glorious freedom, too, and she intended to enjoy it. But she wished there were someone readily accessible to give her a full history of the castle with all the gruesome details of the story the groom had only been able to whet her appetite with. It was so very prosaic to believe that that tower had been sealed up just because it was becoming weakened with age. It was very much more romantic to believe that it held some dark secret or some tormented ghost. All the other towers, she discovered on examination, were open to exploration even if not all of them were in excellent repair.

Mr. Tweedsmuir consented to take a short ride with Daphne in the afternoon and she discovered that Uncle Cyrus had not exaggerated either the height or the spectacular drop from the cliffs to the sea. But they did not ride far across the clifftop as the wind buffeted them quite mercilessly.

Miss Tweedsmuir sat and conversed with her after tea and played a few hands of cards with her after dinner.

Altogether, Daphne thought as she retired to bed, watching the strange dancing shadows her candle cast over the walls of the passageway as she approached her bedchamber, she was enjoying being the owner of her own home. In two or three months' time, she would probably be someone's governess, the pattern of her life interrupted only briefly. But in the meanwhile she was going to enjoy to the full her new and unexpected status and the adventure that was coming

with it. Why spoil these months by reminding herself
that they would soon be at an end?

She wondered if the Earl of Everett really did look
like Adonis and if he had the character to match.
Perhaps she should hope that he was far more ordinary in every way. What would an Adonis think of
her as a bride? She set her candle down on the dressing table in her room and peered at her image in the
looking glass. She looked very ordinary with her short
brown curls and brown eyes and rosy cheeks. And her
figure, though slender, was not exactly the type to
make a man's mouth water. At least, she had never
noticed any of the men of her acquaintance salivating
at the mere sight of her. The two men who had pro-
posed to her had needed housekeepers and breeders.

Daphne sighed and turned toward the warmth of
the fire while she undressed. She was unused to having
a maid and had told the one assigned to her that she
would not be needed until morning. It would be wonderful to see the light of admiration in a man's eyes
at least once in her lifetime. She was twenty years old
and had never been in love or the object of anyone's
love. She had never even been kissed. She really had
led a very dull life so far.

Well, she reminded herself, shivering despite the
heat of the fire, she might experience far more than
just kisses within the next three months if her grandfather's plan came to fruition.

Did he look like Adonis?

She did not know what woke her. At first she
thought it was a sound, but if it was, it had stopped
altogether by the time she was awake and listening
intently for it to be repeated. There was no sound

beyond the ticking of the clock on the mantel. Certainly there was no other sound inside her room or in the passageway, either. But then she had not woken with a wildly beating heart, as she would surely have done if there had been a noise to threaten her, like stealthy footsteps. She could hear no outdoor noise, either.

Perhaps it was just that she was cold or uncomfortable. But she was neither, she realized. She was as warm as toast even though the fire had died down in the grate. It must be very late into the night. Anyway, she had woken suddenly, not with the gradual irritation of some physical discomfort.

Perhaps it was just a dream she had needed to escape from, she thought, yawning and stretching with lazy comfort. There was something rather delicious about waking in the middle of the night and knowing that one could fall back to sleep for hours before there was the necessity of getting up. She wriggled her shoulders more snugly beneath the pillows and settled her mind for sleep.

Except that it would not come. Or the delight of being snuggled into a warm and comfortable bed with chilliness beyond it and hours to go before she must feel obliged to throw off sloth and get out of bed. She had to get up now. She could not resist the urge. She had to get out of bed and huddle quickly inside her slippers and winter dressing gown and light the candle and go—where?

It was absurd, she thought as she lifted the candle aloft, gave her warm and tumbled bed one last regretful glance, and turned the handle of the door. There was nothing to investigate, and even if there were, it was the depth of madness to do so alone with a candlestick her only weapon. And yet it was not a sense of danger that drew her onward. She turned instinctively left outside the door—in the direction of the blank wall.

Except that it was not a blank wall. She stared at the rounded doorway and the stout wooden door with a frown. She could not possibly have overlooked it during the day. It was not even as if she had glanced at the wall absentmindedly. She had looked for a door and had questioned its absence. And yet there was the door, as plain as the nose on her face. Unless it was one of the tantalizing shadows that the candle tended to throw on the castle walls. She lifted the candle higher.

Well, she thought, stepping forward, she had missed it somehow, that was all. The handle was a heavy hollow ring of black metal. She reached out gingerly with her free hand and took hold of it. It was no figment of the imagination. It was solid and cold and felt familiar in her hand. After the merest hesitation—during which time her heart began at last to beat faster than usual—she turned it. She knew to turn it inward to the door rather than outward toward the frame as one would normally do. She knew that the handle was stiff when turned that way.

Daphne caught herself in the thought and hesitated again before pulling the door slowly outward. How could she know that about the handle? She was being fanciful again. It must come of having led a rather dull life and of having read too much, though she had never before noted the tendency in herself to allow her imagination to run riot. Perhaps she was sleeping. *Probably* she was sleeping. But if so, she was walking into what was very likely to turn into a nightmare.

It was pitch black inside the tower, and the candle did rather frighteningly weird things to the twisting stone staircase that went both up and down from where she stood, to the stone wall on the outside and the huge central column about which the stairs wound. Should she go up or down? Or back to bed? Unfortunately, she realized as the beating of her heart started to become almost painful, the latter course seemed not to be an option. Neither did going down, though that was where she decided to go when she stepped through the doorway. Her body turned itself the opposite way and her feet began to climb. Just as if she were a useless traveler inside her own body and had no control over its movements.

There was somebody up there. She stopped more than once, standing quite, quite still and listening, but there was not the slightest sound. But she could *feel* that there was someone there. And that someone— whoever he or she was—had the advantage over her. It was true that she had the light and he or she did not, but by the same token the other person knew for sure that she was there and knew where she was and that she was a mere slip of a girl feeling none too courageous though she continued to climb.

There was a round room at the top, from which a narrow flight of steps led up onto the parapet. The room had doubtless been used by guards years and years ago, when the castle was a fortress. They would have slept in the room while one of their number kept watch above. At least, Daphne thought, that was what she assumed—all of it. She did not know about the round room. How could she? She just felt that it must be there. Common sense told her that it must. Only common sense. She did not know. She had never been to the castle before and there had been no such room in the south tower when she had explored it during the day.

But there it was—the heavy wooden door at the top of the steps, a door that matched the one leading from her passageway. Daphne paused again. It was still not too late to retreat to the safety of her room. What, after all, was she looking for? Why was she here? Whoever was in that room—she could feel that someone was there—might have heard her approach, though she was wearing soft slippers and was not aware of any sound she had made. Anyway he would by now be able to see the light of her candle beneath the door. But if she turned, she could hurry back to her room before he came out. And perhaps he would not come out. Perhaps he did not want her to find him.

So it was *he* now, was it, she asked herself mockingly. She knew that whoever was there was a man? Yes, she knew it was a man. She even knew who he was. Daphne shook her head and decided to go back. Towers were far more comfortably explored in the daytime. She would come back in the morning.

But her hand reached out to the metal handle of the door and turned it slowly—the normal way this time, toward the outside of the door. Her heart was beating so wildly that her whole head pulsed. She pushed the door inward quickly, staying where she was. It swung open on squeaking hinges.

Her candle, raised over her head again, revealed emptiness. Nothing. No one. So much for fanciful imaginings and nightmares, she thought, drawing a deep breath of relief. So much for dull living and too much reading. She had climbed a castle tower, doubtless looking like an eerie specter herself, only to find an empty room at the top of it. Perhaps she should proceed all the way up to the parapet and peer outward to see if armies of ghosts were creeping up toward the castle on specter steeds.

She stepped firmly into the room and took two steps forward—and froze with horror as she heard the door squeak behind her and shut with a soft click.

"I startled you," a man's voice said. He chuckled. "You look as if you had seen a ghost. I had to hide behind the door. It might have been someone else."

Daphne had spun around to face him. He was disconcertingly tall and muscular, and was standing between her and the door. He was dressed only in tight pantaloons and a loose shirt, open at the neck, but it seemed he had probably just risen from the mattress she had not been able to see from outside the door. Two or three blankets were heaped untidily on it.

He was also, she noticed after the understandable first impression of size and strength, extraordinarily handsome. An Adonis, no less. His hair, so blond as to be almost silver, was worn long and tied with a black ribbon at the nape of his neck in a style so old-fashioned that Daphne had seen it only in pictures. His features were regular, his eyes a startling blue, his teeth white.

He stepped forward and took the candle from her one hand and the bundle from her other. *The bundle?* She looked down at it blankly.

"Thank you," he said, depositing them both on a bench and turning back to her immediately. "Have you brought me lots of good things to eat? I am ravenous."

Who are you? The words formed themselves loud and clear in Daphne's mind. Curiously her fear had disappeared. There was nothing sinister about this man. Indeed—

"But more for you than for food," he said, and his eyes softened and kindled all at the same time. He opened his arms to her.

He was mad. *Who are you?*

"Justin," she whispered, stepping forward and lifting her arms about his neck as his came about her waist. She had never been held by a man before. She had never even performed the scandalous waltz, since her aunt considered it quite improper. She was being held now—she could feel him, warm and muscled and unmistakably masculine, from her shoulders to her knees. *Justin?*

"Margaret." The name was a caress, spoken against her hair. "It seems a se'nnight instead of a day since I saw you last. And held you last."

"I am afraid for you," she said, drawing back her head to look up into his blue, blue eyes—oh, so familiar, so beloved. "The hue and cry is growing. Soon they are bound to—"

He kissed her. Lightly. Only enough to stem the flow of breathless words. But she was so afraid for him. Sick with fear. He was under their very noses—the very safest place to be, he had said a week before, when he had first come to hide in the tower. But she could not believe it. Besides, matters had not been nearly as serious a week ago. Every moment of every day she had expected them to search the tower.

"Hush, love," he whispered against her mouth. "Hush. All will be well. As soon as they give up looking, I'll go home and make my confession and my peace and then do some searching of my own. And some questioning. I'll find those jewels if it's the last thing I do. I do not like being accused of theft and seeming to be the cause of the hostility between your family and mine growing into enmity. Especially not now."

"But it is not just theft now," she said. "It is murder, Justin."

"Murder?" His eyes bored into hers.

"Cleeves, Father's man, was found dead yesterday morning with a knife in his back," she said. "He must have known something. Sebastian says Cleeves told him he had seen you take the jewels, but Sebastian would not believe that of you. Now everyone thinks you came last night to kill him."

"Your brother said those things?" he said with a frown.

"So they still believe you are close by, you see," she said. "You must leave, Justin. You must get away to France."

"And leave you?" He lowered his head toward hers again. "Never, Margaret. I'm never leaving you."

She clung to him, waiting for him to kiss her again. Daphne knew for certain now that she was dreaming. She was in the typical world of dreams, where everything was bizarre and totally unreal, where she was someone she did not know, where she knew things she did not know, where no one recognized her as Daphne. In this strange world she was Margaret and about to be kissed by a man Margaret knew but Daphne did not.

She hoped she would not wake up just yet. This was just the type of moment when one usually awoke. Just before his lips touched hers he parted them so that he kissed her with his mouth rather than with his lips. There was the shock of warmth and softness and moistness. Daphne would have broken free in some alarm. But there was the dream. Margaret tightened her arms about his neck and opened her own mouth so that the kiss became a deeply physical and intimate embrace. His tongue slid deep into her mouth, and she stroked it with her own and sucked gently on it.

How could it be a dream? How could one do in dreams what one's waking self knew nothing about? Was this a type of kiss that existed only in dreams? Would such a thing be merely disgusting in reality?

"I'll blow out the candle," he said against her mouth. "It is not wise to risk even that much light being seen through the window or beneath the door. And then we'll lie down for a while."

Lie down?

"I should go, Justin," she said. "What if it is discovered that I am missing from my bed?"

"In the middle of the night?" he said. "Who would be prowling?"

"Anyone," she said. "No one, I suppose."

"Stay for an hour," he said. "I must have you for an hour, Margaret. We have been married for a week and not once have we been able to lie together all night."

Married? They were married?

"Justin." She took a death grip about his neck and hid her face against his shoulder. "I want to be with you all night and all day. I want us to be free. I want to be able to tell everyone. Will the day ever come? Or are we doomed?"

"The day will come, love," he said, loosening her grip and leading her to the bench, where he stooped to blow out the candle. In the total darkness that followed he led her to the mattress and lowered her onto it. "No more talk of doom. One day we will be together and free and will live happily ever after."

"Oh," she said with a sigh. "In this century or the next, Justin?"

He chuckled. "One day," he said. "I promise."

They were lying together on the mattress, their arms about each other. Somehow, Daphne realized, her dressing gown had been shed. Her warm flannel nightgown felt suddenly very thin, though she was not by any means cold. Dream or no dream, she thought, this had gone far enough. In the candlelight she obviously resembled Margaret, his wife. But she was Daphne. She had no business sharing a mattress with him under such false pretenses. She was going to have to tell him who she was and make a hasty retreat.

He kissed her again. And she understood suddenly what all the vague dissatisfactions and longings of the past two or three years had been all about. It was not just, as she had told herself, that she needed an amiable gentleman to marry and a home of her own to set up and some children to fuss over. It was not just that. It was this. Her woman's body had been craving a man's body to love it.

It was a shockingly improper idea. But then in dreams one could not control one's ideas.

His mouth kissed hers as before. And his hands explored, touching her in places she was almost too embarrassed to touch herself. They lingered at her breasts, stroking them, kneading them gently. Her own hands, she realized suddenly, were roaming over his back and shoulders—beneath his shirt. He must, of course, be a dream man. No real man could be so perfectly formed. The excuse for her wanton behavior and her silence was her conviction that he was a dream man.

"Love," he murmured, first against her mouth and then against her ear, causing her toes to curl involuntarily—toes that were no longer inside slippers. "Let's get rid of the encumbrances, shall we?"

She was not sure of his meaning until he sat up and she could hear him pulling his shirt off over his head and then proceeding to dispense with his pantaloons just as fast. And then his hands were at the hem of her nightgown and stripping it up over her body and over her head so that she lay naked on the bed beside him. She had never lain naked on a bed, even on the hottest of summer nights and even when very firmly alone behind locked doors.

"Justin," she whispered, lifting her arms to pull him back down beside her, "make love to me. Make love to me as you did last night."

Somehow, Daphne thought, she had got trapped inside the body of Margaret and could not make her presence known. But then she was not sure she wished to. His hand on her naked breast had her gasping for air. Besides, it was a dream. A shockingly erotic dream for a maiden to be having, but only a dream nonetheless. His thumb was rubbing over her nipple and she could feel it harden almost painfully. And yet it was not exactly pain she felt. A sharp spiral of sensation whirled up into her throat and downward, to set up a throbbing between her legs. When he did the same thing to the other breast, she found the feeling almost too sweet and too painful to bear.

"Ahh," she heard herself say before his mouth cut off the sound.

What followed took her completely beyond the realm of thought into that of pure sensation. His hands and his mouth touched every part of her body, even the most intimate place of all, intensifying that sweet stabbing pain until, at the point when it became finally unbearable, she shuddered into unexpected sweetness. And then building it all over again until once more she went shuddering over the edge into glory. She was only half aware of the fact that her own hands and legs and mouth were not idle, but were drawing gasps and moans from him as he worked on her.

It was only when finally, after what must have been fully half an hour of fondling and kissing and exploring, the full weight of his body came down on her and between her spread legs that thought returned. And awareness. And the realization that her body was about to be penetrated. Daphne's? Or Margaret's? Was she really sleeping? Could this possibly be a dream? But could it possibly be reality? There was no door into the tower. No man, even in candlelight, could really mistake her for his own wife. Even in darkness he could not mistake her unawakened virgin body for the more experienced one of his wife. In reality she could not have called a stranger by name or told him all the things she had told him before they started to make love.

No, it could not be reality. Yet it did not feel like any other dream she had ever had.

"Together," he said, finding her mouth with his again. "Now and always, Margaret. To the end of time."

She was sore and aching. The hard length of him coming into her was painful. But painful only in the

way that all his touches had been that night. Painful
with a sweet ache that begged to be taken to the brink
of madness and over into beauty and peace. There
was not the sharp pain of a sealed passage being
opened. She was not a virgin. She must be Margaret.

"I love you,". she said. "Make us one, Justin. All
the way one. Give me your seed." She twined her legs
about his powerful thighs, tilted herself, and tightened
inner muscles to pull him deeper.

But he would not stay deeply imbedded in her. He
drew out of her—*almost* out—and slid back in again,
and when she sighed, did it again and again and again.
There was a rhythm that her own motionless body felt
and responded to until she was moving with him, at
first slowly, then faster, then with frenzied need. She
could hear both of them panting—an erotic accompa-
niment to the energetic dance of bodies joined at the
core.

She was approaching the precipice again. But this
time they were approaching it together. Her body
could feel that as she tightened the hold of arms and
legs about him. They were going to fall together, their
bodies locked in the deepest intimacy. They were
going together.

He thrust into her and held deep and firm instead
of withdrawing once more. She pushed down onto
him. There was a moment when she feared being
stranded on the edge of pain, when she was afraid he
would fall and leave her alone and lonely. But then
they were over the precipice, together, falling free,
only the freedom and the fall of any importance in
this life. She clung to his damp, panting body, too
exhausted even to wish that they would never land.

"Like last night?" he said ages and ages later—but

how could she have fallen asleep if she already was asleep? "It was many times better than last night, love, just as last night was better than the night before."

"I am still so very inexperienced," she said. "I have had only a week of lessons."

He chuckled. "You learn quickly and well," he said. "An apter pupil I could not ask for. And you have a strong instinct, love. You are teaching me as surely as I am teaching you."

"How long did we sleep?" she asked.

His arms tightened about her and the laughter went from his voice. "We loved for a long time, Margaret," he said, "and slept as long, I am afraid. You had better go. I don't want you in trouble. Each day I vow that when you bring me food at night, I will insist that you return to your room immediately. And each night I do this to you."

"*With* me," she said, kissing him warmly. "With me, Justin."

"You must go," he said. "There is enough food and water to last me for two days, love. Have one safe night at least and stay in your room tomorrow. I did not anticipate having to stay so long when I first came here. Then it was only reluctance to go home and face Paul that kept me here. Now there is all this business of a theft and a murder."

"I'll be back tomorrow night," she said fiercely.

He got up from the bed, and she could hear him striking a flint to light the candle. She sat up and pulled her nightgown on over her head. When the light flared, she located her dressing gown on the floor and drew it on, belting it firmly at the waist. She got to her feet and slid them into her slippers.

"Go then," he said, turning to her and handing her the candle. "Go quickly, my love."

So very handsome he was, this stranger who was so familiar and so dear. This stranger with whom she had been actively and vigorously intimate for more than half an hour on that mattress with its tumbled blankets.

"Justin." Her voice was high-pitched, on the verge of tears.

"All will be well." He framed her face with his hands and kissed her lips softly. "All will be well, Margaret. I promise."

She smiled at him, deliberately swallowing her fear. She wanted him to remember her smile during the coming day until she could come back to him tomorrow night. She turned to the door. There was a box behind the door with a cracked bowl and a jug of water and his shaving things standing on it. And a small looking glass. Daphne moved to one side of the door to glance into the glass.

Her own face looked back at her. It was surrounded by long ringlets of her own hair color, considerably disheveled. There was a frill at the neck of her nightgown, and the gown itself was of a fine material. She wore no dressing gown. She was dressed as a bride might dress when going to her husband to be loved.

He was easing the door open quietly and peering out and downward. Though if anyone had been there, the candle would have betrayed them. No one would be there. No one ever came to the north tower. That was why she had suggested it as a hiding place—just for the one night, before they brought the wrath of both their families down on their heads by announcing their secret marriage. And of course her bedchamber was next to the door into the tower.

"Good night, my love," she said, raising her face for one more kiss.

"Good night, Margaret," he said. "Thank you for the feast." He grinned, making her stomach leap inside her. "And for the food bundle. I am going to raid it now."

She laughed. *She* was the feast? But then so was he.

And then she was making her way down the stairs, holding up the hem of her dressing gown as she descended. Going down the steep stone stairs of a castle tower was always more frightening than going up. She was relieved to see the door into the upper passageway and to be out in it again and then inside her bedchamber. No one had seen her. She closed the door and leaned back against it.

He would be safe. No one would find him there. Who else's room was situated in this passageway? But Daphne could no longer think with Margaret's mind. She tried to. She wanted to let Margaret tell her through her thoughts exactly who Justin was and why they had married secretly a week ago. She wanted to know more about the jewelry theft and the murder and more about the brother—Sebastian?—and the hostility between their two families.

But Margaret had gone as surely as Justin had been left behind in the tower.

Daphne was cold again. She shivered. She reluctantly abandoned her dressing gown and slippers and dived beneath the bedcovers, now cold. That was it, she thought. She was cold. That was what had woken

her. In reality she had just woken up—because she
was cold and because she had had a bizarre dream.

Oh, but what a dream, she thought, turning over
onto her side and sliding one hand beneath the pillow.
She closed her eyes tightly and tried to identify the
leftover ache that his hands and his body had created
on and in her. But there was nothing. Only the memories. The vivid memories that set her to yearning and
sighing and even shedding a few tears.

Justin!

She was lost. Hopelessly lost. Deeply, deeply in
love with him. With a dream man. What a dreadful
and ridiculous fate, she thought with a thread of
humor, to be in love with a dream man. To have the
rest of her life blighted by it. For it would be blighted.
How could she ever love or even mildly desire another
man after knowing Justin?

How would she be able to listen to the addresses of
the unknown Earl of Everett sometime within the next
two months?

Perhaps by morning, she thought, addressing herself
firmly to sleep, she would be able to see the dream
in better perspective. Perhaps by morning she would
not be so achingly and foolishly in love with a dream.

The next day was far milder than the last. At least
the wind was not blowing with such force. She would
go for a ride, Daphne decided after an early luncheon.
She would ride along the top of the cliff and breathe
in some fresh air. Perhaps she could get rid of the
terrible burden of last night's dream. She would take
a groom with her—perhaps the elderly one she had
spoken with the day before. Miss Tweedsmuir, she
was fast discovering, was not an outdoor person. Even

the stroll they had taken about the courtyard during the morning had brought a martyred expression to her face. And Mr. Tweedsmuir had ridden out on some business.

The door into the tower had not been there this morning, of course. The first thing Daphne had done when she woke from a surprisingly sound sleep to find full daylight streaming through her window, was to jump out of bed, race to the door, and peer out and to her left. There was only a blank wall at the end of the passageway. Indisputably blank. There was no possible chance that any shadows hid the existence of a heavy oak door.

And so it really had all been a dream. She had known it, of course. After she had closed her door again, she had lifted her hands self-consciously to her breasts. There was no lingering soreness to suggest that a man had held and fondled and kissed and suckled them just a few hours before. She did not touch between her legs, but she stood very still, pulling in with inner muscles, trying to feel the awareness that a man had been there not so very long before, moving there in the vigorous act of love she could remember so clearly. But her body felt unused. Virgin.

It had all been a dream. Of course it had. How could she even for a moment have hoped—though she had told herself that she was doing no such thing—that it had been real? How could she even have thought it desirable that it be so? To have been mistaken for a man's wife. To have been bedded so very, very thoroughly because of the mistake. To have lost her virtue to another woman's husband. To have risked bearing his child. She could clearly remember begging him— or had it been Margaret begging?—to put his seed in her. Daphne would never even have thought those words, let alone spoken them aloud. Dreams were strange things.

As she rode out, hatless despite Miss Tweedsmuir's reproachful glance and hint that dear Miss Borland had perhaps forgotten to put on her riding hat, she tried to forget those words and the passion with which she—or Margaret—had spoken them. She tried to forget everything that had happened. Erotic dreams must be sinful, she was sure. They were certainly not seemly. How would she ever be able to bear the ordinariness of a real marriage if in her dreams she built such expectations?

She had known for a long time what happened between a husband and wife in the marriage bed. On two separate occasions—and feeling a fascinated guilt both times—she had watched two of her uncle's dogs coupling and had realized that much the same process must be involved when a man and a woman were in bed. But those couplings had been over in a matter of seconds or at the most in one or two brief minutes. She had never dreamed—and perhaps *dreamed* was an appropriate word—that so much could precede the actual coupling. So much that had been delightful beyond words and that had made the final joining of bodies so unbearably sweet.

Perhaps in real life lovers did not play like that. How would she be able to bear real life? And perhaps real life would not even have a husband to offer her. If she could not bring herself to marry the Earl of Everett, or if he would not marry her, then she would become a governess. Governesses rarely married.

How could she go through life without experiencing that again?

Someone was galloping up beside her horse. The groom. And he was clearing his throat apologetically and suggesting that perhaps it was a little reckless for Miss to be galloping on such uneven ground and so close to the edge of the cliff. Daphne smiled her apology and reduced her horse's speed to a safe canter. She had not even realized that he was galloping. The groom faded to a respectable distance behind her again.

But it would not even be enough, she realized suddenly, to experience *that* again. Not with just any man. It was with Justin she wanted to make love. It was Justin she loved. Her heart ached for him. It had been like a lead weight in her bosom since she had risen that morning and seen that blank wall and known that there was no way back to him. She was still as hopelessly in love with him as she had been before she fell back asleep last night.

She was in love with a dream man. Deeply. Irrevocably. She had made love with him. She had given herself to him, opened her body to him, received him and his seed inside herself. More than all that—she had given all of herself, not just her body, and had felt him give all of himself. She could not do any of that with anyone else. She felt as closely bound to him as if he really were her husband. She longed for him, felt that she could not live without him.

The fresh air unfortunately had not done much good, she thought ruefully as she turned finally for home. She would have to try the power of common sense over the coming days. Common sense did not usually fail her. She had had a heap of it ever since she had been old enough to realize that she could not expect a great deal of life because she was poor. It

had been as simple as that. Life had been very simple
until Mr. Tweedsmuir had turned up on Uncle Cyrus's
doorstep.

There was a strange carriage standing outside the
carriage house next to the stables. She looked inquir-
ingly at the groom as he helped her down from the
back of her horse.

"The Countess of Everett, miss," he said.

"Oh." Daphne's heart sank. Her future mother-in-
law come to look her over? And she was rosy-cheeked
and doubtless rosy-nosed, too, from her ride. Her hair
was probably a riot of tangled curls. She hurried in
the direction of the great hall, hoping that she could
slip up to her room and somehow restore herself to a
semblance of respectability before entering the dread
presence of his mother.

She hated the poor man even though she had not
yet set eyes on him. And his mother.

The Countess of Everett was beautiful. And young.
If she was the earl's mother, Daphne thought while
making her curtsy in the drawing room where Miss
Tweedsmuir had been entertaining the visitor, then
the earl himself must be an infant. Heavens, her
grandfather was trying to marry her off to a boy.

"Ah, lovely," the countess said, getting to her feet
in order to cross the room, and extending an elegant
hand to Daphne. She was smiling. "And what an
awful thing to say aloud. It quite gives me away, does
it not? I have been hoping that my son's selected bride
would be young and lovely, almost as if those two
qualities are the only ones that matter. And what have
you been hoping with regard to me, my dear?"

"That you would not be a dragon," Daphne said,

noticing the grimace of embarrassment on Miss Tweedsmuir's face.

The countess laughed. "I don't believe I am," she said. "But that will be for you to decide. Come and talk to me, Miss Borland. Daphne, is it not?"

Daphne followed her across the room and seated herself before accepting a cup of tea from Miss Tweedsmuir. She felt almost as if she were the guest and the countess the hostess.

"It seems very ill-mannered of my son to be from home," the countess said, picking up her own abandoned cup and sipping from it. "He needed to spend a week or so in London, and we really did not expect your arrival quite so soon. I hope you are disposed toward marriage, Daphne, and have no attachment elsewhere?" She raised her eyebrows, but did not wait for a reply. "It is high time my son was married—he is twenty-six years old."

The countess must be at least forty-three or forty-four, then, Daphne thought irrelevantly. With her golden blond hair and flawless complexion and slim figure she did not look nearly so old.

"Of course," the countess said, "he is very eager to acquire Roscoe Castle. Even more so than his father was. Sometimes I think he is almost obsessed with the idea."

So he would wish to marry her even if she looked like a gargoyle, Daphne thought.

The countess laughed. "I have stunned you into silence," she said. "I am sure he will be equally eager to acquire you, Daphne—as a bride. Come, tell me something about yourself."

Daphne did, and the conversation continued for almost half an hour. At least, she thought after a while, if it was of any importance whatsoever, she was going to have a mother-in-law she would like.

The countess got to her feet eventually and took her leave of Miss Tweedsmuir. She smiled at Daphne. "Don't have my carriage brought to the door," she said. "Stroll to the carriage house with me, Daphne."

"How do you like Roscoe Castle?" she asked when they were outside.

"I love it," Daphne said without hesitation. And she meant it, too, though she had not yet been forty-eight hours in her new home.

"It is very ancient and very uncozy," the countess said, "but it does seem to have that effect on people. My son is determined to have it, you know. It is the one fixed goal of his life."

"What do you know of its history?" Daphne asked.

The countess smiled. "You mean the ghosts?" she said. "Has someone been terrifying you with them already? Or have they not been mentioned and I am frightening you?"

"Tell me about them," Daphne said.

"They seem to be confined to the north tower," the countess said. "It is sealed, as perhaps you know. Maybe it is for that very reason that various people have claimed to see a faint light from the top window at night and to have heard the sounds of clashing swords and a scream."

Daphne shivered. "You think it all nonsense?" she asked.

"I think it unutterably exciting," the countess said, "given the history of that tower. No." She laughed and held up a staying hand. "You do not need to ask the question. Folklore has it that a hundred years or so ago relations between Baron Selborne and Viscount

Everett—the earldom came later—were strained because the viscount was poor yet seeking a marriage with the baron's only daughter. They deteriorated ever further when the daughter and the viscount's younger and even less wealthy brother became enamored of each other—the viscount was none too pleased either, from all accounts. The baron's younger son, who had been a boyhood friend of Everett's brother, was somehow caught in the middle. And then, under guise of calling secretly upon the sister, Everett's young brother stole a box of valuable jewels from the castle and then murdered the baron's valet, who had seen him do it—but who first had reported to the baron's son. Or so the story goes, Daphne. There must have been a great deal more to it. The jewels were never found and the accused thief was soon dead and unable to speak up for himself."

Something lurched painfully inside Daphne.

"It seems that the young man was daring enough to hide right in the castle—in the north tower, of course—while the countryside was being scoured for him," the countess said. "His young lady was taking provisions to him there. But her brother followed her one night and there was a terrible fight."

"And the man who was hiding died?" Daphne said, hardly able to get the words past her lips.

"There were no survivors," the countess said. "It all left a terrible bitterness between our families that has never been properly healed, though very few people still know the origin of the feud. I uncovered the story only because I am insatiably curious. There must be some truth to it, I suppose, else why would the tower have been sealed off? It looks stout enough, does it not?"

Daphne looked toward the tower and swallowed painfully. "What were their names?" she asked.

Her ladyship's footman was waiting to hand her into her carriage. But she paused, one foot on the lower step. "That I do not know," she said. "It would be satisfying to be able to give them names, would it not? It has been lovely meeting you, my dear. I do hope you will look kindly on my son's suit when he returns from London and comes to wait on you."

Daphne smiled and raised a hand in farewell. Their names were Justin, Margaret, and Sebastian, she thought. And she had not been dreaming. Somehow last night she had been caught up in events that had happened one hundred years ago. She had not been dreaming.

She was in love with a man who had lived one hundred years ago. And died there in the tower soon after the encounter she had relived last night. She felt a pain and grief as powerful as if she had lost a real lover.

She had not been dreaming.

Daphne explored every inch of the castle during the next three days. Miss Tweedsmuir showed no eagerness to traipse after her since the rooms that were not in frequent use were chilly—no, downright cold would be a better description; the rooms with fires in them were chilly. The long passageways were drafty. Daphne explored alone, and the feeling she had had since her arrival that this was home, that this was where she belonged, grew on her with every passing moment.

She would have to marry the Earl of Everett, she decided, if he would have her. She had been at Roscoe Castle less than a week, but already she knew that if she was forced to leave she would be haunted by it for the rest of her life. And yet it was neither a beautiful nor a comfortable home. She did not know quite what its aching attraction was. Or perhaps she did.

The castle held all that remained of Justin. His spirit. His ghost, perhaps. Or perhaps neither, but only her memories of him—of that night when she had somehow been projected back into history as Margaret and had gone to him in the tower. It had happened only that once. She had awoken each night since and lain in her bed trying to feel the overpowering urge she had felt on that occasion to get up and go from the room. But there had been no compulsion, only painful hope and a longing to relive that night. On each occasion she had got up anyway and lit a candle and opened the door of her room to peer out. But each night the candlelight had revealed only a blank stone wall at the end of the passage.

It seemed it was never to happen again. And yet her yearning grew and her aching, hopeless love for a man who had lived a century before and had loved another woman. And yet Margaret had not been another woman on that particular night. Margaret and Daphne had been one. He had loved Daphne as much as Margaret.

She was never to see him again. But she knew that she would always want to live at the castle so that she could be close to him. Close to his lingering spirit. Of course, if she married the Earl of Everett, she would move to his home. She would live at Everett Park. But still she would be close to Roscoe. She would be able to ride there occasionally to hug close the memories—the memory. Alas, there was only the one.

But it was a memory that she would wrap about herself like a cloak for the rest of her life, she knew.

Miss Tweedsmuir accompanied her on a return visit to Everett Park three days after the countess had called on her. The house was a magnificent manor, she discovered, and the park splendidly laid out and well kept. Even at the end of October it looked neat, its lawns almost free of dead leaves although the trees were already shedding their multicolored load. The house was light and warm, cozy and elegant inside. The countess was gracious. The earl had sent word that he would be home the next day.

"My dear Miss Borland, you are indeed a fortunate young lady," Miss Tweedsmuir said as they rode home in the carriage. "Soon to be married to an earl and surely a personable young man if he is anything like his dear mama."

Daphne hoped somehow that he would not be too personable. If he were, and if they married, she would feel guilt. For she would never be able to concentrate all her affections on him. She would always dream of Justin. Her heart would always ache for him.

"And soon to move to that luxurious home," Miss Tweedsmuir added, "and be able to get away from that dreadful castle if you will excuse me for calling it that. It is a wonderful piece of history and worthy of being visited by travelers. But it is scarcely a comfortable home, I am sure you would agree. I worry that you will catch a chill there."

"It *is* cold there at this time of year," Daphne agreed. But she loved it. It haunted her. It was in her blood although a week ago she had never even seen it. She could not bear to leave it. She felt as if she had lived there for a hundred years and now someone was trying to wrench it away from her.

"You must select your very prettiest dress and have your hair freshly washed the day after tomorrow," Miss Tweedsmuir said. "His lordship is sure to wait upon you. Perhaps he will even make his offer. How like the Cinderella story this is, my dear Miss Borland." She beamed, the first time Daphne had seen her smile. "Just a short while ago you were preparing to become a governess, and now you are to be a countess."

She did not want to be a countess. She did not want to think of marriage just yet, though she supposed she would eventually. She could not grieve for a hundred years' dead lover for the rest of her life. But she would have liked some time to let the rawness of the pain become dull. She did not have that luxury. She had to agree to marry the earl within a month and a half. She had to be married to him a month after that.

"It *is* rather like a dream come true, is it not?" she said, smiling. Despite herself she was becoming rather fond of Miss Tweedsmuir. "But perhaps he will not have me."

"Not have you?" Miss Tweedsmuir's tone was indignant. "If he will not, he must be the most foolish young man in the kingdom. Not only would he be losing Roscoe Castle and all its wealth and properties, but he would be losing one of the prettiest and pleasantest-natured young ladies of my acquaintance."

Daphne laughed and startled her companion to no small degree by leaning across to the opposite seat of the carriage and hugging her.

She knew as soon as she awoke that it was different from the last three nights. And yet she dared not hope too much. Perhaps she felt that urge to get up and go and that deep, deep yearning only because she wanted to feel them, only because she knew that the Earl of Everett was returning home tomorrow and would probably come the day after to force her to a decision.

She was shivering more from nervous excitement than from cold as she swung her legs over the edge of the bed and wriggled her feet into her slippers. She drew on her dressing gown, tightened the sash, and lit the candle with deliberate thoroughness. It had happened once. It could not happen again. She opened the door of her chamber and stepped out into the passageway, looking to the right rather than to the left. She was afraid to look left. She was delaying the moment. There would be only a blank wall there, of course.

But the door was there, looking so massive and solid that she was amazed she could not see it beyond the shadows in the daytime. And yet, real as it was and much as she had longed for three days to see it again, she reached out hesitantly to take the metal handle. She should just turn around and go back to bed, she thought. She should not deliberately step back into history and get herself involved in its passions. Perhaps she would get caught there. Perhaps she would not be able to come back.

She turned the handle. But that would mean that she could stay with Justin. That was what she had yearned for for three days and nights. He had died, though. He had died without ever getting out of the tower. She felt sick with grief again. And with fear.

But for now he was alive. And for now she had found the way back to him. And life, she realized, could be lived only one moment at a time. She would enjoy each moment, then, until she must be separated from him forever by the barriers of death and a hundred years. Lady Everett's words, "There were no survivors," echoed in her mind for a moment, but she ignored them and stepped through the doorway.

He was there. She could feel that he was there above her, awaiting her in silence and in darkness. But she would not have heard him even if he had made some inadvertent sound. The wind was howling beyond the walls and the slit arrow windows. It sounded like a hurricane. She had not noticed the wind when she had been in her bedchamber. There was no light beyond the windows. No moonlight, no starlight. Only total blackness. The light of her candle, guttering in the draft of the stairwell, seemed very fragile.

She pushed open the squeaky door at the top of the stairs and peered inward. The room looked as deserted as it had before. But she could feel his presence.

"Are you hiding behind the door again?" she asked.

He chuckled and stepped around it in order to draw her inside and shut it. He took her candle and bundle of food from her and set them down before taking her into his arms and drawing her close against him.

His warmth, his smell, the firmly muscled contours of his body were so achingly familiar that she merely closed her eyes and sagged against him at first. Justin. Justin.

"I have missed you so very much." She drew her head back and looked into his familiar and dear blue eyes. He was not wearing the black ribbon tonight. His hair was loose and in silver blond waves about his shoulders. "I was afraid that I would never see you again."

His smile softened and he lowered his head and kissed her. Warmly, with opened mouth. She felt suddenly safe and happy again.

"I have got us into the devil of a mess, haven't I?" he said. "At first putting off going home because I did not know how to break the news to Paul that I had married his chosen bride, and then deciding to hide here until everyone had had time to cool down after the disappearance of your father's jewels so that I could find out what had really happened and why Sebastian had accused me. Cleeves did not see me, after all. But now there has been his murder and our two families almost at war with each other. I have done the wrong thing from the start, Margaret. I should not have delayed or hidden for a single moment. I should have announced our marriage as soon as it was solemnized. I wish I could go back and do everything differently."

"But you must not leave here yet," she said, holding him more tightly, panic in her voice. "They are talking about hanging you, Justin. Everyone, except perhaps Viscount Everett, believes that you committed both the theft and the murder. Sebastian swears that Cleeves told him he had seen you, and Sebastian has been telling everyone that I was your motive, that you needed the jewels in order to be able to marry me and get away from both Father and the viscount. If they find out that we actually are married . . ."

"What nonsense!" he said. "My poverty and Paul's have been much exaggerated, you know. And does everyone know me so little that they believe I would steal from my own wife's father? Or from anyone for that matter?"

"They will hang you if they catch you," she said.

Her voice was shaking almost beyond her control. "Let me arrange for you to be taken to France, Justin. I know some people who would do it for me—and for you. I will come with you. We will live there until it is safe to come home again. Or for the rest of our lives if necessary. It will not matter. We will have each other."

"I do not want that blot on my name, love," he said. "And I don't want it to be said that you married a thief and a murderer and that you fled with him because he was too cowardly to face his accusers."

"I would rather that than be a widow," she said.

"Margaret." He hugged her tightly and rocked her in his arms.

"I could not live without you," she said. "Life would have no meaning. It would be too empty. Too painful. I want you alive and in my arms. Oh, please, Justin, stay here and let me make some arrangements."

She wanted to tell him that he would be killed if he tried to leave his hiding place too soon. And she, too. She wanted to change history. Was it possible to change the past? But it seemed that Daphne could say nothing that Margaret would not have known.

"We will talk later," he said, his lips touching hers. "I should send you back to safety without delay. The worst part of my hiding here is that I put you in constant danger. But I must have time with you. An hour, love. We must have our hour together."

"Yes," she said fiercely. "Let's forget all else for an hour, Justin. Let's remember only that we love each other and have been married for just a little over a week. Make me forget everything else. I'll make you forget." Her fingers twined in his long hair.

It was for the last time. She knew that with a dull certainty and was not sure whether it was Margaret or Daphne who knew. Or both. Perhaps they were not after all two different persons. Perhaps they were one. Perhaps she really was Margaret. She tried to push from her mind the knowledge that it was the last time.

But he felt it, too. She could tell he did, though neither of them said anything. There was something a little desperate about the passion with which they clung together and kissed. She could hear the wind howling dismally outside. Nothing mattered but that small room at the top of the tower, sheltered from the fury of the storm, and the two people inside it, pressing into the shelter of each other's arms while the storm of events and passions beyond their immediate control raged outside the room.

"The candle?" she said as he stripped off his shirt and reached down to grasp her nightgown—she seemed not to be wearing her dressing gown any longer—and draw it up over her head.

"I want to see you," he said, his eyes roaming hungrily over her exposed body as he peeled off his pantaloons. "I want to watch what I do to you and what you do to me."

"Is the light not dangerous?" she asked, her eyes feasting on the magnificence of his naked body.

"No one will be out to see it on a night like this," he said. "And anyone who was out would have his head down. Just once, Margaret, I want to see my wife as we make love to each other."

She should have been horribly embarrassed. Her own nakedness often embarrassed even herself. She must be something of a prude, Daphne thought. But there was no embarrassment. She stepped forward and closed her eyes as the tips of her breasts touched warm body hair. His hands drew her the rest of the way against him and turned her chin so that his mouth could continue the process of arousing her. It would not take much to arouse her tonight. What they did would be done for the pleasure of play rather than from the necessity of preparing her as it had been on their wedding night.

"Give it to me the other way tonight," she pleaded as he lowered her to the mattress and came down with her.

"The other way?"

"Yes, please."

"It is good for you that way?" he asked.

"Yes. Good," she said. "Deep."

Daphne did not know what Margaret meant, but she gave herself up with unashamed abandon to the play that followed. She would not feel ashamed. She was both Margaret and Daphne. She need not feel ashamed of making love with another woman's husband. And she need not feel ashamed either of lying with a man when she was unmarried. Part of her was married and there could be no shame in lying with her husband, giving and receiving love and pleasure. Some of it was repeated delights from the last time. Some of it was new and had her gasping with surprise and pain and pleasure. The pleasures of sight as well as touch and sound and smell and taste made their lovemaking somehow more complete.

His skilled hands and mouth had her shuddering into release so many times and with such force that there seemed to be no more pleasure to receive and no more energy with which to enjoy it. Yet they were still at play. He still had not penetrated her body with his. And then he lifted her over him instead of moving onto her, drawing her legs astride his body, her knees snug against his waist.

"Yes, this way," Margaret said and Daphne understood.

"Beautiful," he said, his hands moving up to caress her aching breasts and then feathering down her sides and over her hips and buttocks and along her outer thighs to her knees. "I always want to remember you as you are now. Your eyes are more beautiful than ever when you are being loved."

And his were, too. Blue and dreamy and heavy-lidded.

"Watch," he said, and her eyes followed his as he spread his hands on her hips and brought her slowly down onto him. She inhaled. Yes, deep. There was no place to hide from him if she had wanted to hide. And of course there was after all more pleasure to be taken and more energy with which to give. This was her husband's greatest pleasure. She would make sure it was complete. She clenched her muscles about him, closed her eyes, and dropped her chin.

He lifted her a little so that he could move in her, and she opened her eyes and watched his face. His own eyes, closed at first, opened, and looked back. They both smiled. She soon picked up his rhythm. In more than a week of marriage her body had learned familiarity with his and with his various ways of making love, though each time there was something new. Tonight they could see each other, could watch each other give and receive.

She rode him, watching his face until the frenzy of approaching climax made her close her eyes very tightly. She tightened every muscle in her body into almost unbearable tension.

"Come," he said, his hands on her arms drawing her down until her mouth touched his. "You were too far away. Now we can go. Together. As usual, love. Together. Now!"

They came with a shared cresting of pain, and descended together into the world beyond passion. Daphne was beyond thought except for one intrusive and unwelcome one. It was for the last time, she thought. It was for the last time.

He hooked a blanket with one foot and drew it up over them without either uncoupling them or lifting her off him.

"Justin," she said, "I don't want to lose you. I couldn't bear to lose you. I would die if you died. I would not want to live."

"Shh," he said, his arms coming about her. "Shh. Sleep now for a little while. That was too good not to be savored. We'll talk later."

He felt it, too, she thought, her ear over his heart hearing it gradually slow to its normal beat. He knew. But he was right. What was to happen need not be hastened to its end. They had just shared a loving to end all lovings. They must have just a few minutes to savor the sense of relaxation and well-being. Instead of sleeping, she set herself to remembering the feel of him and the smell of him.

I love you so much it hurts. She did not speak the words aloud, though they were Margaret's words as well as Daphne's. She did not think he was sleeping either, but she was afraid to break the silence. She no longer wanted them to begin talking. Once they began talking, they would begin the end.

They held each other tightly and wordlessly when she was ready to leave, though she already held the candle.

"I'll slip out before it is light," he said. She knew that he meant immediately, as soon as she had gone.

There was no point in remonstrating with him further. They had talked themselves out. And really she supposed he was being sensible. Perhaps the idea of staying for a day or two in the tower had been a sound one at first, but now matters had become too serious. The trouble was not going to go away merely because he could not be found. Somehow he had to force the issue.

But forcing the issue meant danger to him. And unbearable anxiety for her—even more than she had suffered daily with the knowledge that he was in the last place anyone would think to look—Roscoe Castle itself. His leaving would bring heartache, too. Despite everything, this week had been magical. Now it would all be over.

She was thinking as Margaret, Daphne realized suddenly. His leaving the tower would be the end for Daphne. She could never hope to see him again after he had left. *If* he left the tower. History said that he had not, that he had died there.

But he was determined to leave before daybreak. He was going to go to Everett Park first of all to talk with his brother, to break the news of his marriage, to plead his innocence of the charges against him. With his brother on his side matters might not look quite so bleak. Then he was going to confront Sebastian and find out why Margaret's brother was so loud in his accusations. Perhaps Justin could uncover the truth, clear his name somehow.

Perhaps after all they would be able to live happily ever after. He had said that they would be free and happy once he had cleared up a few matters. As if there was nothing serious wrong at all. But she knew he spoke with such confidence merely to reassure her.

"Take care of yourself," she said. "Be careful."

"I'll see you," he said, kissing her once more, "perhaps tomorrow. Certainly the day after. I should have done this a week ago, Margaret." He grinned. "I could not tear myself away from our nightly feasts."

She smiled, too. He needed smiles.

He opened the door and she stepped out onto the stairs and looked back at him. He hesitated for a moment, crossed to the bench, buckled about his waist the sword belt that was lying there, settled the sword at his side, and then stepped out behind her.

"I'll see you to the door into the passageway," he said.

She did not argue. After all, he would be just as unsafe if she was discovered alone on the stairs as he would if he were there with her. The wind was still howling about the tower, she could hear as she descended the stairs slowly. The candle threw strange and shifting shadows on the walls. She felt a fear she had not felt the last time when returning to her room. A fear and a foreboding. *Go back,* she wanted to tell him. *Let's both go back.* But perhaps only Daphne had the feeling of impending doom. Margaret said nothing.

She stopped when she reached the door into the passage. "Go back," she said. "I am safe now."

He kissed her, rubbed his nose against hers, smiled at her, and reached beyond her to open the door. It swung outward. There was a man standing just beyond it, a rather stocky young man with a bared sword in his right hand. Daphne did not know who he was but she could guess.

"Sebastian!" Margaret said, stepping out into the passageway, hoping to block his view of Justin. "I could not sleep. Have you ever heard such a dreadful storm?"

But with his left arm he brushed her aside so that her shoulder cracked rather painfully against the stone wall. He did not even look at her. He stepped through the doorway.

"I am decidedly slow," he said. "It took me until today to realize that if I kept an eye on Margaret by night as well as by day, she was bound to lead me to you sooner or later. An hour and a half ago she was still in her bed. Five minutes ago she was not."

His sword was pointed upward. Oh, God. Daphne clung to the wall, waiting for the nightmare to end. It must after all be a nightmare. But Margaret was still with her and paralyzed by shock and terror. It was real. It was happening.

"I was going to find you today anyway, Sebastian," Justin's voice said calmly. "I want some questions answered. Better sooner than later, I daresay."

"I suppose," Sebastian said through his teeth, "you have been up there the whole time and have been rutting with my sister every night."

"Margaret is my wife," Justin said.

"Your wife?" Sebastian laughed. "Since when?"

"Nine days ago," Justin said. "The same day as someone was busy thieving, I believe."

"She is a slut and a whore," Sebastian said, his voice becoming hysterical. "And you are the worst kind of vermin." He lunged forward and upward with his sword. Daphne's paralysis left her and she rushed back to the doorway with the candle. She was not sure whom the near-darkness favored. But Justin, she could see, was having difficulty drawing his sword free of its scabbard in the confines of the narrow stairwell.

"Wait!" she cried, holding up a staying hand. "Sebastian. Let's talk. Please, let's talk. Can't you see that Justin is virtually unarmed. Please don't."

But he ignored her, his attention focused entirely on Justin, a few steps above him.

"No!" she said as he made to lunge again. And she stepped forward onto the stairs between them, with the intention of staying her brother's arm and protecting her husband, at least until his sword was free and he could meet Sebastian on equal ground.

The strange thing about being wounded, she thought quite lucidly and quite calmly a moment later, was that at first one felt no pain. Some shock, perhaps. Certainly the knowledge that one had been hit. But no real pain. She sank down to sit on the step above her and then lay back against the one above that. She knew that Sebastian's sword had pierced her side. When she pressed a hand to it, she felt the wet heat of blood.

And then she was aware of Justin beside her and over her, his one arm about her shoulders, his other hand touching her, assessing the damage. His face was gazing down into hers. Strange grotesque shadows danced on the walls, like hovering demons. She did not know where the candle was, but clearly it was still lit.

He was crying. She knew it even though she could neither hear nor see him clearly. She was dying, then. She was feeling rather cold. But she was strangely calm. *Let him just hold me while I die,* she thought. *Let his face be the last thing I see on this earth.* She tried to smile at him, but she knew that her facial

muscles were not responding to her will. *I am not
unhappy*, she wanted to tell him. *I love you.*

"Margaret. Margaret." His sobs were torn from him
in what she knew must be painful gasps. But Margaret
could not hear. Unconscious or dead already, she lay
on the stone steps, his arm beneath her neck, her eyes
closed. Daphne, disembodied, watched from somewhere above. She looked down on them—on the
woman who looked exactly like herself, on the man
she loved even over the span of one hundred years,
and on the brother of that other self.

"She asked for it," Sebastian said viciously. Perhaps
he felt horror or remorse, Daphne thought, but could
cope with reality only by masking his feelings thus.
"She should not have consorted with someone as poor
as a church mouse and with a thief and a murderer."

Justin slid his arm slowly from beneath Margaret's
neck. He rose to his feet slowly, disengaging his sword
from its scabbard as he did so. "In descending order
of importance, Sebastian?" he said. "My poverty is
my greatest sin?"

"She should have married money," Sebastian said.
"Lots of it. There are any number of wealthy men
who would have had her."

"For her sake?" Justin asked. "Or your own? Were
you hoping to benefit from your sister's marriage, Sebastian? Are all the rumors I have heard of your gambling and other debts true? And is your father still
the nipfarthing you have always claimed him to be?"

"Worse," Sebastian said. "He is worse. An infant
could not live on what he allows me."

"Is that why you needed the jewels?" Justin asked.
"And why it did not hurt your conscience to steal
from your own father?"

Sebastian laughed.

"Or to kill your father's man?" Justin said. "Did he see you do it? It must have seemed a nice touch to put all the blame on the relatively poor man who has spoiled your plan to prey upon your sister's husband. Where are they hidden?"

"In a secret place that only I know of," Sebastian said. He looked down at the inert form of his sister. "Now that Margaret is dead."

"Then they will remain forever hidden," Justin said. "I am going to kill you."

Sebastian laughed again. "Why not?" he said. "They can hang you only once, after all."

Daphne watched as both men raised their swords and began to fence in deadly earnest, Margaret's body and the guttering candle between them. The advantage should have been all Justin's since he was above Sebastian and looked to be by far the fitter of the two. And indeed, it seemed after a minute or two as if he would edge past Margaret and finish off his weaker, less skilled foe. But Sebastian fought with more than physical strength and skill.

"Ha!" he shouted, just when it seemed that he would overbalance and be forced to drop his guard. "Margaret is stirring."

Justin glanced down involuntarily at her prone body, and in the instant of his inattention, Sebastian's sword flashed beneath his guard and pierced his heart. Daphne watched from above, powerless either to intervene or to close her eyes. She watched him fall dead beside Margaret, slumped against her, on the narrower inner part of the stair.

And then suddenly she felt pain and cold, and she was staring upward from the stairs, Justin's body half across hers. She knew he was dead. And she was glad again that she was dying, that after all they were not to be separated. She closed her eyes.

"Foolish Margaret," Sebastian said from above her. "You could have been my salvation if you had not been so selfish. As it is you have died with your lover. History will not be kind to the two of you." He laughed softly.

He was standing on the step below her. Her feet were brushing against his leg. He had killed Justin. And blackened his name for all eternity. She was dying. She would not have the strength during the minutes that remained to her to uncover the jewels from their hiding place behind the fireplace in his room and to return them to her father.

"Good-bye, Margaret," he said. "Sweet dreams." But whatever his inner feelings might have been, there was no remorse in his voice, only a gloating kind of triumph.

She did not know how she found the strength. Perhaps it was the strength of love, the need to strike one small blow for the husband and the lover he had just killed. As he turned to step out into the passageway, she managed to stretch out one foot and hook it about his leg. She felt him lose his balance. She heard the sound of fingernails trying to claw a hold against the door frame and the wall. And the clattering of a sword bouncing downward from stair to stair. And then there was one long, blood-curdling scream as he fell backward and hurtled downward. It was followed by silence. He was lying at the bottom with a broken neck, she knew.

She tried to push one arm beneath Justin's body so that she could cradle him until she died. But she did not have the strength. She turned her head so that her cheek rested against his shoulder. The pain was going away again. She was very cold. But she was happy. Almost excited. Soon they were going to be together again. Together for always.

Perhaps it was a fanciful idea for a dying woman to have. Perhaps it was the way the dying consoled themselves and prepared to face the inevitable. But however it was, she knew that they would be together again. A love like theirs could not die, could not be snuffed out almost before it had blossomed.

They would be together again. In this world or the next. It did not matter which. They would be together again.

"Until then, my love," she whispered. "Good night until then."

Daphne was above them again. The candle had burned low. Even as she watched, numb with grief, it shivered and went out, to be replaced by total darkness. At last she was able to close her eyes. At last she had hands with which to cover them.

She held her hands over her eyes for a long, long time. When she finally removed them and opened her eyes, she was staring upward at the canopy of her bed. The blankets, drawn up beneath her arms, were gradually warming her chilled body.

She did not try to move. Or sleep.

Mr. and Miss Tweedsmuir talked with some enthusiasm throughout breakfast about the probable return of the Earl of Everett to Everett Park that day. If he arrived home early enough, Miss Tweedsmuir suggested, nodding encouragingly at Daphne, perhaps he would make his call during the afternoon and not wait

for tomorrow. It was very unlikely, Mr. Tweedsmuir
said, since the countess would inform him that he was
not expected until the morrow.

Daphne did not join in the conversation, though she
tried to look as if she were a part of it. She tried to
smile. She tried to appear as if she were anticipating
the earl's visit with some pleasure.

In reality she felt worse than wretched. She had
died the night before and so had her husband, her
dearest love. She had killed her brother. It had all
happened a hundred years ago. All sense of humor
had temporarily deserted her. She could not even appreciate the utter absurdity of her thoughts. In reality,
of course, she was merely a maiden with a vivid imagination, who was prone to vivid dreams. But that was
not right either. It really had happened. Lady Everett
had described at least a part of it. And she, Daphne,
had seen it all happen. More than that—she had lived
it.

She grieved deeply for both of them. For Margaret
and Justin. But more for Justin. Margaret seemed
somehow to have been resurrected in herself. But now
she was separated by a hundred years and all eternity
from the man she loved passionately and totally. It
was not absurd. Had she described it all to anyone,
of course it would have seemed so. Worse. Anyone
listening to her story would think her quite mad. But
she was not mad, and her feelings were not absurd.

"I am surprised you have anything left to discover,
my dear Miss Borland," Miss Tweedsmuir said after
breakfast when Daphne announced her intention of
spending the morning exploring again. "These rooms
are so chilly unless one is seated almost on top of the

fire." She shivered delicately and rubbed her hands together.

Daphne took the hint and assured her companion that she did not expect to be accompanied.

Sebastian's room, she thought. How was she to know which one of the numerous bedchambers had been his a hundred years ago? It would take her months to examine the fireplace of every room in the castle. But Margaret, when she had thought of the jewels and the hiding place, which apparently only she and Sebastian knew of, had briefly visualized a room—a room at one end of a passageway. She had even turned her mind for one moment in the direction of the open door. Was it on that passageway, then, the same one as she herself had occupied? It made sense, Daphne supposed, for brother and sister to occupy rooms on the same floor and in the same wing of the castle. Her room was at one end of the passage. Was Sebastian's at the other end?

It was decidedly silly to go treasure hunting on such slight evidence, of course, and one hundred years after the event. But she had to do something. And she found herself this morning almost obsessed with the need to clear Justin's name. No one remembered him directly—except her—and very few even remembered the story about him. The chances were that no one would be at all interested if she were suddenly to proclaim his innocence and declare that she had found proof of it. There would be a great deal of interest in the discovery of a box of jewels, of course. They would be hers, she supposed—or the earl's soon if she married him. Some unknown American relative's if she did not.

Daphne suddenly felt a deep and unreasoned hatred

for that unknown relative. Roscoe Castle was *hers*.
Justin was there. All that remained of him lingered in
the sealed tower. Oh, not bones. She did not doubt
that his body had been given burial. But he was there.
She would do anything in the world, she realized—
anything—to keep the castle. She would beg and
grovel if she had to to persuade the earl to marry
her—how she hated him, too! Certainly she would
dress with greater care tomorrow than she had ever
done. And she would wear her very best smile.

The room at the beginning of the passage was cold.
But then most of the rooms were. Daphne was growing accustomed to the discomfort. She wore a warm
woolen dress and a thick shawl. Besides, mingled feelings of grief and excitement and dread of the morrow
combined to make her largely unaware of her physical
comfort or discomfort.

The fireplace was large and surrounded entirely by
heavy oak carvings. The artist who had designed it
had decided to decorate it with a riot of heads and
leaves and flowers and cherubs and demons. It was a
monstrosity, Daphne decided, and she was glad that
the fireplace in her room was a great deal more elegant. She stood before this one, her eyes roaming over
the carvings, and tried to feel a familiarity with the
sight. She tried to feel an instinctive knowledge of
where a secret compartment might be. Would it be
inside the grate or the chimney? Or behind part of
the surrounds? Was one of these carved projections a
secret handle?

Alas, Margaret was dead, and Daphne could no
longer think with her mind or make use of any of her
memories. She was not even sure she had the right
room. She was not sure that Sebastian had spoken the

truth. She was not sure the jewels had never been found, though the Countess of Everett believed that they had not.

But she had to do something. If she did not do this, she would be obliged to sit with Miss Tweedsmuir for much of the day, since it was raining dismally outside. And if she had nothing to do but sit, then she would have nothing to do but brood. There was no point in brooding. Life had to go on. She could not spend what remained of hers grieving for a man who had died a century ago.

Daphne spent almost an hour pressing, poking, pulling, twisting. She had touched every single projection of the wood carvings at least twice, she thought finally, sitting back on her heels and rubbing her hands together to restore some warmth to them. It was hopeless. Obviously there was no secret compartment. Or else she was looking in the wrong room. She had told herself at the start that she did not expect to find anything. But she could feel now how much she had hoped. She felt like crying with frustration and disappointment.

"You," she said aloud to the carved head of a particularly hideous gargoyle on a level with her eyes. "Why cannot you be the secret handle?" She jabbed a finger at the rather prominent nose, as she had done at least twice before. She took hold of the nose and twisted.

It would be the easiest thing in the world to have a temper tantrum, she thought, to start throwing things and kicking things. But she was not naturally of a volatile temper. She merely sat on her heels and sighed.

"Justin," she muttered, "I so wanted to prove your

innocence." And she so wanted, she knew, to prove to herself in one more way that she had been neither dreaming nor imagining all that had happened. It had been real. If she could just have found the jewels, the last vestiges of doubt would disappear.

"Well," she said to the gargoyle, "keep your secret. It is all the same to me. I don't need the old jewels anyway. I thumb my nose to you." But instead of thumbing her own nose, she thumbed the gargoyle's, reaching a finger beneath it and flicking upward.

A whole large square of paneling tipped upward and inward to reveal a square, dark hole. Daphne snatched her hand back as if it had been scalded and rubbed both palms over her dress at the knees. Her heart was beating rapidly and painfully. This was it. This really had been Sebastian's room. There really was a secret compartment in the fireplace. It was a little below the level of her eyes, its base almost at floor level. She would have to stoop down farther to peer inside. She was afraid to do so. What if it was empty?

Daphne drew a deep breath and lowered her head. A box. Very much smaller than she had imagined. She had pictured a treasure chest, a pirate's chest. This was a velvet box, long and rather thin. She reached in a shaking hand and drew it out. It was covered with purple velvet, rather faded, not at all dusty as she would have expected. There were two metal clasps at the front. Daphne flicked them upward and opened the lid after a lengthy pause.

Her hand shook more noticeably. She was looking down at what she knew must be a vast fortune. Diamonds, rubies, sapphires, other gems, all set into necklaces, earrings, brooches, bracelets, pins. Even if

Sebastian's debts had been astronomical, there would have been enough left after paying them to have kept him in luxury for the rest of his life. It was no wonder that he had been willing to kill in order to keep them. And no wonder that the hue and cry after Justin had been so persistent.

Daphne closed the lid and bowed her head over it. She knelt where she was for a long time. Justin. Ah, Justin. The pain was raw. It tore at her heart until she felt she could not bear it. This was what he had died for? But now, finally, it was real beyond any doubt at all. She was Daphne, firmly anchored in the beginning of the nineteenth century. And yet she held in her hands very tangible proof that last night and four nights ago she had been caught up in the real and tragic events that had led to the deaths of three people.

To Justin's death.

Something splashed onto the purple velvet of the box top and darkened its color. Daphne set the box on the floor, spread her hands over her face, and gave in to the misery and the luxury of tears.

She was wearing blue muslin, the best color for her complexion, she thought, and her favorite color, too. Of course it was ridiculous to be wearing muslin on the second day of November and at Roscoe Castle of all places, but it was her best and her very favorite dress. Besides, she was feeling too much nervous terror really to be aware of the cold. She had washed her hair and her maid had brushed it into soft curls about her face. The color in her cheeks was high, she noticed at a glance into the looking glass, and her eyes were bright. She looked for all the world like a young girl awaiting the arrival of her suitor—which she supposed was just as well.

He was there at the castle already. She had not seen him arrive, but Miss Tweedsmuir had sent a message to tell her that if she was not ready, she must hurry as his lordship's carriage had just drawn into the courtyard. His mother was with him. They had sent a message that morning.

Of course, Daphne was discovering, she need not have hurried, though all she had needed to do was push her feet into the slippers that matched her dress. The earl was closeted with Mr. Tweedsmuir, and a discussion of the marriage settlement was taking an age. Daphne had wondered if the courteous thing to do would be to go to greet the countess, who would be in the drawing room with Miss Tweedsmuir. She was not sure what correct protocol demanded and had not thought to ask Miss Tweedsmuir at luncheon. She would wait until she was summoned, she had decided. She just hoped it would not be long. There were butterflies dancing in her stomach.

She glanced at the purple velvet jewel box, which was standing on her dressing table. For some reason she had told no one about it yet. It was too much part and parcel of the events in which she had been caught up. And she could never tell anyone about those. Though the compulsion was still there to clear Justin's name. Justin. She dared not think of him. Not now. She hoped she would not be kept waiting much longer.

And then the maid she had dismissed fifteen minutes earlier reappeared at the door to request that Miss Borland attend the Earl of Everett in the library. The girl's eyes were wide with excited anticipation.

Everyone down to the lowliest scullery maid knew why his lordship was calling.

Daphne drew a deep breath. "Justin," she whispered. But she must not think of him. She left her room with resolute steps.

He was standing in front of the fire, facing the door. She was aware of that though she kept her eyes on her hand as it transferred itself from the outer door handle to the inner one and carefully closed the door behind her. She had not once looked at him, and yet she was somehow aware that he was tall and elegant and immaculately dressed. She had caught a glimpse of white-topped, tasseled Hessian boots.

She turned toward him after closing the door and lifted her chin resolutely, remembering the smile with which she had intended to greet him. But the smile never reached her face.

Blond hair. Silver blond, cut fashionably short. Blue eyes. Very noticeably blue despite the distance between them. Regular, handsome features. An Adonis, no less. She stood very still and stared at him. He stared back. Daphne was not sure if seconds passed or minutes before he spoke.

"Margaret?" It was a whisper.

Her mouth opened and closed. She swallowed. "Justin?"

They stood transfixed, staring at each other. One part of Daphne's brain wondered if her own face was as pale as his.

"You have cut your hair," she blurted at last. The foolish words hung in the air between them. They seemed to have been spoken very loudly.

"And you," he said at last.

"You died," she said, her hands going behind her to grip the door handle. "The night before last. A hundred years ago. He tricked you and you died."

"And you," he said. "I thought you died first, but you did not. You were still alive. You died alone."

She stood gripping the handle as if only it kept her firmly anchored to the earth. He stood on the hearth as if turned to stone.

"Are you Miss Borland?" he asked at last.

"Yes." She drew breath. "You are the Earl of Everett?"

"What is your name?" he asked.

"Daphne," she said. "And yours?"

"Andrew."

"I can prove your innocence," she said with a sudden rush of eagerness. "I found the jewels yesterday morning. They were hidden where Sebastian said they were. They were in a secret compartment beside the fireplace in his room. Margaret thought of that room while I was still sharing her thoughts, so I knew where to look yesterday morning. It took me a whole hour of poking and prodding. I thought I would never find them. It was not that I wanted the jewels. I wanted to prove your innocence. And the reality of what had happened. I found them. A whole fortune in gems. I have them in my room. Now everyone can be told that you were innocent."

"That Justin was," he said.

"Yes." Her burst of eagerness faded and she leaned her head back against the door.

"You look so much the same," he said. "And you sound the same."

"And you."

He took a step toward her and stopped. He held

out one hand toward her. She looked at it and hesitated. He was a stranger. She had never met him before. She looked up into his face—his familiar and beloved face. He was Justin. She loved him.

"Oh," she said, and she abandoned the sanctuary of the door and hurtled across the room. His other arm was out, too, before she reached him. Both closed about her as her arms circled his neck and her face buried itself against the elaborately tied folds of his neckcloth.

"God!" He held her so tightly she could scarcely breathe. "You even feel the same."

She tipped her head back and stared up at him in wonder. Up into his blue, dearly familiar eyes. He was the same man. There was no difference at all except for the length of his hair and the style of his clothes.

Even his kiss was the same. His mouth was open when it met hers so that she was enveloped in moist heat. His tongue probed gently against her lips and accepted the invitation of her opened mouth to press inside. She felt the flaring of a familiar passion—and a familiar tenderness—and knew with the instinct of love that it was something shared.

And then they were looking at each other again, each exploring the other's face with wondering, hungry eyes.

"I have been consumed by grief," he said. "It seemed foolish to blight my whole life with love for a woman who has been dead for a century, but I could not stop thinking of you and longing for you. I knew that I must acquire Roscoe Castle at any cost. I had to own it and keep it as a sort of shrine to you. Even if it meant marrying the new owner—Miss Borland."

"I had to keep it, too," she said, "even at the expense of marrying a stranger. I have wished and wished for two days that I could have died with Margaret. Or that if I really was Margaret I could have stayed dead."

His eyes smiled into hers. Justin's eyes. "It happened to you only the night before last?" he asked.

"And three nights before that," she said. "Nothing bad happened that first time except that I could not get back there for three more nights and thought I would never see you again. I felt stranded across an ocean of time."

"We just made love that first time?" His eyes were still smiling into hers. Daphne could feel herself flushing.

"Yes."

"It was wonderful, wasn't it?" he said.

Her cheeks felt as if they were on fire. She nodded. "How did it all happen to you?" she asked.

"I considered buying Roscoe Castle because my father had always wanted it and your grandfather was always hinting about selling," he said. "But there was always that enmity between our families. He was only teasing us, I believe. After the first time I called on him, two months ago, he told me to look around to my heart's content. And so I wandered about the courtyard and into the north tower and up the stairs and found myself in another world in the middle of the night although it was supposed to be afternoon. I found myself clothed differently. And then I heard or felt you come up the stairs and I hid behind the door. When I first saw you, looking like someone out of another century, I wanted to ask you who you were and what was happening. But I found myself

speaking someone else's thoughts and feeling someone else's emotions. Although they felt like my
thoughts and my emotions, too. And then we made
love. You were my wife, I discovered. And I loved
you more than life."

It had been Andrew and Daphne making love as
well as Justin and Margaret, then? Or were Andrew
and Justin one and the same person? Were she and
Margaret one? "There was no stone wall at the bottom of the tower stairs?" she asked.

"Not on that occasion," he said, "and I did not
know there was supposed to be. Not until I went there
the next time and the next and found no way up. That
was when I asked my mother about Roscoe Castle.
She revels in piecing together stories of the past. I
learned that I had got somehow involved in events
that really had happened."

"But you did go back again?" she said. "You know
about our death—about Justin's and Margaret's."

"I called after your grandfather died," he said. "I
went at the bidding of the executor of his will, Mr.
Tweedsmuir, since it seemed that the will had something in it that concerned me. Of course I went to the
tower before returning home—for weeks I had been
sick with longing to find you again. And I found you
and loved you. And lost you."

She rested her face against his neckcloth again. It
was only then that she realized they still had their
arms about each other, that their bodies were still
pressed together. But he did not feel like a stranger.
He was not a stranger. He was Justin—Andrew. He
was her love. He had been her love for a hundred
years and would always be her love.

"Are we the same people?" she asked him.

"Yes and no," he said. "You are Daphne. I am Andrew. We are living in a different century. I am the Earl of Everett rather than a younger son. You are the owner of Roscoe rather than a daughter of the house. We both have short hair." He chuckled and set a cheek against her curls. "But I think that after just a few minutes of acquaintance in this century we already love each other deeply. Because we have loved for a long time. We are continuing the love of Justin and Margaret. We are, aren't we?"

"You always said we would be free to be together and to love one day," she said.

"I remember you asking me if it would be in this century or the next," he said. "I don't believe you realized what a serious question it was."

Daphne sighed. "I was so dreading this meeting," she said.

"Me, too," he said. "I have been hating you, sight unseen."

Daphne sighed again.

"Will you marry me, then?" he asked. "That, after all, is why I came here, is it not?"

She raised her head and smiled up at him again. "But we are married already," she said.

"I believe there is an obscure rule in canon law," he said, "that after each one hundred years marriage vows must be renewed."

They both laughed. And kissed. And rubbed noses. And murmured nonsense to each other.

They were caught in each other's arms when the countess tapped on the door and opened it almost simultaneously. Miss Tweedsmuir was peering over her shoulder.

"Oh, my," Miss Tweedsmuir said, and turned an interesting shade of mottled pink.

"Splendid!" the countess said. "The suspense is over. Daphne must have said yes."

Daphne flushed. But the earl would not release her. He turned her to face the new arrivals, but kept her at his side with an arm about her waist.

"You might say it was love at first sight, Mama," he said. "Was it not, Daphne?"

"Oh, my," Miss Tweedsmuir muttered again. His lordship was already addressing dear Miss Borland with great familiarity.

"Yes," Daphne said, smiling and blushing and breathless.

"In fact," the Earl of Everett said, his blue eyes laughing down into hers while his mother clasped her hands to her bosom and Miss Tweedsmuir fumbled in a pocket for a handkerchief with which to dab at moist eyes, "we have just been agreeing that it feels as if we have known each other for a hundred years. Haven't we, Daphne?"

"Yes, Andrew," she said. "Or at least that we have been waiting that long to meet."

"Miss Tweedsmuir," the Countess of Everett said firmly, "we have a wedding to plan, my dear ma'am."

The earl lowered his head to kiss his betrothed as the two older ladies bustled from the room.

Reflections

by
Maura Seger

1

THE MEDIUM wore red. She was a slender woman in
her midtwenties with an untamed mass of auburn
curls, an oval face ruled by wary eyes, and slim, long-
fingered hands that went about the business of laying
out cards with graceful efficiency.

A fringed shawl of crimson satin crossed over her
bodice. Beneath it was a glimpse of darker, almost
black silk embroidered with jet buttons that gleamed
in the gaslight. White lace cuffs showed at her wrists
where the shawl was pushed back.

Bram Hayes frowned. Standing at the entrance to
his aunt's parlor, he studied the young woman seated
at the oval table. He knew her name and her supposed
profession but very little else. She was younger than
he had expected and far more attractive. Her fresh
innocence and air of quiet elegance belied her tawdry
occupation.

In the fashionably cluttered room filled with over-
stuffed furniture, potted palms, paintings, sculpture,
and every imaginable gimcrack and gewgaw, she was
an island of serenity and self-possession.

He supposed it was all part of the act.

His aunt hurried in, moving as fast as she could while so tightly corseted. Her plumb cheeks were flushed with excitement. "There you are, dear," Georgette Hayes said, taking his arm. "I'm thrilled you came. Do let me introduce you to Miss Butler."

Bram suffered himself to be led across the room, past several of the other guests who were now filtering in. As they approached, the young woman rose and swept the Tarot cards away. They vanished into a pocket of her skirt. The impression Bram had received was reaffirmed as the shawl fell open slightly, revealing a figure that though slim was perfectly formed. His gaze flicked to her face in time to catch her looking at him. Quickly, she turned to her hostess.

"I'm ready to start any time you like, Mrs. Hayes."

Georgette's hands fluttered anxiously. "Are you certain? I presumed you would need to prepare, meditate, whatever."

"I'm quite ready," the young woman assured her. She spoke softly but with unmistakable firmness. Again, her eyes flicked to Bram. This time they lingered for a moment, long enough for him to see that her irises were a startlingly pure shade of blue, light enough to make them look almost like crystal.

"Everyone," Georgette trilled, "this is Miss Nora Butler. She will be conducting tonight's séance. We are very fortunate to have Miss Butler with us. As some of you know, she is the granddaughter of Madame Gitanos and as I am sure we will discover, every bit as gifted as her illustrious forebear."

This pretty speech was received with much murmuring and head noddings around the room. The guests were a varied bunch, ranging from an elderly gentleman Bram recognized as a justice of the state supreme court to several of Georgette's pet artists, down-on-their-luck scavengers always ready for a free meal and a night's entertainment.

He repressed a sigh. He was fond of his aunt, his late mother's only living relative, but there were times when she could be exasperating. This was one of them.

For months, Georgette had been caught up in the spiritualism fad that was all the rage in Europe and the States. She had gone through one medium after another before discovering Madame Gitanos, who she insisted was a genuine seer.

Bram scoffed at the notion. So far as he was concerned, the spiritualists were all thieves out to dupe the ignorant and gullible. Most of his aunt's money was in a trust that Bram managed for her, but she had enough elsewhere to make her ripe for the plucking. He was determined to protect her from that.

Madame Gitanos's disappearance almost on the eve of Georgette's dinner party had thrown his aunt into a panic. He had no idea how she'd managed to find the granddaughter but he presumed Nora Butler was only too happy to exploit the situation. Or at least she would be until she discovered that she was dealing with more than just a credulous bunch of society sycophants.

Bram's smile was grim. He had seen a good deal of the world in his thirty-four years and had few, if any illusions. He despised those who sought to twist the desperate longings of others to their own advantage. Auburn hair, crystalline eyes, and a perfectly formed body made no difference.

He intended to make an example of Miss Nora Butler, one neither she nor anyone else would ever forget.

"Do sit down, everyone," Georgette urged. She nodded to the butler, who began going around the room, lowering the gaslights.

Bram took his place directly across the table from the medium. Georgette was to his right. As the light grew dimmer, he glanced around at the other guests. A few affected to look bored, but most were already entranced, fascinated by some combination of ill-formed hopes and dreads uniquely their own.

"Please join hands," Nora Butler said quietly. She bowed her head. Silence filled the room.

It lasted for several minutes, enough for them to feel the weight of it. At last, Nora said, "We seek contact with the spirits of the departed. We ask for their counsel and advise. We invite them into the circle we have formed, and we open our minds and hearts to them. Let them come forth now."

Her head fell forward. A tremor ran through her body. Slowly, she straightened. Her eyes were wide and no longer fully focused. Her lower lip trembled slightly.

When she spoke again, her voice had changed. It was deeper and with a hint not precisely of an accent but of an older, more mature woman.

"Who summons me?" the voice demanded.

The group around the table stirred. No one wanted to be the first to respond. Remembering her duty as hostess, Georgette reluctantly spoke up.

"We do . . . oh, spirit from beyond." She warmed to her task. "Enlighten us, great one. Reveal to us the secrets of the world to come."

Bram bit back an exclamation of disgust. He found it impossible to believe that seemingly sensible people would take part in such a charade. His instinct was to break the circle and walk out. But instead he stayed, more grimly determined than ever to expose Miss Nora Butler for the fraud she was.

"Who are you?" the elderly judge asked. He leaned forward intently, as though addressing a witness who could shed light on the ultimate truth.

"I am Brigida, priestess of the Morrigan, servant of the goddess. I speak through this earthly vessel."

Bram rolled his eyes. How could they listen to this gibberish? Morrigan indeed.

"Will you answer our questions?" Georgette asked eagerly.

"If I can," the voice replied, "but be warned, my concerns are of a higher order than yours, my knowledge is of the plane beyond. Heed my words. Wisdom demands prudence. Insight requires patience. You may begin."

"My daughter," the judge said. "Is she all right?"

"All are well here. Pain and grief are not of this place. Your daughter loves you. She awaits reunion with you in the natural course."

"If I could speak with her—"

"She has gone on to the world beyond yours. She is content and she wishes you to be the same."

The judge's lined face was taut with concentration. "Another medium said it might be possible to reach her, if I paid enough . . ."

"Servants of the world beyond do not concern themselves with the material. No payment can pierce the veil between you and the departed. Your daughter knows of your love. It is enough."

The judge sat back, clearly surprised but not unsatisfied. His features relaxed and he even smiled faintly.

Bram's dark brows drew together. What was that about not being concerned with the material? No self-respecting charlatan would say that. What game was Miss Nora Butler playing?

"Please," a woman said from the other side of the table, "if you could . . . last month I lost my wedding ring. I have been at my wits' end ever since. Could you possibly . . ."

"Look for it in the place you would least expect to find it. If it still eludes you, remember that everything of this world passes in an instant. Only love and memory endure."

"Is there truly no way to contact my dear husband?" another woman asked, "He left me a great deal of money and I really have no idea what to do with it. I need his guidance."

Bram stiffened. Surely this was too tempting a bit of bait to be ignored. He fully expected the so-called Brigida to suggest a private séance preparatory to robbing the woman blind. But instead the voice replied, "Seek the counsel of a trusted banker. Do not put your faith in those who promise extravagant reward. Prudent investment is best."

While he was trying to come to terms with that, Georgette chimed in, "What is it like where you are? Can you tell us that?"

"This is a place of great beauty and peace. All here are happy. The trials of your world, the disappointments and frustrations, are but a testing. They strengthen you. Bear them in the knowledge that all things have a purpose."

The voice faltered. Gravely, Brigida announced, "The vessel tires. I must withdraw."

Nora's head fell forward again. When she straightened once more, her eyes were clear and she appeared surprised.

"What happened? Did someone speak?"

"She did indeed," Georgette exclaimed. "A woman named Brigida."

"The priestess," Nora murmured. She nodded. "I hope she was helpful?"

"Very much so," the judge said. He had an air of quiet contentment. "Rather surprising, I must say. I've been to quite a few of these and this is the first time I had the feeling I was actually speaking to someone who knew anything."

"A very sensible young woman," another said. "She gave excellent advice."

"I'm glad," Nora said. She stood and gathered the shawl around her. "Now if you will excuse me, it is always a great strain. . . ."

"Of course it is, dear," Georgette agreed. She hurried over and began to guide her from the room. "I can't imagine how you do that. Quite an extraordinary experience. If you would like to lie down . . ."

"I think it would be best if I return to my home," Nora said as they left the parlor. "My strength is restored most quickly in familiar surroundings."

"Naturally," Georgette said. "But you will come back, won't you? Such a lovely person, Brigida. So soothing."

Whatever Nora replied, Bram could not hear her. The guests were milling about, eagerly discussing what had occurred. Despite the complete lack of any of the usual tricks he'd been expecting, they seemed well satisfied with the experience.

It made no sense. Every other medium his aunt had come into contact with—except the vanished Madame

Gitanos—had wasted no time making the table shake, producing spirit visions, and so on, all the while charging more and more extravagant sums. Only "Madame," as Georgette reverently called her, and now her granddaughter had failed to do so.

"Is she coming back?" he asked when his aunt returned to the parlor after seeing the medium off.

"She didn't actually promise," Georgette replied. "But I'm sure I can convince her. Such a lovely young woman and so gifted, don't you think?"

A gifted trickster, certainly. By restraining herself as she had, Miss Nora Butler assured that she would be enthusiastically—and no doubt expensively—pursued. It was a daring technique, but judging by the audience's reaction, it worked. Nora Butler had established herself as someone who could be trusted.

That made her all the more dangerous. And made him all the more determined to stop her.

2

Bram Hayes. The name suited him. He had what Gramma Rianna would have called a golden aura filled with energy and raw male power.

Nora shivered slightly. Seated in the hired carriage Georgette Hayes had insisted on, she leaned her head back against the padded bench and closed her eyes. Visions of the tall, dark man danced before her. Vainly, she tried to banish them.

He was dangerous. She needed no psychic powers to conclude that. Any man who stirred her as he had done—instantly and with absolutely no effort on his part—was a man to stay well away from.

That suited her perfectly. Her involvement with

Georgette Hayes—and her nephew—was over. Gloriously, wonderfully, totally over. She had done it, actually conducted a séance without making a screaming fool of herself, and collected fifty dollars no less in the bargain. Fifty precious dollars that meant the difference between destitution and survival for herself and her younger siblings. Money she had not sought, but which in the end she could not refuse.

The carriage rattled on over the cobblestone street. A light rain had begun to fall. Nora stared out at the pavement shining black in the glow of the gas lamps. The small cold-water flat she shared with her brother and sister was barely fifteen minutes away from Georgette Hayes's luxurious Fifth Avenue apartment, but it might as well have been a world apart. It provided little more than bare bones shelter, but under the circumstances she was fortunate to be able to afford even that.

Money had never greatly concerned her. She was appalled to find herself so obsessed by it. But then she had never had to give it a moment's thought before. Her parents had both been teachers, her father in a lower East Side school serving immigrants and her mother giving piano lessons from their home. They had earned enough to live comfortably.

But not to save, not for the huge medical bills that resulted when both were injured in the fire that destroyed their home and not for the orphaned children they had left behind.

Nora swallowed with difficulty. Even two years after that tragedy, it hurt to think about. She had done her best, learning to operate a typewriter and going to work in a financial firm. But that job was gone, lost when she refused the advances of her employer, and the bills were mounting up with terrifying speed.

Just when she thought things couldn't possibly get worse, Gramma Rianna disappeared. She left behind a battered trunk, a cryptic message, and an hysterical client—Georgette Hayes—who insisted Nora take her place at the dinner party. And why should she not when Rianna had thoughtfully sent Mrs. Hayes a letter suggesting Nora do exactly that? Bless Gramma's heart, wherever that might be.

She had never in her life performed as a medium, never even thought about doing it. Indeed, whenever her mind so much as turned to what it was that Gramma Rianna did, something in her instinctively shied away. It was as though she stood at the edge of a jagged chasm that would swallow her up in an instant if she made one false move.

But it had not. She had kept her thoughts, her feelings, whatever they might be called under strict control. Exercising rigid self-discipline, she had performed a séance with absolutely no psychic content whatsoever. And she had left her audience perfectly well satisfied in the process. Her conscience was if not entirely clear, at least not guilt-ridden.

She could put the experience behind her, forget it entirely. Forget the cold fear she'd felt at the thought of summoning powers she did not want to believe existed. Forget, too, that after all her concerns about what might happen to her, the single genuinely shocking moment in the entire evening had happened when her eyes met those of Bram Hayes.

The carriage rolled to a halt. Nora got out and thanked the driver, Georgette having already paid him. He did not respond, his silence and the speed with which he cracked the reins making it clear what he thought of her destination. The carriage vanished around the corner. Moments later, the sound of the horses' hooves faded away on the night air.

Nora reached into her bag for her key. She unlocked the outerdoor and stepped inside quickly, securing it behind her. Although there was no sign of anyone on the street, it was best to be cautious.

She climbed the steps to the fourth floor, doing her best to ignore the smell of cabbage and other odors that lingered in the close confines of the shabby building. A second key opened the apartment door. She had paid for that lock herself after finding a drunken neighbor waiting for her one evening. It had cost dearly, but she couldn't regret the small measure of safety it provided.

Shutting the door behind her, she tiptoed across the room. Her brother slept in a small curtained alcove off the kitchen. Patrick was soundly asleep, his light blond hair tousled over the pillow and one hand folded childlike beneath his chin. Nora straightened the covers and touched a feather-light kiss to his brow.

Patrick was thirteen and small for his age. He should have been in school, for he had a good mind, but instead he worked when he could preparing vegetables for market and doing any other odd jobs that came his way. He earned little, but they needed every penny they could get.

Deidre shared the second room with Nora. The younger Burke daughter was also fast asleep. At eighteen, six years younger than Nora, Deidre was bidding fair to be a beauty. Or at least she would have been if the drudgery of piecework didn't drain her so completely.

Wearily, Nora removed her clothes and folded them away in the battered wooden chest at the foot of the bed. Clad in a long white nightgown, she washed and cleaned her teeth, all as quietly as possible before slipping into bed beside Deidre.

Her sister woke partly. "Everything all right?" she murmured.

"Fine," Nora assured her. She squeezed Deidre's hand lightly. "Go back to sleep. Everything's fine."

At least for the moment. Tomorrow she would go shopping. They'd have decent food for a change, not the scraps they'd been getting by on. She'd pay the rent for three—no, four—months just to give them that much security. The rest she'd squirrel away to see them through until she got another clerical job, as she was sure to any day now. All she needed was a bit of luck.

She was very tired, more so than the day's work seemed to justify. But sleep eluded her. Behind her eyes, in the hidden places of her soul, she saw the silvery glint of the dark man's eyes. The boldness of his gaze followed her into her dreams.

A mile—and a world—away, Bram retired late. He had returned from his aunt's party to spend several necessary hours going over his investment accounts. The market was volatile, but his instincts were sound. He knew when to take risks and when not. The fortune inherited from his parents had grown considerably under his care.

It was not enough. He was plagued by a restlessness he could neither identify nor cure. Business was only mildly interesting, polite society bored him, the women he enjoyed were pleasant enough, but even they had a tendency to pall.

Perhaps there was no solution for it. He might be fated to go through life wishing for something he could vaguely sense but neither touch nor see. Grimacing, he tossed his frock coat over the back of a chair and unbuttoned his shirt. He had sent his valet off to bed hours before. The large house, further north along the avenue than his aunt's, was silent except for the faint murmurings of night sounds.

He opened one of the bedroom windows wider and stood looking out at the garden below. Something moved between the rose bushes, a cat most likely. The scene was peaceful, the room luxurious, yet it all irked him. Inevitably, after a few weeks in the city he felt the urge to escape.

He unbuttoned his shirt and pulled it off over his head and tossed it next to the frock coat. The remainder of his clothes followed. Naked, he stood tall and powerful and arched his neck to relieve the tension in it.

He needed to get out of the city, to feel clean wind on his skin, to move without the fetters of civilization. He needed sunshine and good rain, towering pine trees and white water pounding through rock chasms. He needed . . .

Nora Butler. He froze, riveted by that stray thought. Where had it come from? He had absolutely no need of the so-called medium. There was nothing at all appealing about a money-grubbing chit willing to take advantage of other people's gullibility. Nothing except for that riot of auburn hair and the startling light blue eyes, that perfectly shaped body and damask smooth skin, that way she had of moving her hands so that a man could not help but think how they would feel on him.

He laughed, a deep, male sound, and shook his head. Definitely, he was overdue for an extended visit with one of the women whose company he enjoyed from time to time. If he'd actually reached the point where he was attracted to a wily Irish lass with a keen eye for the main chance and no scruples to get in her way, he was worse off than he'd thought.

Or perhaps the very unlikelihood of her was part of the attraction. Desire was a capricious thing, seldom inclined to settle where it ought.

With a sigh, he stretched out in bed, his muscled arms folded behind his head, and gazed up at the ceiling high above. He had no doubt that he would encounter Miss Nora Butler again and soon. Before he'd taken his leave that evening, his aunt had gone on at some length about her plans for employing Miss Butler again. Bram intended to be there when she did so.

The chit was cleverer by far than most of her kind. She'd done nothing to trip herself up. It would be a challenge to unmask her. His smile deepened. Honesty forced him to admit that he was looking forward to the contest.

But honesty only went so far. He did not allow himself to contemplate exactly why that should be. In time, his breathing grew deeper and he slipped into restless sleep, pursued by flickering candles and far off in the distance, a flash of auburn hair vanishing just beyond his grasp.

3

"That woman's sent round again," Deidre said.

Nora grimaced. She shut the apartment door behind her and sat down slowly in the battered chair beside the kitchen table. Her feet throbbed. She had been up since before dawn, out at first light, walking the streets with the newspapers clasped in her hand, following every possible lead for a job.

She'd trudged up stairways, bluffed her way past secretaries, ventured through the twisting, turning streets of lower Manhattan, all in vain. There did not seem to be a job to be had anywhere, at least not by a young woman without either influential friends or highly flexible morals.

Deidre gave her a sympathetic look. She set her sewing aside and went to put the kettle on. When she came back, Nora had slipped her boots off and was rubbing her stockinged feet.

"No luck?" her sister asked quietly.

"Not a thing. There's a line for every job."

"And the men have first call?"

"Yes, I suppose so." Nora managed a weary smile. "I'll try again tomorrow." She was silent for a moment before she asked reluctantly, "What did Mrs. Hayes want this time?"

"What has she wanted for the past fortnight? Another reading. The messenger brought this." Deidre held out a heavy envelope of creamy white paper embossed with Georgette Hayes's name and her Fifth Avenue address.

Nora took it, but made no immediate effort to inspect whatever was inside. She was certain that she already knew. Georgette Hayes wanted another séance. She beseeched Nora to come to her aid and the aid of her friends. She avowed her utter faith in Nora's abilities. And she promised "considerable" financial reward.

Of the fifty dollars, twelve were left. She had paid the rent as planned, bought food, and put the rest away. Ordinarily, it could have kept them going for several months.

Then Patrick got sick. He had tried to hide it at first, insisting that he was merely tired. But when the racking cough and high fever appeared, he could no longer conceal the truth.

The tenements were a breeding ground for illness. It was a miracle that they had escaped so far, but no longer. The doctor had been clear, pay eight dollars for his time and another for the needed medicine, or he would not lift a finger to help.

Nora railed against him, calling him every name she could think of, but he would not be moved. He made his livelihood—more likely his fortune—bleeding the desperate poor for every cent they possessed. Whatever oath he had taken, whatever charity had once been his soul, was long since forgotten.

She paid. Patrick improved but only slightly. There was still no possibility of his going out to work again anytime soon. The very thought of him trying to do so made Nora want to weep. She was the eldest, she had to take better care of her family. It was up to her.

She was so tired that her hands shook as she opened the letter. Briefly, her eyes scanned it. As she had expected, Georgette wanted another reading.

Nora's stomach knotted. She did not want to do

this. At bottom, she was fiercely afraid. But what else was left to her?

Slowly, she stood, ignoring the fatigue that threatened to crush her. "I will go see Mrs. Hayes."

Deidre looked startled. "Are you sure?"

Nora shrugged. "I don't see any other way, do you?"

"No," her younger sister admitted regretfully. Her gaze was full of compassion. "I only wish that I did."

Bram walked from his club. The evening air was pleasantly cool. Spring was late in coming but all the more welcome for that. He intended to call on his aunt, who had been feeling poorly of late, then return to his own residence before venturing out for an evening's entertainment.

The thought of diversion held little attraction, but he had decided that he needed to get about more, indulge his senses and his pleasures. Perhaps then he wouldn't be thinking so damn much about Miss Nora Butler.

It was absurd how she haunted his thoughts. In the two weeks since their encounter, he had not managed to go a single day—much less a single night—without thinking of her. He recalled the flash of her azure eyes, the play of light through her russet hair, the damask smoothness of her skin, the sweet curves of her body, all in exquisite, excruciating detail. Absurd. Especially for a man of his age and experience. He was no green boy to be infatuated with the mere notion of a woman. The sooner he sated his hunger, the better off he would be. A quick visit to his aunt, a quick stop at home, and on to a certain blond-tressed music hall singer who was more than eager for his company.

"Good evening, sir," Georgette's butler said as he opened the door to Bram.

"Evening, Wilson. How is my aunt today?"

"About the same, sir," Wilson said, taking Bram's coat. "Mrs. Hayes is in the drawing room."

"I won't be long."

"As you say, sir."

A few quick strides across the marble entry hall, through the open double doors to the drawing room, a cordial smile and—

She was not alone. His aunt had company.

"Miss Butler," Bram murmured with a slight inclination of his head. "Aunt Georgette."

"Bram, darling," his aunt exclaimed as she rose to greet him. "How lovely that you've stopped by, and just in time to help me convince Miss Butler. She is quite unaccountably reluctant to give another séance. Do tell her she must."

"Must she?" Bram murmured, his eyes on Nora. She sat, back erect and shoulders straight, on the couch. Her gaze was averted but there was a slight flush to her otherwise pale cheeks which suggested she was as startled by his sudden appearance as he was by hers.

"Of course she must," Georgette went on. "How can she possibly hide such a gift? I realize she believes her powers are of a higher order and she mustn't benefit from them, but she must be realistic, mustn't she?"

"Must you, Miss Butler?" Bram asked. His mouth curved in a sardonic smile. An unholy light gleamed in his pewter eyes as they swept over her again. She really was astoundingly beautiful even given the drab brown dress she wore. Yet it was clear that she possessed a keen, if unscrupulous intelligence. How else to explain her clever handling of his aunt.

The more she refused, the more desperate Georgette would become. And the more money she would offer. His hat was off to Miss Nora Butler, figuratively of course since he never actually wore a hat even in the coldest weather. She had figured out a scam that would have put the most audacious Gypsy to shame.

"I have a better idea," Bram said. In fact, it had just occurred to him, but he turned the notion over with his usual alacrity. On Wall Street, he was known for the lightning speed of his decisions and their infallible logic. There was no reason he shouldn't do the same in his aunt's drawing room.

Disengaging himself from Georgette's grip, he sat down opposite Nora and continued to regard her. She raised her head, her chin tilted proudly, and met his gaze with her own. They studied each other for several moments before Bram said, "I am considering buying a house north of the city along the Hudson. I have its use while I decide. I'm going to be giving a party there. Perhaps Miss Butler would be good enough to join us."

Nora's color deepened. "I really don't think—"

"I will pay you a thousand dollars."

Georgette gasped. It was an enormous sum. For such an amount, a house could be purchased, a business, a future.

Nora's eyes had widened so that they completely dominated her face. She stared at Bram. "You aren't serious."

It was not a question, merely a flat statement of

her disbelief. He took particular pleasure in correcting her.

"Actually I am. If you're as good a medium as my aunt seems to think, you'll be worth it. The party will last for four days beginning Friday." He leaned forward, regarding her intently. Try though he did, he could not find the slightest flicker of greed in her. All he sensed was deep, abiding shock and something more, something strangely like fear.

That troubled him, but not enough to make him relent. "What do you say, Miss Butler?" he demanded remorselessly. "A thousand dollars for four days' work?"

She was very pale. All the color had fled from her face and her hands were trembling. Again, he felt that odd twinge of conscience that was so unlike him.

"I still cannot believe you are serious," she said. Her voice was little more than a whisper. She regarded him with what could only be described as shock.

"One hundred on account, the rest if you last the four days."

Her finely arched brows drew together. "What do you mean, last?"

"If my aunt still believes you're a medium."

Georgette smiled nervously. "Bram is something of a skeptic, my dear. Don't mind him."

"Something of?" Nora asked.

"Surely you aren't put off by that?" Bram interjected. "Think of me as a challenge."

To his surprise, the corners of her mouth lifted. "Oh, I do, Mr. Hayes," she said softly. "I most certainly do."

4

The house rose above her, a massive stone intrusion into the surrounding woodland. Rolling lawns spread out from it on all sides, keeping the forest at bay. Against the bright blue of the sky, the stone towers were almost black. The sun had slid round to the other side, leaving the windows dark, no light there to ease the sense of terrible weight, no hint into the life of the house.

The carriage bringing her from the train station slowed as it approached, as though neither horse nor driver was eager to reach their destination. Nora couldn't blame them. Although the day was brilliantly clear, the gray pile of stones perched above the river appeared cloaked in shadow. The impression was deceptive, of course, rendered by the heaviness of the large stone blocks and the way they sat upon the earth rather than rising from it.

The house did not belong. She had no way of saying how she knew that, but the sense of alienness was as clear in her mind as the day itself. In style, the turreted walls and twin towers had a medieval air rediscovered in recent decades and made popular again. Nora didn't think one way or another about it, what the rich chose to do with their money was not her concern. But this house was different. It looked less like the fancy of a wealthy romantic and more like something wrenched from its own time and place.

And ill at ease in its present surroundings.

She shook her head to clear it. The last thing she needed was to be having strange fancies about the house. Her wits were her best, indeed her only weapon in the struggle to come. She had to keep them at all costs.

The carriage rolled to a stop. Nora stepped out and took hold of her carpetbag. She stood clutching it in both hands and stared up once again at the house.

Was Bram Hayes truly considering the purchase of this singularly odd-looking house? And if he was, why should she be surprised? She had no more reason to think that he possessed a modicum of good taste than she did to think that he meant her well by offering her this job. Indeed, given his excessive wealth, both possibilities were equally unlikely.

Bram Hayes disliked her. Never mind that he looked at her with a boldness that made her stomach tighten and her heart quicken. His disdain could not have been more evident.

Not that it mattered. She disliked him, too. He was arrogant, self-centered, spoiled, and all-too accustomed to having people do his bidding. That he obviously cared for his aunt and was protective toward her didn't matter. That he was reputed to be a ruthless but imminently fair businessman counted for nothing. She didn't like him, never would, and was glad of it.

Or she would be as soon as she managed to convince herself it was even slightly true.

"Everything all right, miss?" the carriage driver asked. He looked at her uneasily.

Nora straightened her shoulders and summoned a smile. "Perfectly." She paid him, added a tip, and took her leave. As she walked up the gravel path to the front entrance, she heard the carriage driving rapidly away.

Three broad stone steps led up to the front door. Massive stone urns stood on pediments to each side of the steps. Above the door, a carved stone lintel was populated by writhing figures. High above, stone gargoyles glared from below the battlements.

Nora swallowed hard. She had to remind herself that this was the last decade of the nineteenth century. That was the Hudson River twining far below the cliffs, a silver ribbon dotted with the reflections of tiny clouds. She could turn around, walk down the road, and take either a train or ferry back to the city. She was not trapped here, she was not helpless. She would be fine.

Heart in her throat, she raised her hand and before she could think better of it, tugged on the bell pull set within the wall to the right of the massive double doors. Far in the distant caverns of the house, she heard the bell toll.

She waited, as patiently as she could, through what seemed like very long minutes. At last, footsteps approached, one side of the door was eased open, accompanied by much creaking.

A monk stood before her. He was a small, very stooped man with waxen skin, untidy gray hair, and red-rimmed eyes. He wore a brown woolen robe tied around his waist by a length of twine. A plain wooden cross hung from the makeshift belt. He blinked at her.

Nora put her hand to her mouth and took a quick step back. A wave of intense coldness rolled toward her. Had she been able to, she would have run. But she felt frozen in place, unable to do anything except stare at the man.

"Miss?"

Nora squeezed her eyes shut, holding on to her courage with all her strength. The ground seemed to rock beneath her. She smelled—what?—wood smoke and wool, and something more, sweet, faintly cloying. Incense?

"Miss?"

The voice was cultured, imminently reasonable, and slightly perplexed. Slowly, Nora opened one eye and the other. The monk was gone. In his place stood a butler in black frock coat and gray morning trousers, a middle-aged man with pink cheeks and neatly clipped hair, looking at her with concern.

"Are you all right, miss?"

"I . . ." Nora swallowed hard. This couldn't be happening to her. Not here, not now, not with so much at stake. Her knees started to buckle.

"Let me help you," the man said. He stepped forward and took her carpetbag. With his other hand, he touched her elbow lightly. "You must be Miss Butler. I'm Wilson, the butler." He smiled. "I suppose that gives us something in common. Do come in. I expect the journey's tired you."

Yes, Nora thought desperately as he guided her inside. She was tired. All the worry over Patrick, the fear that she wouldn't find employment, the constant concern over money, all that had sapped her natural strength. Fatigue made her prey to fancies. That was all. She'd always had far too much imagination than was good for her. She hadn't really seen the monk, not in such detail, it had only been a shadow or a trick of light.

Yet the smells lingered as though on the still air, fading last of all.

Speaking softly, Butler Wilson guided her through the massive entry hall. He kept gentle hold of her, but his manner was entirely proper. She felt a flash of gratitude.

"A cup of tea, I think," he said. "Your room is ready. Would you like me to send a tray up?"

"That would be very kind," Nora murmured. A high, winding staircase of elaborately carved wood rose up out of sight. They climbed it together. At the top, a broad hallway stretched the length of the house. Wilson led her toward the western end. He opened the door to a pleasant room, very large and comfortably rather than luxuriously furnished, with a canopied bed and wide windows overlooking the river.

"Please make yourself comfortable, miss," he said. "The maid will be up shortly."

When the door had closed behind him, Nora took a long look around. Her first impression of the room was right, it seemed a perfectly pleasant place, reminiscent in some ways of the room she'd had as a child, although bigger. Certainly, there was nothing in the least threatening or ominous about it.

What accounted then for the completely different impression she had at the front door, and to a lesser extent in the entry hall? Was she becoming ill? Could a fever of some sort have caused a brief hallucination?

The thought unnerved her, but not for long. She felt fine despite the shock she had suffered. Her natural resilience was reasserting itself. Indeed, she felt mildly impatient at her own foolishness.

Tea, that was what she needed. Tea and a bit of a rest, unpack, get her thoughts together, and then find out what her host—say, rather her employer—expected of her. No doubt he'd make that clear enough. For a thousand dollars, he'd probably have her conducting séances nonstop the whole four days and nights.

She'd do it, too. For the security it would give her family, for the once-in-a-lifetime chance to escape the burden of dread that had descended on them, for Patrick and Dee-Dee, for herself and—to be fair—for the sheer pleasure of besting Bram Hayes.

Oh, yes, she'd do it right enough and she'd do a damn fine job of it. Briskly, she took her hair down, combed it, and was just rewinding it into a bun on the top of her head when there was a knock at the door.

"Come in," she called and turned to remove the carpetbag from the nearby table where she had thoughtlessly put it. "You can put the tray right here. Thank you for—"

Nora broke off. There was a tray all right, gleaming silver with a little lace cloth and a delicate china cup. But that was no maid holding it.

"Wilson said you weren't feeling well," Bram said. Impossibly, he seemed even bigger and more muscular than she remembered, or perhaps that had something to do with the fact that he was clad only in black riding breeches and a white shirt left open at the neck. His face was stern. He took a few steps into the room, set the tray down, and turned, hands on his hips, to look at her. "What's wrong?"

"Nothing," Nora said hastily. "Thank you for the tea. I'm just going to freshen up, if that's all right, and I'll be down. I won't be but a moment, no need for you to stay. Thanks again, but really—"

"You're babbling," Bram said with a hint of wonder as though it was not a form of behavior he had expected of her. To her dismay, he pulled out an armchair from beside the table, sat down in it, and stretched out his long legs, looking for all the world as though he meant to stay awhile.

And why shouldn't he? This was his house, at least

for the moment. He was in absolute control here and he clearly knew it. Resentment filled her. She turned her back on him deliberately and began unpacking.

"What about the tea?" he asked innocently enough, although from the sound of it, there was nothing innocent about this man, nothing at all. He was enjoying her discomfort.

"It needs to cool," she said, still with her back to him, and thinking that the tea wasn't the only thing with too much heat in it. Her cheeks were flushed and she felt a queer curling sense below her middle. Ridiculous to be that way. She'd been alone with a man before—her father, her sweet old music teacher, Patrick.

All right, she'd never been in a remotely similar position before, but that was no reason to come apart at the seams. At least Bram Hayes was indisputably real, unlike the vision that had greeted her upon arrival.

She inhaled deeply, let her breath out slowly, and walked back to the table. Sunlight pouring in through the rear windows of the house silvered the thick ebony mass of his hair. It curled at the nape of his neck.

He was only a man, real, solid, compelling. Yet he had all unknowingly summoned her to a time and place where something was not right. She could sense that deep within the powerful currents of her being. Something awry, distorted, something—

"Tell me about this house," she said and took the chair across from him.

5

Bram frowned. Why did she look so fragile? Was she ill or merely worried? Wilson said she'd had some sort of shock, but that made no sense. She'd known where she was coming and why. What was there to shock her?

He shifted slightly in his chair. "This house? I'm not sure there's much to tell." Was she trying to gather information to use in a séance? If so, she was going about it the wrong way. No one would be asking about the house. They'd be too preoccupied with their own concerns.

"It was built twenty years ago by—" He mentioned the name of a robber baron who had made a fortune in the fur trade, another in stock manipulation, and a third in railroads before dying in his bed just a few months before, having outlived three wives, sired a dozen children, and cheated unknown thousands of investors. The New York newspapers had covered his demise in depth, even going so far as to print engravings titled "The Death Scene" which suggested the old man had gone to his reward, whatever it might have been, with a satisfied smile on his face.

"I didn't realize he'd lived here," Nora said slowly.

"He didn't. He built it on a whim, spent one night here and never came back." He shrugged. "The house isn't the point, it's the land I want."

"The land? Why?"

"It's one of the choicest tracts left along the river and the closest to the city."

She looked thoughtful. "So you don't actually intend to live in this house?"

"No, I don't, but why should that interest you?" Indeed, it seemed to do more than that. She seemed positively relieved.

"I don't know," Nora admitted. She touched a hand to the teapot. "Will you join me?"

"There's only one cup."

"That's not a problem." She rose gracefully and went over to the bed where she had left the carpetbag. From its depths she withdrew a small wooden box. Opening it, she carefully lifted out a delicate porcelain cup of Chinese design and returned with it to the table.

"This belongs to my grandmother," she explained.

Bram grimaced. "She used it for reading tea leaves, I suppose."

"No, she just likes to drink tea."

He accepted the cup she offered, not the Chinese one, but the one Wilson had provided, and felt mildly ashamed of himself. It was wrong to keep baiting her like this.

"What else did she leave you?" he asked.

Nora flinched. Too late, he realized how poorly chosen the words had been.

"She isn't dead," Nora insisted. "She's just gone away for a while."

Gentled by the sudden force of her grief, surprised by how intently he felt it, he asked, "Has she done that before, just gone away?"

"No, but I'm sure that's what's happened this time. She left a letter, you know. And she sent another to Mrs. Hayes."

"Did she really?"

Nora nodded. "That's how she found me, your aunt I mean. Gramma Rianna recommended me. She didn't just want to leave Mrs. Hayes in the lurch, so to speak."

"I see," Bram said slowly, although in fact he didn't. He was too preoccupied with the way the light touched the curve of her cheek and the faint scent of lavender seemed to cling to her skin. "But she didn't say where she was going?"

"To renew herself, whatever that means."

"Don't you know?"

"How would I?"

"Being in the same line of work, I presumed—"

"But I'm not—" Her eyes flew open. She put the teacup down hastily. "That is, it could mean all sorts of things. Spiritual renewal, for one, or perhaps just a nice rest."

Bram's eyes narrowed. A suspicion was forming in his mind. Was it possible that Miss Nora Butler was new to the medium business? A novice fraud still learning the tricks of her trade? It would explain her failure to drag out the usual table thumping, smoke and mirrors routine.

"You were telling me about the house," she said hastily. "It seems a good deal older than twenty years."

His mind still largely on the possibility that had just occurred to him, he answered absently, "It is. The foundation and the first floor were built from the stones of a medieval monastery shipped over from Europe."

Her eyes widened, azure pools reflecting the flirtatious sunlight. He had a sudden impulse to reach out to her, but restrained it. "What did you say?" she asked.

"You heard me. I know it sounds crazy, but that's what happened. Rich Americans have been buying up portable chunks of Europe for years now. The whole thing was disassembled, every stone marked for its original position, and then it was put back together on this site. The second floor was added and the towers tacked on. Simple."

"Bizarre," Nora corrected. Her voice was very faint. She appeared deep in thought.

"Something wrong?" Bram asked.

"Yes," she said quietly and proceeded to tell him.

The dress was a mistake, she shouldn't have brought it. What had she been thinking of to let Dee tuck it into her bag at almost the last minute when she should have already been out the door? And why in heaven's name had she decided to wear it her first night in the house.

It was too late to change. The maid had left, and try though she did, Nora couldn't reach the intricate buttons down her back. Without help, she was trapped, a stranger in a guilded mirror staring back at her with wide, luminous eyes the same shade as the rich blue velvet that fitted her so snugly.

Surely the bodice hadn't always been that tight? The woman Dee had made the dress for had been about the same size as Nora, a very proper uptown lady who had promised fair payment and then reneged. They'd been stuck with a dress they couldn't afford and which no one else of their acquaintance could conceivably buy.

So here it was, on her, donned to give her courage, but at the moment merely making her doubt her sanity more than she already had to begin with. Yet what else could she do after confronting her employer's cold fury?

Bram hadn't believed her. When she tried to tell him about the monk, he accused her of using the information he'd given her about the house to cook up a preposterous story. He'd warned her that she was a fool to believe he or anyone else would be taken in by such an absurd tale. And he'd stormed out after advising her that she'd have to do her job a damn sight better to have any hope of surviving four days under his roof, not to mention collecting the thousand dollars.

She considered herself a brave woman, she'd had to be since her life had taken such an unexpected turn. But confronted with his rage and disdain, she quaked. How could she possibly face him again?

The dress had seemed the answer, but now staring at herself in the mirror, she was assailed by doubts. She didn't even look like herself, this creature of feminine grace, her auburn hair piled high on her head by the so-skilled maid, and a faint, becoming flush staining her high-boned cheeks.

Where was sensible, reliable Nora, she of the serge skirts and starched blouses, typist par excellence and not a wayward thought to call her own?

Vanished apparently, but not, she had to hope, beyond recall. Far below, down the curving wooden staircase in the cavernous great rooms of the main floor, the dinner gong sounded. The reverberations floated up the steps, echoing again and again, summoning her to her fate.

But first, just for a moment, she delayed, delving deep into the carpetbag, seeking reassurance. From its depths she withdrew another, smaller mirror, source of a second opinion of sorts, comfort that she was not the stranger she had glimpsed, but the Nora she had always known, always seen in this, Rianna's mirror.

Since childhood, perhaps since infancy, she had

looked into this mirror to find herself. It was not anything like the great gilded thing in the corner, but
fitted snugly into her hand, ancient, eternal, blessedly
familiar.

Very old, Rianna called it, being no more specific.
She knew more, of that Nora was certain, but she
divulged nothing. Look, she said, deeply and without
fear, but all Nora had ever seen was her own true
self, smiling back at her, child into woman, growing
steadily in strength and wisdom.

Yet Rianna had always seemed satisfied. Each time,
she put the mirror away with a pleased nod and a hug
for Nora, wrapping it in the length of frayed velvet
and sliding it carefully away into the battered wooden
trunk. From that trunk Nora had taken it and still
wrapped in velvet had brought it along on this journey. Into it now she stared, seeking herself, seeking
truth, while far below the gong sounded again, a
heavy bronze tone rich in memory.

Bronze like the mirror, not remotely modern, part
of a long vanished world even older than this house.
And more powerful?

Please God, she whispered on a rustle of velvet,
wrapping the mirror, putting it away, velvet again
sighing softly as she moved to the door and opened
it. Please let the ancient prevail over the merely old,
the power drawn time out of time from a world long
gone to confront something she did not want to recog-
nize, but feared awaited her below.

Slowly, she gathered her skirts and, careful not
to crush the delicate fabric, walked head high
down the hallway to the well of curving steps and
stone walls, to the confrontation she could no
longer delay.

6

"We are gathered," Nora said softly, "to call upon the wisdom of those who have gone before us."

Although her voice was very low, Bram could hear the tension in it. They were gathered around the table in the vast drawing room, twelve in all including Nora herself. Besides Georgette and an artist friend she'd brought along, the guests were mainly business associates and their wives, the men shrewd and tough-minded, the women even more so. It was as demanding an audience as could be assembled, yet barely five minutes into the séance, Bram sensed that they were being won over.

Perhaps it was Nora's complete lack of dramatics, or the effect of her pale beauty, or simply the strange sense of powers stirring in the shadows of the room that had been the monastery's chapel. Whatever the cause, the guests hung on her every word, hardly blinking as they sat joined in a circle awaiting whatever might happen next.

Bram suppressed a sigh. He was annoyed at himself for staging the whole preposterous business, but even more so for almost succumbing to Nora's charms. Upstairs in the bedroom, he had come dangerously close to forgetting what she really was—a liar, a cheat, and a fraud. Instead, he had for a brief time seen her solely as a beautiful woman he desired to a degree he could never remember experiencing before.

Even now, watching her, raw hunger that dulled the keenness of his thought and threatened to banish reason altogether. Her eyelids, like porcelain, fluttered lightly as her eyes closed. Her head lifted, her slim white neck arched. Softly, she said, "Brigida is here. Speak that I may know your wishes."

"I'll go first," Georgette declared, jumping right in. Having "spoken" with the spirit before, she apparently considered herself most qualified to do so again. "There are others among us tonight who were not present before, oh, great priestess. They long for the benefit of your wisdom."

"Wisdom comes through the trials of this world. It is but a passage to the next, truer life."

"Yes, yes, you said that before. What we would like to know—" Georgette rattled on, something about the exact nature of existence on the spiritual plane. Bram barely listened. All his attention was focused on Nora. Her brow creased and her shoulders jerked slightly. He had the sudden sense that she was in pain or at the very least, uncomfortable. The feeling was so intense that he actually began to rise up out of his seat.

Her eyes flew open. She stared not at him but just over his left shoulder to where the shadows deepened at the far end of the room. Her lips parted. She dropped the hands she had been holding on either side of her and pressed her palms to the tabletop, as though to steady herself.

Georgette broke off. "Brigida . . . ? Miss Butler . . . ?"

Nora started to speak, but only a strangled sound came from her throat. Her lips were suddenly bloodless. Around the table, the guests realized something was wrong.

"I say . . ."

"What's happening to her?"

"Passing strange . . ."

"Miss Butler," Georgette said again. "Are you all right?"

Bram didn't wait to find out. He was around the table in two long strides and taking hold of Nora. Through the rich blue velvet, her skin felt like ice. She was stiff as stone and seemed unaware of his presence. Her eyes remained locked on the far end of the room. A soft moan escaped her. Without warning, she slumped against him.

Cursing, Bram swept her into his arms. Behind him, the guests were out of their chairs, milling about and demanding to know what was wrong. Ignoring them, he carried Nora from the room. Georgette started to follow but he waved her off.

"Get the lamps relit and keep everyone down here."

His aunt's hands fluttered nervously. "But Miss Butler needs looking after."

"I'll see to her," Bram said grimly. Before Georgette could object, he mounted the stairs, taking them two at a time. On the landing at the top, he paused and looked down at Nora. Her head lay against his shoulder. She almost appeared to be sleeping, but she was too pale by far.

Her room was at the end of the hall. His was much closer. Without hesitation, he shoved the door open and carried her inside. Lowering her onto the big, canopied bed, he brushed his fingers across her cheek. Her skin was like ice and she did not react to his touch. Either she was the world's greatest actress or she truly had fainted.

He withdrew slightly, but continued to watch her. She moaned softly. Her eyes fluttered, then opened slowly, widening when she perceived him standing so close by.

"W-what . . . ," she murmured as she tried to sit up.

Bram put a hard hand to her shoulder, pushing her back against the pillows. He sat down on the side of the bed and braced an arm on the other side of her, effectively blocking any chance of escape.

"How are you feeling?" he asked almost cordially.

She swallowed with some difficulty and stared at him in bewilderment. "Feeling . . ."

"You appear to have fainted." His mouth twisted sardonically. "Do you do that often?"

Her cheeks darkened. "I've never fainted."

"You have now. Can you do it on command? That might come in handy."

Her eyes were shards of blue ice stabbing at him. "You think everything I say is a lie. You're so determined to believe whatever fits your preconceived notions that you don't see what's happening right in front of you. This house—"

"Oh, I see clearly enough," Bram interrupted. His gaze focused on her full mouth. Her lips were petal smooth, the precise shade of a rose just before it opens. A lush, tempting mouth, so very close, so enticing.

Her anger pierced his self-control. Resentment for what she was doing to him mingled with desire, which eclipsed all else. Thickly, he said, "I see a beautiful woman who isn't too particular about how she gets what she wants. So why should I be?"

His head moved, dark against the bed hangings. She had no time to withdraw and no way to do so. His arms closed around her, his big hand cupping the back of her head, holding her still for him. With deliberate ruthlessness, his mouth plundered hers.

She stiffened against him, her hands pressing against the wall of his chest. A small twinge of guilt moved through him, but he thrust it aside even as he gathered her more closely. Beneath his lips, her own softened. She made a small sound deep in her throat. A bolt of surprise roared through him as her body lifted slightly, her hands no longer resisting but instead touching him with tentative curiosity.

Tentative and innocent. Any thoughts he'd had to the contrary were banished in moments that, passion-heated though they were, exposed her inexperience. This was no sophisticated woman wise in the ways of the world, but rather an innocent whose artless sensuality pierced him to the core.

They were alone in the room, the door closed and the world held at bay. She was fire in his blood, raging need, a thirst that could not be denied. And susceptible, very, very susceptible. It would take very little effort to brush aside whatever natural reservations she felt and make her completely his.

But afterward . . . His conscience, ever inconvenient, bestirred itself. Afterward, he would have to live with the knowledge that he had taken advantage of her. *Taken advantage?* Which of them was truly the more vulnerable?

She lay beneath him, eyes half closed, mouth slightly swollen, the very picture of feminine power and temptation. His gaze drifted down over the curve of her breasts, which was accentuated by the snug fit of the velvet dress. Summoning all his strength, he forced himself to sit up, drawing her with him.

"I'm sorry," he said, "I shouldn't have done that." His tone was perfunctory, concealing the genuine regret he felt. He had never in his life misused a woman and he wasn't about to start now, no matter how great the enticement.

Yet his body was so hard that he actually hurt. Hands clenched, he moved away from the bed and stood with his back to her until he heard her rise and straighten her clothing.

Only then did he look at her again, noting reluctantly that she was still pale and that the self-possession he normally associated with her seemed to have disappeared entirely. Because of him? Gratifying as that might be to his vanity, he suspected there was more to it.

"What happened down there?" he demanded.

She touched fingers to her lips, staring at him. He watched as she struggled to contain—what? Fear, shock, dismay? Desire?

"Sit down," he said and pulled a chair out for her, "before you fall."

Her head lifted. She stared at him disdainfully. "I assure you I won't. Now please leave me. I need a few minutes—"

"Damn it, I said to sit down." More gently, he added, "If you could see yourself, you wouldn't argue."

She stared at him for a moment, as though wondering at his sudden concern. "Perhaps it's just as well that I can't." Without further ado, she took the chair. He kept his distance, giving her that much. If he went closer, he would touch her again. And if he did that—"

"I asked what happened."

"Will you hear me out? Not just dismiss what I say?"

Bram leaned back against the table. "That depends."

"On what?"

"Whether you can give me some reason to believe you're telling me the truth."

Nora took a deep breath. "I see." She straightened her shoulders and looked directly at him. Quietly, she said, "Well, to begin with I'm not a medium."

7

"I guessed that," Bram said. Lounging against the table, he was a dark and devastating presence. His chiseled features, the breadth of his shoulders and chest, the long, tensile strength of him all combined to steal her senses.

Too vividly, she remembered every exquisite detail of what had happened on the bed. Or almost happened. She was not so naive as to be ignorant of what he had wanted. Nor could she pretend that he had been alone in his desire.

Minutes ago, he had wanted to possess her. Now he wanted truth. In which lay the greater danger?

"You brought me here to try to prove that I was a fraud, didn't you?" she asked.

He shrugged, as though it was a matter of small importance. "Georgette is too trusting. I don't intend to let anyone take advantage of her."

"I would never do that. Your aunt hired me for an evening's entertainment. That's precisely what she got."

"No, she got the illusion that you were somehow more than you really are."

"Did she?" Nora demanded. "Or was that merely the image she cast in her own mind out of her private yearnings?"

Were they still talking about Georgette? She was no longer sure. All she knew for certain was that in this time and place, none of the usual rules seemed to apply. It was as though she had stepped out of the world she had always known and into an existence in which all things were possible. Even long-dead monks appearing in the drawing room.

"You accused me of making up the story about seeing a monk at the front door after you told me the history of this house."

"It seemed obvious."

"Then you won't believe me if I try to tell you what happened downstairs."

"You saw the monk again?"

She shook her head. "A group of monks, perhaps six in all. They were standing at the far end of the room. Their hoods were pulled up over their bent heads. They appeared to be praying."

Bram frowned. He stepped away from the table, but did not approach her. Instead, he paced over to the windows and stood looking out at the night-wrapped landscape.

"You've admitted you're not a medium but you're still sticking by your story?"

"Odd, isn't it?"

"Decidedly." He glanced at her over his shoulder. "What do you have to gain?"

Softly, she said, "The same thing you say you want—truth. Why are they here? How *can* they be here? And why do I see them when no one else seems to?"

"Why indeed?" His gaze swept over her, hooded so that she could not read his emotions beyond that same possession—that presumption that he had the right to possess her—brushing aside all other considerations. The sheer primitiveness of any such emotion, so out of keeping with the ordinary world, quickened her pulse. She had to stop herself from rising and seeking some avenue of retreat, for indeed there was none.

"You could leave," he said, giving her the uncanny sense that he had a window into her thoughts.

"No." Her voice was quiet, filled with certainty, "I cannot."

He smiled, white against the burnished tautness of his skin. "The thousand dollars."

"Having just confessed to not being a medium, I would think any payment is forfeit."

Her logic was unassailable. It bewildered him, a fact which gave her much pleasure. "Then why?" he demanded.

"Truth. I have to know."

"Whether this place is haunted?"

"That and the other." She hesitated, hands folded in her lap, so calm, so serene. So terrified. "About myself."

He came away from the window, standing surely too close to her. Very large against the darkness outside. She should have been frightened after the bed. Instead, she was oddly reassured.

He was being very reasonable, passion in check now, mind fully engaged by her and the problem she represented. He thought he knew the world, every aspect of his life pointed to that. Yet suddenly, in this place out of place and time out of time, hitherto denied possibilities were stirring.

"You just said you aren't a medium."

"That's right. I refused to be."

His brows knit. In the light of the gas lamps, his eyes had a pewter sheen. Nice eyes really, not at all as cold as she had once thought them. Indeed, fire shone against the silver, the steady flame of the lamps and a steadier one from within himself.

"You made a choice?"

"Somewhere along the way. I don't think I ever consciously thought it out, but Gramma Rianna presented certain possibilities to me, made me aware of certain things. I rejected them." She sighed, looking down at her hands, thinking of the way it had all been back then, safe and secure, predictable.

"I liked my world the way it was. My parents were good people, they took care of their children and prepared us for a life much like their own. That was fine with me." The corners of her mouth twitched. "I suppose you could say I lacked any instinct for rebellion."

"What changed?" he asked, dropping suddenly on his haunches, the fine fabric of his trousers straining over heavily muscled thighs. Looking at her so intently.

"They died." Such simple words, such a wealth of pain. "I assumed responsibility for my younger brother and sister. I got a job." This last part proudly, it was something too few women were still able to do. "Then I lost it. Gramma Rianna knew. She left me her trunk and disappeared, *after* writing that note to your aunt."

"She was trying to force you to change your mind, to accept what you had previously rejected?"

"To rebel? Well, perhaps, but also to be sensible. To do what I had to and I did, but I tried to do it on my own terms." Earnestly, she went on. "I truly don't believe I cheated your aunt. After that evening, I never intended to present myself as a medium again and I wouldn't have if you hadn't made that absurd offer of a thousand dollars."

He was so close she could see the pulse that leapt once, twice in the square line of his jaw. See the quick sliding away of his eyes concealing what—regret?

"The offer stands."

She did not try to hide her surprise. "Why should it?"

"If you prove this house to be haunted, don't you think you'll deserve it?"

"Do you even admit to the possibility of such a thing?"

He hesitated, mulling it over. She watched the play of thought behind his eyes and knew an instant before he decided. "I can be convinced," he said and held out his hand to her.

Bram told the guests she was resting. It seemed to satisfy them. They were content to talk over what they had seen, turning it this way and that, each contributing some item of imagined insight. On one point they all appeared to agree: something had happened. Miss Nora Butler had clearly been intensely affected by some presence in the room. He was congratulated for having found her.

Out of sorts, he sought out the den he had taken for his own and armored himself in solitude until they had all gone off to bed. Georgette was last, pausing at his door with an admonition.

"Now, Bram," she said, "I know you're out of sorts about all this but it was your idea. You really must be more open-minded."

"I'm trying," he promised because she was his mother's sister and not without merit of her own, a kind if sometimes too gullible woman who loved him as the son she had never had herself.

"Good," she said with a fond smile and went to her bed, leaving him alone in the study, listening to the ticking clock and thinking of long dead monks.

But not for long. Soon enough the object of his thoughts shifted. She would be asleep by now, he supposed. The day's long journey and the upset of the evening should guarantee it. Wilson had been instructed in the making of a soothing herbal tea from leaves gathered by Gramma Rianna and stored away in the trunk she left. Carried to Nora an hour or more, the tea should have done its work by now.

What other potions did she possess, he wondered. Something to explain this strange unsettled yet pleasurable feeling he was experiencing? Something to explain why a man as strong-willed as himself seemed unable to think of anything but a woman he should not in all honor approach.

She was an orphan, supporting a younger brother and sister. About that he had no shred of doubt. She had spoken with a too simple starkness and honest pain for that particular truth to be denied. Misunderstanding her, presuming the worst, he had made her an offer beyond her wildest imaginings, a chance for a life not merely for herself but for all three of them that she could not deny.

She had taken it courageously. He admired that, new for him who had liked many women, desired more than a few, but had seldom been moved to genuine admiration. She provoked that along with so much else. So much unsettling.

There was a brandy decanter on the sideboard. He glanced at it, briefly considering it, then decided no. He needed nothing to befog his thoughts.

The clock in the stone-floored hall chimed midnight. He rose, stretching his long, lithe frame. The day had been long for him, too. It was time to retire.

But first—Pausing in front of his door, his eyes drifted down the shadowed hallway. She was there, in her own room, in bed, no doubt soundly asleep. Were he to merely check on her, see for himself that she was all right, she need never know. And besides, his duty as both host and employer seemed to require him to make such a gesture in light of her recent disability.

So did he rationalize the need, all the while grimly aware that he had never needed such excuses before, but had merely followed his own will wherever it happened to lead. Not this night though, as he walked pantherlike in silence down the hall and stood before her door. A strip of light shone beneath it.

Had she left a light on to help her sleep? The glow was steady, betokening a gas lamp, not a candle. Even so, he worried. She did not know the room. What if she woke in the night, and rising, upset the lamp?

Slowly, he eased the door open, intending merely to assure himself that she was well and to check the position of the lamp. He need not have bothered. The lamp was fine, situated dead center in the table beside the bed, well enough back from all sides that no sudden jarring would upend it.

As for Nora herself, she, too, was perfectly well. A little startled to see him there, at her door, in the night and the silence. But not so much so that she couldn't rise from the chair where she had been sitting, and lifting the mirror she held in her hand, beckon him to enter.

8

"What are you doing?" Bram asked. She had taken off the blue velvet gown of earlier and wore instead a simple white lawn dress. Her hair was swept back from her face and secured by a blue bow the same shade as her eyes. She looked absurdly young and innocent, the last person to be cast in the role of searcher after long-dead monks. The last woman to be the object of his own unbridled desire.

"Nothing," she said, setting the mirror aside. She rose gracefully, smoothing her skirt. "I couldn't sleep."

"Neither could I."

They stared at one another, full of unspoken questions. Finally, Bram said, because he could think of nothing else remotely safe, "It's an odd hour for it, but would you care for a tour of the house?"

She agreed at once, anything rather than stand there so close together with the stillness all around them. "Has everyone else gone to bed?" she asked as they stepped into the hallway.

"Some time ago. I apologize for coming in as I did, but I truly thought you would be asleep. I had some concern about the lamp."

As explanations went, it wasn't terribly much, but she accepted it all the same. Better that than to venture down the slippery slope of why he had really come and what he had really intended.

She shivered slightly as they reached the ground floor and drew the shawl she'd brought along more closely around her shoulders. "You said the stones from the monastery were used in the foundation and for this floor?"

Bram nodded. "So the family's lawyer informed me. In addition, there are some wall hangings that were brought along as well as some of the original plate and a few other items."

"Is there anything to tell us more about the history of the monastery?"

"Not that I'm aware of, but we might take a look in the library. The books date from much later than the monastery, of course, but there could be something useful."

"That's an excellent idea. After all, we could search the house itself from now to doomsday and not find anything."

He opened the heavy oak door to the library and stood aside to let her enter first. "I'm surprised you're not more optimistic. Don't these things usually have to do with restless dead, bodies requiring proper burial, that sort of thing?"

Nora wrinkled her nose. The lamp he carried to light their way flickered as he set it down on a nearby table. It cast a huge shadow along the high wall of the library, the shadow of a man and a woman vastly larger than life, their shapes merging into one another.

"Think about it," she said, turning away from the shadow to concentrate on the tier upon tier of books that ran up to the ceiling. "Any bodies that were buried at the monastery surely weren't moved when the buildings were dismantled. Even if someone had been immured in the walls, their remains would have been found then."

"Ghastly thought. Did that sort of thing happen?"

"Fairly frequently. At any rate, there can't possibly be any human remains here. This has to be a case of some sort of spiritual energy remaining in a place long after all else is gone."

"Why would it?"

She shrugged. "Who knows? To finish some task, right some wrong, serve out a sentence of some sort. There are any number of possibilities."

"What do you mean, serve out a sentence? These were supposed to be holy men."

She fingered a volume bound in rich Moroccan leather, the title embossed in gold along the spine. "Hmm, supposed to be. Monks were only human after all. Some of them proved to be pretty frail."

"You said you saw a half-dozen or so in the chapel. If there are that many still around, wouldn't that suggest some sort of general crime, not merely an individual backsliding?"

"Let's not jump to conclusions. First, I'd like to find out if anyone wrote down a history of the monastery."

Bram glanced around at the vast tiers of books fading off into the darkness beyond the circle of light. "That could take a while."

"You don't have to help," she said softly. "I realize none of this is really believable to you."

"Fine. I'll just go on to bed then and leave you down here alone."

The quick flash of apprehension across her delicate features made him shake his head wryly. "Do you honestly think I'd do that, Nora?"

It did not escape either of them that he had used

her given name. His voice was low and gentle but with an edge of roughness that made her stomach tighten. She was glad of the large room, the space between them, and all the hundreds upon hundreds of books to provide distraction.

"I don't know what to think," she admitted softly.

Firelight danced in his eyes. She turned away and reached out blindly toward the books.

They searched for an hour at least, perhaps more. The books were dusty, making them both sneeze. Some of the titles were amusingly quaint, they read them out to each other. Bram found a volume of poetry he particularly liked and quoted from it. Nora discovered a playwright she had always enjoyed and described her very first trip to the theater.

There were books about other parts of the world, many of which Bram had seen for himself. He was in the midst of a story about sailing down the Ganges when Nora reached for a volume just beyond her grasp. The high ladder on which she stood was attached by rollers to the shelves. It moved smoothly—too smoothly—picking up speed surprisingly fast. She was startled at first, then laughed and pushed herself along so that the ladder fairly flew along the wall.

Her white skirt billowed behind her as she finally came to a stop in a far corner near the windows. "This is more fun than I thought it would be," she said gaily.

Bram grinned, watching her with unfeigned enjoyment. She was being silly and knew it. The circumstances demanded decorum, but that was beyond her, off there somewhere in the proper world where men and women who desired one another did not linger among dusty volumes of distant worlds.

Here, perched high on the ladder, sailing past her sensible concerns, she was merely, completely, startlingly happy. Without reason, to be sure, but happy all the same and content for the moment to let that happiness be without questions or regrets.

She gazed down at him even as he looked up at her. He was very fit, she thought distantly. Not the sort of man who spent his days behind a desk or at his club. There was a hard, tensile strength about him that spoke of wild places.

He held himself very still, looking at her, but she felt his desire as intensely as she felt her own. She would have been less a woman if the knowledge that this strong, proud man wanted her so powerfully hadn't evoked a certain secret pleasure.

Perhaps if she hadn't been so absorbed in him, she would have sensed something wrong sooner. But all her attention was focused on Bram. Distantly, she felt the ladder move, but thought nothing of it until it shook again, more strongly. Suddenly, the ladder quaked violently. Nora reached out a hand to hold on but too late. A surprised cry escaped her as she lost her balance and fell from her high perch straight toward the stone floor.

9

Bram lunged. One moment he was standing several yards away watching Nora, the next he was directly beneath her. She landed in his arms, caught safe.

Or not. The shock of the fall made her cling to him. Made him hold her tightly. Made them both vividly aware of how easily things could change in an instant, for better, for worse. How terribly fragile it all was.

Put her down, his mind said. Set her feet on the ground, step away, put your hands behind your back and keep them there.

No, his heart declared, body and spirit in agreement. No, flatly and without discussion. He was a man of reason who would shun it at this moment torn out of time, possessor of an indomitable will that had unaccountably gone missing now when he needed it most.

She was warm in his arms, slender and yielding, hands still entwined in the fine linen of his shirtfront, eyes pools of startled light. It was a well-appointed library, having both books and a convenient couch on which to sit to read them.

Or not. Couches had other uses. He crossed the room in half-a-dozen strides and lowered her onto the velvet-covered horsehair. She was very pale. He sat down beside her, arms holding her in gentle captivity.

"What happened?" he asked, the words grating slightly as he considered for the first time what could have happened to her. At the very least, a fall from such a height onto a stone floor would have left her badly injured. At worst—

He would not think of that. She was here, close beneath his hand. It was enough.

It was not. He was a fool to pretend otherwise. She was exquisite, enthralling, a fire in his blood and a hunger that would not be denied. Yet for all that, he moved slowly, still holding himself in strictest check.

Let her protest or express the slightest fear and he would withdraw. It might require a long walk in the cool night, but he would manage it. Honor demanded no less.

Slowly, very slowly, the back of his fingers brushed her cheek. She raised a hand—to stop him? Her hand curled around his, fingers entwining, holding him to her.

His breath stopped, resumed raggedly. He kissed her curled fingers, the curve of her ear, the pale line of her throat. Her skin was damask smooth, faintly scented with lavender. He clutched handfuls of the soft, billowing white dress, tracing the shape of her beneath, high full breasts, a tapered waist pliant without the stiffness of a corset, rounded hips and slender thighs. Gaining knowledge with his hands, learning the way of her, claiming her as his own.

She moaned and clung to him, passion meeting passion, as strong in her own right as he was in his. Tiny pearl buttons marched down the front of her bodice. One gave way to him, another, and another. His mouth followed, dipping into the sweet hollow at the base of her throat, exploring the swell of her breasts.

Sweet, unbridled madness drifted on the night air, wrapped round in stillness, measured by the deep groan of a man and the soft, surprised cry of a woman. She was fire in his arms, silken heat, a promise and a dream wrapped in stunning reality.

The barrier of their clothing was rapidly becoming intolerable. He was tempted to rip it all aside, lay her on the ground, and take her then and there. But the ground was stone and the thought intolerable. She deserved far better, this woman of courage and strength.

Upstairs in his room was a wide bed with silken covers only waiting to receive them both. But first—

His hand slipped inside her bodice, cupping her breast. He pushed the fabric down further, exposing the exquisitely formed peak. His tongue flicked over her, tasting, savoring. She twisted beneath him, hands tangling in the thick mane of his hair.

The dress yielded further until both her breasts were exposed above the lacy fabric, her nipples taut. He moved from one to the other, suckling her deeply. When at last he raised his head, her eyes were slumberous with desire. Auburn hair, filled with lambent fire, spilled across the couch. Her eyes were heavy, her shoulders and breasts bare, her nipples moist from his caresses. She was the image of female sensuality, there for the taking.

Not there. On that he was determined. Despite the fire raging in his blood and the hardness straining against his trousers, he stood—just a bit shakily—and lifted her.

"Where—?" she murmured dazedly.

Speech was almost beyond him, so great was the effort to maintain even a shred of control, but he managed. "Upstairs. I want you where we won't be disturbed."

Her cheeks flamed, but she offered no objection. He yanked the library door open and strode out into the entry hall. Swiftly, he mounted the curving steps. Never had he thirsted for a woman with such driving obsession. Never had the need to wait even briefly so threatened to overwhelm him.

His jaw clenched. The top of the stairs was directly above. A few quick paces down the hall and they would—

A scream shattered the night stillness, echoing off

the paneled walls and frightening the blackbirds from
their nests in the eaves.

10

"A mouse?" Bram repeated. Disbelief curled through
his voice.

A flushed and still semihysterical Georgette nodded, clutching her *robe de chambre* about her, looking
apologetic and defiant all at the same time.

"You know how much I loathe those horrible
things. When I couldn't sleep and went to light the
lamp, one of them"—she shuddered convulsively—
"Horrible, just horrible. What possessed God to create such vermin?"

Nora pressed her lips together hard. The hasty rear-
ranging of her clothes did little to mask the turmoil
of emotions still coursing through her. Had Georgette
been even a little less preoccupied with her own concerns, she would undoubtedly have realized something
was amiss.

Something concerning her nephew and the hired
help.

How could she have behaved so shamefully, thrown
away the strictures of a lifetime, forgotten honor and
duty, sense and sensibility in a firestorm of passion
that still resonated throughout her?

And he— She dared a glance in Bram's direction.
He appeared completely self-possessed except for the
disarrangement of his hair and the flush of color staining his high-boned cheeks. Surely she had imagined
the man of unbridled passion, the dark lover guiding
her through hitherto unimagined realms of desire?

Sweet lord, her mind was going. She had come to

the very brink of disaster, but thanks be to Georgette—and the mouse—there was time to draw back.

But no will to do so. Regret threatened to swamp her. Even as her mind struggled to reassert itself, her wayward body still yearned for what it had so briefly experienced. Beside her, she felt the tension in Bram and marveled at his control. Not a flicker of anger or regret showed in his manner toward his aunt. He was the sole of patience and consideration.

But why shouldn't he be? She was a woman of his own class, deserving of every possible regard. Whereas Nora—

Oh, God, what a fool she'd been. To forget everything that had been drummed into her since childhood, to ignore her duty and responsibilities, to throw it all away on a whim—?

No, not a whim. Whatever had driven her, it had not been remotely a whim. She had to acknowledge that and deal with it or there would be no hope for her.

"I don't know how I'll get back to sleep," Georgette said, fretting. "Every time I shut my eyes, I'll see that dreadful thing."

"Why don't you come to my room?" Nora suggested. She ignored the quick glance Bram shot her and went on, "You're welcome to sleep there. I'm sure we won't be disturbed."

"Why thank you, dear," Georgette said. She beamed a grateful smile. "That is very good of you."

"Not at all," Nora murmured. She took the older woman's arm and walked with her down the hall. Behind her, she felt Bram's eyes boring into her, but she did not look back.

Morning came too soon. Nora woke from a fitful

sleep, stiff-backed and more tired than when she had
nodded off. Not so Georgette. She slept deeply.

Bram had gone riding. So Wilson informed her
when she descended to breakfast. The other guests
were also still asleep or off after their own
amusements.

She was left to herself. And to the library.

There was an alternative, she could spend the morning moping about, thinking about what happened the
night before. Down that path lay confusion, shame,
thwarted desire, and bewilderment.

The library beckoned. She would lose herself among
the books and perhaps in the process even find some
clue to the mystery of the monks.

In daylight, the room was at once more dramatic
and more prosaic than it had been at night. Its dimen-
sions stood starkly revealed, no longer the vast cavern
of imagination. But the books still ran on, rank after
rank, stretching to the ceiling almost twenty feet
above and down two facing walls. Thousands of volumes, each leather-bound, a world unto itself.

Sternly, she resolved on discipline. With such a
wealth of reading, there had to be a guide of some
sort. The library, apparently never used since the
house's abandonment decades before, must have been
intended as more than an amusement. Someone at
some time must have thought to use it.

Such was her faith in the motives of the vanished
robber baron, but it proved misplaced. An hour later,
she had at last admitted the inescapable. The books
were for show, nothing more. They had been brought
to this place, and left there, because they were no
different from the wallpaper or the flooring. They existed merely to be seen.

Still, she refused to give up. There had to be something ... some clue ... some hope. Eyes itching from the dust, she kept looking, until at last just when she was about to give up, she found hidden away in a desk drawer a crumpled sheaf of papers. Upon examination, they proved to be an inventory written in the neat, crabbed hand of a long-forgotten clerk. An inventory of the books.

And there it was, halfway down on page eight: *The Monks' Tale, Being a History of St. Alban's Monastery, Late of Infamous Regard.*

Late of Infamous Regard? Sounded promising. Now where—? Twelfth case to the right on the north wall, nineteenth shelf. Which put it up near the ceiling. Right about where she had fallen the night before.

Nora hesitated. It was all very well to decide to go detecting on her own, but did she really want to risk another encounter with the shaking ladder without Bram there to save her?

Did she really want to wait for him to return?

She would be very careful, go slowly, hold on tightly. It would be fine.

And so it seemed to be. She reached the top shelf without incident and managed to locate the volume. Climbing down with exaggerated care, she breathed a sigh of relief when she reached the bottom, the book clutched tight in her hand.

It was smaller than many of the other volumes in the library, being no more than six inches in height and three across. The leather bindings were badly cracked, but the pages when she opened them were unfrayed and the ink unfaded.

The type style was centuries old and difficult to read at first, but soon enough she was able to proceed with greater speed. St. Alban's founded in 1211, favored by various nobles over the years, a respected place. Until—

Bram drew rein on the ridge above the house. He had been riding for hours but felt as tautly drawn as when he set out. The day was pleasantly cool. Clouds gathering on the western horizon suggested a storm before nightfall. That would suit his mood perfectly.

Despite the sleepless night he had spent, he felt almost too alert. The world all around him had taken on a more vivid hue, each leaf more sharply etched, each brush of wind more keenly felt.

He was losing his mind. Over a fey charlatan, no less, who couldn't even manage to be a good fake medium. A woman given to strange visions, inopportune falls, and the unholy ability to fracture reason.

Three more days. The house party had that much longer to go and he was damned if he'd end it a moment early. If she could stick it out, he could bloody well do the same. And then—

Oh, yes, then. A grim smile curved his mouth. There was a reckoning to come. Like it or not, he could not deny what Nora made him feel. Trying to escape it was useless, as the long ride had shown. It would have to be confronted and dealt with, which meant—

He preferred not to think about that. The keen bite of irony would have to wait. Never mind that he, a man of the world, had been brought low by an untried girl. It had happened before and it undoubtedly would again. He would last out these few days and then—

His eyes narrowed. Looking toward the house, he thought he saw . . . Surely he was mistaken? That stray wisp of gray must have been a trick of the eyes. No, there it was again, thicker now and unmistakable. Smoke was coming not from the half-dozen brick chimneys peppering the roof, but from the first floor, near where the old chapel had been.

Smoke that grew denser and more ominous by the moment.

11

Nora's finger touched the rough stone pillar, part of the underground vault beneath the first floor of the house. Nearby, the lamp she had brought flickered. Long ago, the vault had been used to store all manner of materials used in the construction of the house. Very little effort had been made to remove what was left. Stacks of paneling, wooden moldings, cabinet doors, and the like littered the floor and were stacked against the walls. She'd had to climb over them to find what she was looking for.

It was here, exactly as the book described, the markings of the pentagram carved into the stone long ago by the hands of heretic monks drawn to call upon a very different sort of master.

A sigh escaped her. Surely there was enough evil in the world without misguided people trying to conjure up even more? Yet the monks of St. Alban's had done exactly that, succumbing to the temptations of the flesh, forgetting their holy vows and trying to summon evil into their very midsts.

Had they succeeded? A cold shiver ran down her back. Gramma Rianna had always told her that their power came from the light, one with the renewing strength of the world born again each spring. Nora no longer doubted that. She felt the strength of birth and life deep within her being, flowing out into the dark stone vault to challenge whatever twisted forces had dwelled there.

Despite what they had done, she felt a spurt of sympathy for the poor, twisted minds that had condemned themselves to such a barren eternity. If there had been anything she could do for them, she would have. But this was no simple restless spirit who could be assuaged and sent on his way. This was beyond her ability to help.

Regretfully, she bent to pick up the lamp. Bram meant to tear the house down, but that would not solve the problem of the stones. Nothing she knew of could solve it.

Her fingers touched the metal ring on top of the lamp. It was within her reach, she was straightening up, when the same unexpected vibration she had felt on the ladder struck her again. Quickly, she reached out a hand to steady herself. Her palm touched the pentagram.

The vault shook. It vibrated so forcefully that Nora could not keep her hold on the lamp. It fell, the glass globe smashing on the floor, flame and oil running together straight toward a pile of waste wood.

Nora screamed. Too late she felt the full rage and insanity of the trapped monks. Doomed as they were, they did not intend to spend eternity alone. Unseen spectral hands reached out to clutch her as she ran, back the way she had come, stumbling through the darkness to find the door.

It was locked. She had left it open, she knew she had. But now no amount of strength could budge it. Behind her, the fire fed greedily, inching ever closer to where she stood even as billowing smoke began to fill the narrow space between the floor and the low ceiling.

Desperately, she realized that she would not burn to death. The smoke would kill her first.

"Is everyone out!" Bram shouted. He leaped from the saddle before the horse came fully to a stop. Wilson was there, his arm around a frantic Georgette. Several guests and servants milled around, pointing to the smoke billowing out and shaking their heads in confusion.

"I haven't seen Miss Butler, sir," Wilson said. "She went into the library a short time ago. When we realized there was a fire, I checked there first but there was no sign of her."

"Her room?" Bram demanded. Dread filled him. He fought it down.

"I banged on the door," Georgette said, gasping. "There was no answer."

"I don't understand what could have started this, sir," Wilson began. "We have been most scrupulous—"

Bram barely heard him. He raced into the house. Smoke was already thick on the first floor and drifting up the stairs to the second. He put a hand over his mouth and nose and kept going. The library was empty, as Wilson had said. Swiftly, he mounted the stairs.

"Nora," he shouted, thrusting her door open. "Are you here?"

No answer, only silence to mock him and the acrid stench of the smoke. He looked around hastily. The bed was neatly made. Beside it was the carpetbag she had brought. He grabbed it, distantly thinking she would not want to lose her grandmother's belongings, and hurried out.

She might have already escaped the house. Surely, that was what had happened. She couldn't possibly have stayed.

But why hadn't Wilson or anyone else seen her? What had she been doing in the library? What had she found?

The smoke was even thicker on the first floor than it had been just minutes before. His breathing was ragged and his eyes burning as he went into the library again, searching for any sign of Nora. A book lay open on the desk, *The Monks' Tale, Being a History*—

She'd been right, there was information on the monastery. But that didn't tell him where she had gone. Lights danced before his eyes. He bent over, coughing harshly, and staying low made his way from the room.

Sweet lord, where was she? Outside and safe or trapped inside? The house was enormous, the smoke spreading rapidly. But where was the fire? He had found no sign of it. Where—

His foot caught on the doorjamb right outside the library. He tripped, began to fall, stopped himself, but not before the carpetbag slipped from his hold and spilled across the floor. The bronze mirror landed right in front of him.

Cursing, he scooped it up, intending to tuck it into his shirt and— He frowned, squeezing his eyes to try to clear them. Something moved in the mirror. The smoke?

Pain seared his lungs. He had to get out himself soon or he would die. But instead he stood, rooted in place, staring into the mirror. Behind the polished bronze, deep within it, light shifted. He saw not his face, not the smoke, but eyes wide and lustrous, terrified, a sea of auburn hair, and lips full and soft that shaped a single word: *Bram*.

He heard her, impossibly through the thick walls her voice reached out to him. He thrust the mirror under his shirt and ran, heedless of his starved lungs, toward the far end of the hall.

Ancient hinges creaked resentfully as he wrenched the heavy oak door open. Flames licked at the base of the stairs leading down into the vault. Nora fell into his arms. Her face was covered with soot and she was unconscious, incapable of making any sound.

Yet he had heard her. He must have for what he had seen in the mirror could only have been a trick of his desperate mind. Couldn't it?

The bronze was cool against his skin as he turned and with Nora held safe in his arms, ran from the house. Behind him, the fire leapt high.

He laid her on the fragrant grass. Georgette, Wilson, and others clustered around, but he brushed them away and bent, trembling over her. Please God—

She was so pale beneath the soot and grime. Her breasts seemed to barely move. Was she breathing? Or had life—precious, exquisite life—fled on the curling smoke?

Pain corkscrewed through him. He could not bear it. Better not to live himself than to exist with such anguish. A fierce strength rose from deep within him, hurling defiance against his darkest fear. She could not be gone. He would not allow it. To keep her, he would face the howling maw of death itself.

He bent, head dark against the smoke-grimed sky. His hand cupped her cheek, so tenderly, another slipped beneath her neck. His mouth touched hers, so

cold were her lips, unmoving against his. And yet—
Surely, the essence of Nora, proud, beautiful, and defiant, still flickered there.

The wind shifted. A breeze blew out over the river,
crisp and clean as the nearby sea. He filled his lungs
with it, seizing her close, and on a silent prayer, gathered her to him, never to let her go, not while the
breath remained in him.

Time ceased. He was aware of nothing except Nora
in his arms and close at hand, far too close, that dark
and howling presence, hungering for her. The battle
began.

His weapons were few. Breath, to be sure, filling
her lungs, but behind each breath was the fierce
strength of his own spirit. He claimed her in this most
powerful way possible. Yet he also gave, unstintingly
and without hesitation, life to life, soul to soul, until
at last the howling faded, growing faint, retreating.

She stirred, so slightly that at first he didn't feel it,
but then again. He raised his head, hardly daring to
hope. Her eyelids fluttered, opened slowly.

"Bram?" she whispered and raised her hand, fingers
catching the tear that slid soundlessly down his burnished cheek.

EPILOGUE

"It's done," Bram said. He crossed the bedroom,
shrugging off his robe as he went. By the time he
reached the bed, he was gloriously naked once again,
his hard, muscled body resplendent in the light filtering through the gauze curtains.

Nora smiled and reached out a hand to him. Wilson
had brought the message—a very discreet Wilson who

had adjusted surprisingly well to the recent changes in his master's household. The news had not been unexpected, but she was glad to have it all the same.

"Done," she murmured, holding up the sheet for him. He slipped beneath the sheet and drew her close, their bodies nestling against each other with ease that belied how new this still was to them, this sweetly heated familiarity, this blessed privacy, this thing called—

"It's for the best," he said, interrupting her thoughts. His lips brushed hers. She could feel his smile. "Although the workmen may have thought I was mad."

The fire had destroyed the house. Only a few charred timbers were left. Those and the stones. Bram had given the orders. The ruin was completely razed down to the ground. Even the foundation was removed, the vault disassembled, and everything piled into carts to be hauled away.

The final resting place for St. Alban's monks was a disused quarry hard on the New England shore. There the stones were thrown down, not one standing upon another, and the pit filled in with more stones, gravel and dirt until nothing remained but a smooth, untroubled surface waiting to be sown with wild grasses.

On the ridge above the sea, a new house would be built, shaped by love and free of the past.

Nora moved slightly, her hips brushing Bram. He groaned, then shook his head wryly. "What you do to me."

Her eyes widened in pretended innocence. "Whatever do you mean?"

"This," he said and firmly guided her hand to the

proof of his desire. She flushed but did not draw back, so swiftly did her passion mount to meet his own.

"We're due at Georgette's for supper in a few hours. She's being very good about all this."

"Hmm."

"Some people wouldn't have been so accepting." Indeed, much of New York society was still reeling from the news that Bram Hayes had married his aunt's medium. That might have caused a problem except that Georgette—and Bram himself—had made it clear they would tolerate none.

Fickle as the wind, society agreed. It was new, daring, unexpected. In short, marvelous. Nora was welcome everywhere, but wanted to go nowhere, only here in the quiet room and the wide bed where passion soared and love was fulfilled.

A soft gasp broke from her. Would she ever become used to this? Sixty, seventy years, who knew, she might even be a bit blasé?

Bram raised his head. His silvered eyes devoured her. "What's so funny?"

"Nothing."

He touched his mouth to her rib cage, along the indentation of her waist, to the underswell of her breasts. "I felt it, the laughter, deep inside you."

"What else do you feel?" she asked softly, hands tangling in his ebony hair. Gold gleamed on her finger, gold poured through the light, gold and bronze mingled in the clutter on the dressing table. All that jewelry he insisted on giving her, and Rianna's mirror.

"I mustn't forget," she murmured, forgetting already, all else swamped by the exquisite sensations he unleashed.

"What?" he whispered against her skin.

"The mirror . . . tonight . . . Rianna . . ."

She meant to say Georgette had received a note, Rianna was returning, might even be at the supper, "looking forward to meeting Bram at last," she'd said, and added a postscript "so glad everything worked out as it was meant to be."

Had she known then, seen it all somehow, and even taken steps to bring them together? It was doubtful Rianna would ever say. But Nora could wonder. Or would have had not wonder of another kind filled her, not of the mirror and the power, but of this man and this life, so miraculously made hers. Wonder to last a lifetime and beyond.

A breeze billowed the curtains, blowing them into the room. Outside, birdsong mingled with the muted sounds of the city. The man and the woman did not hear. They were lost in a world of their own making. Lost in wonder.

The Demon's Bride

by
Jo Beverley

"SO THE GIRL was burnt to a cinder," concluded Lord Morden impassively.

The Reverend Joseph Proudfoot rubbed his plump hands together. "Fascinating, my lord. Fascinating."

The vicar's daughter, however, gazed at the earl in shock. How could any human—even a soulless rake—be so unmoved by such an event?

As if Rachel had spoken, the earl met her disapproving gaze and she was the focus of startlingly blue and wicked eyes. He raised a brow and said with derisive gentleness, "It was nearly a century ago, Miss Proudfoot."

Rachel hastily lowered her head and recorded the grisly details, wishing her color wasn't always so ready to betray her. She found her writing was not as neat as usual, but it wasn't all the fault of the disreputable earl. She had been prey to a morbid fear of burning to death since it had happened to an aunt when Rachel was but a child. She had not witnessed the event, but her parents' whispered comments had made a deep impression. The thought of a poor girl being consumed by the flames of a Walpurgis Night bonfire was truly horrible.

"And no one was ever brought to book over it, my lord?" her father asked.

"Back in 1668 matters in this corner of the country were primitive, Vicar. Inquiries were made, of course. . . ." The earl had been standing by the fire, one booted foot raised on the scuttle there, but now he moved restively to sit in a chair. "The people here are secretive by nature, Vicar. They claimed that their innocent revels turned tragic when the girl fell into the fire. It may have been true."

Rachel flicked a surprised glance at Lord Morden. It was not just the local peasantry who were secretive, it would appear. She noted in her record that the earl had concealed something, probably some matter concerning his family. How peculiar.

Her father pursued it. "Do you doubt that it was a simple mischance, my lord?"

The earl made no other betraying move, but every arrogant line of his body seemed to say, I have been gracious enough to consent to speak to you, and to tell you of the customs in my land. Do you presume to interrogate me?

Such a man could not be pressured for details, but a silence would often bring out information just as well as questioning. Rachel spent the small hiatus flexing her tired fingers and exchanging her pencil for a fresh one. Then she allowed herself the indulgence of admiring the pleasantly modern room in which they were seated. The earl might be a rake and a wastrel—which is what local gossip said—but his house was very fine.

Instead of somber paneling, the small drawing room was finished in the new style, with white paint and plaster. It gave the chamber a sense of air and light even on a rather gloomy October day. With a large fire in the beautiful marble fireplace and a thick carpet over the floor, it was the epitome of modern comfort.

Rachel was not a young woman who hankered after luxury, but she couldn't help thinking that a little of this elegance would be pleasant at the vicarage. Their new home was a warren of small, darkly paneled rooms with bare floors.

Her wandering eye was caught by a portrait directly opposite her. It featured a handsome young man somewhat arrogantly posed beside a very fine black horse. His blond hair was unpowdered and carelessly dressed so that strands blew loose in the breeze, and his bright blue eyes shone with the joy of living. The artist appeared to have captured a moment when his subject had just dismounted after an exhilarating ride, ready for more adventures.

It was astonishingly lifelike, and Rachel found the subject's direct look and challenging half-smile compelling. It was as if he were about to invite *her* to share in his next mad-cap scheme. . . .

"Miss Proudfoot." The earl's voice abruptly captured her attention. "Are you admiring the artist, or the subject?"

Rachel colored, as much at having given the earl an excuse to change the topic, as at being caught staring. "It is a remarkably fine portrait, my lord."

"Indeed it is. The picture was executed by a local man, a Mr. Gainsborough. He has recently removed to Bath, where I predict a fine future for him. The subject is myself some twelve or more years ago—in my innocent youth."

Rachel felt her face heat, and was hard put not to

stare between the portrait and the earl in astonishment. How had the golden youth turned so to dross?

And yet now that it had been pointed out, she could see the resemblance—the same lean, fine-boned features, startlingly blue eyes, and careless energy.

The earl spoke again, and Rachel concentrated on her recording.

"To answer your question, Vicar, I have wondered about that tragic event. But Walpurgis Night is celebrated on Dymons Hill every year, and there is no other record of tragedy. The festivities appear innocent, or as innocent as such things ever are."

The earl looked again at Rachel, but she was ready for him this time and smiled innocently back. She was twenty-four years old and had acted as assistant and amanuensis to her father for eight years. She was perfectly aware that these local revels always included excessive drinking, and often grossly lewd behavior.

"Walpurgis Night revels are not unknown in England, my lord," prompted the vicar. "And despite their roots in the worship of the demon Waldborg, and their connection to witchcraft, I have found no case of one that was anything but an excuse for unseemly jollity."

"Ah," said the earl with a glint in his eye, "but here we have a refinement."

Rachel came to full alert.

The earl smiled slightly, and seemed to be speaking directly to her. "There is a local tradition that when Walpurgis Night falls on the feast of the Ascension, it is of special significance. They call it Dym's Night."

"But St. Walburga's day is May first," said the vicar with a frown. "That would make Walpurgis

Night April the thirtieth, which is far too early for Ascension Day, my lord."

"I think you will find that it is not, Vicar."

Rachel's father performed some rapid calculations. "It would mean that Easter would have to be . . . March the twenty-second!" he announced, eyes bright. "The earliest possible day! Rare, but it does occur."

"The last occurrence being in 1668," pointed out the earl gently. "The year the girl died in the fire. The next occurrence, I am told, will be in 1761. Next year."

"By the stars!" exclaimed Reverend Proudfoot, sitting up straight. "This is most fortuitous, my lord. What an opportunity to record a rare ceremony!"

"Burning and all?" asked the earl dryly.

Reverend Proudfoot flushed. "No, no. But . . ." His voice dropped almost to a whisper. "My lord, you cannot suppose that we have here a tradition of *human sacrifice*?"

Despite her training, Rachel almost dropped her pencil. She stared at the earl, and his sardonic face became macabre. Despite the fire, the room was turning decidedly chilly.

Then he looked at her, and she saw that he was enjoying his effect. Was his story even true?

"It does seem unlikely in this age of reason and enlightenment, doesn't it?" he said to her. "It bears watching, though." He turned to her father. "Perhaps by the shepherd of the flock?"

Rachel saw now why they had been so readily afforded this interview with the earl, and perhaps why her father had been offered this living. The Reverend

Joseph Proudfoot's interest in superstitions was well known.

Her father nodded. "I will keep a close eye on events, my lord."

"It will have to be very close, Vicar. The people here are wary of strangers. Even though my family have been here for nearly two hundred years, we are considered strangers still. And you and your daughter are very new here indeed."

Again he looked at Rachel, looked her over in fact. She was not the sort of woman men directed such looks at, and yet she was embarrassed. Perhaps it was just that she was unaccustomed to a man like the Earl of Morden. Despite his dissipated way of life, the earl was a remarkably handsome man and yes, that vital force she had detected in the portrait still flowed through him. . . .

He spoke abruptly. "There are some records of the events in 1668 in the muniment room. Perhaps you would care to examine them."

This was a dismissal, and Rachel was pleased to escape. The once chilly room was now too hot.

She and her father rose with many expressions of appreciation of the earl's graciousness in speaking with them. They were shepherded by a footman down one floor, and along a number of corridors to the bleak but dustfree room wherein the earldom kept its records.

The journey gave Rachel an opportunity to regain her wits. For pity's sake, the Earl of Morden would never even give Rachel Proudfoot a moment's thought!

No matter how rakish the owner, his muniment room was well organized, with record books on shelves, loose documents in boxes, and maps and charts in narrow drawers. It had even been catalogued by a family amateur, and so it did not take Rachel and her father long to find the records of the enquiry into the unfortunate death on Walpurgis Night, 1668.

The earl had not made up that story, at least.

"Her name was Meg Brewstock," said Rachel, taking notes. "There are still Brewstocks, aren't there, with a farm out near Haverhill? She was a dairy maid here at Morden Abbey. . . . Goodness. She was only sixteen."

Her father was flicking through a sheaf of papers which had been found with the records. "This general account of local customs says that a girl is selected every year to play a part in the Walpurgis Night festivities. She is called Dym's Bride—the Demon's Bride, I fancy. What's the odds Meg Brewstock was Dym's Bride in 1668? As usual, the bride is supposed to be a virgin, so probably they are all quite young. . . ."

"The Demon's Bride!" exclaimed Rachel. "That's horrid."

The vicar smiled. "A fancy only, my dear, I'm sure. I doubt the people here think as much of it as did the writer of these notes. I detect an excessive interest in the strange and lurid, and," he added, waggling his eyebrows, "in tales of young virgins."

Rachel chuckled. Her father's dry common sense could always bring these fanciful matters into focus. "But I still think it unpleasant to be forcing any girl into such a role, especially in the light of what happened to Meg."

"I'm sure that was pure mishap. See, this writer recorded the Dym's Brides from 1669 to 1680. All came through the experience hale and hearty. He does note, however, that all these girls married before the end of the summer, and many produced a babe rather sooner than would be proper."

Rachel was not surprised. "Giving birth to little devils?"

Her father reflected her grin. "Only in so far as it is in the nature of children to be imps. See, here is a note that in 1673 the Demon's Bride was Pru Thurlow, who in July married Nathan Hatcher, and who gave birth to a son on Epiphany Day 1674."

"The ancestor of our dour gardener, Tom Hatcher?" Rachel exclaimed in delight. "For all that I find him taciturn, I cannot see him as a descendent of Waldborg the Demon."

Her father laughed. "Nor can I, pet." He replaced his papers in the box. "I do wonder what happened to poor Meg Brewstock, though, on Dym's Night in 1668."

Rachel gazed at the few dry words which seemed to be the only record of a young girl's life. "So do I, Father. So do I."

Back at the vicarage, Rachel sat at a small table near the fire, transcribing her hastily written record of the day's events in her best handwriting. Her father sat opposite her consulting his books and notes in search of similar customs elsewhere. She spared a moment for a fond glance.

He was never so happy as when he was digging to the bottom of a strange tale. He excused his investigations as a search for the ordinary explanation for superstitious customs and beliefs. Rachel knew it was a simple, childlike fascination.

That was the main reason they were in Suffolk,

which Rachel was inclined to think a rather boring part of the country, being generally flat and windy. She had lived all her life in the milder climate of Somerset. After her mother's death, however, and with her two brothers out in the world, her father had begun to slide into a decline. The intriguing puzzles of their locality had been long exhausted, and so she had encouraged him to look for a new living elsewhere.

The living of Walberton was serving its purpose admirably. It was fairly riddled with peculiar beliefs and notions. Over the past two months, the Reverend Proudfoot had grown as plump and hearty as he had ever been. In the light of this improvement, Rachel could even forgive the local people their secretive natures.

Mrs. Hatcher, their housekeeper, came in with a tea tray, square face set in disapproval. Rachel had found that disapproval quite daunting at first, but now recognized it as the woman's habitual expression.

"Ah, Mrs. Hatcher," exclaimed the vicar. "Excellent. Sit down, dear lady. I wish to talk to you."

The woman was clearly taken aback. She placed the large tray on the central table and said, "I'd rather not, sir. What did you wish to say?"

The vicar sighed. "I don't wish to *say*, Mrs. Hatcher. I wish to ask. I am gathering information on a local matter which is, I believe, called Dym's Night, or Demon's Night."

Rachel would not have believed that the woman's stony face could become even harder, but it managed it. "Demon's Night, sir? Sounds right ungodly to me."

"Come come, Mrs. Hatcher. No need to be like that! Such strange names occur all over the country.

They mean nothing. I know that the people here gather on Dymons Hill on Walpurgis Night."

"Aye, sir. We do that. It's just a bit of fun."

"But what of this matter of Walpurgis Night falling on Ascension Day?"

"I don't know, sir. What of it?"

"Is not that what you call Dym's Night?"

"I've never heard it called so, sir."

Reverend Proudfoot becoming exasperated, so Rachel took a hand. "Apparently a girl died during the Walpurgis Night revels some years ago, Mrs. Hatcher. . . ."

The housekeeper's pale eyes swiveled to her. "Not in my time, miss, no."

Rachel now shared her father's impatience. She knew the people here could probably talk of the Conquest as if it were yesterday—a mere matter of seven hundred years. "It happened nearly a hundred years ago, Mrs. Hatcher, but I doubt the memory of such a tragedy has faded. The poor girl burned to death."

There was a moment's hesitation. "Oh, that. Yes, well, it's a wonder it hasn't happened more, the way young people will frolic near the flames, drinking and all like they do."

"I suppose that's true. Was Meg Brewstock Dym's Bride that year?"

The woman's eyes widened with alarm for a second. "I wouldn't know, miss, would I?" She turned firmly to the vicar. "Will that be all, sir? I've bread rising."

The vicar sent her off and grimaced at his daughter. "All the informativeness of a turnip."

"Oh, I don't know, Father," said Rachel as she poured their tea. "I thought her discomfiture very informative."

"Yes," said the vicar as he took the cup. "She wasn't at ease about it, was she? First the earl keeping something back, and now Mrs. Hatcher." He stirred a lump of sugar into his tea with relish. "This could prove to be a most enjoyable investigation."

Rachel was pleased that her father had a juicy puzzle to solve, but she found the death of poor Meg Brewstock more haunting than intriguing. She desperately wanted to know what had happened to the girl. She kept her ears alert for any mention of Dym's Night, and whenever possible, she questioned the local people. She found out nothing.

It was not that all the people in Walberton were as dour as the Hatchers; most were quite pleasant. They smiled and joked and passed on local gossip, but no one would even admit the idea of a Demon's Night. Oh, certainly there was Walpurgis Night, and the Dym's Bride, but nothing more than that. And no one remembered any details about Meg Brewstock's death.

Rachel listened to one long, detailed tale about a family feud that dated back to the Wars of the Roses, and then was blandly told that the speaker had never heard anything particular about a girl who'd burned to death here less than a hundred years before.

It was both ridiculous and suspicious.

But why would such a matter be a dark secret? Even if someone had killed Meg nearly a century before, what need to conceal it now? The culprit was surely in his or her grave.

When Rachel heard that old Len Brewstock was ailing with his chest, she took the opportunity to drive out with her special cough syrup. Old Len must be over ninety himself. He was quite possibly a brother, or at least a nephew, of Meg's. Surely he must have some memory of that time.

She half expected the Brewstock farm to be a gloomy, secret-ridden place, but it proved to be solid, prosperous, and welcoming in the autumn sun. Rachel took up her basket of help for the sick and knocked at the door.

Ada Brewstock, the current ruler of the farmhouse, greeted her pleasantly enough. "Why, that's right kind of you, Miss Proudfoot. Come you in and take a cup of tea. Grandad's here by the fire. Grandad!" she called to wake the wizened little man. "Here's the parson's daughter come to see you."

The old man blinked, face slack with sleep, then perked up. "Always like to see a pretty girl," he wheezed, then went into a paroxysm of coughing.

"He's not well," said Ada as an aside. "But then, at his age . . . Sit you down and have a chat, miss."

Rachel sat across the fire from the man. "Please don't try to talk if it bothers your chest, Mr. Brewstock."

"No, no," he wheezed. "It's none too bad."

"I've brought some of my syrup for you. It may help."

"That's kind of you, miss." He peered at her a moment. "Yous new here, ain't yous?"

"Yes, my father and I have only been here since August. It's a very interesting part of the country."

"That it is. That it is. Were lively here once, back afore the Normans came . . ."

Rachel did not want a lecture on Anglo-Saxon Suffolk. "And has many quaint customs," she said briskly. Then winced. It was highly inappropriate to describe something as quaint when it had resulted in a gruesome death.

"Aye, aye," the man nodded. "We keep to the old ways pretty well. Important, that is. Keeping to the old ways. Don't hold with these newfangled notions. Changing crops. Changing seasons. When I were a lad, we knew what day it was. . . ."

Ada Brewstock brought the tea over. "Grandad's still fretted about the way they changed the calendar ten years back, Miss Proudfoot. Reckons they stole eleven days, he does."

In 1752, September 3rd had become September 14th to correct the calendar. It had created a lot of resentment among the ignorant.

"But days are days," said Rachel. "Changing the date doesn't take anything away."

Even sensible Ada looked skeptical. "If you say so, miss. Are you wanting to ask Grandad something special?"

Rachel colored at that perception. "Actually, yes. As you may know, Mrs. Brewstock, my father collects information about local customs. We recently heard of the death of a member of the Brewstock family on Walpurgis Night many years ago. I was wondering if old Mr. Brewstock remembers anything of it."

"Well, it was before his time, of course. Grandad," she said. "Miss Proudfoot wants to know about Meggie."

"Burnt Meggie?" the old man asked in surprise. "That were afore my time."

As if the Normans weren't, thought Rachel. "But what did people used to say about it, Mr. Brewstock? Back when you were a boy."

He slurped his tea and gave her a surprisingly

shrewd look. "Same as they say now, miss. That folk shouldn't mess in things they don't understand. . . ." He fell silent and sat staring into the fire, sipping tea.

Rachel tried to puzzle out his comments. She wished she could take notes, for often the precise words were useful, but she feared it would make these people nervous.

Then the old man muttered something else. It sounded like, "Could have been worse."

"Worse than being burned to death?" Rachel asked.

"Nay." He peered at her. "Who said Meggie were burned to death?"

Rachel realized she had been thinking more of her aunt, whose clothes had caught from the fire, turning her into a human torch. "Mrs. Hatcher implied that Meg's clothes caught at the fire."

"How would *she* know," grunted the old man. "Mere snip of a thing, she is."

Rachel had a struggle to keep a straight face at the thought of solid, fifty-year-old Mrs. Hatcher as a snip of a thing. "So how *did* Meggie end up burnt?" Rachel asked. As she framed the question, horrid thoughts gathered. Sacrificed on an altar, then her corpse flung into the flames?

The man didn't answer, so Rachel asked again, "How did Meggie die, Mr. Brewstock?"

He seemed to peer back through the years. "Died from getting above her station, as I heard it, and from people messing around with things they don't understand."

"Who? What people?"

But the man gave all the appearance of dropping off to sleep.

"He's asleep more often than not these days," said Ada, coming over with her own cup of tea. She pulled up a stool. "Did you find out what you wanted to know, miss?"

Rachel considered the woman, who appeared sensible and honest. "Not really. I cannot understand why there is so much secrecy about such an ancient affair, Mrs. Brewstock. My father's interest is simply scientific. He records these customs because we live in a time of progress, and soon these traditions will be forgotten."

The woman's look was wry. "I doubt much'll be forgot round here, miss. Folk have long memories."

"Then they presumably remember what happened to Meggie."

"Some might."

Rachel tried a shot at random. "They say Meggie worked at the Abbey."

"Aye." Ada stood abruptly and pulled Rachel's cup and saucer from her hands. "I've work to do, miss. Thank you kindly for bringing the cough syrup. I'll see he takes it."

Rachel cast a regretful look at the somnolent old man, and allowed herself to be firmly shepherded outside. She knew Old Len could tell her all about Burnt Meggie if he chose.

It was a fine day for October, so Rachel took a detour on her way home, and passed close to Dymons Hill. This corner of Suffolk was fairly hilly, but Dymons Hill was an abrupt mound of chalk, and she could quite see how it would seize the local imagination. It told her nothing about Meggie Brewstock's death, however.

On impulse, she stopped her gig and tethered her

horse and began to pick her way across the rough sheep pasture toward the hill. She met up with a path which appeared to link the village to the hill. It was faint, but had the depth and permanence of the ancient. There were so many of these paths in England still, trodden for thousands of years so that their mark would never really leave the earth. Many were the only record of a ceremony once crucial to the people. Rachel had to admit to sometimes wondering if those old ceremonies had been valid, if once gods other than the Christian Trinity had linked themselves with humans, for good or ill.

Her father would be ashamed of such thinking.

As Rachel neared the rise, she could see that there was a clear path up the hill as well. It wound slightly, and appeared to have been carved out in places to make it easier, but it, too, looked very old. Could Dym's Night be pre-Christian?

Rachel had no intention of climbing the hill today, but she wandered around the base pondering what she had learned.

Certainly the old man didn't believe Meggie had been burned to death. That could only mean that she had been burned after she was dead. It did conjure up very unpleasant notions.

But what had he meant about her getting above her station? The most likely interpretation was that she had become romantically involved with one of the family at Morden Abbey. If she had shamed herself, would her family kill her and use the revels to dispose of the body?

And what of the matter of not messing with what one did not understand? Had that been a warning directed at her and her father?

Had it, in fact, been a threat?

But why? Why? Why would anyone think such old history of any importance? Even the earl had concealed something, probably the fact that an ancestor had seduced Meggie Brewstock. Why should such a man care about a thing like that? Doubtless he'd worked his way through the dairy maids like a sultan with a harem.

Rachel was distracted by the beat of a galloping horse, carried to her by the earth. Threats, demons, and funeral pyres all leapt panic-powered into her mind.

She turned to flee, but could not tell from what direction the danger came. By the time she had fixed it, the black horse and caped rider were in sight, galloping with magnificent speed along the base of Dymons Hill toward her.

A scream caught in her throat and the rider charged her like a cavalry officer.

However, the man reared the steaming horse to a halt some yards away and Rachel instantly recognized him. It was the earl. He sat arrogantly on his steaming, sidling horse and looked her over as if she were a prize ewe, and one he was planning to slaughter.

He was rather more alarming than a demon.

He slid off the horse and walked toward her, reins held slackly in one hand. Rachel stepped back nervously. Even casual country wear could not disguise his rank, and she was not accustomed to dealing with the high nobility. He was a good foot taller than she, too, and being tall, she was not accustomed to that. In his long black riding cloak he was positively menacing, especially as his courteous smile did not reach his eyes.

"What a blessed chance," he drawled. "It's the vicar's pretty daughter."

Rachel stopped her retreat and frowned at him. No one had ever called her pretty in seriousness, including this man.

Before she could frame a reply, he further disconcerted her by drifting his gaze up and down her body and adding, "No, I mistake the matter, Miss Proudfoot. You are not pretty."

This was even more impossible to respond to. Rachel was experiencing a strong desire to box his ears, earl or no.

Sharp-edged humor touched his heavy-lidded eyes. "Magnificent, I think, is more the word."

That liberated Rachel's tongue. "My lord, pray stop this foolishness!"

"Is it foolish to call a lady magnificent?" he asked, supremely at ease. "If so, all London is foolish." He glanced around at the bleak landscape scattered with sheep. "But this assuredly is not London, Miss Proudfoot, and our company is not the glittering throng."

Rachel knew he could be up to no good. She dropped him a stiff curtsy and turned to pick her way back across the field.

The wretched man kept pace with her, saying nothing, his horse stepping neatly behind. Rachel could not bear it. She stopped to face him. "Please, my lord, this behavior is *intolerable*."

A sudden smile lit his face, making him look a great deal more like his portrait. "I have merely been waiting for an opportunity to apologize, Miss Proudfoot."

"You could have apologized at any time, my lord."

"Shout at a fleeing lady? I think not." He placed a hand on his heart. "However, Miss Proudfoot, on reviewing our brief encounter I am forced to conclude that I was discourteous, and I most humbly beg your pardon."

Rachel didn't believe a word of it, most particularly, the "humbly," but in the face of such a superficially gracious apology, she could do nothing but say, "It is forgotten, my lord."

He bowed, with a true London air. "Thank you, dear lady. You have distressed me, you see, which naturally leads me to resent you deeply."

"I? I have done nothing."

"Indeed you have. You have looked at me with honest eyes, and tilted that firm chin at me."

Rachel colored, wondering if he was accusing her of boldness.

"And you blush," he said with a sigh. "What am I supposed to do with a strong-minded woman who can still blush?"

He dropped his horse's reins, pulled Rachel within the compass of his arms and his cloak, and kissed her.

For a crucial moment, Rachel was frozen by shock. When she tried to struggle, she found herself powerless in his strength. She also found that her struggles only served to make her far too aware of his body. His strong, hard, exciting body.

She turned instead into a statue of icy disapproval.

That, however, only pulled all her attention to his mouth. To begin with, his lips had merely captured hers; now they released her and started to play across her cheek to her earlobe.

"My lord!" she gasped.

His open mouth swooped back to cover hers as he simultaneously swayed her stiff body off balance, so that she had to clutch at him or fall. Her mouth opened further in a scream and became joined with his without restriction. She lost control. She was plunged into a pit of wicked sensation, swirling ever deeper into a spicy heat unlike anything she had ever known.

And she liked it.

In the dim recesses of her mind, her well-trained conscience struggled to assert that this was wrong, was *terrible,* but her wanton body betrayed her. It surrendered itself to his skill. It drank in the heat and smell of him as her mouth learned from his shockingly intimate attentions.

When she was lost, entirely lost, and was willing to sink with him to the damp grass and do anything to continue this delight, he began to raise her back toward the vertical. As he did so, he released her lips gently, with many parting, flickering kisses.

Rachel realized she was returning those kisses in full measure, and stopped it.

She stared up at blue eyes dark with sin. She thought, perhaps, that her own drowning disbelief was strangely reflected there. . . .

Then the cool cynicism snapped back. "So, the vicar's daughter knows how to kiss."

Rachel snatched herself out of his arms. "I know no such thing!"

His lips twitched. "You do now."

Rachel began to swing to hit him, but thank heavens, she stopped herself from that final idiocy. She turned to march away with as much dignity as she had remaining. He did not follow, and when she reached the gig she could not help but turn back.

He was still standing where she had left him. Now he gave another of his exquisite bows, swung smoothly onto his horse, and rode away.

Rachel collapsed against the side of the vehicle and covered her face with shaking hands.

That couldn't have happened. . . .

She *couldn't* have. . . .

She shouldn't have. . . .

But underneath it all was the honest truth that the kiss had been magic. Devil's magic, perhaps, but magic all the same, the sort of magic that could drive a person wild. She recognized now what could make a virtuous woman act wantonly, stupidly, dangerously, for the sake of kisses like that.

And to see that strange expression in a man's eyes. . . .

And there was more, there was worse. The Earl of Morden was a known rake, gamester, and duelist, and the sort of man every sensible young woman avoided, but Rachel could not shake off the memory of that portrait. She could not resist the notion that somewhere inside the cynical man was that magical youth, waiting to be set free.

This was madness, madness of the sort that could ruin a woman. She had, after all, read Mr. Richardson's *Clarissa Harlowe,* in which the heartless rake Lovelace had played just such games to ruin a virtuous lady. She loosed the reins, dragged herself into the seat, and set off home, praying for the strength to resist her own devastating Lovelace.

Thoughts of Dymons Hill and Meggie Brewstock were lost until an insight shocked her. Had Meggie perhaps felt like this for another member of the earl's family? Had she surrendered to the temptation to act against all sense and virtue?

And had she died for it?

When Rachel arrived back at the vicarage, she would have liked to take refuge in her room, but her father called her into his study. She found him dutifully beginning a sermon for the next Sunday, and glad of an excuse to pause.

"Why, my dear, you must get out in the fresh air even more. You are looking very fine with roses in your cheeks. So, have you discovered anything new about our little mystery?"

Rachel recounted her visit to the Brewstock farm. She thought her tone and manner were admirably composed until she became aware that she was pacing the room.

She froze and caught sight of herself in the mirror. Her round cheeks were unusually red, and there was something wild in her eyes. Apart from that, however, she was just her ordinary, unremarkable self—too tall, too plump, brown hair, blue eyes, snub nose . . .

Why *had* the earl kissed her?

Because he was a London rake amusing himself in the country, that was why. He'd have kissed a passing goose girl!

"Rachel, my dear, has something upset you?"

In the mirror, Rachel saw her father observing her with concern. She turned, gathering her wits. "Oh, not really. But I don't like the thought that Meggie might have been burnt after she was dead."

"You'd rather she had been burned alive?"

"Of course not! But . . ."

"But there is that taint again of human sacrifice," said the vicar, sobering. "I know." He met her eyes very seriously. "If it was a matter of rough justice, then that is a sorry matter but long past our help. If there is evil superstition involved, then it is our God-given duty to make sure it never happens again."

Rachel nodded.

Her father was still looking at her curiously, so Rachel claimed that she needed to change her gown, and she escaped his perceptive eyes.

As she took off her muddied gown, Rachel tried to exorcise the Earl of Morden and that kiss, but did not find it easy. She was horrified by her behavior, but if the earl stole a kiss again, she wasn't at all sure she could be any wiser or stronger than she had been today.

Rachel had hoped that her wisdom and willpower were not to be tested, for Lord Morden rarely stayed at his estate for long. The next day, however, she encountered him as she was walking across the footpath between the Fletcher farm and the churchyard. He reined in his horse beside her. It truly appeared that he had sought her out, and a wicked thrill tingled through her at the thought.

"A fine morning, Miss Proudfoot."

"Indeed it is, my lord." She eyed him warily. "May I help you in some way?"

"It is more a question of me helping you, Miss Proudfoot."

"Yes?"

"I have discovered that there are some papers at the Abbey that concern that death on Walpurgis Night in 1668."

Rachel's breath caught at such a blatant ruse. "Then my *father* and I will be interested in them."

"They are confidential, Miss Proudfoot." It was a swordsman's parry.

"We are not to be allowed to read them, my lord?" she riposted.

"I could show them to *you*."

Rachel sucked in a breath. "Why?" Foolish question, but she could hardly believe this was happening.

"For the pleasure of your company, of course."

Rachel's mind was spinning. She could not believe that the earl was trying to seduce her. She could not believe that she was even considering going with this man—this *rake*—when his intentions could only be of the worst. She could not believe how much she *wanted* to go with him, and it was nothing to do with Meggie Brewstock's death.

Just then, a salve for her conscience appeared in the form of young Hal Fletcher strolling back from the river with a string of fish dangling from his rod. He grinned and touched his forelock to them both.

"Good morning, Hal," said Rachel. "Could you be so kind as to stop at the vicarage and tell them that I have gone up to the Abbey with Lord Morden to check on some papers?"

"Right, miss," the lad said cheerily and went on his way.

Rachel looked up triumphantly at her thwarted abductor. He seemed merely amused and held down a hand.

Rachel regarded it with alarm. "You want me to *ride* with you, my lord?"

"It would be tedious for me to dawdle beside you for the three miles to the Abbey doors, would it not?"

Rachel berated herself for not thinking of this, and considered the size of the horse nervously. She rarely rode and had no idea how to manage.

He swung down and presented his hands. "Foot in here and I'll toss you up."

"But then I'll be up there alone!"

"Only for a moment, and Waldborg is a well-trained devil."

Rachel had raised her foot into his waiting hands, but now she clutched his shoulders. *"What?"*

He tossed her up willy-nilly, almost immediately grasping her waist so that as she hit the saddle she could not fall off. She again clutched his shoulders.

"Waldborg," he said, eyes bright with laughter. "The famous demon." He swung up and arranged her so she was sitting in his lap. Rachel knew then with certainty that she was being most unwise. But she had known that from the first moment, and rushed madly on as if possessed.

He set the horse to a canter that rocked her against his body with every stride. His right arm was tight around her waist, but instead of objecting, she clutched it to her for safety.

"Not much of a rider, are you?" he said.

"No."

"You'll learn."

"Will I?"

"I'll teach you. . . ." But he murmured it in a way designed to wear down virtue.

"Why did you call your horse Waldborg, my lord?" she asked in a desperate attempt to control the conversation.

"Why not? He can be a devil. He has a daughter, and I called her Walburga after the German saint the

Church tried to plaster over the old beliefs. I fear she takes her nature more from the pre-Christian demon than from that pious nun. She reminds me of you."

"*What?*"

"Which would you rather be, Rachel Proudfoot? A sainted virgin or a wild earth spirit?"

Sealed to his body by his strong arm, rocked to madness by his horse's speed, Rachel had no reply she cared to make.

When they arrived at the Abbey, Rachel's legs were unsteady. She told herself that it was just the novelty of riding, but she knew she lied.

What now?

What did she want to happen now?

The earl disconcerted her, however, by leading her straight to the muniment room and unlocking a drawer.

He took out an oilskin package, and handed it to her. "The memoirs, scribbles—call them what you will—of the mad third earl."

So he had not been lying about this. Rachel was aware of a chill hollow inside her that could be acute disappointment if she were a wicked woman. She made herself be glad that his intentions were, perhaps, honorable.

She sat at the table and began to open the package. "Mad?" she asked.

"He was after Walpurgis Night, 1668."

She looked up sharply. "What happened?"

"Why don't you read, and then we'll discuss it."

He lounged in a chair across the room, watching her. Rachel did her best to put him out of her mind and concentrate. The writing was a mere scrawl, and little attention had been paid to the state of ink or pen, but she could make out most of it.

Meggie Brewstock had been the earl's lover, if that was not too grand a term for an assistant dairymaid seduced by the master. The earl seemed to have felt something more than the casual for her, however. Rachel came across a lock of hair—dark and vibrantly curling still. There was even an attempt at a sketch, but the earl had been no artist.

As usual, the present Earl of Morden was restless, and Rachel was aware of every move he made. She noted when he rose to wander the room, and when he moved behind her. She could as well ignore him as she could a roaring fire.

She wanted to draw him back into her field of vision, where he seemed to be less dangerous. "Are there any records here of the previous Dym's Night? The one in 1573?"

He spoke from behind her. "Not that I know of. My family did not hold the property then."

Then he was closer. He placed one hand on the left arm of her chair and leaned forward over her shoulder, pressing lightly against her. "Do you think he loved her?"

"He is grieving. . . ."

"Or perhaps just mad. Perhaps love drives us all mad. . . ."

Rachel turned another page, begging her hand not to tremble. A finger touched her hair and she stiffened. "My lord . . ."

"Mark. My name is Mark Brandish. There is no need for formality between us, Rachel."

Rachel wanted to protest, but the words faded on her lips. She focused desperately on the page in front of her. "Oh . . ." Was that because his hand was traveling her shoulder, or because of what was on the page.

"Oh?" he queried in soft amusement.

"The earl mentions Dym's Night. . . . My lord . . . Mark . . ."

"What does he say?" His hand was stroking her shoulder gently, backward and forward. Surely that was not so very wicked, and yet it seemed to be melting all her resolve.

Vicars' daughters are not prime candidates for flirtation, never mind seduction. Some men had shown interest and taken time to talk to Rachel, even to dance with her at local assemblies. None had been to her taste, and so she had hinted them away. She had never been kissed on the lips until this man had kissed her. She had never had a man touch her as this man touched her.

"He wanted to stop it," she said. "He thought he had stopped it." The earl slid his hand beyond the limit of her gown to her neck—flesh against flesh. "When he realized it was still going on, he rode out. . . ."

He raised and turned her chin. ". . . he rode out to save his lover," he murmured against her lips, "and was deprived of his senses by a blow on the head. Meg, of course, perished in the flames."

And he brought the flames to Rachel in a kiss that melted her like sealing wax.

It was the thought of flames that saved her, though whether it was the flames of the Dym's Night bonfire or the flames of hell, Rachel couldn't be sure. She pushed him away. "My lord, you *must* not!"

He fell to one knee. "Alas, you wound me! When you tear yourself away, you leave an open wound, that only you can heal." His eyes were bright with passion and laughter.

Rachel leapt to her feet and put the solid chair between them. "And you wound me, sir, with your insincerity. And your . . . your *unwanted* attentions!"

"Unwanted, Rachel? Oh come now, can we not have a little honesty between us?"

"Only if it starts with you. What do you *want*, my lord?"

He leapt lightly to his feet, smiling almost with honesty. "I want you, of course."

Rachel's foolish heart leapt. "And why, pray?"

His lids lowered, making his eyes mysterious. "To see if those kisses are the extent of it, or if the fire goes deeper. . . ."

Rachel came back to earth. "We are not, I assume, speaking of marriage, my lord."

"No, my dear innocent, we are not speaking of marriage."

Rachel turned and gathered the papers together with unsteady hands. "Is it not a little foolish to be trying these tricks with a vicar's daughter?"

"Not at all. As I recall, they worked admirably with a Bishop's daughter just a few months ago."

She glared at him, not knowing whether he was honest or not, but fearing that he was. "You, my lord, are beyond despising." She held out the papers. "Here. Take them. I am not so cheaply bought!"

He laughed. "I have not yet sunk to bribery, my dear. Take the papers with you. Perhaps they will teach you something of the mysteries of passion."

Rachel hesitated, then grasped the escape he offered. As she hurried out of the Abbey, she reminded herself that he was a dangerous, worthless rake. But

she wanted him. She could not believe how she
wanted him. She walked the three miles home berat-
ing herself furlong by furlong for being a foolish, wanton woman.

The next day she learned that Lord Morden had
returned to London. She swallowed acute disappointment and offered a prayer of thanks on her knees.
And may he find his true level, she thought waspishly,
in the stews and hells of the city.

She and her father studied the third earl's papers
and learned little more. The vicar shook his head.
"There's nothing here, pet, except that something deprived the earl of a large part of his wits, and left him
with a great fear of the dark. It was doubtless just the
effect of being hit on the head."

"The earl said his ancestor was assaulted because
he tried to rescue Meggie. Rescue from what?"

Her father nodded. "That is the question, isn't it?
It all bears watching, pet."

In December, Rachel and her father received an
invitation to spend New Year's Eve at Morden Abbey.
Rachel suspected that a wise woman would refuse to
go, but she told herself such a flattering invitation
could not be refused, and that her own private demon
would have lost all interest in her by now. It was two
months since their last encounter, after all, and she
had shown him that his tricks would not work with
her.

And if she was going to attend, it would not be
appropriate to go to the Abbey plainly dressed. This
meant that she must wear her new pink silk even if it
was a little skimpy in the bodice for a crisp winter's
evening. And she must certainly wear her mother's

pearls, and the matching earrings her father had recently given her. . . .

Rachel prepared for the event aware for the first time of how a virtuous and generally sensible person could play games with their conscience, and rush headlong toward the fires of Hell.

She entered the drawing room at Morden Abbey almost aquiver with anxiety and longing, and froze when she saw the earl. She had no reason to be dumbstruck to see him there, so perhaps it was his grandeur that halted her. It was the first time she had seen him in the full elegance of silk and satin, with his hair neat and powdered, and gold and jewelry glinting as he moved.

Across the room, his bright eyes held hers as if he had been watching for her. Another rakish trick, she warned herself.

His knowing gaze wandered lightly over her and seemed to approve of her new gown, which had fashionable hoops, and a richly embroidered stomacher done by her own hand.

Oh foolish, she berated herself. He's fresh from London, where they doubtless give such as this to their servants!

One of his brows rose, and he raised the wineglass in his hand in a secret toast before coming forward to greet her.

The other guests were already well known to the Proudfoots: Sir George and Lady Pritchard; Mr. and Mrs. Home-Nowlan and their son and daughter; elderly Mr. Cathcart and his sister, Miss Diana; and an ancient great-aunt of the earl's, Lady Ida Brandish, who made her home at the Abbey.

Rachel greeted each in turn, hoping she appeared

more composed than she felt. She took a seat by young Lady Pritchard and engaged her in talk about her children, which could always be relied upon to avoid silence.

As the lady's rambling discourse on teething and the colic washed around her, Rachel wondered what the earl was doing and thinking. She refused to look in his direction.

She caught a flicker of movement in the corner of her eye and turned just as he sat beside her with a flick of his mulberry-brocade coattails and a discreet waft of perfume.

She could not help but take in his magnificence.

His breeches and stockings were pristine ivory silk, his waistcoat a masterpiece. The flow of lace at wrist and neck was the finest Mechlin, and every fastening of his garments seemed to be made of gold and diamonds. Not only was his hair powdered, but there was a light dusting of powder on his skin as was the fashion. It merely made his blue eyes more jewel-like. His long-fingered pale hands carried a gold signet and a large sapphire.

He looked not one bit like the young man of the portrait, or the wild rakish seducer who had twice assaulted her. Tonight he looked the aristocrat he was, and that aristocrat could have no decent interest in prosaic Rachel Proudfoot.

"It's novel to see you at the Abbey, Morden," said Lady Pritchard without any particular awe. "London must be a mighty fine place, the way you like to stay there."

"It is indeed, Lady Pritchard." His lazy smile was a masterpiece of subtle intimacy. "You should per-

suade Sir George to bring you. I will guarantee to
squire you about to any number of novel amusements."

"None of that, Morden," said Sir George, coming
over hastily. "We don't need such foolishness." Sir
George was clearly of an age with the earl, but much
more rotund—a different type altogether. A more
worthy type, Rachel told herself firmly, though her
heart was already racing just from Lord Morden's
presence beside her.

"Assuredly we don't," said Lady Pritchard cheerfully. "I have my home and my children, Morden, and
want nothing else. There's nothing to London but
time-wasting and frippery, if you ask me." With this
amiable dismissal, she turned to Ida.

Rachel sipped her Madeira. "That should put you
in your place, my lord," she remarked to her demon.

"Do you, too, see only frippery?" The earl produced a silk-and-ivory fan from his pocket with which
to fan himself. "And after I dressed like this just for
you."

Her eyes flew to his, startled. And found his teasing. He turned the fan on her. "That pink becomes
you. It is bringing out the roses in your cheeks."

Rachel cast an alarmed look around. "Please
don't . . ."

"Did you wear it just for me?"

Rachel pulled herself together. "Certainly not.
Being a simple person, I have only one fine gown."

"I see," he murmured. "I am put in my place indeed . . ." He suddenly stood. "May I show you the
portrait gallery, Miss Proudfoot?"

"No." Rachel's refusal to go apart with him was
instinctive.

He smiled slightly. "It is merely around that corner.

Impropriety would be virtually impossible." He was standing there, hand outstretched and attracting attention. Rachel must either comply, or create a scene.

She put down her glass, placed her hand in his, and rose.

Capturing her eyes, he raised her hand and brought his lips much closer than propriety allowed, so that his breath warmed her there. Then he led her from the room with a distinct air of challenge.

Rachel was aware of speculative looks from all quarters.

Once around the corner and in—as he had promised—the portrait gallery, she pulled her hand from his. "I do wish you would stop playing this game, my lord. You embarrass me."

"Game? Perhaps I am serious."

"Serious?" Her heart was doing a mad dance in her chest. "Can there be such a thing as a serious seducer?"

"Oh, assuredly. It's generally devilish hard work. But I was referring to my more honorable intentions. I am considering you as my bride."

"Bride?" Rachel echoed, knowing her ready color was flooding her face. "Do not try to make a May game of me, my lord. I am no bride for an earl."

"Are you not?" His smile was a masterpiece of cynicism. "Why should not any fine healthy specimen with wits and virtue intact be acceptable as an earl's bride? It would do the aristocracy a great deal of good."

It should have been possible to take that as a compliment, but his tone made it into an insult. Rachel stamped on an urge to lose her temper, for it seemed to be his intent.

"Enough of this, my lord. Everyone here knows you consider marriage a fate worse than death."

She saw a flicker of appreciation which was surprisingly pleasing. "Been asking about me, have you?" he murmured. "I'm sure, however, that if it came to a choice between death or wedlock, even I could be persuaded into the trap."

Rachel's alarmed—and slightly hopeful—heart settled. Talk of marriage was just another game to him. She turned to stroll along the gallery, studying the pictures. "Why do you find marriage so repugnant, my lord?"

"Why? Because women are the very devil."

She turned. "Well, really!"

"Excluding the delightful company in which I find myself, of course." He gave her a distressingly charming smile.

Rachel felt her foolish heart quiver again. Oh, how perilous he was. A rake, after all, must have a host of tricks at his disposal. She stared at a very horse-faced lady of some fifty years past. "You must intend to marry one day, my lord."

"Must I?"

"It is surely your duty."

"To the devil with duty."

She stared at him, aghast.

"Do you always do your duty, Miss Proudfoot?"

"To the best of my ability, my lord."

"Then perhaps I will make it your duty to marry me." The glint in his eyes told her exactly what he meant.

"Cease this, my lord! You will not seduce me, even with talk of marriage. The very clothes you wear would doubtless pay my father's stipend for a year."

"Then think how advantageous it would be to wed me."

Rachel decided to call his bluff. "Should I consider that a proposal, my lord?"

To her astonishment, he said, "Why not?" He offered an elegant bejeweled hand. "Marry me, Miss Proudfoot."

Rachel stared from hand to sardonic face, her heart thumping madly. "Repeat that invitation in public, and I may accept, my lord. It would serve you right."

"You tempt me greatly. . . ."

"I doubt that." Rachel turned sharply to study the closest portrait before she allowed him to tangle her wits entirely. *Marriage!* Though she knew it was a trick, the notion caught at her, and not for rank and riches.

She reminded herself ferociously that even were he serious, marriage to an unrepentant rake would be a certain road to misery.

Then she felt his fingers brush lightly at her nape again.

After last time, Rachel knew where this would lead, and yet she was snared despite her good intentions. She allowed the murmur of nearby conversation—promise of aid if needed—to deaden her conscience. She stood staring sightlessly at a portrait as first fingers then lips tantalized the very topmost layer of her skin.

"The gentleman who so enthralls you is the third earl," he whispered, his breath warm against her skin. "Another rake and scoundrel. True follower of his friend, Charles II."

"Oh." His lips were traveling further down her back, exposed as it was by the low neckline of her gown. Deep between her shoulder blades he blew against her heated skin.

She felt his lips move as he said, "The one who was bashed on the head for Meg Brewstock's sake."

Rachel was snapped out of her dream state. She moved forward a step to better study the florid, hook-nosed man. He certainly wouldn't tempt her to wanton irresponsibility, but tastes differed.

"He was a rake, you say?" *Like you,* she reminded herself.

"So one gathers." Lord Morden's voice was rather strange. "May I ask how you can possibly find him so much more attractive than I?"

Rachel turned on her high heel to face him. "*He's* dead, my lord."

Anger flashed in his eyes. His hand snared her carefully arranged curls, so she could not move without pain. "Have claws, do you, my Rachel? I can show you better ways to use them."

Instinctively, futilely, she gripped his wrist. "Release me or I will scream."

He made no move to obey. With only this to face, Rachel could not create such a scene, and he knew it.

"Then I will use my claws." She began to dig her nails into his skin.

He did not flinch, but tightened his grip on her hair, meeting her eyes unwaveringly. Rachel dug her nails harder, though she was struggling not to cry out from the pain on her scalp.

He suddenly smiled and looked very like the youth in the portrait. "You are, as I said, magnificent. I believe I *will* marry you." He released all the tension in his hand, but did not remove it. Rather, it seemed to caress her skull.

Rachel swallowed. "Not without my consent." She remembered to loosen her claw-grip on his wrist. A horrified glance showed dark nail marks, one of which oozed blood.

"You'll consent," he said softly.

Rachel tried to deny it, and failed.

He pulled her slowly toward him and she went, recognizing that their battle had roused her passions, and that he knew it. He seemed to know her better than she knew herself.

She would never have thought that Rachel Proudfoot even had such passions.

His lips brushed softly over hers, teasing in her a brutal desire to be kissed with violence. What kind of a woman was she? What was he turning her into?

Without satisfying the need he had caused, he released her and turned her to face the portrait, his hands resting on her shoulders. "So, what did you make of the third earl's insane ramblings?"

Rachel closed her eyes in despair. She had been vanquished by one of far greater experience and skill. But at least she managed not to follow her true desire and impose a violent kiss upon him. Instead, she told him of the earl's deductions about Meggie's death.

"So, my ancestor seduced the maid, and for that her family killed her, disguising the murder by throwing the body into the flames?"

"It is the better explanation." The one branch of candles and the winter light was creating entirely the wrong atmosphere for this discussion.

"What other is there?"

Rachel could not speak the words. He turned her to face him. " 'Struth. Is my practical Miss Proudfoot really envisioning human immolation? Little Meggie Brewstock with her throat cut on an altar, thrown onto the fire to appease the angry god? What god?

Of course." He dropped his voice to an eerie level. "Waldborg, the ancient one, raised on Demon's Night."

"Don't jest about it!"

He laughed. "Why not? We live in a modern age, and the old gods are dead. I fear you have a romantic imagination, after all, my sweet, but that gives me hope. I find it hard, however, to imagine the third earl riding to the rescue of a dairy maid just because she'd warmed his bed."

Rachel raised her chin. "*Your* ancestor, sir."

"I've never seduced a maid in my life."

Flustered, Rachel tried to move away from him. "We must return—"

He captured her hand and raised it to his mouth. "I'm willing to turn over a new leaf for you."

"What?" He had turned her hand and was kissing her palm.

"Reform. Try new ways . . ." He tickled her skin with his tongue.

Despite her better instincts, she was tempted. "You will become a sober, virtuous citizen?"

He captured her other hand and held them both against his heart. "Of course not." His blue eyes shone with laughter. "I mean I'm willing to try seducing a maid. If you are that maid."

Rachel dragged her hands free. "Never!" she snapped, and fled down the gallery. At the last minute she recollected the waiting company and stopped to compose herself, hand on unsteady chest. She glanced back and found him strolling after her, appearing unmoved by their time together, and by her denial.

He escorted her back into the drawing room with perfect propriety.

Rachel avoided the earl by sitting by old Lady Ida.

"He's a rare rascal," the old woman said.

"I fear he is, ma'am."

"Needs a good wife. In my day he'd have been shackled when he was too young to fight it."

Rachel did not want to talk about the earl and marriage.

The raddled old woman grimaced at Rachel, though she supposed it was meant to be a smile. "I can tweak his chain, though. You'll see. You'll see."

Rachel had no idea what this was about. What a fool she had been to come to this affair.

She was heartily relieved to find that she was to go into dinner on the arm of young Mr. Home-Nowlan. This was completely appropriate to her lowly station and she could be comfortable in his company.

When the meal was over, everyone returned to the drawing room and the wine circulated along with the tea. Rachel took care to be sure that she sat nowhere near the earl. He did not pursue her, but seemed to regard her maneuvers with disquieting amusement. Rachel felt horribly like an animal being stalked by a very patient but surefooted predator.

The conversation soon touched on the New Year, the various local superstitions of the season, and the long memories of country folk. Sir George spoke up. "My people are still in a fret about their lost eleven days."

"Indeed," said Reverend Proudfoot with a chuckle. "Only the other day, James Crowbourne's widow told me that he'd have lived another week and a half if the government hadn't taken to fooling with matters best left alone. It is strange, though," he continued. "The resentment does linger here. Back in Somerset,

I had hardly heard the matter mentioned in years, but here it has come up again and again. Why only the other day the gardener was pressing me as to when Easter would have been in the old style."

"Simple enough question, I'd think," said Sir George.

"On the contrary, my dear sir. It is a very complex calculation to do with the phases of the moon. I am not sure, were I to attempt it, that I would do it correctly. I am happy to follow the liturgical calendar sent out by the bishop."

"If you want my opinion," said Sir George, "they're still fretting about Dym's Night."

Rachel was having difficulty ignoring the earl, especially as he was sitting in her line of sight, wielding his absurdly beautiful fan, and watching her. . . .

At this, however, she snapped to attention.

"So you know of Dym's Night, Sir George," her father was asking with considerable interest.

"Course I do," said Sir George with some affront. "Family's been in these parts for centuries. Can trace the line back before the Conquest."

"And Dym's Night goes back that far?"

"Aye, Vicar, or farther. Back before . . . Well, just before. Everyone knows that."

"Can you tell us what you know, Sir George?" Reverend Proudfoot looked around. "If no one else objects to my indulging my curiosity."

"Not at all," said Lord Morden. "I, too, am very interested in the subject, as you know." But his eyes never left Rachel.

Sir George looked a little taken aback at being the center of attention, but he was game. "Well, sir, let me see. What I know, eh? Demmed if I know what I know." He scratched beneath his brown wig. "Well, you all must know of Walpurgis Night."

"Yes, George," said the earl. "We all know of Walpurgis Night, though it is an interesting question whether it is the eve of St. Walburga's feast day, or the night of the demon, Waldborg."

Sir George swiveled to face him. "What does that matter, Morden? What matters is that Dym's Night is a Walpurgis Night that falls on Ascension Day. There's not been a Dym's Night in my lifetime, nor in my father's, and with the fiddling with the calendar, I'll go odds no one knows if there will be a real one again."

"A *real* one, George?" Morden's voice was distinctly irreverent.

Sir George flushed. "A proper one. I mean . . ."

Rachel interrupted out of kindness. "But you've been at a Walpurgis Night, Sir George?"

"Aye," said Sir George, smiling at her in relief. Then he glanced at his wife and added hastily, "Before me marriage, of course."

"Can you describe it, Sir George?" Rachel asked.

"Well, there's Dym's Bride, you see. Sort of like a wedding, really, I suppose. It's a young village girl chosen for the part. She gets a pretty dress and flowers in her hair. Then everyone goes up to Dymons Hill where a fire's been lit. There's dancing, and drinking, and songs. Lots of jollity. When the sun rises, it's over."

"Come, George," said the earl, "that's not much of a tale. What of Dym's Bride? What becomes of her?"

"Becomes of her? Why nothing, Morden."

"She does nothing special? Nothing special is done *to* her."

It was clear to Rachel that the earl was poking fun
at all this, and angling for embarrassing details. She
frowned at him and he winked unrepentantly. She reminded herself wickedness was no affair of hers.

Sir George, oblivious to the undercurrents, looked
back ten years or so. "Nothing special, no. As I recall
the Bride dances a lot. . . . Oh yes, she leads a special
song, then. . . ." He straightened and looked at Rachel's father. "Yes, now I think on it, this might be of
interest to you, vicar. You like these curiosities. She has
this knife. She sort of plunges it into the earth."

They all waited, but after a moment it became clear
the man had finished.

"Into the earth," said the earl thoughtfully. "But
Dymons Hill is solid rock. There's mighty little earth
up there."

"Aye, Morden," said Sir George. "That's what I
thought the first time I saw it. I was sure that blade
would snap, and it's a fine one. Old-looking. But there
must be a crevice. Seems to me some older women
showed her where to stick it. . . . But there's more."

"Yes?" Rachel realized the impatient voice was
hers.

"The Bride cuts herself. Just a little cut on the
hand. One of the years I was there the girl made a
silly fuss over it, and had to be helped. You could see
the people didn't think much of her for that."

There was another silence. Rachel glanced around,
wondering if anyone else desperately wanted to wring
information out of Sir George like a washerwoman
wringing water from a cloth. Her father clearly did.

"And what happened after she cut herself, Sir
George?"

The man blinked. "After. She stuck the knife in the

ground. Didn't I make that clear? She cuts herself, smears the blood on the blade, then sticks it in the ground."

"And then what?"

Sir George frowned. "Everyone goes back to drinking and dancing. It's a grand affair."

And that appeared to be all Sir George had to add, despite having been at the event on a number of occasions. He clearly didn't realize the year just beginning was a year that would include a Dym's Night.

But then would it? What was the effect of the changed calendar on such matters? No wonder the local people still fretted about the government's interference in days and dates.

When it was time to leave, the earl usurped the footman's place, and wrapped Rachel's woolen cloak around her shoulders as if it were velvet lined with fur. "I will give you a pretty gown and flowers in your hair," he murmured.

Rachel clutched the cloak at her neck, unable just yet to manage the clasp. "Like the Demon's Bride?" she asked shakily.

"I'd make a good demon, don't you think? Would you lie on the ground for me and smear my blade with your blood . . . ?"

She wrenched herself out of his lax hands and glared at him. "You *are* a demon, my lord."

His eyes twinkled. "A compliment at last!"

"I don't consider it one." She swung to face the mirror and managed to clasp her cloak.

He appeared behind her, beautiful, irreverent, and devilish. "Will you marry me, Rachel?"

She met his eyes in the glass. "I give you fair warning, Lord Morden. If I do marry you, it will be to reform you. I'll drive the demons out entirely."

He blew her a kiss. "What amusing battles we are going to have, my sweet savior." He captured her hands and placed his fan in it. "A gift to greet the New Year . . ."

Rachel broke free and hurried out after her father, clutching the fan. She should have thrown it in his face, but with the Earl of Morden she never did anything she should. It was terrifying. Somewhat to her surprise, the vicar said nothing about the attentions the earl had paid her.

Rachel spent a restless night struggling with her feelings for Lord Morden. He was a rake, with no shred of decent modesty, and far, far beyond her touch. He *couldn't* be serious about his talk of marriage. But his mere presence set her heart pounding, and his touch turned her body to fire. . . .

What should she do when next they met and he pressed her again to marry him? She rather thought she would say yes.

When she came downstairs the next morning she was in a state of nervous anticipation. Mrs. Hatcher slid her a look and said, "I hear the earl's gone back to Lunnon, Miss Proudfoot. Never stays long, do he?"

Rachel went into the parlor and deliberately smashed a very ugly pottery vase. Then she stared aghast at what she'd done.

Her father came from his study, pen still in hand. "Are you all right . . . ?" He looked at the broken pottery. "Ah well, it was a distressing piece of work."

"I smashed it," said Rachel.

"So I gather."

"Deliberately."

Reverend Proudfoot twinkled. "I know. Your mother was much given to such things in her younger days. Threw a cream bowl at me once. Would have done for me had it hit, I think."

"Mother?" Rachel queried. "I cannot imagine it."

"Emotions do tend to settle once people are wed," said the vicar. "Though not entirely, thank goodness."

Rachel could feel the heat rise in her cheeks at her father's perception. "He's gone back to London."

"Ah."

"I *can't* marry a man like that."

"You certainly can't marry a man who is in London."

"I can't marry a man who spends most of his time in London, either! He's a rake and a reprobate. He drinks, he gambles, he fights duels. I'm sure he . . . You know what I mean."

"Consorts with loose women," said the vicar calmly. "Undoubtedly."

Rachel knelt and began to pick up the shards of pottery, fighting tears. "I don't even know why he pesters me so. We are worlds apart." She got to her feet and looked sadly at the broken fragments.

Her father smiled at her. "Rachel, my dear, you will do as you think best, and I have great faith that you will do what is best. But I confess I would not be displeased to see you wed to Lord Morden. Of course, in worldly terms it would be a great thing, but we will not consider that. I think, though, that he is a man of many qualities. Those qualities may be drowned in excess, or rescued to flourish. I believe you can rescue them if you try, and be very happy in the result."

"He teases me to death!"

The vicar nodded happily. "As I said, I think you could be very happy with the result."

Rachel was left in even more confusion than before. Her father's approval of the match must count with her, but how was she to really settle her mind when her suitor was not here suing? How was she to know him better, and be able to make this fateful decision, when he was in London, and she was in Suffolk?

Surely any suitor whose intentions were honorable would stay close to the object of his attentions!

She threw herself once more into her researches, though really she and her father seemed to have drained the well of available information about Dym's Night in general, and Meggie Brewstock's death in particular. The death in February of old Len Brewstock from a winter chill seemed to close the final door.

Two days after his burial, Rachel went to stand by the old man's grave, pondering the way people's knowledge died with them. He had known things, she was sure of it, but now they were irretrievably gone.

There were a number of new graves, for winter took its toll. Over there was the raw mound that covered Thomas Caldwell, crushed when his chimney collapsed. And two small graves marked the Grigham children who had died of the fever. In the crypt lay the remains of Lady Ida Brandish who had been carried off by pneumonia. Her great-nephew had returned to see to her burial, but had not sought out Rachel at all.

Rachel looked around the gravestones of people great and small, young and old, and thought about the finality of death. It could come at any time, stealing secrets and leaving so many things unexperienced.

Like marriage, and children, and the fullness of the passion to which a certain wretched man had awoken her senses.

Spring came to Suffolk with its usual magic touch, and soon the green and fertile land was cheered by birdsong and the bleating of newborn lambs. Apart from remaining observant for any hint of wickedness in the congregation, Rachel and her father had put aside their enquiries about Walpurgis Night until closer to the event.

For her part in her father's work, Rachel was now collecting songs. These were interesting in themselves, but often related to customs, sometimes long-forgotten ones.

Rachel sat one day with Widow Tufflow as the old lady spun fine thread despite the fact that her sight was almost gone.

"Ester, ester, egg is bester," chanted the woman in a cracked voice as the wheel hummed, "green is swester dimmy's wife. Bester dancer, ester chancer, blood agrounder dimmy's knife."

Rachel had recorded it mindlessly, just making sure to get the sounds down, but now she looked in fascination at what she had written. "That's an interesting song," she said carefully. "Was it sung at any particular time, Mrs. Tufflow?"

"Children sing it," said the old woman. "It's just a bit of nonsense."

"But what of this dimmy?" When the woman didn't respond, Rachel resorted to a direct question. "Could that have anything to do with the Dym of Dymons Hill and Dym's Bride?"

The milky eyes turned toward her. "Why, that it might, miss. Dym. Yes."

"And Ester would be Easter. And on Easter Sunday, I understand, one household finds an egg on the doorstep. The youngest unmarried woman of that house will then be the Dym's Bride that year, yes?"

"Aye, miss." The woman nodded amiably.

"Do you have any idea what 'green is swester' might mean, Mrs. Tufflow?"

The wheel spun steadily, bewitchingly on. "Well, the bride mun wear green, miss."

"Must she? I didn't know that."

"Aye, green and simple. No hoops or anything. Like in the old times."

How old, Rachel wanted to ask. Druid times? "And she dances and chants. That's dancer and chancer," Rachel mused almost to herself. "And put's blood and earth on Dym's knife! This is all about Walpurgis Night."

"Doubt not it is," said Mrs. Tufflow, unexcited. "I were a Dym's Bride once, you know."

And the woman sat there and calmly recounted the whole event in detail. Even as she scribbled it down, Rachel was aware with some apprehension that Widow Tufflow had always intended to tell her all about it.

The bar on the village's knowledge had been broken.

Sure enough. From having to scratch for every scrap of information, now Rachel and her father were drowning in it. It seemed every person in the locality had a song or story they wanted to share, many of them connected to Walpurgis Night. Rachel, who was distressingly inclined to pine over an absent, heartless rake, threw herself into this torrent of information with enthusiasm.

They soon had a complete picture of the festivities. They did not contradict Sir George's account, but merely filled it in. The bride was dressed in a simple green robe of rather medieval style, and wore flowers in her hair. She was taken in precession to Dymons Hill where the fire was lit. There was a lot of dancing, drinking, and singing up until midnight. At that time some special songs were sung, the bride cut her hand, smeared the blood on the blade, and plunged the knife into the earth.

Then the festivities went on until dawn. The people believed that by the ceremony the earth had been fed, and good crops and kine were assured for the next year.

It appeared no more wicked than any other country festival. Just to be sure, Rachel and her father compiled a list of all the Dym's brides since 1668, and interviewed those still living. There was no suggestion of anything untoward.

"So that is that," said her father one evening, making a final note in the book in which they had recorded everything. "Whatever happened to Meggie Brewstock was to do with her personal affairs, doubtless her liaison with the earl. Quite possibly the attack upon him was for the same reason, and it was intended that he end up on the fire with her. It is a serious enough matter to require secrecy, but not at all mystical. Our investigations of Walpurgis Night here are complete except for our direct account of this year's rites."

Lord Morden returned in the week before Easter.

The first Rachel knew of it was when he walked into the vicarage parlor where she was transcribing a song. She was so startled she forgot his rank. "Where did you come from?"

He brought a hint of fresh spring air, but his eyes were dangerous. "I materialized from a hole in the ground like the demon I am." He grasped her chin and kissed her.

His skin was cold, his breath was warm. Rachel saw two choices. She could be outraged, or she could play him at his own game.

She snaked her arm around his neck and rose to kiss him back.

Unwise.

With no start of surprise that she could detect, he deepened the kiss and collapsed her onto the new carpet with him on top of her. Rachel struggled then, but he carried her forward into passion with the irresistible force of a river in full flood. . . .

It was a very loud, repetitive coughing that gained their attentions. The earl broke the kiss and they both looked up.

Mrs. Hatcher stood in the doorway, blank of expression. "I'm sure, miss, you'll think better of what you're doing, given the chance."

Rachel felt hot color flood her body. She pushed fiercely at Lord Morden, and he rocked to his feet with an unrepentant grin, helping her up in turn. "You were so eager, my sweet," he said. "It seemed a shame to waste it."

Rachel turned all her embarrassment into fury. "Get out!"

"Oh, don't be predictably prudish, Rachel. I'll leave if you can deny that you invited that."

She glared at him, but then collected her dignity. "Very well, my lord, I did. It was foolish. I thought to teach you a lesson."

"Remarkably foolish. In this, I am the master, and you are a mere infant."

"I would not be so proud of that if I were you."

"Do you want tea, miss?" interrupted Mrs. Hatcher, who was radiating disapproval. And not surprisingly.

Rachel wanted to throw him out—or a part of her did—but there was no chance of removing the Earl of Morden before he wished to leave. She had best tame him with tea. "Yes, please. Thank you, Mrs. Hatcher." She meant the thanks to be more for the interruption than for the tea, and the woman nodded.

Rachel returned to her seat, directing the devil in her midst to a seat a safe distance away. He took one closer. "What were you so busily engaged in, my Rachel? More demonic enquiries?"

"A song, only." She kept her voice cold.

"Sing it to me."

"I do not have the music."

"Then how can it be a song? Recite it to me."

With a sour smile, Rachel picked up the paper. " 'One ewe, two ewe, three ewe, dim. Round up, still tup, ring tup, lim.' More?" she queried sweetly.

"That's the nonsense the shepherds chant when they're counting the sheep. Why on earth are you recording that?"

"I record everything. That's the way it is done. One never knows when it might be of interest. And it does say 'dim.' "

"Still obsessed with our local demon? If you want to be a Demon's Bride, be mine."

Mrs. Hatcher came in at that moment and put the tray down with a thump.

Rachel turned to her. "Mrs. Hatcher, you heard that, didn't you? He offered me marriage."

"I heard nothing, miss."

"Miss Proudfoot," said the earl clearly, "please marry me."

Rachel stared at him.

"His lordship's making a game of you, miss," said Mrs. Hatcher. "Why, the first thing he did on arriving yesterday was to visit his daughter, Catty Hesset."

The flash of fiery anger from the earl's eyes seemed to bounce off Mrs. Hatcher, and she turned and left the room.

Rachel looked at the tea tray, unable to pour because she was sure her hand would shake too much. "Is it true?"

"That I have a daughter? Yes. Did you think I was a virgin?"

Her cheeks were hot with mortification. "I think you should have married the mother."

He laughed out loud. "My father would have had me shot! I was sixteen and Catty's mother was the assistant dairymaid."

Rachel stared at him. "Like Meggie Brewstock! I suppose your victim was fortunate not to be thrown into a fire, too."

"Don't be idiotic."

"I thought you said you had not seduced a maid."

"I haven't. She seduced me."

Rachel gave an unladylike snort of disbelief.

"Can't imagine a woman making the first moves? Nan knew what she was doing, certainly rather better than I did, though I was willing enough. We had a merry month of May, as I remember, and when she was with child both she and her family were pleased as punch. The dowry she got from my father set her and Jed Hesset up for life."

"And that makes it right?"

"If all parties are happy, can it be wrong?"

"Of course it can. What of the poor child?"

"Cattie's twelve and pretty as a picture."

"And known far and wide as the earl's by-blow!"

"It won't do her any harm to be blood-bound to the big house."

"It would not do her any harm to be raised a lady, but I don't suppose your beneficence would stretch that far, would it, my lord?"

His eyes narrowed. "I hope this vinegary disposition is the consequence of shock, Rachel. What would you have had me do? Snatch the babe from the mother's breast? Take her from her loving family as a child and raise her at the Abbey with no other children? Or try to change her life in a year or two, when she will be equipped for something else entirely."

Rachel's cheeks stung under the rebuke and she had no reply.

"There are worse things," he said, but more moderately, "than to be the well-loved daughter of a prosperous yeoman family. Be assured, if she ever were in hardship I would take care of her."

"I'm sorry," she said, though she could not feel that all this was right. She poured him a cup of tea. "Do you have other children?"

"Not as far as I know, though there are quite a few junior sprigs of the aristocracy who could be mine. They could be fathered by half the men in London, though. Are you going to marry me?"

"No."

"Why not?"

"After a saga of dissipations such as that? Need you ask?"

"Yes. Perhaps it's my unmarried state that leads me into wickedness. It could be your Christian duty to marry me."

"I do not have the disposition of a Holy Martyr, my lord."

He stood restlessly. "What the devil do you want from me? I am offering you a marriage far beyond your expectations."

"I want an honest reason for your pursuit, my lord. You do not love me, and I have made it clear that I will not marry for rank and fortune."

For a while, she realized, the cynical mask had been lowered. Now it slid back into place. "If you want the truth, you shall have it. My financial resources are becoming stretched. Due to the peculiarities of the Mad Earl, a large part of the estate was left to his daughter, my dear Great-Aunt Ida. Upon her death, it was to have come to me, but the old witch has tied it up with a condition. I will only get free access to it when I wed. If I must marry, I would rather it be to you."

Rachel swallowed against a bitter lump in her throat. "I see. I am a slightly better option than debtor's prison, am I? I recommend economy instead, my lord."

"Even marriage would be preferable." He leaned forward on the table. "Have some sense, you foolish woman, and take what is offered. Marry me."

Rachel made herself not quail backward. "I am

sorry, my lord, but I must decline your oh so flattering offer."

He hissed in a breath and she thought he would pounce on her, but then Mrs. Hatcher appeared in the doorway as if she had been hovering. "Did you want something, miss?"

With a muttered curse, the earl swept out of the room.

Mrs. Hatcher came in and sugared Rachel's tea. "You drink this up and put that young man out of your mind for the while."

"For the while?" echoed Rachel, clutching the cup. "Forever! I want nothing to do with such as he."

"Now, now. No need to be hasty. But he'll do better for you in a while."

"When he reforms? Ha! That will be on Doomsday, or never!" Rachel downed the strong, sweet tea and promised herself that no matter what tricks the earl played, what maneuvers he attempted, she would marry no man just so that he could stay out of the Fleet!

She turned her mind to another line of thought. "Mrs. Hatcher. About the earl's daughter . . ."

"Yes, miss?"

"Is it true that she will feel no shame at being his?"

"Aye, true enough. Such things happen."

Rachel stared at the leaves in the bottom of her cup, wishing she had the gift of reading them. "So if a girl were to behave improperly with the Earl of Morden, she wouldn't be a cause of shame to her family?"

Mrs. Hatcher's glance was sharp and rather alarmed. Rachel realized with embarrassment that the woman thought she was speaking of herself.

Before she could correct the impression, the housekeeper said, "No, miss, not really. But that's the farming families. For someone of higher station," she said pointedly, "it'd likely be different, wouldn't it?"

"Yes, I'm sure it would."

When the housekeeper had returned to her kitchen, Rachel pondered the fact that Meggie Brewstock's immoral behavior might not have been cause for anyone to kill her. True, it was a hundred years ago, but had matters changed that much?

She waited anxiously for her father to return home so that they could discuss the matter, but his first words drove it out of her mind.

"The earl has invited himself to dine with us, Rachel. I met him in the village."

"No!" Rachel wailed.

"My dear? Why not?"

"He was here earlier and offended me grievously."

"What did he do?"

"He offered me marriage." At her father's raised brows she added, "He made it perfectly clear that the offer was only made because I am the means to keep him out of the Fleet."

"Tut, tut. Foolish man. But," said the vicar, "we cannot refuse to host him, and it would be petty for you to stay up in your room. You must act the hostess with dignity, my dear. It is the only way to handle such matters."

The Reverend Proudfoot rarely directed Rachel's behavior, but when he did, it was wisest to obey. Rachel refused to dress in something fine, however. She greeted their unwelcome guest in the same workaday high-necked gown of blue-striped jaconet that she had worn all morning.

He showed no trace of his earlier anger, and bowed

with courtly elegance. "You look so charming when you glower, my intriguing Puritan. I still want you to marry me."

"And I still refuse."

"That seems clear enough," said the vicar, "so we have no further need to discuss the matter just now."

"On the contrary," said the earl, and already the anger was bubbling to the surface, "I was hoping you would make your daughter see sense, Vicar."

"Rachel has excellent vision, my lord, especially in matters of right and wrong. She does not wish to marry against her inclinations. As *she* is too prudent to run into debt, there is no reason she should."

The earl stared at the vicar as if he'd grown horns. "I could have you thrown out of this living for that."

"Perhaps so," said Rachel's father calmly, "but I would be a poor sort of fellow to allow you to bully my daughter for such a reason, wouldn't I?"

Mark turned to impale Rachel with cold eyes. "You hold yourself damnably high."

Rachel was shivering in her shoes, for she had not thought that her affairs could ruin her father, but she would not let her demon know it. "Are you saying you hold me low?"

His chin rose. "Believe it as you may, Miss aptly named Proudfoot, but there are a great many ladies in this land who would jump at the chance that you toss back in my face."

"More fools they!"

"I will not grovel to you." It was almost a snarl.

"I expect no man to grovel to me. Pray tell me, sir, what do you have with which to tempt me? I don't care a snap for title and riches."

He did not allow her father's presence to deter him. "Rapture of the senses," he said.

"That is no reason to marry," said Rachel, face burning.

"It is an excellent one. Is it not, Vicar?"

"It is an important part of marriage, yes," said Rachel's father calmly.

Rachel stared at him. "But there has to be more, Father."

"Assuredly."

Rachel turned back to focus a politely inquiring look at her arrogant suitor.

"Oh, be damned to you for a prude and a stiff-rumped idiot! I will not ask you again." He stalked out of the room.

"Good!" Rachel shrieked after him, then sat down and burst into tears.

Her father patted her back and plied her with a dry handkerchief. "It really is better this way," he said when her tears had subsided to sniffles.

"I know. Such a marriage would never work."

"That is not certain."

"He's an unrepentant rake."

"He is certainly reluctant to change his ways."

"He makes me so *angry!*"

Her father just patted her hand. "He certainly does. See, dinner is ready. As there is enough for three, we must address it heartily."

"I'm not hungry."

"You need to keep up your strength for future developments."

Rachel looked up sharply. "What developments? He said he'd never ask me again."

Her father led her into the dining room. "That does

not mean that he will give up." The vicar seemed almost amused by her predicament.

He was correct, though. The very next day as Rachel was returning from a visit to the Dilbury cottage, where there was a new baby, she encountered the earl on foot. She was taking a shortcut by the river and the location was alarmingly isolated.

"Are you afraid of me at last?" he asked with an unpleasant smile. "Perhaps you are wise."

"Why should I fear you?" But she did.

"I could deprive your father of his living."

"That would be below contempt, my lord."

She tried to walk past him, but he seized her arm. "Perhaps you could reform me . . ."

"Oh, come now, *Mr. Lovelace,* I am no Clarissa to be taken in by that ploy."

He flinched. "You are infuriating."

"Only to a spoiled child who must have his way. Release me!"

"No. I must have my way."

Rachel didn't even resist when he drew her to him. She'd been aware from the first moment of seeing him that he would kiss her, and her blood had been singing with the wanting. If he hadn't kissed her, she suspected that she would have dragged him in for a kiss herself.

His lips were clever, but now his hands, too, showed their skill, first at her throat, but then sliding down to her breasts. She wore no stiff stomacher with this gown and the merest brush of his fingers seemed to start a fire of longing.

She cried out against his hot mouth and knew she was mad. Mad to surrender, mad to deny them both . . .

" 'Scuse me, miss. Milord . . ."

The young voice shocked Rachel back into her wits and she tore herself out of the earl's wanton hold. Standing on the path were the three Fletcher youngsters needing to pass. They grinned cheekily. She heard the earl hiss with anger, but he stepped back. The two lads and a girl passed by and stopped to inspect the water for fish.

Lord Morden muttered something and moved to drew Rachel away to a more private place.

"No," she said shakily. "I admit your power over me, but I will not go willingly to ruin."

"Plague take it, I want to marry you not ruin you!"

"But only for money. It will not do."

He looked at her darkly and she sucked in a breath. "You were going to seduce me, weren't you? Here, on the path! I suppose you think that once you've had your way I would be bound to marry you."

He maintained a bold stance, but she could see that her words had hit home. "It seems a reasonable assumption."

"I'd rather *die!*" she declared. "If I think it wrong to marry you, my lord, then nothing will persuade me to. Neither threats, nor seduction!"

"Now you're sounding just like that damned Clarissa! I suppose you would pine away from the shame of your fate."

"Not before I'd killed you, sir!"

He suddenly laughed. "Gads, but you *are* magnificent! Are you really going to force me to make do with some simpering London miss?"

It was the hardest thing she had ever done in her life, but Rachel said, "Yes." And walked away.

The next she heard he had gone back to London. She knew he had gone back to find some other woman to marry him so he could get his hands on his inheritance. A handsome earl would have no trouble finding a bride. She wept many a bitter tear, and berated herself for being a complete fool, but knew that given the time over again—and the remnants of her virtue and sanity—she would have done the same thing.

Still and all, she could hardly bear the thought of the earl's return to the Abbey with a bride.

"Plague take the man," Rachel muttered as she took out her frustration on the weeds in the garden. "And plague take me for a fool for caring."

On the night before Easter, Mrs. Hatcher said, "I wonder what house will have the egg this year."

"To pick Dym's Bride?" said Rachel, who couldn't even summon much interest in that matter anymore. "How is it done?"

"There's someone as has the job of choosing, but none knows who."

"No one knows? But I suppose if it were known, there would be pressure. It must be an honor, being Dym's Bride."

"That it is, miss. Something to be right proud of."

The next morning, Mrs. Hatcher came to Rachel as soon as she came downstairs. "Miss Proudfoot! You'll never guess. The egg were on this very doorstep!" She proffered a small blue robin's egg.

It took a moment for Rachel to understand. "Dym's Egg? Here? But . . ."

"Yes. You've been chosen to be Dym's Bride!"

Rachel felt a shock of icy horror. "No! I mean, it's impossible. I'm not even from these parts. . . ."

"That don't matter, miss."

"But what if I don't want to?" Images of Meggie

Brewstock in the flames were dancing before Rachel, and Mrs. Hatcher appeared ghoulish.

The woman's frowned. "Nay, miss, you couldn't spoil a tradition that's gone on for centuries."

The Reverend Proudfoot came in at that moment, and when he heard the news he looked very thoughtful. "But is not the Bride generally young? Rachel is twenty-four years old."

"Nay, sir, just unmarried." Mrs. Hatcher turned to Rachel. "It's a great honor, miss, and," she added slyly, "it's said that all the brides wed within the year."

"Perhaps we could have breakfast now, Mrs. Hatcher," said the vicar calmly, and the housekeeper had to leave.

Rachel stared at her father. "A virgin, she means. I'm to be a sacrificial virgin! Though I fear I am not supposed to end the night that way!"

"Now, now, don't fly into alt over this, my dear. I'm sure it is right that they assume that you are still a maid, being the vicar's daughter, but if you choose to act the part of Dym's Bride, I will be in attendance at these rites. I will make certain that no harm comes to you. This development is most intriguing, though."

"It's terrifying!"

"Come, come, dear. You cannot really suppose the people here would intend harm to you."

"I don't know what to think any more. But Dym's Night . . ."

"We are agreed that there is nothing to this Dym's Night, Rachel. Of course, we will not let them force you into this role if you do not care for it, but there could be benefits. We could show that there is nothing to whatever superstitions they hold, and at the same time gain a completely accurate record of the event."

Rachel recognized that it was the latter temptation that was first in her father's mind, though he certainly would not allow her to be placed in any danger. His calm good sense was steadying her, however.

"As a further safeguard," the vicar said, "I think we will send the record of our researches to the bishop and make sure that everyone here knows that we have done so. Moreover, I will ask Sir George to attend this year, and also Mr. Home-Nowlan. They will be additional representatives of reason." He considered her kindly. "I really think there is no cause for concern, but if you do not wish to do it . . ."

Rachel could see how much he was looking forward to it all. "It will be rather exciting," she made herself say, "to be the center of it all. And after all, I am becoming something of an old maid. I can't afford to turn up my nose at a guarantee of marriage within the year."

But then she was assailed by the image of the only man ever to propose marriage to her. If she would not marry him, where would she ever find a man to her taste?

After church that day, Rachel was the center of attention as everyone congratulated her on being Dym's Bride. What struck her, though, was that no one seemed surprised by the choice, and none of the other eligible women seemed at all jealous.

Her worries resurfaced. "I don't know," she said to her father later as they were assembling the record of their research. "It all seems very strange. And do you know what I have realized—" She broke off, for she had been about to reveal something embarrassing.

"Yes, dear?" Her father looked up from his letter to the bishop.

Rachel licked her lips. "The earl has kissed me. A number of times . . ."

"Yes?"

"The last two times, he was stopped. . . . No, *we* were stopped by local people interrupting. If we had not been stopped . . ."

Her father's brows rose, but he was not shocked. "You think that perhaps the people here have been preserving your, let us say, eligibility."

Rachel's face was burning. "Yes."

"While Lord Morden was trying to remove it in order to force you to the altar. What a great deal goes on in a simple country village, to be sure. But perhaps the Bride is chosen, however that is done, long before Easter."

"I suspect *I* was. I do wonder why."

At least the days between Easter and Ascension passed quickly, for Rachel was harried with preparations for her role. There were a number of chants to learn, ones that she would have picked up naturally if she had lived here all her life, but which she had to learn by rote. This was particularly difficult as many of them were gibberish.

"Miggeth, hibby, degeth ru," she repeated to Mrs. Hatcher one day as the housekeeper helped her cut out the bright green fabric for her Dym's Bride robe.

"Degeleth ru," the woman corrected.

"But what does it *mean*?" Rachel demanded.

"No one knows, miss."

"Then what does it matter?" Rachel complained. Her patience was generally very thin these days.

"Maybe it don't."

Rachel looked at the woman across the big kitchen table and asked the question she'd avoided. "Do you think this is to be a Dym's Night?"

The woman looked up with an anxious crease above her eyes. "None knows, and that's the truth. But we mun be prepared, miss."

"And if it is, what will happen?"

"Things'll be better."

"What will happen to *me*?"

"To you, miss? Why do you ask?"

But her eyes shifted and Rachel could see that she'd get no more truth out of the woman. Rachel strongly suspected that she'd been picked to be Dym's Bride because no other woman in the parish would take the role. Whatever the truth, the people here were not at ease about what had happened to Meggie Brewstock. If she believed in superstitious nonsense, she'd doubtless flee the area until long after May the first.

She reminded herself that they lived in a modern age of reason, and that there were no demons. Except a certain sort of man who could tear a woman's heart in two.

When she put on the dress, it felt strange because it had no hoops or heavy petticoats, but hung against her skin with only her thin shift as barrier. "It's hardly decent," she muttered.

"That color's right pretty on you, miss," said Mrs. Hatcher. "Now for the neckline." Before Rachel realized what she was doing, the woman cut away a great deal of the bodice.

Rachel ran in front of the mirror and gasped. "Mrs. Hatcher, that is far too low! I will have to fill it in with lace." And that wouldn't stop her nipples pressing against the thin cloth. She *needed* a stomacher.

"Nay, miss, it's no lower than your best silk."

"But I look . . . indecent!"

"Nay, miss. It'll look right fetching, and what's the harm in looking your best one night in your life? Your man'll like it."

"I have no man."

"The Bride always marries within the year, miss."

Another superstition about to be proved hollow, thought Rachel bitterly. Oh, why didn't Lord Morden come back to the Abbey with a bride and get it over with?

On Walpurgis Night, Rachel found her nerves in a better state than she had expected.

This was in part because the waiting was over, but also because Sir George and Mr. Home-Nowlan had come over to dine, wanting to be in on the business from the start. Rachel watched Sir George in particular and simply could not believe that he had any secret knowledge. With the solid good-worth of these two men, and her father's keen eye for the bogus, it did seem impossible that there would be any mischief.

She must have still looked anxious, however, for Sir George patted her arm. "Don't you worry about a thing, Miss Proudfoot. Both Hubert and I have a pistol in our pockets. And I've been at these affairs. There's no harm to them, none at all."

"Thank you, Sir George. But don't be too quick to react. I expect matters to be boisterous, and will not take offense."

"Good girl. Good girl."

Rachel went up to her room and changed into her

green dress. It was completely simple but clung to her full figure in a way she found strange. She tied the green sash at the waist and acknowledged that the effect was becoming. She brushed out her hair and let it fall loose to her waist. Her thick hair generally went from its knot on the top of her head, to the plaits she wore for sleep. It looked rich and wild when loose and seemed to suit the gown. After a moment's consideration she decided that it formed enough of a cloak to screen the low neckline, and she did not add a neckerchief.

When she returned belowstairs, she saw Sir George's eyes widen in honest admiration and felt both self-conscious and pleased. She couldn't help wishing that a certain other gentleman was here to see her in this wanton deshabille.

The light was fading and they heard the drums and pipes of the band coming down the street. The tune seemed primitive to Rachel and she shivered even as her toe tapped to the insistent beat. As she had been warned to expect, it stopped outside the vicarage, and there was a great cry of, "The Bride! The Bride!"

Heart thudding, Rachel sucked in a deep breath and walked out to be greeted by a thunderous cheer. "Good Lord," Rachel said to her father, "how many people are there here?"

"All the village, and half the area besides, from the look of it."

Indeed, just counting the lanterns that made a river of light down the road, there must be hundreds. Rachel saw children, though, and even babes in arms, and that eased her fears. Would anyone bring a child to an evil event?

Some young women ran forward and crowned Rachel with flowers, tossing a chain of fragrant blooms around her neck. Then, laughing excitedly, they pulled her out to the front of the procession.

A roaring beast leapt at her.

Rachel screamed, then realized it was only the mummer's horse. As her panicked heart steadied, she saw other people present in the traditional masks and disguises and the Morris dancers with their bells. She had to keep hold of her sanity.

She checked to see that her father, Sir George, and Mr. Home-Nowlan were close by and then set to lead the way to Dymons Hill.

It was not hard to find, for the fire was already lit there like a beacon.

The atmosphere for weeks had been tense, but now Rachel could only find it merry. The music was impossible to resist, and many people were dancing their way along the road. Even Rachel could not help walking in rhythm and keeping the beat with her hands. She grinned at her father, and he twinkled back.

As they followed the path across the field, Rachel tried hard not to think of the Earl of Morden, and their first kiss here. She almost succeeded. She found the climb not as hard as she'd feared, but kept a careful eye to be sure her father was not left behind.

Once on top of the hill, the magnificence caught her.

It was just high enough to give the illusion that one could see forever, and the lanterns behind were still winding along. Back in the village every house was lit, and nearby she could see the big houses—Walberton Grange and Morden Abbey—blazing from every window.

She turned to Sir George. "I didn't know about the lights."

"Have to greet Waldborg properly," he said cheerfully. "How else would he know where to visit?"

"This is done every year?"

"Of course."

"How do you know if he visits?"

He smiled, seeming to acknowledge the foolishness. "By the good fortune that comes, of course."

"And if bad fortune visits?"

He winked. "Then perhaps a candle went out."

"I presume everyone has left someone at home to tend the lights."

"Of course. Mostly the elderly, who have no taste for the climb and the night air anyway. And it's more to try to guard against fire, my dear. With all those candles left burning, it's amazing places don't burn down more often."

His practical common sense robbed the occasion of any lingering shadows.

There was a great deal of space on the top of the hill, but even so there would not be room for all. Rachel saw the lights turn into a ring around the base of the hill as people settled to have their revels down there.

Or to guard the hill from interference.

Was that where the third earl had been hit on the head?

Stop it, she told herself. You'll drive yourself mad if you think that way.

The musicians changed their rhythm to more ordinary country dances, and people took partners. Rachel allowed Sir George to lead her into the patterns and was soon enjoying herself mightily. She had never even attended an open-air dance. To attend one on the top of a hill was exhilarating indeed.

She danced next with Mr. Home-Nowlan, and then with her father, but after that she danced with everyone. There was familiarity, yes, but no improper behavior that she could detect.

There were a great many flasks and bottles going around, but despite the exercise of the dancing, Rachel refused all. She had no intention of being made drunk or worse. She no longer had any fears of murder, and certainly none about demons, but she had to be concerned about wanton behavior.

After having resisted the Earl of Morden, she had no mind to be ruined by a local farm lad.

Mark Brandish pulled up his steaming horse in the stables of the Abbey. He was not surprised to find the place ablaze with light—he knew the local customs. He was furious, however, to find the stables totally deserted. Someone should be here to keep an eye on things.

In the kitchen he found his three oldest retainers toasting themselves by the fire. Even though two were retired, he sent one to keep an eye on the stables and commanded the other two to patrol the house to make sure there was no danger of fire from the many lamps and candles.

Damn Waldborg and all to do with him!

He downed a mug of porter then saddled a fresh horse. He'd have been here hours ago if the other one hadn't cast a shoe. As it was, it was close to midnight, and this was Dym's Night.

He'd scoffed at all these matters for years and teased Rachel for her concerns, but when he'd received his steward's report, and it had contained the news that the vicar's daughter was to be Dym's Bride, he'd been flooded with alarm. The very choice raised questions.

The people here would never choose an outsider for such an important role without reason. Perhaps the reason was that none of the local girls were willing to risk Meggie Brewstock's fate. In fact, he remembered Nan saying that she was glad Cattie was too young to be in danger.

In *danger*.

Plague take it, why hadn't he forced the issue of marriage, then Rachel wouldn't have been in danger either?

As he thundered out of the stables on a new horse, he knew why. Because Rachel had demanded that he woo her, and he'd been too damned proud.

He'd expected the vicar's daughter to accept the tarnished honor he offered her without cavil. When she hadn't, he'd tried to wash his hands of her. Three times. Each time, the painted London beauties had appeared less and less appealing, and he had wanted only Rachel with her strong chin and firm standards.

And the blasted woman would try and reform him. She'd want him to stay here in the wilds of Suffolk breeding sheep and draining land. She'd limit his drinking to a glass or two of wine at dinner, and his gaming to a hand of whist for penny points. . . .

He must be mad!

Dymons Hill looked like a scene from hell, with the great fire leaping on top and showering the black sky with golden spangles. Around the fire, tiny figures cavorted. Around the base, more people danced, lit faintly by their lanterns. 'Struth, the whole parish must be here.

He pulled up his horse at the ring.

"The earl!" someone shouted, but it was greeting not alarm. "May Waldborg come to ye, milord!"

"And to you," Mark muttered, and thrust his reins into the hand of a lad. "Hold him awhile. I want to go up."

"Aye, milord," the lad said willingly. "You don't want to miss Dym's Night."

Mark took the steep path at a run.

Rachel was thoroughly enjoying herself when the music changed. She half moved to choose another partner, then realized that this wasn't dancing music. It was that pounding, haunting music that had greeted her at her door.

Someone nearby nudged her. "The chants, miss. It's time for the chants."

Feeling rather foolish, Rachel began the first of the chants she'd learned. "Refter coma, refter coma, her-ilk dimi moder droma . . ." It was immediately picked up by all the women so that she did not have to struggle anymore but could let them carry her. She saw women with young girls coaching them to follow the words.

Coaching future Demon's Brides? Yes. This was a passing on of the chants. Rachel glanced at her father, and saw him busily scribbling in his book. She smiled. It was all innocent, after all.

But somehow the meaningless chants were different with the drums beating and the earth vibrating beneath her feet.

The earth vibrating?

She almost laughed in relief when she realized it was just the men stamping their feet in rhythm.

Now the women held hands and made a big circle around the fire, dance-stepping as they chanted. Rachel had a moment's qualm, but then she realized she had a five-year-old by the hand. Surely if there was any intent to throw her into the blaze, she would not be holding on to an innocent child.

Back in 1668, Meggie Brewstock had followed these rites, though. At what point had the pattern been broken, and how had she ended up in the flames?

The circle suddenly stopped turning, leaving Rachel standing alone, but safely away from the fire. Three people came forward: two older women and a man bearing a box. She recognized the man as Michael Bladwick, a prosperous local farmer, and the one most interested in new scientific ideas. She was astonished when he opened the old carved box to present a knife.

"As keeper of the blade," he said prosaically, as if a bit embarrassed by his task, "I give it unsullied to the bride."

"Take it, dear," said one of the women. Sally Fuller, the innkeeper's wife, known far and wide for the tough bargains she could strike.

Rachel picked up the knife. It looked extremely old. The blade was shining silver covered with worn-down runes, and the hilt was made of carved green quartz. The music pounded in her ears and her blood matched the beat.

"Cut yourself, dear," said the other woman, Mary Heyman, the carter's widow, and the most devout member of the parish. She was neat as a pin tonight in cap and hat, and it was bizarre to see her in these surroundings. "Now just a little nick," she said. "I'm sure Michael has the blade well-sharpened, and we don't want you to do yourself damage."

Rachel almost giggled at the contrast between this and her imaginings. Really, she had been absurd. She wincingly applied the blade to the ball of her thumb. It *was* sharp, and she didn't even feel the sting before blood beaded.

"That's a girl," said Mary cheerfully, and called out, "She's blooded and not a moment's hesitation!"

There was a great cheer.

Grinning as if she had done something wonderful, Rachel smeared the blood on the blade. She remembered a certain lewd comment about blood and blades and knew her cheeks were reddening. "Now what?" she asked quickly.

The two women knelt and their four hands seemed to mark a place, though there was nothing to be seen but the scrubby short grass. "Plunge the knife here, dearie," said Sally. "Don't hesitate. You won't harm it."

Rachel knelt, too. Despite the woman's words, she was worried about driving the blade into what appeared to be hard earth over rock.

"Just imagine it's a big, thick cheese," said Mary, "and stick it in there, dear."

The music pounded on, but the people were still and silent as they waited for her to complete the rite.

Rachel took a deep breath and thrust the blade into the hill. It sank in as if indeed cutting into cheese and she grinned with relief.

Then a heat rippled up the knife. It ran into her hands, along her arms, through her body . . .

She tried to pull back, but the two women put their hands on her back and pushed down.

"Just lie a moment," she heard Mary say, but far far away.

She heard the woman cry out.

Rachel would have cried out herself if she'd had voice to do so. She was sucked down onto the earth and her body was being invaded by something, something rushing up with elemental force, flooding her, expanding her. . . .

Even in her terror she was struck with wonder.

Then it was gone. She was torn from the earth and screamed at the agony. She was being dragged. She writhed in a grip of steel.

The fire? Was she being dragged to the fire? Hands tore at her, but she was forced on, away.

A shot? Was that a shot?

Not to the fire. Into the dark, the cold, cold dark. Down the hill, fighting through demons.

"Don't worry. I've got you."

Morden! What was the earl doing here?

He threw her up on his horse, and she clutched the mane, afraid of falling. Then he was behind her and the horse was galloping.

The loss. The loss hit her. With every stride she was torn further from herself, and the spirit was loose and adrift. . . .

"Take me *back*. I must go back!"

"What the devil have they done to you?"

"Can't you feel it? It needs me!"

"By heaven, it does not. The church. That'll stop it."

Rachel was half fainting with the pain that was more mental than physical. The earl dragged her off the horse and carried her into the church, to put her gently on her feet by the altar. She felt her body and was astonished to find herself whole. "Oh no, oh no . . ."

He grabbed her and held her tight. "You're safe now."

"No, no! I'll never be safe again!" She was shuddering and her teeth were rattling together like bones in a bag. "The demon is real, and loose!"

"No, love. It's all superstition."

"Then why are we in a *church?*" she demanded wildly, tearing herself out of his arms. He made no answer. "It's seeking me!" She gripped his arms. "Help me!"

"Hush, hush. It can't get you here."

Rachel shivered. It seemed true. She could sense that here what sought her could not enter, but it waited outside, beyond the limits of consecrated ground.

"We'll wait for dawn," the earl said soothingly. "Presumably then whatever it is will have to return to its own private hell."

"No." She shook her head. "No, it won't."

"Come now, everyone knows the rule of these things."

"How can you laugh? Can't you *feel* it?"

"No." But she sensed he lied.

"I have to go back."

"What?"

"It *needs* me!"

He grabbed her. "I need you. Be damned to whatever demon they've raised. You aren't going to be its sacrifice."

"But it *needs* me," she repeated, and the keening demand sang in her mind and through her blood. "I must, I must—"

He silenced her with a kiss. Rachel felt the humming swell in her and engulf them both, as if the demon were here in the church with them.

They fell rolling to the floor.

When the kiss broke, Mark stared at Rachel, wondering if she were just drunk, or had run mad, or if he had. He didn't care. Her passion had always amazed him, but now she was aflame with it and he could not resist the power.

He spoke loudly and clearly, "You are going to marry me, Rachel, but we are going to make love here and now. That will put an end to any question of you being the Demon's Bride."

He was prepared for resistance, but she said, "Yes," and her eyes were fierce. Dear heaven, what had they done to her? Drugs?

He would do it anyway. It was the only way to be sure of keeping her safe. He didn't attempt to undress but Rachel's thin dress was little barrier to his touch. He wished he had time to introduce her to love more skillfully. "I'm sorry, sweeting," he murmured as she moved sinuously beneath him, "I'll show you all my skills and graces another time."

She opened her clear eyes and focused on him. "Now!" she commanded with an urgency and knowledge that shocked him. She opened her legs and dragged him on top of her. Was all this for naught? Was she no virgin anyway? When he entered her, however, he felt her maidenhead tear.

There was no cry of distress, though, just a manic delight. "Yes, oh yes," she whispered, then shrieked, "Yes!" so the church rafters rang.

Then the tempest took them both—a storm that was

more than human, and deeper than the earth that mankind tilled; a power that blew bodies and minds apart and mingled them with another whole.

Mark became slowly aware that he was both human and alive, and was surprised. For some moments there he had not been human, and in the climax—if it had anything to do with sexual climax—he had not been sure he would live.

In sudden concern, he opened his heavy eyes and rolled to cradle Rachel. "Rachel! Love?"

Her eyes flew open. "The earth," she said, staring at him. "I was the earth. . . ."

He wanted to make some boastful, flippant remark, but it would seem like spitting in church. Then he realized they had just fornicated in a church, before the very altar. There was a madness here. He tested the atmosphere but found nothing but echoes of their bonding.

"The demon has gone at least," he said.

"No, no!" she laughed. "It's in us. The earth is *in* us." She leapt to her feet and whirled, green skirts dancing. "The earth is reborn!"

He grabbed her. "Rachel. This is very flattering, but calm down."

She clutched his arms, suddenly serious. "I must go back to the hill."

"Oh no. We'll wait here until dawn to be safe."

"I must be there *before* dawn, or it will all be wasted."

"All what?"

"All this! Stop denying it. You know."

"Know what?" he demanded.

"Waldborg. The earth. The spirit of the earth. It is to be renewed, and I am its vessel."

"Not anymore, you aren't. You're not a virgin anymore. Waldborg will have to make do with someone else."

She shook her head. "I don't have to be a virgin, just fertile. And I am fertile," she said in a rapture. "I am as fertile as the buds of spring and as the seeds of autumn . . ."

She was going into a trance. He shook her. "*Stop it*! God damn them all, I'll tear that hill down."

Her eyes focused. "No, no," she said almost gently. "The spirit is the earth, and the earth is us. I am just needed for a little while, and then I will be yours forever."

It was almost as it were not Rachel speaking at all.

"I'm not letting you out of here before dawn."

"Poor Mark," she said, and his name was beautiful from her lips. "Are you fighting the beautiful mystery of it all? Look inside and see what you have become."

"What have *you* become?"

"I am the bride. I could be any fertile woman, but now I am . . . I am *prepared* to be the bride. I am the key. It has to be me, and I must go."

The power of her conviction shook him. "What if this is madness? What if the demon wants you in the fire?"

"It doesn't."

"How the devil do you know?" he shouted. "I love you, dammit. I've been fighting it for months. Now I've finally admitted it, am I to let you walk away to perform some ungodly rite that might destroy you?"

She looked at him with tranquil eyes. "Yes."

"Oh, God."

"If for nothing else, for your land, Mark. You have your duty to your land."

"Plague on the land. I care only about you."

She shook her head in gentle reproof. "I do love you, but it's not very noble to love such a frippery fellow. I am going to have to change you. I am going to nag you about your gambling and your drinking, and demand that you spend more time here looking after the land. When I do that, it will be because I love you, but also because I am one with the land."

He pulled her into his arms. "I'll do my best to be worthy of you, Rachel, but I'm a wastrel at heart, you know."

"Yes."

He groaned. "Could you perhaps come up with a polite lie for me?"

"Not tonight." But there was a hint of humor in her eyes.

"And you feel you must return to the hill?"

"Yes. Absolutely. I don't know what will happen if I don't, but it will not be good for anyone."

He should be able to overwhelm her physically, but he doubted it would work. She had within her the force of storm, flood, and thunder. He surrendered. "But I come with you."

"Of course."

They went finger-twined out of the door of the church. There seemed nothing there to fear, but against all reason, Mark could sense the waiting presence. They mounted his horse and he kicked it to the gallop toward the beacon on top of Dymons Hill.

The fire still burned, but all was quiet. The people around the base of the hill looked at them with eyes full of reproach and grief.

"It's all right," Rachel said, touching hands with two people nearby. "It's all right. Waldborg is here among us, and the earth will be renewed."

The word and the touch rippled around the hill. *Waldborg is here. Waldborg is here.* As Mark followed Rachel up the path, the music began again below them. He was in awe of her just now, but terrified. What if the end of this was for her to be consumed by fire? He fingered the pistol in his pocket just to be sure it was still there.

As soon as they arrived on the hilltop, Reverend Proudfoot hurried forward, looking years older. "Rachel, my dear, are you all right? You screamed most terribly when Lord Morden seized you and poor Mary Heyman has a numb hand."

"I am quite all right, Father. It was just the interruption. Now we must finish." She spoke almost absently and headed straight for the place where the knife still protruded from the ground. She was like a parched person seeing water, and Mark knew no one could stop her now. She lay over the knife, facedown.

Mark could not simply watch her do this. He ran to sit beside her, placing his hand on her back in comfort. "Rachel?"

She turned her head and smiled. "It is all right. You'll see."

And then the spirit poured through her.

It was more than before, and different. Mark tried to break free, for this was too strong even for his cynicism, but his hand was sealed to Rachel and through her to the earth. He knew now why Rachel had screamed. If he was separated from her, the skin would surely be ripped from his hand.

He tried to resist, to cling to reason, but the rapture

was too great. He collapsed down over her—his bride, his love, his dear destruction—and every point of contact became a new annihilation of his self.

He was the hill, and he was the beating heart of the earth, full of the fearsome energy of life. When he was lost, when Mark Brandish was no more, he was expelled with newborn agony like a seed breaking through the soil, suffering for the first time the glorious triumph of growth.

He saw the air in all its wonders, full of dancing magic, and rode the wind through the living trees. He brushed over water, the blood of the earth, and sank drowning-deep into the salt oceans.

He was with Rachel now, joined to her more poignantly than in sex as they played with fish and dolphins, then spouted free to race through clouds. At last, at last, the new day was beginning and they must spiral arrow-swift back down and into a hill in Suffolk.

Mark opened his eyes slowly and stared at the watching faces. Plague take it, he was intimately wrapped around his future countess and being grinned at by a silent crowd of yokels. He shook her and said, "Rachel."

She rolled onto her back and smiled at him.

He hoped that one day she would open her eyes like that after lovemaking, and smile in that way that spoke of recent heavenly delights. "Oh my," she said.

He straightened her skirts. 'Struth, but her gown was scarce decent, being so thin and without petticoat or stomacher. "Are you able to stand?"

She looked around and her delicious color flooded into her face. She scrambled to her feet, completely the vicar's practical daughter caught in the most unthinkable situation.

He kept an arm around her, even though she tried to struggle free. "Miss Proudfoot has done me the honor of agreeing to be my countess," he announced.

"I have not!"

He put an edge of command into his voice. "You most certainly have."

And she hid her face against his chest and did not deny it. The music on top of the hill picked up the jollity already ongoing down below.

"You'd no need to tell us, milord," said Mrs. Hatcher dryly. "We knew you were the one."

"The one for what?" asked Rachel, coming out of hiding.

"Why, the one for the Bride. The Bride is always one on the point of marrying. Has to be really, the way it can take them."

Rachel gasped. "You mean. . . . It usually . . . ?"

"Tends that way, yes, miss, though there's some as say that it's just the excitement and the excuse. I've never seen it take anyone like tonight, that's for sure. I reckon tonight were a proper Dym's Night. The land's all set for a while now."

It astonished Mark that anyone could be in doubt.

"Yes it is," said Rachel clearly. "I have to tell you something. Dym's Night comes of the joining of the Christian rhythms with those of the earth. No calendar change can alter it."

There was a murmur of relief.

"But there is no need for the Bride to be a virgin, only that she be fertile. That is why a virgin is better. If a woman is with child, her . . . her powers are turned to that, and cannot be used by the spirit. But any woman who is not with child, but is still able to conceive a child, can be the Bride."

"Was that what happened to Meggie Brewstock?" Mark asked. "Was she with child, and did the spirit kill her?"

"No," she said fiercely. "The spirit will *never* kill. But the earl came later than you, and the bond was too great. She died of the shock."

Mark could imagine being torn from the earth in the midst of that experience, even though it was rapidly fading into a magical dream. He was appalled to think that moments later he could have done the same thing to Rachel, and killed her.

"Aye," said Ada Brewstock, stepping forward. "Grandad told me before he died. Said to tell you, miss, but I reckoned it were a matter best left alone. They had to knock out the earl, you see, to try to save her, but it were too late. Said poor Meggie looked so awful they couldn't have people see her, so they threw her on the fire and claimed it were an accident. But she had done her part."

"Yes," said Rachel, "she had done her part, and the earth was renewed." She turned to Mark. "But I think your ancestor felt some of what you felt this night and it drove him mad. It's not a mystery for men, you know." Her lips twitched. "Are you still sane?"

"No, I'm madly in love." He kissed her, despite their audience. "I think he was driven mad more by grief and a sense of what might have been, than by horror."

"You don't regret it, then?"

"No," he said, and it was true. "I regret nothing."

She turned and drew the blade out of the earth and handed it to Michael Bladwick. "Keep it safe."

"Aye, lady," he said, not at all prosaically. "That I will."

People seemed to want to gather around Rachel, talking, but mainly touching. He noted how they all called her "Lady" and he didn't think it was a reference to her future as his countess. It was as if she were magic, and perhaps tonight she was.

He knelt and tested the ground with his fingers, the ground from which she had just drawn the blade. It was hard earth over chalky rock, with no crack or crevice that he could detect.

Was he to believe this? That spirits could rise in the eighteenth century? Whatever had happened, though, he knew he was changed without hope of recovery. His land was no longer maps and ledgers and rents to be spent, but a living thing in his charge. He was called to cherish it as potently as he had ever been called to a woman.

Except one.

He stood and looked across at where she was talking to her father. Probably duly reciting all the details for one of his damned books. That dress outlined every lush curve of her passionate body, the bodice was far too low, and no woman with hair like that should be allowed to let it hang free in public.

He commandeered Sir George's cloak and went to wrap it around her. "No details of all this are to be published," he said to her father.

"The routine details, perhaps," countered the vicar calmly. "But as for the rest, I doubt it would be believed. However," he said with a direct look, "I think a wedding is in order."

"Indeed it is, and as soon as possible." Mark dared Rachel to refuse. He'd carry her off and hold her prisoner until she consented.

But Rachel blushed and smiled. "I am to be the Demon's Bride again, I see."

"For all time and beyond, without hope of escape. Yes?"

She raised her firm chin. "Yes please, my lord."

Author's Note

Walpurgis Night falls on April 30th and is a well-known festival associated with witches and the raising of demons. April 30th is also St. Walburga's Eve, for Saint Walburga's feast day is both the 25th of February and the 1st of May. This was an attempt by the Christian church to appropriate a pagan festivity and make it harmless. A common practice.

Ascension Day did fall on April 30th in 1573, 1668, and 1761. It happened again in 1818 and will occur next, I think, in 2027. (Could that long gap be what is wrong with the world today?)

The calendar was changed in 1752 in Britain to correct accumulated errors, and it is possible that the change is responsible for the shortage of early Easters.

Apart from the above facts, and despite my humorous speculations, this story and the customs described in it are complete invention.

The Haunting
of Sarah Gordon

by
Anita Mills

Near Balaklava, the Crimea: October 31, 1854

THE LANTERN LIGHT in the surgical tent was dim, but the attending physician saw enough to shake his head as he bent over David Gordon. The young officer bit his lip against the pain and tried to focus his eyes.

"Captain Gordon?" Without waiting for acknowledgment, the doctor spoke gravely, "We have delayed as long as we can, sir—in another day, you'll be dead of the infection, I am afraid."

"My leg?" the younger man gasped.

Chief Surgeon Major Dennison nodded. "And the arm at the elbow."

"No!"

"The leg's cold and black, and the arm's streaked with poison. I'm sorry—I wish I could have better news for you," Dr. Dennison went on matter-of-factly. "Today we might save you." He paused for a moment, then added significantly, "But tomorrow will be too late."

"No!"

Turning to his assistant, Dennison ordered, "Half a

pint of rum, followed by three drops of laudanum."
Under his breath, he muttered, "I would it could be
more, but we are nearly out of the drug. God knows
I have tried to be sparing with it, but there have been
so many, so very many in need."

"No!" Gordon shouted, trying to sit.

As the young man fell back, the doctor shook his
head again. "None of 'em wants to lose a limb, but
when it's done, most of 'em thank me." He reached
to pat David Gordon's shoulder in a fatherly manner.
"Buck up, and with the Almighty's aid, we'll pull you
through yet."

"I cannot go home without my leg," Gordon protested painfully. "I cannot."

"That's what they all say." As he spoke, Dennison
nodded to his assistant. "Pour the rum."

"I won't—"

"You will, sir—if it takes ten men to hold you.
Should have been done six days ago, but you were
not in the worst case, and—well, I had hopes . . ."
The doctor's voice trailed tiredly, then he recovered.
"But God willing, it is not too late."

David closed his eyes and clenched his teeth as they
raised him and put the cup to his lips. "Don't be a
fool," Dennison said curtly. "Pain's bad enough with
it. As it is, you'll feel the cut and wish you'd taken
twice what you were given."

"I'd rather die."

"Got a young wife, as I hear it. You want to go
home to her, don't you?"

"Not like that—not like that." As he tried to turn
his head away, the physician's assistant slid an arm
beneath his neck. David swallowed hard, then managed, "I promised her to come home whole."

The aide used the opportunity to pry open his jaws and pour the rum down his throat. David strangled for a minute, then as the fiery liquid hit his empty stomach, he retched, but the man held his head back, forcing it down again.

"Wait a few minutes before you give him the laudanum," Dennison advised, moving away to the next pallet. Over his shoulder, he added to David, "I won't take any more of the arm than I must. She'll understand."

"When he comes back, you'll be dashed grateful for everything you got," the tired aide said as he measured out the precious opiate and stirred it into a canteen cup of water.

They were going to take his leg. And half his arm. David Gordon's fevered thoughts turned again to Sarah. He couldn't go home like that—he couldn't. He couldn't go home half a man. What would she think of him? Would she turn away, sickened by the sight of him? He'd rather die than tie her to an invalid. But he didn't want to leave her.

He tried to remember the feel of her in his arms, but instead he saw the tears sparkling in her dark eyes as she whispered her good-bye. And he heard her beg him to take care, to come home again whole. And, fool that he was, he'd made the promise he could not keep.

"Go on—drink it," he heard the man murmur, this time more gently. "You'll need it."

He managed to swallow the nasty drug, then lay back, trying to keep his thoughts on Sarah. His Sarah. Sweet, pure, loving Sarah. The dearest love of his life. He could not remember when he had not loved her.

His stomach churned when they came for him, and

he did not protest when they laid him on the hard trestle table. Somewhere in the dim distance, he heard someone say his leg was a putrid mess, and he stiffened as the saw bit into bone. He heard someone scream a raw, agonized scream that cut through the fetid air. Merciful oblivion enveloped him.

For a time, there was no sound beyond what they did, and as tired as he was, the military surgeon worked carefully, until his aide touched his arm.

"He's not breathing."

Dennison stopped, leaned over his patient to listen, then felt David Gordon's neck, searching for a pulse. When he straigtened up, there was no mistaking the defeat in his face.

"He's gone, poor devil."

London: November 22, 1854

Even as she listened to the words and heard the sympathy in the man's voice, Sarah Gordon gripped the arms of the chair, every fiber of her being denying what he told her. Beside her, David's father wiped his streaming eyes, swallowing before he spoke, his voice little more than a whisper.

"He was my only son."

The smartly dressed officer rose uncomfortably and reached for his hat. "He died bravely of wounds sustained for his country, sir." As his gaze rested briefly on the face of the young widow, he wanted to offer some solace, but he could not. "Yes, well, I expect I should be going. Deuced nasty business, I can tell you—and there are a dozen more on my list for the day."

Long after he left, they remained sitting silently in the dark-paneled study, Sir Charles staring miserably into the fire, Sarah telling herself it was a mistake, that it was someone else's body, not David's that was being sent back to her. David could not be dead. Not David, who was so strong, so full of life. Not David, who had promised to come back to her.

She leaned back, closing her eyes, seeing him as he'd been when he left, his blue eyes bright beneath the dark red hair, his smile warm, his body straight as he sat his saddle so proudly. No, he could not be gone from her forever.

She felt Sir Charles's hand grip hers tightly for a moment, then withdraw. "First Janet, and now my David," he said, his voice breaking. "We've naught left, Sarah." When she said nothing, he sighed heavily. "I know he would wish me to provide for you, and you are welcome to stay here or at Groseby with me." Looking away, he added, "I know he loved you, Sarah."

He loves me still, she cried silently.

He sighed again. "Though it was not for long, you were a good wife to him—aye, I'd be the first to admit it. I know you loved him, and that is enough for me."

His words did not come easily, not when he'd opposed the marriage earlier, not when he'd argued with his son that "Sarah Jane Kendrick will not do, I tell you! For the one thing, she's got no family—and for the other, she's penniless! Oh, she's a good enough girl, I grant you, but you could do better." The argument rang in his ears now, making him ashamed. He'd forced them to elope, to wed over the anvil, rather than admit that David had loved the girl beyond reason ever since she'd been a small, orphaned waif in her uncle's house the next property over.

But since she'd lived with him in David's absence,

the old man had changed his mind almost completely. She was lovely in heart and mind as well as face, reminding him almost daily of his own beloved Janet. No, David could not have done better.

"Would you stay with a lonely old fool, Sarah?" he asked finally.

She looked up at that, her bewilderment written on her face. "He cannot be gone forever—he cannot."

"We'll heal together, child," he said softly. "At least we will have memories to share."

Her chin began to quiver, and tears filled her eyes. "But I want more than that, sir!" she cried. "I don't want memories! I want him to hold me, to—to—" She choked for a moment, then sobbed out, "I want him to love me again—I want his sons and daughters! I cannot accept this! I—I cannot!"

"In time we shall both have to do so." Unable to deal with her grief and his own, he rose and reached for his cane. Earlier he had been contemplating going out to his club, but now he felt far too old, far too weary to live. With his free hand, he reached out to Sarah, then his hand dropped helplessly. Time—it was going to take time. For both of them.

She sat still as stone now, her tears flowing unhampered down her cheeks. As though it had been but yesterday, she could remember the tearful parting, the feel of his strong arms around her, his shaven cheek against hers, and she could still hear his promise to come back to her. For an instant, she felt a surge of anger at him—if he had not gone, he'd still be alive, they'd still face a lifetime together. Instead, he'd made a promise he could not keep, and now she had naught to do but mourn him.

"Is there anything I can get fer ye, Mrs. Gordon?" the maid asked timidly from the door.

Sarah wanted to scream out that there was nothing—that inside she was as dead as David, but she could not. Instead, she shook her head and managed a calmness she did not feel.

"No. No, thank you, Betty," she answered, her voice tight now, controlled.

The girl moved closer, standing before her. "Sir Charles is taking it hard, ma'am." She raised her hand, then dropped it helplessly. "It just don't seem right, does it? For him to lose the missus, then Master David in the same year, I mean."

"No—no, it isn't."

"We're sorry—all of us, ye know."

"Yes."

"Seems like he could walk through that door right now," Betty went on. "He was so—so—" She caught herself guiltily, for she'd been about to say "alive," and somehow she couldn't. Instead, she finished lamely, "so good." When the young mistress said nothing, she sought the familiar words of solace, adding, "At least ye had 'im fer a bit, and that was a blessing, wasn't it?"

Sarah's brief composure cracked, and her voice rose as she cried, "It was not nearly enough—not nearly enough! It was but a taste of what was to be! Now I shall never know the rest—never!" Unable to bear it, she rose and walked to the window, where she stared unseeing into the dead garden. When she spoke again, her voice was distant, haunted. "We wanted children, and now I shall never hold his child in my arms."

"Oh, mum!" The girl burst into tears. "It was not

my meaning to overset ye—I swear it! All of us is mourning him, and—"

"I know."

"Sir Charles said I was to help ye, but—" Betty stopped to wipe her eyes.

"You cannot. Nobody can help me." The odd, bitter thought crossed Sarah's mind that the sun ought not to shine, not now, not ever again. "Just go on. Please."

She did not turn around until the maid had shut the door, then she sank to her knees, burrowed her face in the fullness of her sea green skirt, and wept uncontrollably. It was over—everything was over. David was dead. David was dead. David was dead. But no matter how many times her conscious mind repeated the thought, she could not accept it.

"You lied to me, David," she choked out. "*You lied to me!* You promised you would come back to me! You promised it!" she sobbed.

In the next room, Charles Gordon winced as he heard her, and he blamed himself for guiding his only son into the military he himself had loved. He should have used his influence instead to keep David at home for her. He knew what she felt now, for his own breast would ache forever for Janet.

He stood there, his knuckles white from gripping his cane, listening to her anguish until he could stand it no longer. "Tell Mrs. Potts to fetch the laudanum," he ordered a hovering footman. "And tell her to see that she gives Mrs. Gordon enough to make her sleep."

"Would you have the doctor, sir?"

"What the hell good would that do?" Sir Charles demanded angrily. "There ain't a quack alive as can mend what's broke in the girl!" His own eyes wet again, he lowered his voice. "I know. For twenty-nine years, I had the best wife a man could have. I would that David could have said the same." He swallowed hard, then looked up. "You might bring me a mite of the laudanum, too, after the young mistress is gotten to bed."

Sarah . . . Sarah . . .

She awoke in the darkness, the taste of the opiate still in her mouth. Thinking she'd heard David's voice, she sat up as the room spun crazily about her, but she was alone. Someone had laid more logs on the fire that burned in her fireplace, and that surely must have been what had awakened her. Then she remembered. *She would never hear David's voice again. Never.* And the horror of it all washed over her again.

Barely a wife, she was now a widow. At two-and-twenty, she was a widow. Odd, but she'd always considered it a circumstance for the old, not for her. She couldn't be a widow, she argued with herself. Her life with David was still unfinished.

The shadowy figure of her maid moved silently across the room, then stopped by the bed.

"Ye're awake," the girl murmured. "Mrs. Potts said to give but six drops, and I gave ye eight. Ye ought to be asleepin' like a baby."

"I just woke up."

"Well, sleep's the thing for ye, ye know. Helps heal the heart, me mum said." The girl moved closer. "I know what ye're feeling, mistress—I lost my Tom ere we was married even."

"I'm sorry." Sarah's voice was scarce a whisper. "I didn't know—you never spoke of him."

"It wasn't the war. He caught a chill and died of the fever." Leaning over, she plumped Sarah's pillow, then stood back. "I know it don't help to say it, but ye'll go on. The Almighty don't give us no choice in the matter." The girl's mouth twisted for a moment, then she recovered. "Would ye be wishin' for more of the laudanum, mistress?"

"No."

"Ye got to try not to think on it," the maid advised softly. "Ye got to wait until it don't pain ye."

"I thought—I thought someone was calling for me."

"No doubt you was dreaming, ma'am—or else it was the rainin'. Ye know laudanum allus makes me dream real odd," the girl added, stoppering the small bottle. "Had the toothache once, and after they gave it to me, I thought I was being chased by a mad dog. Only when it got to me, it wasn't a dog at all."

"What was it?" Sarah asked grudgingly.

"A handsome gentleman. He gave me a guinea, then he left me."

"How very strange."

"I never did know what the guinea was for," the maid went on. "Paid a sixpence to have my fortune told, thinking I might find out, but there wasn't nothing about no guinea in it."

"I expect you are right—that it was the laudanum that made me dream," Sarah admitted reluctantly. "Go on—I am all right," she lied.

As the door closed behind the girl, Sarah lay back and closed her stinging eyes. She was never going to be all right, and she knew it.

Sarah . . . Sarah . . .

This time, it was as though David spoke again. She

bit her lip to still the sob that tore at her, then strained to listen.

I never meant to leave you, Sarah . . . never. . . .

"David?" she whispered tentatively. "David?"

They are calling it bravery, but it was folly. I didn't want to fall. It was a terrible, terrible mistake—all of it. The Valley of Death, they are calling it, Sarah. The Valley of Death. No one could survive. There was a pause, then she heard him again. *I am sorry, my darling—I wanted to come home to you whole.*

She sat up in bed and looked about wildly. "David!" she cried out.

The rattle of wind and rain struck the windowpane suddenly, breaking the renewed silence, and she knew she was alone. He hadn't been there at all. She'd heard his voice in her mind. But he'd never said those words to her, he'd never spoken of dying. Was this some freak occurrence? Had God allowed him to enter her mind to explain?

"David! *David!* Please do not go, for I cannot bear it! I want you to hold me—I—I want you to love me!" Her voice dropped to a sob, then she whispered brokenly, "I wanted your child so much—I did not want to lose you ever." She spoke desperately, hoping that somehow, somewhere he listened to her. "Please, David—let me believe you are with me yet."

It was as though she could feel his arms about her, comforting her much as he had done the night before he'd left. She closed her eyes, savoring again his breath against her hair, hearing his soft words of love whispered above her ear. And she could almost believe he was there with her. Finally, as new warmth enveloped her, she drifted into sleep.

*   *   *

It was cold, and sleet carried on the icy wind bit into the mourners' faces the day David Gordon's sealed coffin was lowered into the earth. The churchyard, which clung to a hill overlooking the Tweed, had been one of his favorite places. The ancient chapel, a remnant of a ruined monastery, had been the place where he'd wanted his children christened. Children he'd never have.

Sarah stifled a sob and clenched her hands tightly at her side as she fought to control the awful anguish she felt. Beside her, Sir Charles's shoulders shook terribly, but there was no sound. His gloved hand sought hers as the first clods of cold Scottish soil were tossed onto the plain military casket.

"Well, 'tis over," he said finally, straightening. Releasing her hand, he offered his arm. "Come on—you'd best get inside ere you catch your death." For one long, last moment, he stared down again, then turned away. "He wouldn't want you to sicken, you know."

They walked back down the hill in silence to the waiting carriage. About halfway, she heard the beloved voice, his words echoing in mind.

I would you did not weep for me, Sarah, for I am with you always.

She stopped. The old man turned curiously.

"What is it?"

"Did you hear something?" she dared to ask him.

"It is the wind." As he spoke, he shivered. "Damned cold day for a burying. Sleet's in my eyes until I can scarce see."

"It was David," she declared positively. "I should know the sound of his voice anywhere."

"It is the wind," he insisted more forcefully. "It plays false with the mind."

"Then you heard it also."

"No." For a moment, his mouth twisted as though he might cry, then he regained his composure. "The boy's dead, Sarah," he said heavily. "We shall just have to face the fact, no matter how much we wish it otherwise."

"He said he will be with me always."

"Sarah—"

"And I want to believe him!" she cried out. "I must—else I shall go mad! I want to think he knows—that he knows I shall always love him."

Having no words capable of comfort, the old man handed her into the carriage, then waited while his coachman laid the woolen blanket over her lap. With an effort, he heaved his own body in after and sank back against the cold-hardened leather squabs. Silently, he cursed Kendrick for not coming back from London to share his niece's grief. It wasn't right that he himself should be all she had left.

"You think I imagine I hear him," she said finally. "That I want to believe something remains of him, don't you?"

"He is gone from both of us, my dear."

"I cannot—"

He sighed. "You are yet young, my dear. In time, David will be but a memory to you, and you will go on. I daresay there will be another husband, and I will not blame you." He stretched his hand to touch hers. "You deserve children, Sarah—you were meant to be a mother. There is too much kindness, too much love in you to waste." His eyes clouded briefly, then he cleared his throat. "Indeed, but it is my fondest wish that you will bring your sons or daughters to visit me. I should want to know you are happy."

Her throat constricted painfully, making speech difficult. She shook her head. "No. There is none but David for me—none but David for me," she whispered.

It was too soon. He exhaled fully. "I merely wished you to know I shall not blame you if you discover another, Sarah. In the months you have lived in my house, I have come to love you, first for David's sake, then for my own."

The journey from the churchyard to the small manor house was a short one, for which he was thankful. The raw, icy cold gnawed at his bones, paining him. As the carriage turned into the narrow lane, he spoke again.

"What we need, Sarah, is a dose of good Scottish whiskey warmed with a mite of butter in it." As she wrinkled her nose, he conceded, "Or rum, if you prefer—Mrs. Crowe can spice it for you until you scarce know it is a toddy."

"I am all right," she lied.

"No, you ain't," he said. "And I mean to see that you get warmed, if I have to tell your maid to put you to bed with a wrapped brick. All I got left, you know. Cannot have anything happening to you."

She lay abed, listening to the high-pitched wail of the wind and the beating of ice-covered branches against the thick glass panes. Above the ceiling, the ancient rafters creaked and groaned, but she didn't care. This was the house where David had been born, the place he had called home.

Despite the storm, she was diffused with warmth,

and her thoughts were hazed by the effect of Mrs. Crowe's hot rum punch. She could scarce think, but she supposed it was just as well. She had nothing to think on anymore. Nothing.

With an effort, she rolled over and cradled her head against her arm. Tomorrow she would cry again, but today she would sleep. She closed her eyes.

Sarah . . . Sarah . . .

He spoke so softly she wasn't sure she heard his words. For a long moment, she held her breath, waiting for more.

I have always loved you, Sarah—from the first moment I saw you, I have loved you.

"David?" she whispered. "David, we buried you— today we buried you!" As she spoke, new tears burned her eyes.

I couldn't leave you—not like that. I swear it.

She wanted to believe. "But how—? How can you be, when—?"

It wasn't my time, Sarah.

"I cannot go on without you—I cannot! You promised—you promised you would come back! And I cannot even see you!"

She began to weep uncontrollably, drawing her knees up against her chest, much like a child. Pressing her balled fist against her teeth, she sobbed until she could not breathe.

Sarah . . . Sarah . . . I am not worth such grief.

There was no one there, and she knew it, but she could hear his voice in her thoughts so clearly, so very clearly. She was losing her mind, that had to be what was happening to her. And yet not even for the sake of her sanity could she let him go again. She rolled over to look at the ceiling, to search for some sign of him.

"If I am not going mad, show me you are here," she whispered finally. "Please. I hear, but I do not see."

What would you that I did?

"I would have you hold me." She swallowed visibly, then turned her face toward the pillow. "I would have you love me."

I have always loved you.

But even as his voice echoed once more in her mind, she could feel his presence, the enveloping presence of his arms around her, the tautness of his body pressed against hers.

"Love me, David," she implored desperately. "Let me remember how it felt."

The old man was truly worried. In the more than two months since they'd buried David, Sarah had become more and more withdrawn, keeping to her room both day and night. It was becoming the conclusion of nearly everyone in the house that what she was experiencing was not the grief of a young widow, but the depravity of madness.

Whispers of the goings-on in Sarah's bedchamber had been heard as maids shared salacious bits with one of the more amorous footmen, and the fellow had proceeded to regale the lower servants with a few of the details. In the end, after obtaining a thoroughly embroidered tale from Mr. Crowe, Mrs. Crowe had taken it upon herself as a "decent Christian female" to inform Sir Charles that "Young Mrs. Gordon appears to be amusing herself with Philip, the lower footman. And while I would not ordinarily concern myself with the behavior of my betters," she went on, sniffing disdainfully, "I quite count it my duty to see that a mere footman who presumes to such behavior is discharged. It will not do to have an underling taking airs upon himself simply because he is boasting of what can only be called a utterly reprehensible liaison with the young mistress. There—I have said it." But as the fire of anger had flashed in his eyes, she hastened to add, "Not that I fault her for anything, sir. Her mind ain't what it used to be, what with her a-losing Master David."

His first inclination when his temper had cooled had been to turn off Mrs. Crowe, but in doing so, he would have to part with her husband also, and a good butler was indeed a treasure. As was a good housekeeper.

Informing the woman that she'd overstepped her authority in gossiping about his late son's wife, Sir Charles nonetheless found himself observing the comings and goings of poor Philip, concluding in the end that while the fellow was indeed a rather immoral fellow, there was nothing to indicate that Sarah was more than passingly aware of his existence.

But he had paid a visit himself to her bedchamber, and what he had seen had disturbed him. Instead of packing away David's things, she'd set them up, making it look as though he were there. And when he'd casually observed that perhaps she would recover better without them, she had refused to consider parting with anything that "belongs to my husband." As though David were not dead.

Finally, he'd badgered poor Betty into blurting out, "She talks to him, she does—all the time. Poor thing."

"What does she say?" he'd wanted to know. "Can you hear?"

"Oh, I can hear her, all right." Then, as though she'd perhaps said too much, the girl had reddened.

"Hear what?" he'd asked bluntly.

Betty had looked at the floor. "I would ye did not ask me that, sir."

"I am asking."

Her color had deepened, flushing her face to the roots of her hair. After a long moment of hesitation, she sighed. "She thinks he's there with her, she does."

"I am aware she believes he speaks to her," he'd interrupted dryly. "I had quite counted it to be related to her grief."

"There's more'n talk, sir."

"I beg your pardon."

"It—well, it's like they—well, like a man and a woman—"

"Like a man and woman what?"

The girl had bobbed her head and ducked away, mumbling something to the effect that if he wanted to know, he ought to listen for himself. And he had.

At first he'd been shocked by what he'd heard, but now he was like everyone else in the house, utterly convinced that his daughter-in-law's mind was severely affected. Despite the fact that she was verifiably alone, the sounds that came from her chamber were those of the physical side of love. And there was no question who she believed was with her.

For a time, he considered ignoring the matter, ordering everyone to leave Sarah be, but he knew that for the sake of David's memory, if not for her well-being, he could not do that. And, given the delicacy of the situation, he could not consult a local doctor.

In the end, he had dragged an extremely reluctant Sarah back to London, and he had engaged an utterly discreet, thoroughly reputable physician to examine her. To Sir Charles's disgust, the man pronounced her "shy and withdrawn, inclined to hallucination induced by grief, but otherwise young and healthy." It was a diagnosis anyone could have made.

The prescription was simple. "Given that her surroundings must surely remind Mrs. Gordon of her late husband, she must be removed from them entirely, perhaps through a visit to partake of the waters at Bath, or by a visit to the seaside in Cornwall."

"In late winter?" Sir Charles had inquired acidly.

"I have found the sea to have a healing power," was the reply.

"They think me mad, you know," she whispered into the darkness.

Does it matter?

She fell silent for a moment, then sighed. "Sometimes I think I *am* mad. Sometimes I think you are not here at all, that I merely have wished it to such a degree that I have deluded myself."

And yet you can feel me touch you.

"Yes—but what if that is but a delusion also?"

How could I prove otherwise?

She turned away, hugging her body with her arms. "I have always wanted a child, David—your child."

It was as though the room had gone empty, as though he were no longer there. She'd asked the impossible, and she knew it, and now she knew also that she'd driven him away. If he'd ever been there.

Tears of loneliness spilled from her eyes, wetting her cheeks as she clenched her teeth against the pain she felt. Outside, it had begun to rain—a steady, cold, windless rain, the only sound until the clock below struck the hour of midnight.

She was mad—she had to be. Only she could hear David's voice, only she could feel his touch. Only she believed he had come back to her. And now Sir Charles thought her insane also. For a moment, the thought crossed her mind that she could kill herself, that she could somehow join David, that they would once again be of the same world. But she could not know that, not for certain. This way, she could at least believe she still had him.

"Don't leave me, David," she whispered brokenly against her pillow. "I'd still have you love me."

She felt his hands smooth her hair, her gown over her shoulder, and his breath was soft by her ear. His arm slid around her, brushing her breast, as his hand moved over her body possessively. Her breath caught as he traced the bones of her rib cage, the flatness of her abdomen, moving lower. She closed her eyes more tightly when she rolled onto her back to relive again the memory of his touch, to savor again the weight of his body over hers.

Eager kisses awakened the familiar desire, sending hot, exquisite shivers coursing through her, while the heat ran like fire through her veins once more, fueling the aching need within her. She could feel his hands on her breasts, and she wanted to cry out for him to hurry, that she would not wait. Then, as she spread her legs, she felt him love her with his body.

She writhed beneath him with abandon, her breath coming in great gasps, as wave after wave of ecstasy washed over her, then there was peace. Long after she felt him leave her, she lay there, her arms crossed over her breasts, listening contentedly to the rain. Finally, daring to believe that just this once she could somehow see him, she opened her eyes.

And once again she was alone in the bed. Her hand slid over the cold sheets, seeking the warmth of his body, finding none. The clock below struck the quarter hour.

"Dear God, but I am mad," she told her pillow.

Sir Charles sat on a chair perched on the cliff, ostensibly to watch the pounding surf below, but his thoughts were elsewhere. May's warmer weather had not brought much improvement in Sarah's condition. Indeed, since their arrival, her spirits and appetite had plummeted, making him fear she would soon be but skin and bones.

He longed for Scotland, for the quiet peace of Groseby. He was getting too old for holidays, preferring instead the comfort of familiar surroundings. But he could not abandon Sarah. He could not abandon David's wife. And the doctor did not think it wise to take her back to Groseby. Not yet.

"Rather cloudy for the season, is it?"

Startled, the old man looked up into eyes as blue as David's, and for a moment, he felt a pang. Recovering, he nodded his agreement.

"Well, it is warmer than Scotland."

"I did not think you were from here."

"No. Since I left the army in '44, I have divided my time between Groseby and London."

"Groseby?" The intruder wrinkled his brow for a moment. "Oh, I collect it is near the border."

"Aye." Sir Charles studied the young man curiously, judging him to be nearly the same age as David would have been, then he looked once more into the wildness of the sea. "You don't sound much like a Cornishman either," he said gruffly.

"No."

The fellow moved closer to the edge, as though he would see what drew the old man. Sir Charles saw his limp and had to turn away.

"You were wounded, sir?" he managed to ask. As soon as the words escaped, he was ashamed of his rudeness.

But the other man did not seem to mind. He smiled ruefully. "Yes."

"In the war?"

"Yes."

When no more information was forthcoming, Sir Charles could not pry further. Instead, he nodded again. "I lost my son at Balaklava."

"Deuced nasty place, from all I have heard of it. It was folly to send so many to their deaths."

"Yes. Yes, it was." Not wanting to explore the rawness of his own feelings, the old man returned to the earlier subject. "You are visiting friends, I collect?"

"No." Again, the rueful smile. "I have come to regain my soul."

For a long moment, the old man struggled against the pain in his breast, and finally he lost. Tears welled in his pale eyes. "I miss him terribly, you know."

There was instant sympathy in the young man's face. Despite the lack of acquaintance, he reached to touch Sir Charles's shoulder. "I'm sorry—truly I am."

"It is the wages of war, isn't it?" the old man asked,

his voice raspy with emotion. "Your soul or your life, I mean."

"Or both." There was a pause between them before the stranger spoke again. "Do you ever speak much of him—of your son?"

Once again, Sir Charles's gaze sought the sea. "I cannot," he answered slowly. "If I think on it, I cannot survive. And survive I must, for he left a wife."

"As did many."

Sir Charles shook his head. "In this case, I fear her grief robs her of her health." He looked up once more. "I would that I could help her, but I know not what to do. She is too young to wither with none but an old man for company."

"It has not been yet a year. Perhaps her grief will pass."

"No. And what's to become of her when I am gone, I do not know. David would not forgive me if she were to go to an asylum." The old man straightened, suddenly self-conscious. He was telling a stranger too much. "I beg your pardon—not your affair, is it?"

"The wages of war bind many in shared sorrow." The younger man stared up at the gathering clouds. "I'd best go before it storms."

"Do you have far to walk?"

"Yes."

There was the smell of fresh rain in the sea breeze. Sir Charles stood with an effort and reached for his cane. "Got to send a fellow back for the chair," he muttered under his breath. "Get more useless every day." Already the stranger was walking away, his limp slowing him. "Wait!" he called out.

The young man turned back. "Is something the matter? Do you need help?"

"No, but—" Once again, something in the blue eyes drew Charles Gordon. "Yes," he said changing his mind suddenly. "If you'd get my chair before it blows away, sir, I'd be pleased to offer you shelter from the rain." Before the stranger could demur, he hastened to add, "A good day to share a bit of Madeira, don't you think?"

"I'd be pleased." Taking the chair in one hand and Sir Charles's arm with the other, the stranger started back up the narrow path. "I'm glad enough of company, truth to tell."

"I'll send round to your lodgings, so there'll be none to worry."

"I'm afraid I am staying alone in a cottage let for the summer." As he spoke, the younger man gestured vaguely toward the south. "At the time I signed for the place, it seemed the thing to do, you know. But now it has become rather lonely."

"Oh. Well, then it is a good thing you happened by—for the both of us, I mean."

"Yes."

As they crested the path, Sir Charles nearly stumbled, but the young man steadied him. "Terrible lapse on my part," he said, "but I should have introduced myself, sir—Charles Gordon. Don't suppose you might have heard of me, eh? I served in India with some distinction—knighted for it by the Queen, in fact," he declared proudly.

"Order of Bath, wasn't it?" The stranger smiled, then added, "Andrew Lovett at your service, sir. My acquaintances call me Drew—or worse."

"Andrew—a good Scottish name," the old man murmured approvingly. As he walked, he had to lean.

"Old war wound," he admitted. "But I cannot complain, can I? After all, I lived."

"No small accomplishment, I think," Andrew Lovett said softly.

Sarah stared miserably out into the rain, thinking the day fitted her despair. Yesterday, when she'd admitted to the physician that she no longer heard David's voice, he'd pronounced that she was in the first stage of being cured.

But the ache in her breast told her differently. Cured? No, her heart was but breaking again. And this time she could scarce bear the guilt.

If David did not come to her anymore, it was that he'd tired of her begging him for a child he could not give. For some proof that she was not mad. And now she had not even the feel of his arms around her, the soft feathery feel of his breath against her ear, nor the sound of his voice in her mind. No matter how tightly she closed her eyes, no matter how tightly she clasped her arms about her, she could not make him come to her.

He was gone. And if she had not truly been mad before, she was fast becoming so. Had it not been for Sir Charles, for his determined devotion to her, she would have flung herself from the cliffs into the sea. But over and over he insisted she must get well, that now she was all he had left of David.

"Oooh, mum!" Betty squealed excitedly behind her. "Ye got to come see! Sir Charles has brought a young man home, and right handsome he is, I can tell ye! Makes m'heart flutter, it does. And he's staying t' dinner, the master says."

Sarah did not turn around. "That's good," she said dully. "Now I shall not have to come down."

"Not come down!" the maid fairly gasped. "Oh, but—"

"Sir Charles shall have company enough."

"But ye're the mistress of the house! The master'll be expecting ye!"

"Tell him I am—tell him I have a stomach complaint." When Betty came to stand before her, Sarah shook her head wearily. "Tell him what you will. It doesn't matter."

"But ye ain't even seen him!"

"Betty—"

"Oh, I know ye ain't about to set yer cap, but—"

"There is none but David for me." Even now, Sarah could not bear to speak as though he were truly gone.

"Och, but ye're young yet," the maid protested. "When yer grief—"

Sarah stood angrily. "Don't say such a thing! Do you hear me? Don't ever say such a thing! I don't want anyone else!"

"Mistress, I didn't mean to overset ye," Betty said soothingly. "I just—"

Moving closer to the window, Sarah touched the cold panes as though she could dry the water streaks from the inside. And as abruptly as the anger had come, it left her. Her mouth twisted as though she would cry.

"You think me better, don't you?" she said, her voice nearly a whisper. "Neither you nor Dr. Merritt can accept that if it means I must lose David forever, I don't want to be cured. At least when I heard him, I could believe him here with me."

"Oh, mum!"

Sarah swung around. "I should rather be mad than lose him, you know."

There was a tapping, and as the door was not entirely shut, it opened inward. The old man leaned heavily on his cane. His eyes rested on his daughter-in-law for a moment, then he said quietly, "It would please me greatly if you would dine down tonight." To Betty, he added, "And I'd have you see she is properly gowned."

"Please, sir—" Sarah began.

"Got a guest," he said, interrupting her. "I think you'd like him, my dear."

"I—I cannot. I—"

But he'd already turned around, and was walking back through the door. "For my sake, Sarah—for my sake," he said. Pausing briefly, he added, "He reminds me of David—and I'd have him stay. Besides, it will do you good to have someone besides an old fool for company."

She felt uneasy, then an intense resentment of the unknown stranger took root in her mind. How dare he come into Sir Charles's life. How dare he remind an old man of his only son. And suddenly she was afraid.

In the end, to please the father-in-law to whom she owed so much, she came reluctantly down to dine. But, despite Betty's protests, she had conceded little to the presence of company. Her dark hair was worn plain, parted in the middle, and pulled back into two separate coils that covered her ears, and she'd utterly refused to wear the rouge that Betty had insisted would "make you look alive."

She walked down the narrow stairs, her whalebone hoops brushing the walls, making her grateful that she'd not chosen to wear silk. Instead, her gown was a simple dark gray cotton trimmed in black grosgrain. It did not become her, and she knew it, but she was in mourning. In any event, it did not make any difference, for she had not the least interest in attracting anyone.

As she entered the small receiving salon, a stranger stood apologetically. "You must forgive me," he said, "but it was not my intent to stay to dine. You find me not at all dressed for it."

"She does not mind at all—do you, Sarah?" Sir Charles spoke up. "No need to walk about in the rain, is there?" Rising with an effort, the old man made the introduction. "Sarah, may I present Andrew Lovett, a fellow border man?" Turning to his guest, he added, "Drew, my daughter-in-law, Sarah Gordon. Well, no need to stand on ceremony, eh? All on holiday, aren't we?"

"Mrs. Gordon," Andrew Lovett acknowledged gravely. "I'm so very sorry to intrude. And my sincerest condolences on the loss of your husband."

"Thank you, sir," she managed to murmur. Looking up, she met his eyes briefly, and she felt an intense pang. His eyes were so like David's. Recovering, she moved back a bit. "He was lost in the charge of the light brigade at Balaklava."

"So Colonel Gordon told me."

The old man sighed his relief. Perhaps the local quack was right, perhaps she was finally accepting that his son was gone forever.

She moved further away, as though she could distance herself from the warmth, the life, in those bright blue eyes. "Yes," she said, "he was very brave—so very brave."

"Forgive me. I should not have mentioned him. It was not my intent to give you more pain." Without warning, he stepped closer to take her hand. "You've had quite enough, haven't you?"

There was such sympathy in those eyes that she could not bear it. And yet the warmth of his hand was comforting. She pulled away self-consciously.

"I'm sorry—terribly presumptuous of me to touch you, Mrs. Gordon," he murmured.

"She's still on the mend, I'm afraid," Sir Charles insisted. "And I don't fault her for that—not at all, sir—not at all. Damned—*dashed* fortunate to have her, you know. All we got left is each other, and it cannot be very pleasant for her to have naught but an old man for company, can it?"

"And you are such an old curmudgeon," she said, grateful to turn the conversation away from Mr. Lovett. "If any is poor company, it is I."

"I cannot think that, Mrs. Gordon," Lovett responded gallantly.

"Well, unless I am mistaken, sir," Charles Gordon decided, "Mrs. Birks has dinner prepared. Country hours, you know."

"I am used to them." Standing back, Andrew waited for Sarah Gordon to pass, then he followed, ready to hold her chair.

"Not much," the old man admitted, "but if you've traveled with an army, it's a dashed sight better than that."

She noted Lovett's limp then, and an unexpected wave of sympathy washed over her. "You were wounded, sir?"

He nodded. "In the war."

"You were in the Crimea?"

"Yes."

"Were—were you at Balaklava, Mr. Lovett?"

The blue eyes sobered. "Yes—yes, I was."

With an effort, she brought herself to ask, "Did you know my husband, perhaps? Did you know Captain David Gordon?"

He looked down briefly, then raised his gaze to hers. "Yes. He was much admired."

"Dammit, but you did not tell me, man!" Sir Charles protested. "I'd hear of him."

"I was in the Dragoons, sir. But for the wisdom of a sane commander, I should have perished also." For a moment, he stared distantly, then he recovered. "As it was, I am here, and he is gone. Too many perished. Too many," he repeated softly. "I try not to think on it. All I wanted to do was live."

"We have spent dashed near an afternoon together, sirrah, and you did not tell me of this," the old man persisted.

This time, without thinking, Sarah put her hand on Andrew Lovett's arm, stilling his explanation. "I do not think I could bear to listen." Turning her attention to her father-in-law, she said, "No doubt the horror is still too great to speak on, sir."

"Aye. But my boy was dead nigh to a month ere I ever knew it," the old man said, his voice low. "I would I had been there to hold him at the last."

"No." The word was little more than a croak. "No."

"Beggin' yer pardon, sir, but the turtle soup's coolin'," Mrs. Birks announced. "And if ye don't sit down to eat it, I cannot vouch for the fish as yer havin' with it."

Sobered by the earlier conversation, dinner was a quiet affair, with each subdued by his own thoughts. It wasn't until the sponge cake and cream was served that the old man spoke up, his manner sudden and eager.

"Seems to me as you are a godsend, sirrah," he declared. "You've got Sarah down to dine," he went on, explaining himself, "and you've given me a chance for kindness to one as knew David, don't you see?" Before either of them could stop him, he arrived at his point. "You got no one either, you say, and the house is big enough for three. And Sarah's got me to play propriety—not that she needs it, of course," he added hastily. "Be the very thing to chase the blue devils away for the both of you."

"Well, I—"

"Don't know why, but I like you. Liked you from the first, in fact." Afraid the younger man was about to refuse, Sir Charles spoke more urgently. "Oh, I don't mean to throw her at your head, you understand. But we all need company to heal, don't we, Sarah?"

Embarrassed, she looked at her half-eaten cake. "Really, sir, if he does not want—"

But Andrew Lovett was looking at her bent head, an odd expression on his face. "No—no, I should like it very much," he said softly.

"Well, then it is settled. I'll send a man to fetch what you need from your cottage, and you can tell them you've changed your mind." Beaming now, Sir Charles rang the bell beside his glass. "Mrs. Birks, the Madeira, if you please!"

*   *   *

She lay awake, listening, wondering if Andrew Lovett was coming back this night, or if he meant to wait until morning. Unable to bear looking into those bright blue eyes, she'd retired early, but now could not sleep. Rising, she went to the window to look out into the darkness.

The rain had stopped, and there was no wind, only the steady pounding of the surf against the rocks. In the distance, someone's dog bayed at the moon, which rose somewhere behind the house.

Unwelcome, unwanted thoughts crept across her mind, bringing with them the image of Mr. Lovett. It was the eyes—it had to be those eyes. And now they haunted her, reminding her so much of David, making the longing so intense that she could not bear it.

And this night, like so many of late, she knew David would not come to her. She knew that even if she tried to recall every small detail, every nuance of his touch, he would not come. Dear God, if this was healing, if this was sanity, she'd rather be mad. As it was, she had nothing of him left to her.

"David, where are you?" she whispered into the darkness. "Has my memory faded so much that you cannot come back to me?" Backing away from the window, she turned again to her empty bed. "David, I need you so very much."

There was only silence and the howling of the distant dog. Finally, unable to bear the small room, she pulled on the plain woolen robe that David had said was better suited to an Amazon than to her, and she tied it over her tucked and pleated cotton gown. She would get milk and leftover cake in the kitchen, and she would not think of him for a few moments. And when she came back, she would sleep. If she had to take laudanum, she would sleep.

Once downstairs, she heard the banging of a side door, and she went to close it. The night air was cool, almost cold, but there was a fresh, clean smell to it, as though it had been washed by the earlier rain. Drawn by the sound of the surf, she slipped outside, and closing her arms over her chest, she walked toward it, until she stood on a small rock promontory.

The moon shone from behind her, reflecting far out across the water, while below the sea crashed again and again upon the rocks. There was such a wild, barren beauty to it.

"A long time ago, there were smugglers down there."

Her heart in her throat, she spun around. "What—?" It was Andrew Lovett. "You startled me, sir."

"Cannot sleep either, eh?"

She started to deny it, but turned instead back to the sea. "No," she said finally. "Sometimes it seems as though my room is too small."

"And your memories overwhelm you," he said, nodding.

"Yes." Moving away from him, she asked, "And you, sir? Do you regret nothing?"

"Too much to tell," he admitted. "I suppose most of all that I did not come back whole."

"I beg your pardon?"

"A manner of speaking. I regret the leg."

"At least you came back."

"Did I?" he asked, his voice soft.

"I don't understand—"

"Those of us who faced death, those of us who saw

so many die—I wonder that we did not leave too much of ourselves there."

"It must have been terrible for you."

"It was. But you loved your husband very much, I collect."

"Yes."

"So what great regret can you have, Mrs. Gordon?"

She ought not to be out here, and she ought not to be baring her soul to a stranger. But she could not help it. "I regret that he is gone from me—and that I have nothing left of him!" she blurted out. "If there had been children—a child even—"

"And you think you could have borne that better?" he asked curiously.

"Yes—no, of course not," she had to admit. "But at least I should have something of him! I should have something to love!"

"We all have memories, Mrs. Gordon."

"Memories!" she cried. "Memories fade, don't they? One day I shall scarce be able to remember his face! One day I—"

She felt his arms close around her, and she buried her face against the soft wool of his coat. He was solid, real, and yet she felt as though David held her once more. The memory of how he'd held her before they'd parted elicited raw, hard sobs that would not stop.

"Sarah . . . Sarah . . . please don't," he whispered against her hair.

"But I cannot bear it!" she choked out. "And do not tell me I will heal! I may forget what he looked like, but I shall never wish for another!"

He held her, letting her vent her anguish until she

had no more tears. "Sarah," he said, lifting her chin, "you've got to begin again."

"I cannot—dear God, but I cannot."

"You will never see David Gordon again." As cold as his words were, his voice was gentle. "His body lies in the ground at Groseby."

"But I have heard him! He—he talks to me!"

"An illusion."

"No! I have felt—" She stopped guiltily and looked away to finish lamely, "I have felt his presence."

"Still?"

"I don't know! He—he promised to come back to me!"

"He did not have the right to make that promise. Wars kill and maim, Sarah."

"Did you never make such a promise?" she cried out. "Was there no one you told you would come back?"

"Yes."

"And you came back!"

"Not without pain, Sarah—not without pain."

She drew in her breath and let it out slowly for calm. "No, I suppose not," she said finally. "I suppose it was wrong of me to ask it."

His hand slid down her arm to take her elbow. "Come on—you'll catch your death," he said more kindly.

It was not until they were nearly to the house that she heard him murmur so low that she wondered if her ears tricked her, "You are so lovely, Sarah—so young, so lovely." Suddenly, he stopped, and his eyes reflected the moonlight eerily. "If you had but one wish, Sarah Gordon," he said more loudly, "what would it be?"

"That David should have given me a child," she answered. But even as she said it, she knew it for nearly a lie. What she would have wanted more was to have David Gordon back. But somehow the knowledge that he lay in the church cemetery at Groseby made that wish seem even too macabre for words.

For the first time in six months, she came down to breakfast. Sir Charles looked up over his paper to smile encouragement at her.

"Feeling more the thing today?" he asked her.

"Yes."

"Sun's out," he observed. "Probably helps."

"I don't suppose Mr. Lovett is up yet," she ventured.

"Eaten and gone. Fellow's a damned artist, he says. Took an old sketchpad with him."

"Oh?"

"Terrible shame, it is."

She sat down and laid a napkin in her lap. "What?"

"Seen it before. They go to war, and when they come back, they cannot adjust for a time. Daresay the boy's just now coming round."

She reached for the teapot and poured herself a cup of the strong, dark liquid. "I thought you liked him."

"A great deal. Reminds me of David." Once again, he looked over his paper. "You can see it, can't you?"

"Yes. I think it is his eyes."

"He'll come about. Been thinking about asking him to go back to Groseby with us, you know."

"On one day's acquaintance?"

"Think me an old fool, don't you?" he countered. "In my own way, I guess I'm more like you than I'd care to admit. I'd do anything to keep a spark of David alive in my mind."

Sipping her tea, she tried not to think of all she'd told the stranger. When Mrs. Birks sat an egg cup on her plate, she began to eat silently.

"Said to tell you he was going to be sitting in my spot above the sea—took the chair," Sir Charles said conversationally. "Said it'd do you good to get out."

"In that respect, he is not like David at all," she retorted acidly. "David was never a meddler."

"You aren't going back to bed, are you?"

There was a certain disappointment in his tone. "No," she said grudgingly.

"Need something to do, you know."

"Perhaps I shall read."

"Lovett's right—ought to get out. Get a little color in those cheeks. Take a walk."

"Sir—"

"Don't have to go to the sea, do you? Take Betty and walk into the village."

"I might."

He eyed her again, then shook his head. "You are a good girl, Sarah, and you were a good wife to my boy, but damme if you are not contrary when you want to be."

"And sometimes you can be a bully," she reminded him. But as she said it, a corner of her mouth tried to smile. "Tell me," she asked him, "do you spend all your time talking about me to strangers?"

"No. Half of it I talk about my boy."

"Oh."

As he disappeared behind his paper once more, she rose. Without looking up, he inquired, "Going upstairs?"

"No. I am going for a walk."

"Best throw on a shawl. And if you are going into the village, I should like some of those sweet buns from Mrs. Baxter."

"I don't—"

"She makes good ones. Not that you would know it," he added slyly. "Time to get some flesh on those bones, Sarah."

"One walk does not a new life make," she muttered.

"Every day is a start. Every day. Besides, I'd like to see you get better. Getting deuced tired of that quack a-coming around."

In the end, she did not take Betty. But she did put on a fresh gown. Carrying a shopping basket over her arm, she started down the narrow path to the lane, but as she got to the fork, she looked up and saw Andrew Lovett. His back was to her, and he was hunched over, sketching something. She took the sea turn.

"Good morning."

"You are in better spirits," he murmured, moving the piece of charcoal over the paper.

She moved closer to peer over his shoulder, then gasped, "But that is Groseby!"

"Is it? There are many piles of stone on the borders, Sarah."

"I do not know how or why, sir, but you have drawn the house at Groseby," she declared, daring him to deny it. "And you have no right to call me Sarah."

"All right. You *were* in better spirits, Mrs. Gordon. Satisfied?"

"You've been to Groseby, haven't you?"

"I don't know. Would you care to sit down, Mrs. Gordon?" he inquired politely.

"Perhaps."

"If you do not mind it, I should like to sketch you."

"Me?"

"After all, you are a devilish fine-looking woman, Mrs. Gordon."

"You don't have to say Mrs. Gordon in every sentence."

"Well, if I cannot call you Sarah, there's not much else, is there? Would you prefer the word 'madam'?"

"No, of course not."

"Then I am afraid you will have to choose between Sarah or Mrs. Gordon, won't you?"

"On one day's acquaintance?"

"The choice is yours, Mrs. Gordon."

"Sarah," she decided, capitulating.

The sun was shining, the air pleasant enough. Adjusting her hooped skirt around her, she sank to sit upon the rock. Turning her attention to the sea, she noted a boat on the horizon.

"I hope it does not come in too close, for the light cannot be seen by day," she murmured.

"It won't."

"Tell me, Mr. Lovett—do you always presume to know everything?" she said tartly.

"Drew. And no, but I would assume there is a pilot, wouldn't you?"

"Yes, of course."

"Sit still, will you?"

"Mr. Lovett—"

"Drew. If you are Sarah, then I am Drew. It rather fits me, don't you think?"

"I wouldn't know. I scarce know you at all."

"More's the pity."

"And I have not the least intention of engaging in the mildest flirtation," she added dampeningly.

"A mild flirtation had not crossed my mind, Sarah. Hold still."

It seemed she sat there for the better part of an hour, watching the sea as he drew her. Finally, she could stand it no longer. Rising, she adjusted the wide skirts of her dark cotton dress, then dusted them with her hands.

"Let me see what you have done."

He held out his pad, and once again she was stunned. He'd drawn her as a young girl of sixteen, wearing a dress much like one she'd had. "But it has been years since I wore my hair like that. Indeed, but—well, not since I was married, anyway."

"You ought to." He looked up, his blue eyes studying her for a moment. "I can imagine you with it down, you know. I can see you running on the banks of the Tweed with it streaming down your back. I can see you without those hoops to encumber you. And your gown ought to be green."

"It was green. Who *are* you?" she asked hollowly.

"Andrew Lovett."

"I don't believe you."

"Do you want to touch me, Sarah? Do you want to see that I am a flesh and blood man?"

"No, of course not." Shaken, she looked down at herself as she'd been when David had first truly noted her. And she saw once again a green girl in a green dress. "This is a trick, isn't it? Well, you can take your sketchpad and go elsewhere, Andrew Lovett—I have no wish to know you!"

"Sarah—"

"You frighten me!"

He laid the pad aside and rose to face her.

"Sarah . . . Sarah . . . do you not know you have nothing to fear of me?" he asked softly, moving closer.

Before she knew he meant to do it, he reached to twine his fingers in her hair, loosening the pins that held it. While it fell, rippling down over her shoulders, he bent his head to hers. For a moment, she was mesmerized by the look in his eyes, then as his lips met hers, she slid her arms about his waist to hold him.

"Sarah!" Sir Charles called out, breaking the spell.

She jumped back guiltily, her face reddening, as the old man huffed down the path. And Andrew Lovett hastily closed his sketchbook. But if David's father had seen them, he gave no sign. Instead, he sank into the chair.

"Sun's too good to waste." He looked up at her. "Thought you were walking into the village, Sarah."

She picked up her basket. "I am, but the sound of the sea drew me. I could not resist seeing the sun on the water." Still nearly overcome by her response to Andrew Lovett, she licked her dry lips. "Uh—how many buns do you suppose Mrs. Birks wishes?"

"A baker's dozen at the least," the old man answered. "And tell the Baxter woman to be liberal with the icing."

"Yes, of course." She managed a self-conscious smile at Andrew Lovett. "And you, sir—have you a penchant for sweets also?"

"Most definitely. And currants would make them even better."

Her hands shook, for David had always preferred

currants. "I shall see if she has them," Sarah promised him.

"You'd best take Betty with you," the old man reminded her.

Despite the fact that Sir Charles had saved her from her own folly, she felt cheated. As she climbed the narrow path, she could not help wondering, even dreaming, of what might have happened had he not come. And for the first time since David's death, she felt alive, truly alive. And yet frightened.

Not wanting to betray the tumult of emotion within, she chose to walk the village path alone.

For a long time, she sat, torn by indecision. Already the moon was high in the sky, and somehow she knew he would be out there, waiting for her. Indeed, at supper, he'd said as much, telling Sir Charles that he always walked before he sought his bed, that it was to him a release from the tensions of the day. Sometimes, he'd said, he even took a blanket, that he could sit and listen to the roar of the sea. Then he always slept better after.

The sketch on the pad still haunted her. How could he have known? And those eyes of his—how very like David's they were. But he was a stranger come home from the same war that had taken the love of her life from her. No matter how or no matter what he knew of her, he himself had told her he was not David. David was dead. This man was Andrew Lovett, a fellow countryman, a soldier come home from the war.

He was from the borders also, and he'd served at Balaklava, he said. Could David have told him of her? Had it been mere coincidence that he'd come upon

Sir Charles? It was useless to ask herself these things. She had no answers.

Rising, she moved about her bedchamber restlessly, wanting to relive the morning's kiss, wanting to know again the feel of a man's body against hers, a man's arms about her. For the first time in six months, she wanted to live.

She could hear Mrs. Birks moving about, turning down the lanterns, checking the doors, and then the woman's steps creaked on the stairs, passing down the hall past Sarah's chamber. The same dog that had howled the night before bayed again at the moon. But this time, far in the distance, he was answered.

The room was too close, too confining. And the silence hung heavy in the air, leaving no sound within beyond her own breathing and the rhythmic beat of her heart. For a moment, she considered the bottle of laudanum on the table, then she reached for her robe, and her fingers fumbled to knot the ties at her waist.

As she let herself outside, the night air felt cold against the heat of her skin, but it did nothing to quell the almost feverish fire within her. She walked as fast as she dared, given the treachery of a rocky path at night.

He was there, his body silhouetted against the starlit sky. Her foot dislodged a rock, and at the sound, he turned to face her, and even in the night's darkness, his eyes glittered. For a moment, she was afraid again, then he smiled.

"I was afraid you would not come," he said, his voice so soft the surf nearly drowned it.

She pulled her robe more tightly, then closed her arms across her breasts defensively. "I—I could not stay away. God help me, but I could not stay away."

He nodded. "Nor could I." He moved closer, reaching again to twine his fingers in her flowing hair, bending his face so close to hers that his breath caressed her cheek.

She felt wooden, awkward, until his lips met hers with a tenderness nearly forgotten. Her own lips parted for his kiss, and suddenly it was as though nothing else mattered. Her pulses pounded, sending heated blood coursing through her veins. A small, dim voice echoed in her mind that she was being a fool, but she wanted desperately to pretend that it was David who held her. And for that alone she was willing to pay the price of passion.

Her arms held him, her hands clasped his shoulders as though he were life itself. His hands moved over her back, her hips, smoothing her robe, pressing her closer, urging her desire, and all the while his mouth tasted, leaving her breathless and wanting.

"Sarah . . . Sarah . . . ," he whispered, tearing his mouth from hers. "You do not have to do this for me." But even as he spoke, his hands found the ties at her waist, releasing them, freeing her robe.

For answer, she pulled his head back to hers, and she returned his kiss eagerly. And as she felt his hands slip beneath her robe, she whispered against his lips, "I do this for me, David—I do this for me."

For a moment, he seemed to hesitate, then he dropped to the blanket on the ground, pulling her down after him while he undid his clothes. And again his eyes glittered, this time with desire, as his hands moved over her, pushing up her cotton gown, eliciting her eager passion.

And, as the surf pounded against the rocks below, as the stars shone above them, she rocked and writhed, twisted and bucked shamelessly beneath him, seeking the completeness of physical union. It did not matter that she was giving herself to a stranger with utter abandon. Nothing mattered as long as she could pretend he was David.

When it was done, he pulled away wordlessly, rolling onto his side, where he gathered her against him. Drawing her woolen robe over both of them, he held her, and for a time there was no sound beyond the crashing surf and their mingled gasps for breath.

She lay there, her eyes closed, listening to the rapid beating of his heart, his labored breath. Despite the damp chill around them, he was so alive, so warm, so real that she felt her own heart would burst. It had been so long since she'd been held like this.

When she dared to open her eyes, to lift her head to look into his face, he was watching her, and the yearning she saw was real, unmistakable. And she sensed somehow that it was for more than what they'd done.

"David?" she whispered wonderingly.

He did not answer. Instead, his hand crept to smooth her hair where it tangled against her back.

She rubbed her cheek against his solid shoulder, murmuring, "I would you never left me. I would that it could always be like this."

He released her and rolled to sit, his shoulders hunched, his face profiled in the moonlight. When he spoke, his voice was strained.

"You'd best get back before you catch your death, Sarah. It is too cold out here for you," he told her.

"No." Untwisting her gown and robe, she crawled to face him on the blanket. "No," she repeated softly, reaching to put her arms around his neck. "Give me this night at least. I'd be held again." Her lips touched his unresponsive ones, and she whispered, "Please— love me again."

Groaning, he caught her to him, and it was as though the fire leapt between them, rekindling desire. He was pressing kisses on her lips, her face, her throat. And this time, instead of lifting the hem of her gown, his fingers were fumbling with the small buttons at her breasts, undoing the neck of the cotton nightdress.

As the placket opened and his hands slid inside, he lay back to watch the pleasure his touch gave her. "Oh, yes," she gasped, leaning to kneel over him. "Yes."

He loved her slowly, languorously, exploring her warm skin, prolonging every moment, and all the while she demanded more. Finally, unable to stand the wait, she slid over him to take what she would have.

It was nearly dawn before she made her way back to the house. Her robe and gown were damp and muddied, her hair was a wild, tangled mess, and her lips swollen from a night of stolen kisses, but she was too sated to care. For the first time since David had left for Crimea, she felt complete again.

At the crest of the hill, she stopped to look back down the path to where he still sat on his blanket. As she watched, he rose slowly and moved to stand, coat- less now, on the rock promontory that overlooked the sea. The cold, damp wind caught at his shirtsleeves, whipping them.

She shivered and pulled her robe closer, then hur- ried inside to her bed.

*   *   *

When she awoke, it was well past noon. But instead of going downstairs directly, she bathed leisurely, then sat before her mirror, studying her face.

She ought to feel shame, as though she were the greatest sinner on earth, but she could not. Instead, she stared dreamily at herself, pulling strands of her hair down about her face much as she'd worn it years ago, much as it was in Andrew Lovett's sketch of her.

"It ain't like ye to lie abed so late," Betty observed behind her. "If ye wasn't able to sleep, I'd have fixed yer laudanum for ye."

"I slept better than I have in months," Sarah murmured, reaching for her brush.

"And longer," the girl countered. "But it's good to see it, it is."

"Yes, it is," Sarah agreed absently.

"Ye going to wear it down?"

"I think so."

"Well, it does become ye. I remember the first time Master David brought ye home to dine, ye know. I was but a tweeny then, and no hope to be a ladies' maid," Betty went on. "But we was all a-watchin' and a-hopin' for ye. Ye made a right smart pair, ye and Master David."

"Thank you."

"Mrs. Crowe said ye was the prettiest female she'd laid her eyes on, ye know."

"Well, I—"

"Oh, but ye was—and ye still are." Moving behind her mistress, the girl took the brush and worked out a tangle. "There."

"Thank you."

"I laid out yer black dress for ye—the one as has the obsidian buttons at the neck," Betty continued conversationally. "More's the pity ye cannot have color. He always liked ye in the brighter ones, ye know."

"Green—he liked me in green."

"Aye—I remember. It don't seem but yesterday, does it? When he brought ye to Groseby, I mean?"

"Yes." Rising, Sarah stood for Betty to slip the lawn chemise over her head, then to lace the corset over it. "I shall forgo the hoops today, I think," she decided.

"Forgo th' hoops?" the maid echoed incredulously. "But why? The dress'll hang on ye!"

Sarah turned to the gown and sighed. She'd not been wearing anything but a horsehair petticoat beneath the green gown when he'd first seen her. And if she could not dispense with her mourning dress, she could at least leave off the hoop. She wanted to be as much as she could the way he remembered her.

Once Betty had buttoned her into her gown, Sarah stared again at her reflection. On impulse, she reached for her jewelry case, opened it, and drew out a strand of perfectly matched pearls—David's betrothal gift to her. Fastening them on over the black dress, she pushed back her dark hair from her forehead and started to go down.

"Ye like him, don't ye?" Betty said softly at her shoulder.

She stopped, prepared to deny it, then nodded. "Yes—yes, I do."

"Aye. Reminds us all of Master David, he does."

Downstairs, Sarah found Sir Charles sitting alone in the small front room, and he looked as forlorn as she'd ever seen him. Trying to hide her own happiness from him, she crossed the room quickly.

"Not feeling quite the thing today?" she inquired solicitously. "Does your old wound pain you?"

When he looked up, his faded eyes were reddened. "He's gone," he answered simply. Before it sank in whom he meant, he added, "Guess I cannot complain, can I? While he was here, he made me forget how much I miss my boy—aye, he was so like David, I wanted him to stay."

"What—?" But even as she asked, she felt the hollow ache beneath her breastbone. "Who's gone?" she asked cautiously. "Surely—"

He nodded. "Lovett."

The ache nearly took her breath away. "But—but *why?*"

"Wish I knew," he said wearily. "Wish I knew. I asked him to go to Groseby with us, but he said he had Lovett business to attend." He looked away and his shoulders slumped. "I liked the boy, Sarah. Oh, I knew he wasn't David, but there was something there to remind me—the eyes, I guess."

Andrew Lovett was gone. After loving her passionately, recklessly more than half the night, he'd left without a word to her. Hot, bitter tears stung her eyes, and she had to grasp the back of Sir Charles's chair for control.

"Even thought in time—" He hesitated, sighing again. "Know you wouldn't want to hear it, but I thought you could come to like him. Thought he might be the one as could bring you out of your grief, Sarah."

"Please don't," she whispered, her throat aching nearly too much for speech.

"You are still young, my dear." He reached up to pat her hand where it gripped his chair above his shoulder. "I thought he might be a second match for you."

She'd been such a fool. Such an utter, complete fool. She'd given herself to Andrew Lovett and he was gone. She felt sick all the way to her soul.

"Guess it don't matter," the old man decided finally. "We've still got each other, Sarah."

"When—? When did he leave?" she choked out.

"Just before noon."

"Did he—did he say where—?"

"I expect he means to collect his things, then return home to Scotland," he answered, his voice flat, toneless. "Penderly, I think he said. Aye, Penderly."

All the while he'd been loving her, how Andrew Lovett must have been laughing up his sleeve, how he must have thought her nothing but a lonely, silly woman. A hard knot formed in the pit of her stomach, and bile rose in her throat. Covering her mouth, she had to run from the room.

Before she reached the stairs, she began to retch violently, bringing up nothing. Steadying herself with the newel post, she managed to master the awful sickness. And a deep, bitter anger welled inside, spilling over in tears that burned her eyes and scalded her throat.

"No!" she shouted. "No! He shall not do this to me!" Running up the stairs, she went into her room, where she searched almost feverishly for her shawl. "He shall not—he shall not!"

"Is aught amiss?" Betty asked, alarmed.

"Everything!" Throwing the tasseled paisley shawl about her shoulders, Sarah raced back down, nearly oversetting Mrs. Birks. "I wish I were dead!"

The old man had come into the hall, but she didn't

even see him. His knuckles were white where he held on to his cane. "Sarah! Sarah!" But she was gone. With his other hand, he wiped wet eyes, then turned to a stunned Mrs. Birks. "Best send someone after her," he said heavily. "Her madness has returned."

She ran all the way to the village, where she went from house to house, asking, "Does anyone know where I can find Mr. Lovett? Have you seen him today?"

Most just shook their heads, but one woman looked her up and down as though she'd lost her mind. "He ain't here."

"You know him?"

"Aye, but—"

"I must find him! Do you understand? I *must* find him!" As though the woman might not know for certain, Sarah described him quickly. "He walks with a limp—a war wound—and—"

"He took a bad chill—went into a fever—"

"No—no, I am speaking of Andrew Lovett!" Sarah interrupted her. "A tall man with dark hair, blue eyes—young—I should not say above his twenties—"

"Aye." The woman nodded. "Let a seaside cottage from Mrs. Philpot down the lane. Her children was grown, so she'd moved in with her sister. Mr. Lovett took sick more'n a fortnight past. Real bad, they say."

"But he cannot be sick! I saw—"

"Nearly died. They took him to Plymouth, some twenty-five miles away. Ain't come back yet," the woman insisted. "Doubt he's traveling any. Be a stroke of luck if he's alive."

A ripple of apprehension ran through Sarah. "Plymouth?"

"Aye. But you can ask Mrs. Philpot—daresay she knows more about it all."

"Where?"

"Next to the last house ere you are out of the village."

Stammering her thanks, Sarah left, this time walking slowly to seek out Mrs. Philpot, Andrew Lovett's landlady.

The woman was outside, sweeping her sister's stoop. She looked up curiously when Sarah inquired, "Mrs. Philpot?"

"Aye." The small woman's face was guarded. "And ye?"

"Mrs. Gordon. Sarah Gordon."

"The old gent—?"

"My husband's father." Thinking to impress the Philpot woman, Sarah added, "Colonel Sir Charles Gordon."

"Aye—heard of 'im, I have."

"I would ask of Mr. Lovett—Mr. Andrew Lovett."

The woman's expression sobered, and she shook her head. "Bad business there—bad business. They was giving him up for dead, ye know."

"But where is he now?" Sarah demanded hurriedly. "I must find him."

"Can't say. He ain't been back since he was took to Plymouth out of his head."

"You have not seen him since?"

"No."

"Where—where is the cottage he let from you?"

Mrs. Philpot shaded her eyes against the sun, then pointed vaguely toward the sea. "Ye got to follow the lane, then turn at the big tree. Ye can't see it from the lane, but there's a path up. Now, it's a bit big for a man, but I allus supposed he meant to bring his family down, ye know."

"His family?" The awful thought that Andrew Lovett might have a wife came to Sarah suddenly. "He has a family?"

The woman nodded. "There's more to 'em than just him—he said there was Lovetts a-plenty at Penderly."

"Oh." But he did not have a wife. "Do you mind if I walk up there—to your cottage, I mean?"

"I don't—"

"I shall not disturb anything," Sarah promised.

"His things is still there, and—" For a moment, the Philpot woman regarded her doubtfully.

"Mr. Lovett is a friend of my father-in-law's. And he was in the military with my husband."

"Oh, aye. Well, there ain't much there, I expect. He didn't even keep a servant, as I know it. Was looking for one, he said."

"Thank you."

The path was rocky, treacherous almost, but at the top, the thatched-roof cottage sat overlooking the sea. The view was breathtaking, and it was easy to see how Andrew Lovett could have chosen the place. When she reached the house, Sarah had to rest from the climb. Sitting on the small rock stoop, she looked out at the white-capped waves, seeing a fishing boat bobbing among them, its small crew engaged in shark-angling.

Rising, she touched the door handle with trepidation, afraid of what she might find. He'd never claimed to be David, after all. It had been the sketch—and his eyes—that had led her on. Now, what if this cottage yielded proof that he could not be David come back to her? What if he still had proof of his love for his dead wife?

It was unlocked. The door creaked inward on rusty iron hinges, revealing a musty gathering room. Sunlight struggled to penetrate thick, distorted windows. But it was as he'd left it—neat, reasonably clean, with an open book still on a table, a small penknife, an inkpot, and several sheets of paper nearby.

Curious, she moved closer to read an unfinished letter, written in bold, masculine hand.

Dearest Jane,

It is the end, I suspect, and yet I do not mind it. Odd, isn't it? That I should survive the war, only to perish of some stupid complaint? The quack who passes for a doctor here would have me bled, but I shall not allow it. He says it is but some thing I have carried home from Crimea, but I must doubt that. Never in my life have I felt quite so ill, I swear it.

If it should prove to be my time, you must not mourn me, for I shall be going to join Arabella, I hope. And if Tom thinks to sell Penderly, I pray you will not hear of it. Just because he has not the feeling nor the passion for the place does not justify denying Jack and William the pleasure of it. You must remind him that there have been Lovetts at Penderly since Jamie Stuart succeeded Elizabeth on England's throne, and so there must be when we are all dust and ashes. If he does not want it, Tom should deed his heritage to Jack. You must tell him that.

*   *   *

Ruffle Will's hair for me, and tell him to keep his hands clean if he would be a gentleman. You and the boys are never far from my thoughts, and

The letter stopped there, leaving her to wonder about Jane and the others named in it. Was she his wife? His lover? Or merely a relation? She did not suppose she would ever know.

In the main bedchamber, the bed was unmade, and his clothes were hung on the back of a crude chair. She picked up the shirt and held it close before laying it aside. Opening the wardrobe, she stared at the braid-trimmed uniform hanging there, then she could stand it no longer. She let herself out again, taking care to latch the cottage door.

She'd found no answers, only greater questions. Walking back through the village, then up the more familiar path, she found that much of her earlier anger had left her. And yet she wished she could see Andrew Lovett one more time. She wished she could demand the answers that eluded her. But she could not.

At the division in the path, she hesitated, then she chose to go to the sea. Her feet crossed the very place where she'd lain in his arms full half the night. And the emptiness, the loneliness within her was nearly too great to bear.

Sir Charles sat in his usual place, his chair positioned so that he could watch the sea in the sunlight. He half turned in his seat when he heard the small rocks scatter beneath her feet.

"What did you find?" he asked soberly.

"Nothing. I walked."

"We shall survive, you know. Together, we shall survive."

She walked around him, then dropped to her knees at his feet and leaned her head against his leg. His hand touched her hair, stroking it. For a long time, she just sat there, saying nothing, then she sighed.

"I should like to go back to Groseby, if you do not mind it."

His hand stopped. "I should wish it above all else," he told her.

Life at Groseby was quiet and filled with days of reading and nights of a game or two of whist before retiring. And since their return, neither she nor Sir Charles ever spoke of Andrew Lovett.

Nor did she call out in the darkness anymore for David. It was as if that night above the sea in Cornwall had been the catharsis that had stopped the intense physical yearning. David was in the ground. At least once every week, she visited his grave to sit there in the peace of the place, accepting that which she could not change.

But as the weeks turned into a month, she had another problem to face. The sickness came, and with it the realization that she carried a child. Andrew Lovett's child. And soon Sir Charles would have to know it, something she did not think she could bear.

Had it only been she who had to bear the certain public condemnation of her sin, she could have stood it. But David's father was an old man, one who'd wed relatively late and had had but the one son. A man of exemplary morals tempered by a great well of humanity. He did not deserve a scandal. And yet there was now no way to avoid one.

"Ye've got the sickness again?" Betty asked one morning.

"Yes."

The girl eyed her sympathetically. "What are you going to do about it?"

Betty knew. Wearily, Sarah pushed her hair back from her damp forehead and straightened up.

"I don't know."

"Well, if it was me, I'd be telling the father, I would."

"I cannot." Sarah closed her eyes and swallowed. "I cannot. He would not care."

"Then ye've got to tell the old man—ye've got to tell Sir Charles."

"I cannot. He loves me. For what I was to David, he loves me."

"Fiddle," the girl declared dismissively. "He loves ye for yerself. He's got a big heart, he has."

"Not that big." Sinking into a chair, Sarah held her head and tried to quell the waves of nausea that continued to wash over her. "There is no telling what people will say."

"If it don't matter to him, what do you care?" Betty countered practically.

"It will matter to him. He'll think me—he'll think me no better than a common—" She stopped, unable to say it. "But I wanted a child, Betty—I wanted a child!"

"And by the looks of it, ye got one," the girl murmured. "If it was me, I'd tell the old gent."

"I cannot."

"Well, ye'd best be doing something. Now if ye was to wish it, ye could send me to tell him."

"Betty, it is not the sort of thing Sir Charles would speak to you of. No, the consequences are my own."

"Ye could say ye were mad," the girl suggested helpfully.

"I *was* mad. I wanted David's child desperately. I had nothing left of him—nothing."

"Tell him," Betty urged. "Ye got to."

By dinner, Sarah had nearly screwed her courage to the sticking point. Yet when she came down, her father-in-law was still in his study. She hesitated outside his door, then decided to put it to the touch, knowing full well he would be within his rights to turn her out of his house.

"Sir—"

He looked up, then smiled. "You are down early."

"I—uh, I—I have something to discuss with you."

"Later, my dear," he responded mildly. "Do you remember Mr. Lovett?"

It was as though her heart were in her throat. "Yes," she answered, her voice barely audible.

"Quite a family, the Lovetts. Didn't realize it at the time, but Penderly ain't too far from here."

It was as though her blood had turned to ice. "What—what made you think of Mr. Lovett?" she asked cautiously.

"Nothing. Just came to mind, I guess. Went out to visit David in the churchyard and remembered how much the Lovett boy reminded me of him."

"Oh." It was her opening. She could have told him that Andrew Lovett had reminded her so much of David that she'd lain with him. But the words would not come. "How far is Penderly?"

"Twenty-two miles, Taggett tells me."

"Mr. Taggett was here? Whatever for?"

"He's my solicitor," he reminded her. "Asked him to come."

"Oh. Yes, of course."

"Hard thing to do, but David's gone, Sarah. It's taken me nigh to a year, but I've commissioned a new will, my dear." When she said nothing, he cleared his throat. "You are like a daughter to me, Sarah—I could not value you more if you were my own flesh and blood."

She felt utterly sick.

"Got nobody else, and if I did, it wouldn't change my mind," he declared. "Groseby's going to be yours, Sarah. Know you'll take care of it. And one day you'll remarry—I know that also, but it doesn't make any difference."

"But I do not deserve it!" she burst out.

"I'd like to live to see it, in fact," he went on mildly. "I'd like to see your children here."

She could not tell him then. She could not. Clasping cold hands together, she walked to stare out into the old walled garden. "You honor me too much, sir," was all she could manage to say.

"I know he'd want me to do it," he said quietly. "I know he'd want you to stay here, Sarah. And I know he'd be pleased if you had your children here." His smile twisted as though he might cry, then he held out his hand. "Come—give an old man a kiss and tell him you are happy to accept Groseby."

She walked back to brush a kiss against the wispy hair that still shaded his forehead. "You may outlive me, you know," she warned him. And as much as she knew she could not tell him, she knew also she had to screw up her courage and do it.

"You are overquiet," he chided finally.

"You may wish you had not seen Mr. Taggett quite so soon, sir," she said, turning away that he could not see the shame in her eyes. "There will be a child."

He did not move, nor did he speak.

She closed her eyes, blinking back tears. "I'll go away," she whispered. "I—I'll not shame you. I'm terribly sorry," she added lamely.

The silence was more damning than words. Yet as much as she wanted to flee, she could not. Then he sighed heavily and spoke, his voice sober.

"I'd have you tell me how this came to be, Sarah."

"I—I wanted a child—David's child—so terribly." Her hands felt like ice at her side. She let out her breath, then rushed to explain. "I let myself believe Andrew Lovett was David."

When she dared to look at him, his shoulders were slumped forward, his eyes wet with tears. "As did I, Sarah—as did I. You did not wish to believe any more than I."

"I'll go," she said again.

"No," he answered. "We shall rear the child."

"The scandal—"

"Scandals are the broth of gossip for the young, Sarah." He reached to clasp her hand, holding it tightly. "I am old. The pain I feel is for you."

She was going to call on Andrew Lovett, no matter how much she did not want to do it. And if Jane should prove to be his wife, she would simply pay the call, say nothing of the child, and just return to Groseby.

Yet as she dressed carefully, scandalizing Betty by putting off her widow's weeds for the green dress she'd worn so long ago, she could not help feeling the excitement of seeing him again. She would look into those bright blue eyes once more.

"Lud, but ye look like a young girl," Betty gasped when Sarah was ready to leave. "Just like when Master David brought ye here to dine with Sir Charles the first time."

"I hope so—I sincerely hope so." Silently, Sarah prayed that she looked like Andrew Lovett's sketch of her. Taking one last, quick look into the mirror, she tossed her hair for effect, trying to see again a green girl in the green dress. As the dark hair rippled over her shoulders, she was as satisfied as she dared to be.

"Ye ain't going to wear no hat?" Betty asked, scandalized.

"No."

"They'll be a-thinking ye're too young to be out alone," the maid declared.

"To use your own word—fiddle."

The journey took longer than expected, owing to the roughness of the roads, and with each passing mile, Sarah's courage was tested. More than once she wanted to tap on the compartment ceiling, to shout for the driver to turn around. But she wanted Andrew Lovett to know. But by the time the coach had turned down the lane toward the stone house that a farmer had pointed out as Penderly, she was not at all certain she could bring herself to go inside.

What if Andrew Lovett considered her no more than the commonest trollop? What if what had passed between them on that Cornish cliff had been no more than an opportunity taken by him? What if—? No, she could not dwell on those things, not if she would keep her sanity.

She would merely see him, and if there was no Mrs. Lovett, if he gave her any encouragement at all, if he even so much as smiled at her . . . But even as she thought the words, she wondered how on earth she could bring herself to tell him that they would share a child.

The manor house was large, stone, and very old. Vines crept up the walls, reaching for the tiled roof. The place looked welcoming despite the turmoil in Sarah's heart.

As the carriage pulled up to the end of the drive, two boys ran around the corner, chasing one another, squealing. When they saw her, they stopped to stare. At almost the same moment, the front door opened, and a young woman stepped onto the painted wooden portico.

"You must not mind them!" she called out. "Jack! Will! Mind your manners!" She came down the steps, smiling, waiting for the coachman to hand Sarah down. She stopped suddenly, and this time it was she who stared. "You look just like one of Drew's drawings!"

There was no help for it. There was no place to run. With an effort, Sarah forced her own smile and held out her hand. "I am Sarah Gordon," she said, introducing herself.

"Sarah," the other woman acknowledged warmly. "I am Mrs. Lovett—Jane Lovett."

It was as though the ground swayed beneath her. "Actually," she lied, "Mr. Lovett and my father-in-law are acquainted. And," she added hastily, "Mr. Lovett knew my husband, Captain Gordon."

"Ah, yes. Drew has told us about you."

"Us?"

"You must forgive me. Jack—Will—both of you come here and make your bows to Mrs. Gordon."

There was a decided resemblance to Andrew Lovett in the boys. Now Sarah could only wish fervently that their father did not come home before she managed to flee.

"I collect you have come to see Drew on a matter of some import," Jane Lovett said, beckoning Sarah inside. "He is not at home, I am afraid." Seeing that her guest had paled, she was instantly concerned. "Naught's amiss, is it?"

"Actually, it is nothing," Sarah said, recovering. "I—uh—well, I was on my way to Edinburgh, and I thought perhaps I ought to pay a call. My father-in-law's health is declining, and—" Sarah floundered a bit, then lied baldly—"and I thought Mr. Lovett might wish to know of it." The thought crossed her mind that she ought to leave, but there was that within her that wanted to know more of the woman he'd wed.

"I'm terribly sorry." Leading the way into a spacious reception room, the other woman waited for Sarah to sit before she reached for the bell pull. "Would you care for tea perhaps? Or a glass of wine?"

"Tea, I think."

Jane Lovett took the chair opposite, sinking back. "There is so much to do here, and since Drew has come back from Cornwall, he's been so terribly preoccupied."

"Yes, he was taken ill there, wasn't he?" Sarah murmured politely.

"He nearly died. Some sort of fever they believe he brought back from the war. And after his other wound—the leg, I mean—well, we quite despaired of him."

The younger child peeped around the corner, then scampered away. Jane Lovett sighed. "Poor Will. When Drew is gone, he cannot stand it. He believes my—" Distracted by the entrance of an elderly woman carrying the tea tray, she did not finish. Instead, she waited until the tray was before her, then she began to pour. "Do you take much sugar, Mrs. Gordon?"

"Actually, I like it rather sweet."

"So do I." Jane passed the cup and saucer across to Sarah, then sat back. "Tell me—what ails your father-in-law? I should very much like to be able to tell Drew."

"Well, it is mostly his age, I suspect. And he has an old military complaint." Aware that that did not appear enough to justify a visit between near strangers, Sarah groped for something appropriate. "And the gout, of course. He suffers greatly."

The other woman nodded. "I know. Before Drew left for the Crimea, his father passed on. I expect that explains the difference."

"The difference?"

"Well, he used to be quite engaging, you know." Jane Lovett set her cup aside. "He had such charm, such verve for life, and now—well, there is so much to do, and—"

"The war seems to change everyone."

"Yes. Of course that must be it. And the responsibility. We are quite a large family, you see. And like all families, there is a bit of discord. Poor Tom had hoped to sell this house and the land that he might go to London, but as head of the family, Drew will not hear of it. He has the boys to think of, you know."

"I see."

"I'm sorry. How I run on."

"No." Although she'd scarce been there above a few minutes, Sarah started to rise. "Thank you so much, Mrs. Lovett. It has been an enjoyable break from my journey, but I really must go on."

"So soon?" The other woman was clearly disappointed. "I wish you could delay a few minutes longer. I expect Mrs. Johnson has some sweet buns left, and I am sure we don't need all of them."

"Uh—no." Sarah glanced out the window and saw the two children playing roughly on the lawn. Andrew Lovett's sons. "Really, but I cannot stay. As it is, it will be quite dark before I get h—before I reach Edinburgh," she amended hastily.

"Well, at least you must allow me to send some of them with you," Jane Lovett insisted. "It is such a long journey when one is alone."

"Yes—yes, it is." Sarah looked outside again, then said painfully, "They look very much like him, don't they?"

Jane followed her gaze, smiling. "Yes—it would be hard for him to deny them, I think."

Sarah had to escape. "Thank you, but I really am afraid to travel after dark. Perhaps I shall stop again and partake of the buns, but just now—"

"You could stay here," Jane said impulsively. "I am sure Drew would not mind it. And certainly any acquaintance of his is more than merely welcome."

"No—no, I could not." This time, she rose. "You must tell Mr. Lovett I am sorry I missed him."

"I wish he had told me where he was going." The other woman furrowed her brow as though she might think of it, then shook her head. "No, I am certain he did not mention it. Only that he should be back before the first of the month."

"I did not mean to pry."

"No, of course you did not!" Jane reassured her. "It is only that since he came back, he has been so terribly restless. Sometimes, I think neither his heart nor his mind is entirely with us."

"At least he came back," Sarah managed. Holding out her hand, she forced a smile. "Thank you so much for your hospitality, Mrs. Lovett."

"Oh, I shall quite hope to see you again, Mrs. Gordon," Jane murmured.

By the time the carriage pulled into the drive at Groseby, the sun was setting. It had been a day utterly wasted, Sarah reflected wearily. Utterly wasted. She had screwed her courage to the sticking point and gone to face Andrew Lovett, and he had not even been there.

Instead, she'd seen his wife and his sons. And if he *had* been at home, she knew she could not have told him. Not after that.

Dispirited, she pushed her hair back and stepped down. She'd had Sir Charles's blessing, encouragement even, for the journey, and it had come to naught. Settling her shoulders, she prepared to tell him that Andrew Lovett was married.

He was sitting in his study, waiting for her. "Thought you were never getting home," he murmured as she bent to brush a kiss against his cheek. Then, before she could tell him of her useless trip, he smiled up at her. "Sunset's magnificent, don't you think?"

"What? Oh, I had not noted it," she admitted. "He was not at Penderly, sir."

"Oh?"

"It is just as well, you know. He's wed to a lovely woman named Jane, and there are two sons who look much like him."

He patted her hand affectionately. "It doesn't matter, Sarah."

She wanted to cry at that. Didn't matter? It mattered too much to put into words. Defeated, she started for the door.

"A sunset's God's gift, Sarah—a reminder we have survived another day. You ought to look at it," he said mildly. "Beauty lifts the heart, after all."

"I don't—"

"Just look out the back terrace—you can see the reflection on the water."

"I did not know you to be such an ardent admirer of the Almighty's work," she chided him.

"Some things have to be seen to be appreciated, Sarah."

She left him and started up the stairs, then stopped. Abruptly, she turned and went to the back of the house. As she stepped out onto the landscaped terrace, the soft, cool evening breeze carried the scent of Sir Charles's flowers up to her.

The sky glowed in layers of bright pink and orange, casting a rosy glow over the deserted hillside, making the River Tweed seem like silver reflecting a fire. It was breathtakingly beautiful. God's work it was, she had to admit it. Then she noted the man walking beside the water, and her heart nearly stopped.

Catching her full skirts in both hands, she ran down

the hill to confront him. At the bottom, she pushed back tangled hair, hesitating almost shyly.

"Hello, Sarah," he said. His face was sober, his bright blue eyes intent on hers. "I could not stay away."

As much as she wanted to be held, as much as she wanted to be loved again, she backed away. "I have been to Penderly—I have seen Jane!"

"She is my sister-in-law."

"Your—your sister-in-law?" she repeated incredulously. "She is your sister-in-law?"

He nodded. "The late Alan Lovett's wife."

"And the boys—do you deny them?" she demanded, trying to force anger.

"No, I'd not deny them," he said quietly. "I cannot. Jane has cared for them since Arabella died several years ago."

"I wanted to believe you were David! Otherwise, I should never—" Blood rushed to her face, heating it.

"I know."

"I wanted to believe—I wanted to believe!" she cried.

"Sarah . . . Sarah . . ." His arms closed around her, holding her close against his chest. "I have always loved you, Sarah—from the first time I saw you, I have loved you." His hand combed the tangles from her hair. "And I have always loved this dress. I can still see you walking barefoot in the mud, your shoes dangling from your hands," he whispered against the crown of her hair.

"David?" she asked. "If you are not, I beg you will not lie to me. I could not bear it!"

For a moment, he stared unseeing past her shoulder, then he tried to explain, his words coming slowly.

"I cannot be David anymore, Sarah—I cannot. I tried to tell you that night, I swear it." As he spoke, he nuzzled her hair, much as David had done.

"Then why—?"

"I came back to give you the child," he answered simply. "I heard you weep for me, and I could not stand it. I took the only way, Sarah—I took the only way. I took Andrew Lovett's body when he died of a fever."

"Then you *are* David!" she all but shouted at him. "You are!"

"No. I am and will be Andrew Lovett. And now I have Penderly—and Will and Jack, too." His mouth twisted as he tried to reason with her. "I could not take his body and not accept all that comes with it." Very gently, he set her back from him, pausing to look into her eyes. "David Gordon cannot come back to you, no matter how much you may wish it." Then as he saw the tears well in her dark eyes, he smiled, adding, "But you can come with me, Sarah." His knuckle lifted her chin, bringing her face so close to his that his breath caressed her cheek. "I will always love you—always."

His lips brushed against hers, stifling the sob that welled within her, and as her lips parted for his kiss, he whispered, "Marry me again, Sarah. Marry me and make Andrew Lovett the happiest man on earth."

It wasn't until he'd kissed her thoroughly, completely, that she was able to look through the mist of her own tears and see again David Gordon's eyes. For answer, she twined her arms about Andrew's neck, pulling him closer.

"Yes," she answered against his lips. "Oh, yes."

*   *   *

The two men waited, the one pacing, the other sitting, his fingers tapping on his cane. It had been only hours, but it seemed more like an eternity. Finally, the thin, high-pitched wail of an infant pierced the air.

Despite his limp, the younger man bolted for the stairs, taking them with the help of the bannister two at a time, while the old man hobbled after. Betty came out of the bedchamber door, beaming at the both of them.

"Ye got a fine boy, Mr. Lovett!" she announced loudly. "A fine boy!"

"And Sarah?" he asked quickly.

"As fine as she can be, sir. But wait until ye see him!"

Sarah lay abed, her dark hair spilling over the pillow, her swaddled son in the crook of her arm. When she saw Drew, she trembled with unspoken emotion.

He dropped to his knees beside the bed and took her hand, unable to speak either. For a long time, he knelt there, utterly overwhelmed.

"My God!" Sir Charles gasped. "Would you look at this? The babe's redheaded!" He leaned closer, lifting a corner of the swaddling blanket with his finger. "He looks just like David!"

Midnight Lovers

by
Patricia Rice

THE LARGE, spindly wheels of the ancient barouche rattled beneath the cathedral of massive oaks and magnolias. Although the calendar said it was autumn, the humid air in this tunnel of foliage had yet to release the summer's miasma. Adrian Doncaster sat back against the cracked leather seat and gazed at these bizarre surroundings with a feeling of alienation. His sanity might require peace and solitude, but the oppressive air felt anything but peaceful.

Except for the sound of the horses and the squeaking of a wheel, the jungle was as silent as he could wish. To his northern eyes, this tangle of vine and cypress and Spanish moss spreading across acres of marshy field could be nothing else but jungle. Compared to the cultivated fields spreading clear to the horizon of his home, this lush greenery was as foreign as a herd of camels or a Venetian canal.

He had stepped into a different world the moment he had walked off the boat in New Orleans. The exotic faces and swirling colors had been enervating in his current state of mind. The slow voices of the people, the fierce frowns of warning that he had startled from those he questioned had made him understand more than ever that he was an outsider. He couldn't help but remember one old black man with a face like a dried crab apple shaking his wooly head in dismay when he heard Adrian's destination. The man had made a gesture against the evil eye and offered to sell him an amulet to save his soul. Adrian had been tempted to buy it, but not because of any foolish superstition. His soul had been lost long ago.

The land on either side of the sandy road began to clear as the carriage traveled on. The oaks took on a formal pattern as they approached the house. Through the shroud of gray moss dangling from the trees, Adrian caught a glimpse of the shadowed galleries of the mansion ahead.

He had seen houses of this size during the war, and he had always admired their sprawling elegance, even though his Yankee heritage scoffed at the waste of time and money involved in their upkeep. As the carriage drew closer, he could see that the ravages of time were taking their toll and the postwar economy had drained away the funds needed to correct the situation. Still, the mansion was imposing as the barouche drew parallel to the gracious steps leading up to the first gallery.

Emile himself appeared in the towering doorway as Adrian climbed down without the assistance of the black carriage driver.

"You are here at last! I feared the temptations of New Orleans had led you astray, or the alligators had eaten you. Welcome, my friend. Was your journey difficult?"

Adrian climbed the stairs and grasped Emile's hand with affection and gratitude. They had met as rebellious youngsters at the university, had corresponded through the years of war that had cut the country wide open. The easy friendship that had formed between them had not faded with the passing of time and conflict. Emile was a little older now, there were slight wrinkles from the sun beside his eyes, but his hair was still the natural dark of his ancestry, and though his shoulders were a little broader, he was still as trim as he had been as a student.

They were very much alike in stature. In school, they had once combined both their allowances to buy a particularly elegant frock coat that they took turns wearing to impress the ladies of their dreams. The years of war had made Emile a little leaner and Adrian a little broader, but the experience was more noticeable on their faces. Emile's easy smile was still there, but not as frequently and sometimes with signs of strain. In Adrian, the war had left a more arresting mark: a long, thin saber scar down his left cheek. Beside the physical scar, the other scars were less apparent to anyone who didn't know him, but the opaque gray eyes and drawn features were not the same as those before the war.

Emile took all this in at once, and clasped his arm around his friend's shoulder. "Come inside. You are weary."

"How could I be weary? I have done nothing but sit and watch the miles go by. I did not know idleness could be so tiring." Adrian picked up his valise and followed Emile into the spacious, high-ceilinged hall. He had never been inside the few plantation houses he had seen during the war, and he took a few minutes to admire the artistry of the architects.

The imposing circular stairs on either side of the hall would have done credit to an English manor house. But the floor-to-ceiling windows in every room as far as the eye could see added a light and airy touch that no manor house could proclaim. He liked the effect, and Adrian smiled for the first time that day.

"I see now why you are so proud of your home, my friend. It is truly magnificent."

"That is because we Southerners have a generosity and pride that you Yankees will never learn. It is reflected in our homes." Emile directed the carriage driver to carry Adrian's trunk to the upper level. His tone was that of scoffing, but the words rang true.

"Generosity and pride isn't going to keep these monstrosities up," Adrian pointed out, unnecessarily. Although the house was well tended, even he could see the moisture stains on the faded wallpaper and the threadbare state of the carpet.

Emile grimaced as he gazed around him, seeing his home the way a stranger must. "We will contrive. I have already done many things that would make my ancestors roll in their graves. I will take you about as soon as you are ready. But you have come here to rest. Let me show you to your room and you can be idle until the evening meal."

Adrian met the other man's sympathetic gaze with gravity. "I appreciate this, Emile. Don't let me give you any other impression. We fought on opposite sides during the war. This can't be easy for you."

Emile pounded his back and turned him toward the stairs. "We fought all the way through the university, also, but we have always been friends. Differences in opinion cannot change that. The matter is settled now. You have won this time. Next time, you may not be so lucky."

"I hope to heaven there is no next time." Adrian trailed his hand up the polished banister, trying to absorb the peace that he had come so far to find. Despite the airy spaciousness of the mansion, he still felt the oppressive gloom he had carried in with him from outside. He knew the gloom had nothing to do with his surroundings. He had brought it with him.

"I will second that notion," Emile replied with a favorite phrase of their youth. "We will fight it out the democratic way—through politics. The South will be a force to be reckoned with as soon as Congress gets its foot off our necks."

"Which is why its foot will remain there for some time longer," Adrian answered amiably. "But I don't think politics are a discussion we need to get into just yet. I mean to sit here and admire the scenery and sip some of that fine bourbon you tell me you keep on hand. And when I get tired of watching the birds in the trees, you can show me round. Maybe I can find something to do so I won't turn into a stump of wood."

Emile looked concerned as he watched his friend take in the imposing tester bed and the layers of mosquito netting that adorned it. "Your letters did not explain much. I hope sometime you will let me know enough to help."

Adrian strolled to the wide window overlooking the second-floor gallery. "My family thinks I need a rest. They have said I try to do too much at once."

"And?" Emile had never met Adrian's family, but he had heard all about them. They were a fiercely competitive brood who ran numerous industries as well as a shipping business and interests in the railroads. Adrian was one of the younger sons and always something of a misfit. He would rather sail a ship than own it. His family found his attitude a trifle disconcerting, so Emile knew there was more to the story than a matter of a needed rest.

Adrian turned and his smile was slightly warped by the line of the scar. "And I horsewhipped one of the company foremen for forcing higher productivity from some of his crew."

Emile lifted an inquiring brow.

Adrian's smile disappeared. "The crew was all under twelve years of age and had already worked ten hours that day."

"I see." And he did, all too well. "You are still opposed to slavery," he stated matter-of-factly.

Adrian's grin was more its normal self. "You catch on quickly."

"Well, the only slave you see around here is me, unless you listen to my sister or my aunt. They are quite certain that they are the ones in bondage now that the staff has been reduced to a minimum. But they will not complain so much now that you are here. I think it is the company that they miss the most. The war scattered everyone, and there are few left to visit, and those few are often too depressing to speak to. I hope your family did not think you would spend your time enjoying a jolly round of parties."

"I could have that at home were I so inclined. Coming here was my idea. As long as I was being banished, I thought it would be pleasant to go somewhere I could fish in solitude and growl when I feel like it."

"Then you have found the right place. I will send someone up to help you unpack and bring you a bottle of that bourbon I promised. The fishing can wait until tomorrow."

Adrian watched as Emile left. He had not told his friend the whole truth. He wasn't at all certain that he knew the truth himself. He just knew that he was dead inside, drained of all desire of any kind. He had thought it would be peaceful to be dead; he should have realized that peace was found only in heaven, and he was very correctly in hell.

But it was a hell of his own making, so he might as well learn to deal with it. He turned back to stare out the window.

Through the shade of the gallery he could see the long slope of lawn leading toward the fields. Closer to the house he could see the kitchen gardens, a grape arbor, and the various outbuildings for kitchen and laundry and bathhouse. He assumed the narrow tower he could barely see off to the corner of the house was the bachelor's quarters that Emile had said was deteriorating from lack of use. A maze of hedges led to a garden that still held a color or two, although he could not discern the flowers from here.

The setting was as idyllic as he could wish. But Adrian had a strange notion that peace wasn't what he sought.

He had spent four long years fighting. He had seen more conflict and bloodshed than he ever hoped to see again in a lifetime. He had lived in dread of the day he might come face-to-face with old friends in battle. He had never known hatred in his life and could not summon it for these people who were fighting for their way of life. But he had never been the victim of hatred before either, until his regiment had ridden through Richmond and he had felt it in the eyes of every woman and child he had passed. The experience had been unnerving, but it had only been one of many.

He knew he wasn't a coward. He had fought bravely. The scar on his face was a reminder of the man's life he had saved with his impetuous dash to rescue a fallen friend with neither sword nor gun at hand. But he had hated every minute of it, had felt the fire and fury warping his soul, and was glad when he had been wounded seriously enough to prevent him marching with Sherman on his mission of destruction. It had been a senseless battering of innocents and had disillusioned him for life on the glory of war and country.

Perhaps he had lost a piece of his soul for every soul that he had taken. Whatever was the matter, he couldn't summon the energy or desire to rise from bed in the morning or sleep when he was supposed to. And if he drove himself to perform as he ought, he indulged in irrational tempers that kept everyone around him on edge. So it was better for all concerned that he just remove himself entirely.

He wished Emile hadn't mentioned his sister and aunt. He would have to govern his temper and be polite and endure their company and their questions when he had no desire to ever see a woman again. He didn't hold anything against the gender in particular, other than that they were the ones who brought men into the world. He was beginning to think that the world would be much better off without people in it. He would never change human nature of course, but he could do his small part. No child of his would ever wake to the chaos and destruction that was war. He would grow old and gray before he would even consider bringing a child into this world.

Clenching his teeth, Adrian called for the maid to enter. It might be easier if he were a hermit.

Emile's Aunt Marguerite was tall with a back as rigid and straight as a fencepost. Garbed in yards of stiff black, she made a formal nod when introduced and took a place in a corner of the front parlor where she could keep a protective eye on her niece.

Camille LeFebvre was as close to a nonentity as one could be and still be alive, Adrian observed as he bowed over her hand without seeing more of her face than the creamy expanse of her brow as she kept her eyes averted. In contrast to her aunt's stiff black, she wore the soft silk of gray mourning. Her aunt was at least vivid in her contrast of black and white. Camille merely faded into the graying wallpaper.

Despite her demure appearance, Adrian sensed hostility in Camille's quick pull of her hand from his and her deliberate choice of seats as far from his as she could manage. He understood she had lost her fiancé and several close cousins during the war. He should have known better than to expect Emile's family to place loyalty to a friend over loyalty to a cause. It didn't matter. He would have as little to do with the women as it was possible to do.

Unfortunately, his upbringing required that he follow the customs of his host, and it quickly became apparent that Emile liked to gather his small family around him in the evenings. As the days slowly drifted by, Adrian learned that—as improbable as it seemed—Marguerite was the mother of a small infant and was not as formidable as she first appeared. Her husband had died shortly after the war, but from wounds he had acquired in battle. She treated Adrian politely if formally, but he sensed more than reserve behind the dark glitter of her eyes. She made him uneasy. Or perhaps it was the child that made him uneasy. He caught himself staring in fascination at tiny fingers and toes and the blissfully sleeping features when he stumbled across the infant resting in the sun with his nurse nearby. He hurried away as if chased by an adder.

He often saw the two women accompanied by a young mulatto maid with flashing dark eyes and a figure she made no effort to conceal. Although she met Adrian's gaze boldly, she made no attempt to speak to him as she hurried about her daily tasks. He would almost have preferred to speak with her than the other women in the household.

Camille LeFebvre was more ephemeral, less earthy than her maid, more elusive than her aunt. Adrian often caught glimpses of her gray skirts disappearing around corners when he approached, but the only time they shared a room was in the evenings when the family gathered over the last meal of the day and retired to the front parlor afterward.

The first few nights Camille said nothing or very little. She sat beside her lamp neatly hemming gowns or mending linens. Adrian finally decided her hair was a golden brown beneath the heavy net she kept it in, and he wondered that the weight of it did not give her neck an ache as she bent over her sewing. Her nimble fingers never ceased their in-and-out motion as she smoothed the fabric and wielded her needle. Sometimes he found himself staring at her fingers with the same fascination with which he had stared at the babe. And he wondered if he was losing the last part of his mind.

Over the passage of a week's time, Camille began to speak more frequently during these evenings. She never said anything overtly hostile, but her words were seldom addressed to Adrian. He could have been a ghost sitting in the corner for all she noticed.

Which was why it was so fascinating when she finally opened up and began to tell him ghost stories.

Perhaps her inbred courtesy required that she sit with him in the evening gloom as was the custom, even though Marguerite had retired to look after a fussy infant and Emile had been called out on some emergency in the workers' quarters. Adrian would have preferred to go out on the gallery and smoke his cheroot and listen to the night sounds in the distant bayou, but he didn't wish to give Camille any further reason for offense. Her soft words caught him by surprise.

"Do you believe in ghosts?"

Adrian glanced up from his contemplation of the book in his lap. "Ghosts?" He felt like an idiot parroting her words, but she had never before addressed him directly.

"The house is full of them. Has Emile not told you?"

Amused, Adrian closed his book. Her fingers were flying over the material as usual, but he could see the smooth oval of her face in the lamplight, and it was as serene as ever. Did she mean to frighten him away? "Emile has told me nothing of them. Have you seen ghosts?"

"They are there, whether you see them or not. I've seen the general. He looks quite bloodthirsty racing through the house with his sword drawn. He died defending his home from Indians."

"His home? This house? How old is the house?"

"The first cabin was built in the late 1700's, on this same spot. I think it burned, but my great-grandfather built a larger one, and my grandfather added to it, and so on. The spirits stay with the location, I suppose."

She actually looked at him, and Adrian could see that her eyes were of a particular shade of violet-blue that made his heart stand still. Eyes like that were capable of seeing ghosts. They were capable of seeing through walls. He was very much afraid that they saw through him.

To cover his embarrassment, he led her on. "What other spirits linger here besides the general?"

She shrugged and went back to her sewing. "The usual sort, I suppose. The one I've always wanted to see is the haunted lady. They say she sits in the rocker, humming to herself, knitting baby clothes. She is a gentle spirit, I understand, heavy with child, and happy about it."

For some reason, Adrian preferred the grouchy general to this gentle ghost. He opened his book again. "What tragedy brought about her demise, I wonder?"

"She died defending herself and her unborn child against a gang of thieves who caught her alone. They say there were four of them and she killed two before they cut her throat."

"She doesn't sound precisely gentle to me. That's an appallingly bloodthirsty tale. I suppose one sees the blood dripping from her throat when honored with her presence?"

Camille ignored his scorn. "I've not heard of such. I should think it would be a trifle difficult to hum with your throat cut. I think she has just reverted to a time when she was happiest."

"If only we all had that choice." Adrian gave up on the book and set it aside, rising to stare out the long, heavily draped windows.

"Perhaps we do, after we die. That would be my

concept of heaven." She neatly folded the gown she was working on and returned it to the basket.

Adrian sensed her leaving the room without a parting word. He used to have a way with women, but not anymore. It seemed just his presence was an offense to this one, not that he could blame her particularly. She had lost her lover and her family to the army in which he had fought. He would hate him, too, if he were her.

The desire to smoke his cheroot died, as all his desires did eventually. He didn't know what to do with himself. There had been no outbreak of uncontrollable temper during this past week, but there had been no occasion for one, either. The plantation was eminently peaceful, efficiently run, and without any need of his help. He could only stand back and admire the process and wonder what any of it had to do with him.

Perhaps what he needed to do was travel, see something of the world. But he'd had enough of traveling during the war. He'd seen more than he wanted to see. He could travel until the moon turned blue and he still wouldn't find a place for himself in the world that he saw. The problem was inside of him, and he didn't know how to root it out.

He started up the stairs to his room. The sound of humming from above gave him a moment's pause, then he grinned at his foolishness. Camille would laugh herself silly if she knew she had caused him to hesitate with her silly tales of ghosts.

Marguerite must be trying to put the child to sleep. Although she behaved with strict formality in his presence, Adrian sensed that she was a good mother. If he could ever break through her shell, he might discover an interesting person. He had seen her directing the servants in the kitchen, picking herbs in the garden, and walking the infant in the sun. She was a real woman, unlike her niece.

Adrian wondered if perhaps Camille might not be as lost in her mind as he was. Shutting his bedroom door and reaching for his cravat, he smiled again at her ghost stories. She probably hid in her room and read Gothic novels all day. He seldom saw her about except in the evenings. He would ask Emile about her sometime.

Removing his cravat and wandering out to the gallery with a glass of bourbon from the bottle that was mysteriously filled every day, he noticed the moon was in its rising phase. It would be full in a night or two. The light it shed was pale across the treetops, a perfect light for seeing ghosts. Adrian studied the landscape and decided no sensible ghost was going to risk alligators and mosquitoes out there tonight.

Undressing, he listened for the sounds the old house made at night, but there was nothing out of the ordinary. He was just bored, and Camille's stories had appealed to his imagination. He had seen many things in this world, but he had never seen a ghost. It might be amusing to encounter one.

He threw back the covers and lay on the cool sheets, but his mind wasn't ready to rest. Neither was his body, but that was nothing new. He wanted to sleep; he was eager for it. Sleep was the only thing that took him out of this gray world into oblivion. But he had difficulty even closing his eyes.

He must have finally dozed off because the next time his eyes opened, the room was full of moonlight, and the air was strangely disturbed. Adrian closed his eyes again and frowned, searching for the source of the disturbance.

The sound of distant drums caused the frown to deepen. He had picked up a small book on voodoo in New Orleans, but it had been a lot of superstitious nonsense. He found it reasonable that slaves might have sought their own religion and practiced it in secret. He understood the instinct to seek security with one's own kind against the hostility of the world. But black magic and ancient gods were just the usual mumbo jumbo used to control the ignorant. It had been going on since time immemorial.

But the distant thunder of the drums was real. The war had ended nearly six months before, but that didn't mean the people freed by the conflict would give up their strange religion. If anything, they would need it more in the chaos and anarchy that the end of the war had brought.

Adrian got up and wandered to the window. It might be interesting to watch a voodoo ceremony. His intellectual curiosity had not died with his soul.

Wandering the bayou in the moonlight was probably a foolhardy thing to do, but he had little to lose but his life, and that didn't seem worth much anymore. He wasn't a coward and would never consider suicide, but he was quite capable of seeking dangerous situations just to see if anything could ever stir his blood again.

He reached for his trousers and began to pull them on. For the first time in weeks, maybe months, he felt a surge of interest in something outside himself.

The pounding of the drums seemed to increase as Adrian slipped from the house into the moonlight. He scarcely needed the lantern he carried. The silver swath guided him, opening the path into the jungle, making it easy to see.

Once inside the heavy forest of cypress, the light was less, but Adrian could still discern the sandy path above the gurgling waters and the odd plip-plops of animals scurrying away. The drums were strangely muffled, but he didn't doubt that he had the right direction. He could almost feel the vibrations from here.

As he drew closer, he could hear the notes of other instruments, some kind of reed that keened and piped, making eerie notes that curdled the blood, and a constant thrumming of some stringed gourd that added an insistent rhythm. The music was devastatingly effective, and Adrian followed it eagerly.

He could see the clearing ahead, heard the chants accompanying the music as dark figures circled and danced in time to the beat. A fire lit the clearing in an unholy red, throwing off fumes that reached him even here in the woods. Smoke surrounded a high platform, obscuring all but the movement of the writhing figures upon it.

Drawn by the compelling oddity of the scene, Adrian stood on the edge of the clearing, forming a shadow among other shadows. The eroticism of the dance he watched and the sensual beat of the music affected even his frozen desires. The combination was wreaking havoc among the participants, who were obviously heavily imbibing in some substance from the pot over the fire.

Adrian's gaze drifted unwillingly to the shadows outlined in the smoke of the platform. There seemed to be only one figure left standing there now, a woman. She danced in graceful symmetry with the music, her hips swaying provocatively in a gesture that was as old as mankind.

Adrian couldn't tear his gaze away. He was scarcely aware of the other dancers, and hadn't located the musicians. His attention was entirely on the shapely curves revealed by whatever tight gown she wore. It appeared to be little more than a bolt of red cloth wrapped to cover her most intimate parts. He felt a fullness in his loins as a large man loomed behind her, reaching around to cover her breasts with his hands. He wanted to be that man.

When he realized what he was thinking, Adrian tried to tear himself away, but the figure on the platform danced lightly away from her partner and seemed to beckon Adrian, as if she sensed his lust. The urge within him was strong. He hadn't had a woman in well over a year, hadn't felt the need for one. Suddenly, he was bursting with needs and desires, but his mind had always been stronger than his body. He stepped backward, farther into the shadows.

He wanted to run up to that platform, take the woman into his arms, and join the dance that the others were performing. The fires of his banked passions were suddenly blazing. His body knew the ultimate outcome of that dance. Even now, couples were slipping away from the fire, falling into the grass, and the night sounds of the bayou joined with the moans and shouts of human pleasure. He wanted that pleasure for himself, but not with a woman he wouldn't know come morning.

Although his body was willing to surrender to temptation, his rebellious mind refused. He wasn't joining in some damned fertility rite to guarantee the productivity of the fields or whatever the hell this was all about. He wasn't going to play stud for some voluptuous goddess with the morals of a rabbit. His soul might be lost, but he still retained some remnant of his mind.

Adrian turned and fled the clearing.

The music continued behind him. He could hear the laughter and the chanting even when he was too far for it to be possible to hear them. His heart was pounding erratically, but he moved swiftly, putting as much distance between himself and temptation as he could. His body throbbed with the need to turn around and go back. Only his relentless will kept him going forward.

Ahead, a slight wisp of white caught his eye. It disappeared around the bend, slipping between the dark silhouettes of trees until he almost thought he had imagined it. Then it would appear again, racing frantically in the same direction as he.

Adrian increased his speed, but he never got close enough to determine the identity of the wraith. By the time he reached the broad front lawn of the mansion, he was panting breathlessly, and there was no sign of the ghostly figure anywhere.

He laughed aloud, wondering which of Camille's ghosts he had chased through the bayou. His laugh sounded strange even to him. It had been a long time since he had heard it.

Chuckling at the foolishness of the night's adventure, Adrian let himself into the house again. The house was dark and silent, the high open space of the hall giving a feeling of whispering presences. But Adrian was accustomed to his grandmother's tall town house and the strange noises of ancient history, and he climbed the stairs without trepidation. His blood was stirred and rushing through his veins, and he would welcome any encounter with the mansion's ghosts.

This time, when his head hit the pillow, he slept.

She buried her head under the pillow but the drums only pounded louder. Or perhaps it was her heartbeat. She was quite sure it was going to jump right out of her chest. It was beating in her ears and driving her crazy.

She flung off the pillow and covers and turned over restlessly. It shouldn't be so hot this time of year. She was burning up. Her skin was flushed with heat and oversensitiveness. Perhaps she was coming down with a fever.

Only a fever would explain the aches, but they weren't muscle aches or headaches. She couldn't explain what they were, even to herself. They were afflictions of parts she had scarcely known existed until these last months.

Her breasts burned and she feared to touch them, because the other parts began to burn and grow hollow with those strange aches. Remembering what she had seen tonight, she tossed and buried her head under the pillow again, but the images wouldn't go away. She could see herself joining in that restless dance, becoming half of one of the couples in the grass.

It was worse since *he* had come here. The drums had never affected her like this before. She had never been tempted to investigate their source. But now they were driving her mad just as he was driving her mad.

Whyever did Emile have to invite a damned Yankee? Didn't he have other rich friends from that school he'd gone to? But of course, all the ones from the South would be as cash poor as they were. It would have to be a Yankee.

By morning her head pounded as loudly as the drums had, and she felt as if she hadn't slept in a week. She probably hadn't slept for a week, if she thought about it. Maybe months. But she refused to hide in her room any longer. Perhaps if she got out of bed and worked long and hard all day, she wouldn't hear the drums tonight. Or she could bathe in the pool if the heat continued. That would stop the fever.

Marguerite took one look at her niece when she came down and called for their maid. She pointed wordlessly at Camille's dark-circled eyes and Esther gave a brisk nod and swept out to the kitchen to fetch a tisane.

Camille wasn't in the mood to drink the nasty black stuff Marguerite swore was the cure for all evils, but her aunt watched until she had drunk every last drop. It didn't solve a thing, but it made her aunt happy. Although Marguerite was only a few years older than Camille, she had developed an air of authority that successfully ran the household. No one dared disobey a direct order.

Refusing anything more than a muffin, Camille was about to escape to the safety of the garden when Marguerite called to someone behind her. She knew at once who it was, and she hastily judged the distance to the door, but it was too late. She was trapped.

"My goodness! You look as if you've had as rough a night as Camille. I do hope there isn't anything going on here that I should know about?"

Marguerite's voice was playfully girlish, and Camille

grimaced. Marguerite had always been a flirt, although there was every evidence that she had been faithful to her father's youngest brother. She even teased Emile upon occasion. It was just her way; there was no harm in it, but Camille didn't like hearing that tone used on the damned Yankee.

She missed the man's reply. Grudgingly, she turned and made a polite nod of greeting. Before she could escape, Marguerite grabbed her arm.

"Why don't you take this poor boy out in the garden? Esther can mix him up a tonic and bring it to him there. The fresh air will be good for both of you."

Camille wanted to ask why he got off with just a tonic while she had to swallow the tisane, but she was too furious to say anything. The man looked at her as if she were a curious bug on the wall. What was she supposed to do with him in the garden, bat her eyelashes and smirk politely while he told war stories?

He offered his arm but she ignored it, sweeping past him and out the door, not caring if her displeasure was evident. He didn't have to follow.

But he did. Marguerite was right. He did look as horrible as she felt this morning. He had a long, drawn ascetic face that was only emphasized by the scar, and it seemed more drawn and weary than usual. It was a pity some brave Confederate soldier hadn't slashed a little lower than his cheek. She was developing a fascination with throat-cutting.

His eyes were gray and empty, but occasionally she surprised a flicker of a smile on his lips. It could have had a very devastating effect had she allowed it, but she wouldn't. She despised him.

Adrian's presence only added to her misery. Removing shears from her garden basket, she lopped off a dead rose head and did her best to ignore him. He was impossible to completely ignore. She was very aware that he was large and extremely masculine and therefore, exceedingly dangerous. Images from last night flickered briefly through her mind before she ruthlessly cut them out. But she couldn't shut out the man beside her.

When Adrian woke that morning, it had taken him a fraction of a minute to remember where he was and why before visions of the prior night leapt vividly to mind. For the first time in months his body ached for physical release. Perhaps he should have taken the voodoo witch up on her offer, if offer it had been. Surely witches knew how to prevent conception. He had nothing against sex, just babies.

But one tended to bring the other eventually, and he had ruthlessly repressed his desires as he dressed. He'd heard if one did without long enough, they lost the need. He would reach that plateau someday.

Downstairs, his meeting with Marguerite left him oddly disturbed. Her silent gaze seemed to take in his neat cravat and tan frock coat with a strange avarice before she smiled into his eyes. Not until she left him with Camille did he realize she had never smiled at him before. Perhaps he had passed some test of which he wasn't aware.

Adrian took the glass of what appeared to be tomato juice from the solemn maid and followed Camille for lack of anything better to do. He had done nothing to harm the woman to cause her to despise him so, and he was bored as hell sitting around all day with no one to talk to. It was time they came to an understanding of some kind.

He watched as she gathered dried flower heads in her basket, preserving their seeds for the next year. Outside in the sunlight, her hair was more of a molten gold, and Adrian admired the picture she made as she swept through the narrow paths in her long skirt and billowing petticoat with the basket on her arm.

"I looked for your ghosts last night but didn't see any," he said conversationally, sipping at his juice.

Camille gave him a sharp look. "I suppose you heard nothing either?"

His heart quickened as he regarded her carefully. He would know more of the scene in the bayou, but he didn't think this unassuming woman would know of such licentiousness. He was cautious in his reply. "I heard drums. Do you have entire armies of ghosts on parade?"

She gave him what could only be termed a scowl. "You are facetious, sir. Why don't you go eat your breakfast and sulk in the library for a while?"

Was that what it looked like he'd been doing? Sulking? Insulted, Adrian reached over the hedge and took her basket. "Why don't I carry this for you? Then you can tell me about the drums in the bayou while you work."

"There is nothing to say. You would do well to stay away from them. And I can carry my own basket."

She didn't attempt to take the thing away, and Adrian stubbornly kept his claim. He needed some kind of challenge to stir his interest, and this prickly sister of Emile's suited him for the moment. "Humor me, if you would. Do they still practice voodoo around here?"

"I couldn't say. It's not something a lady would

know about." She snipped a dead head off a rosebush as if she wished it were his.

"That's not what I understand. In New Orleans, they were talking about any number of ladies who indulged in magic."

She attacked a wisteria vine at the end of the garden. "Magic will not bring back the dead or return faded beauty, no matter how much the silly fools would like to believe so. If they wish to waste their time and money on such nonsense, it is none of my business."

"You believe in ghosts and not in magic, then?"

"If magic or voodoo gods worked, we would never have lost the war and the people who died would live again. I do not see them rising from their graves."

Adrian leaned against the garden wall and watched as she pruned the vine with vicious slashes, never once looking in his direction. Still, he felt as if all that hostility were directed at him. "Did you ever consider that the ones with the real magic didn't want you to win the war?"

That made her stare. Recovering, she dumped her shears into the basket he was holding and started briskly down the garden path. Adrian admired the flash of stockinged ankles as she lifted her skirt to avoid a puddle, then followed obediently where she led.

"You can't possibly understand," she muttered as she washed her hands in the bowl outside the kitchen door.

Adrian set the basket down where she directed. He was beginning to wonder why he was even trying, but anything seemed better than whistling around the house all day or getting under Emile's feet again.

"What don't I understand? Do you think I didn't lose friends or relatives in that war? Do you think I enjoyed seeing the devastation such senseless violence left behind? Just what exactly do I stand accused of?"

"Of killing our future." Shaking her hands dry, Camille sailed into the kitchen. With only a nod to the black cook, she took down a large bowl of dough from its place near the warming oven and set it on the wooden table in the center of the kitchen. Briskly, she began scattering flour over the boards.

Adrian lingered awkwardly in the doorway, leaning against the frame. He felt out of place in this woman's world, but he didn't want to drop this argument without a protest. Still, her words struck poignantly at his heart, a little too close to home. The future did indeed seem dead.

"Do you think I am personally responsible for killing that future?" he asked conversationally. "Or is it really dead at all?"

Camille slammed the bread dough into the flour, sending up a shower of white dust. "It's dead all right. An entire generation died in that war. It is only by a miracle that Emile survived, if you can call this survival. He works from dawn to dusk with no time to court a wife, so there still may be no future."

He watched with interest as she folded the dough in half and pounded it with her fist. It looked like an exercise he could very much appreciate himself, if he didn't have the feeling that it was his face she was seeing as she smashed her fist into the dough. Her frustration was certainly coming through loud and clear. "The possibility is still there, though, not dead. And your aunt's child—he is part of the future. And you can always marry and have children."

He wasn't allowed to continue that thought. Camille threw him a furious look and picked the dough up and slammed it onto the table again. "It's that easy to you, isn't it? You can have your choice of women. There are women to spare everywhere. But the one man I'll ever know or love is gone, and there will be no other to take his place. What future is that for me?"

So that was what this was all about. Tentatively, Adrian stepped into the room and examined the dough remaining in the bowl. He dipped his hand in flour as he had seen her do and gingerly lifted it to the table. She stared at him coldly but made no effort to interfere.

He folded the dough in half and found it less sticky with a coating of flour. He folded it again until he had a dusty blob, then gave it a gentle punch. With fascination, he watched the dough explode upward around his fist. Perhaps he needed a punching bag to relieve some of the tension building inside him as much as she did.

"It rises into bread from this?" The lumpy ball seemed too heavy for the deliciously light bread they ate at meals.

"Come back in a few hours and you will see." She molded her kneaded dough into a loaf and dropped it into a bread pan. "It will be over the top of this pan."

"If a lump of flour and shortening can rise above its confines like that, why shouldn't you?" he asked innocently. He was actually enjoying this battle of wits.

"You're a fine one to talk." Camille grabbed the dough from his hands and briskly kneaded it. "You won the damned war and still you sulk. Now get out of here. I've got work to do."

Adrian rested his hands on the table and leaned over her so she had to step back and look at him. "For all I know, I was the one who killed your damned fiancé. I lost count of how many men I killed. Try living with that for a while."

He stalked out, leaving Camille to stare after him. She shook her head and blamed the kitchen's heat for the flush spreading across her cheeks. She no longer had the excessive warmth of the summer to blame for these irrational heated fantasies. Even when Phillipe was alive she had not thought of him in such a way as to make her cheeks burn and more intimate parts of her ache. She was certain these strange desires were immoral, but they seemed to be growing stronger. Now that the heat of summer was gone, her blood still boiled. Remembering last night, she punched the ball of dough again. If her mind was slipping, she didn't have time to sit about and rest it like the damned Yankee. She would ask Esther for a restorative.

Emile joined Adrian for lunch, but there was no sign of the women as they sat down to eat. Emile had explained that they frequently took afternoon naps and ate in their rooms, and Adrian had accepted that, but after last night he was beginning to wonder what else went on around here that he didn't know about.

"Did you know you have a voodoo cult practicing their arts in the bayou?" he asked as they lingered over their coffee and cigars after the meal.

Emile blew a smoke ring at the ceiling. "As long as they harm no one, I see no objection to it. I lose a goat or two upon occasion. I don't know why alligator blood wouldn't be just as magical; I'd certainly like to see a decline in their population. But as long as they don't go leaving shrunken heads on my doorstep, I leave them alone."

That was the cynical outlook Adrian would have taken just yesterday, but after what he had seen, he had to wonder if Emile knew just exactly what one of those ceremonies entailed. What if they took to sacrificing innocent virgins or something else equally scandalous? But he didn't dare broach his suspicions so broadly to his host. "How do you know they cause no harm? Do you know who belongs to the cult? Have you watched any of their ceremonies?"

Emile looked amused. "Did you stumble across one last night? I bet that got your blood stirring. Shall I take you into New Orleans to find a woman or do you want to go back and join them tonight? I believe the full moon has some significance to their meeting, and it should be almost full tonight. I don't have a taste for orgies myself, but my workers seem well satisfied the day after. Perhaps they put hexes on their enemies and think everything is in control after one of those get-togethers. Who's to say?"

"It's just your workers then? I couldn't tell for certain, but there seemed to be light-skinned people there, too."

Emile shrugged. "Quadroons, octaroons, and some of my neighbors for all I know or care. We are a very superstitious people. If you wake up to find a doll stuck with pins on your pillow, you can figure it came from one of the neighbors. Most of the blacks think Yankees were sent by God."

"Thanks. You're very reassuring."

Adrian let the topic drift from there, but he couldn't

keep his mind off what he had seen as the day grew longer. He had always prided himself on his control. Even when he thought he was losing his mind along with his temper, he had been able to control his desires, to suppress them until he rarely thought of a woman. But the image of that beckoning woman on the platform kept taunting him, and the sounds of lovemaking echoed through the recesses of his mind along with the pounding of the drums. If there were any ghosts around here, they were in his head.

He took the bottle of bourbon from his room and sat on the gallery contemplating the countryside as he steadily emptied the bottle's contents. When he didn't appear for the evening meal, Emile had a tray sent up. Esther smiled invitingly at him when she delivered the tray, but though he found her attractive, he wasn't tempted to take up the invitation. It was damned odd considering his present state of semi-arousal. Perhaps he just wasn't drunk enough.

Adrian nibbled at a piece of chicken as he gazed out over the landscape. Beside the plate of food on the tray he recognized Esther's tomato "tonic." He wasn't certain it helped, but he tried some as he continued staring through the early evening gloom. He didn't know what he was watching for, but he'd know it when he saw it.

From one of the open windows off the gallery came the crooning of a woman's voice over a babe's fussy noises. Adrian squirmed uncomfortably in his chair, not wanting to think about women and children. Perhaps he ought to persuade his family to build a westward line for the railroad. He could scout the land, buy the properties, and be useful while working off this cloud that blotted his thinking.

He had done what he had to do in war. Thousands of others had done the same and they managed to live with it. Why couldn't he shake off the memories of all those bloody corpses?

He took another swig from the juice. If it had just been the bodies of men killed in battle, perhaps he could have handled it better. But he could still remember vividly the woman with her pale skirts flung over her head, and the dried blood staining her stiffened legs, the victim of deserters, no doubt, but a victim just the same. And there had been both women and children on that train they had wrecked—not armed soldiers, but women and children. Their screams still echoed through his mind at night.

Camille could very well be right. There was no future. It would be criminal to bring children into a world that could treat them like that. It was better for all concerned that there were no men left in the South. If only the same could be said for the North.

As he blew smoke at a distant star, Adrian wondered if he really believed that, or if he was hiding behind cynicism. He was too drunk to really care. The singing in the other room had stopped, and he was grateful. The sound had begun to stir his blood, and he preferred to feel nothing.

He watched the moon begin to rise over the horizon, casting the heavy thickets of the bayou into shadow. There was something almost obscene about the lushness of the vegetation around here, or was that just the unconscious meanderings of his mind?

The drums began to pound again, and he straightened to alertness, or whatever manner of alertness he could summon after drinking away the afternoon. He could see the beginning of the path from here. He would watch and find out who roamed the grounds when the drums pounded.

The bourbon had gone to his head. He could feel it throbbing in time to the drums. Restlessly, Adrian rose and leaned against the railing, confident he was no more than a shadow against the night and could not be seen. Images of that erotic dance still swam in his head, but that wasn't the reason he waited here. He only wanted to know who from this house attended that ceremony.

A flicker of something caught his eye in the darkness not yet reached by the moon's faint light. He couldn't focus on it, and he stepped down the gallery steps to better see. Something was moving against the heavy bushes near the pathway. Would the black servants use this path from the front lawn?

He thought not. Fighting to keep himself erect, Adrian stumbled down the stairs and out into the moonlight before entering the tunnel of live oaks and moss. He would reach the path from the shadows, he thought cleverly. The only problem with that notion was that he couldn't see the path from here, or know who traversed it.

Cursing at this obstacle, he hurried down the sandy drive to the point where he guessed he was nearest the shrubbery from which the path led. An owl called overhead, and he started. Recovering himself, he waited in the shadows to see if anyone was coming.

The flicker of movement was gone. Disappointed, he hurried across the short expanse of grass to the path that would ultimately lead him into the bayou. He wished he'd brought a gun. The idea of meeting a gator in these swamps at night didn't appeal.

But the drums ought to keep any sensible animal

out of sight. The noise vibrated the ground he walked on. The compelling rhythm urged him forward even when he was reluctant to continue. He had no desire to join in any drunken orgy. He simply wanted to know who that woman was.

He didn't have a lantern, and he cursed the darkness. The moon's light didn't reach beneath this curtain of moss and trees and hanging vines. He hoped he could stay to the firm ground of the path, because he had a feeling that the ground to either side was a marshy pool that could suck him in. He could hear the croak of a frog and the cry of some wild bird beneath the constant thrum of the drums.

And then there was another noise. Adrian came to a halt, swaying slightly as the drums and the whiskey pounded through his brain. The emptiness that had plagued him since he had come home from the war seemed to expand and to encompass his surroundings. The whole world might as well be empty, except for that deliberate sound of splashing.

He didn't think it was an animal. The noise was too regular. Clenching his teeth in concentration, he walked silently until the sound seemed to be closer.

The night air ought to be cool, but he felt sweat forming on his brow. The airless humidity pressed around him even as the drums pounded in his brain. He was drunk, not crazy, he reassured himself as he heard the splashing a little closer now.

And then he saw her, and he had to grab a low-lying limb for support as he stared.

She rose from a small pool of water like a naked nymph, hair streaming in shadowy cascades down a back as slender and supple as a willow wand. Adrian gulped and held the branch tighter as she turned slightly and he could see the upward tilt of rounded breasts and the reckless curve of narrow waist and full hips. He hadn't a prayer in hell of resisting that much temptation.

Perhaps she was one of the mansion's ghosts. There wasn't enough light to see more than shadow and form. He stepped closer, waiting to see if the silent figure would disappear into thin air. He must be drunker than he'd ever been in his life to be chasing ghosts, but he wasn't about to turn around now.

The oppressive heat made his coat uncomfortable, and he pulled it off. The motion didn't disturb the water nymph, who didn't seem aware of his presence. With drunken clarity he realized he felt much better without the coat, and he would feel even better if he were as naked as she was and bathing in the pool. Swimming naked in the moonlight sounded like the best idea he'd ever had in his life. He would have liked it much better if the moon would just shine on her.

He discovered billows of skirts and petticoats beneath a tree and added his own clothing to the collection. Had he been in his right senses, he would have been warned by these prosaic garments, but drums and liquor were beating through his veins and a water nymph beckoned. He would take a living breathing nymph over a ghost any day.

The rhythm of the drums was a part of him as he waded into the pool. The water was warmer than he had expected, and the alcohol fumes provided a pleasant haze as he spotted his prey. Adrian was certain she had seen him by now. She stood now with arms crossed over her breasts, but she wasn't running.

Surely lust with a water nymph didn't count in the

way of things. Adrian held out his hand in a beckoning gesture. His loins ached and throbbed even with the water lapping over them. He swelled when she tentatively put her hand in his.

She was shy, but he was drunkenly persuasive. She came into his arms and he kissed her hair and cheek, while she wonderingly caressed the streams of water wetting the hair of his chest. His nipples grew hard and she discovered them, touching them with curiosity. He bent his head and took her mouth with his, and found she was very, very real.

The emptiness that had brought him out here exploded at the impact of her lips against his. She was all heat and light, slender against his larger frame, but just the touch of her tongue shattered every defensive device he had ever erected. Adrian clutched her close and devoured her mouth hungrily.

It wasn't enough. Her breasts left wet imprints on his soul. They burned right through his chest until he had to lift her to taste them. Her gasp of surprise and gurgling murmurs of pleasure urged him to greater glory. He found the small triangle between her legs and caressed her there, and she gave a wild cry that almost made the jungle drums disappear.

There wasn't any escaping what was going to happen. They were already inside each other, tearing at each other's skins to get closer, twining and clutching with a fierce heat that denied relief. Adrian couldn't remember later how he got her there, but soon they were sprawled across the layers of clothing, and she was beneath him, all hot crevasses and moisture.

Their joining was swift and sure and a relief in itself, although she cried out at the first insistent pressure. She was tight and he felt enormous. He tried to make it easy for her, but neither of them could wait. The blood boiling through their veins insisted that the time was now, and they responded without any further reservation, seeking those high planes only two souls joined can reach.

A night bird cried in the distance, and the moon slipped behind a cloud. Adrian closed his eyes, his soul sated, his body relieved. As he slipped into slumber, the nymph in his arms gently caressed his chest and explored with curiosity the place where they were still joined. He felt her hands on him and he smiled—and slept.

When he woke, he was back in his room. He stared in puzzlement at the yards of netting above his head. There was a slight pounding in his head, but not as much as would be expected after drinking a bottle of bourbon. He remembered drinking the bourbon. He wasn't certain of anything else.

Reluctantly, he moved a leg, and then an arm. They still functioned, and they were unclothed. Perhaps one of the servants had found him in a drunken stupor and put him to bed. Or perhaps he had wandered naked through the bayou and into the house after having the most erotic dream of his life.

He glanced quizzically down the length of his body to see if any evidence of his lust remained, but there were no particularly obvious signs to give evidence that it had been any more than a dream. That he had spent himself, he was certain. He hadn't felt this relaxed in years. But whether the floor of the bayou or his bed had received his seed, he couldn't say for certain.

Sunshine poured through the open draperies on the other side of the netting, making a pathway across the floor. It was past time that he rose, but he was half afraid to see the state of his clothing. Convincing himself that it had just been a drunken dream, Adrian pulled himself to the edge of the bed and stared at the jumbled mass of clothes on the floor.

Even from here he could see the wrinkles and the mud stains. Holding his head in his hand, he forced himself to rise and inspect the ruins more closely. The sunshine danced along the white gleam of his shirt, and he picked it up first.

The dried red stain across the ruffles sent him reeling into a chair.

"Come, ride with me this afternoon and I will show you how we get sugar from the cane." Emile patted his lips with his napkin as he pushed away from the table.

His head ached and any other time Adrian would have refused the offer, but he felt hemmed in by women today.

Marguerite had laid her soft hands against his forehead earlier, declared he looked feverish, and ordered a tonic. The cloud of her perfume had lingered for hours afterward.

Esther had brought the ordered drink, smiled provocatively, and stroked his scarred cheek. She didn't leave until he drank the provided medication.

Camille had drifted in and out of his vision, seldom speaking, always on some errand or another, but the air seemed to vibrate with her presence whenever she was around. Flowers sprouted on the hall table. Draperies were thrown back to fill his head with sun. And the sultry scent of gardenias crept up on him long after she was gone.

Suddenly, all he could think of was women. After months of emptiness, he was bubbling over with lurid desires. He didn't know whether to run screaming from his own lust or bury himself in the first willing woman to cross his path.

Since the most available women were respectable ladies, Adrian opted to accept Emile's offer to go riding.

By the time they returned late that afternoon, he was almost beginning to feel like a normal human being again. Before going upstairs to wash, Adrian took Emile's hand and shook it.

"You have been good for me, my friend. I hope someday I can return the favor."

Emile grinned. "Now that I have you down here, we will discuss ways and means. I have only been waiting until you are more yourself again to tell you my grandiose plans."

Camille entered the room and hesitated in the doorway when she saw the two men. Emile gestured in her direction. "If you could only persuade my little cabbage to like Yankees, you could bring your family down here. I would show them what can be done once the railroads are all open again and shipping returns to normal."

Violet eyes widened, then shuttered closed again. "Dinner is waiting," she murmured, before hurrying away.

Emile shook his head. "She has changed greatly. I worry about her. She used to be filled with the joy of life. The house echoed with her laughter. Now . . ." He shrugged. "Now, she behaves much as you do, with her smile turned upside down."

Not only upside down but tensed with hatred and

. . . frustration? Adrian considered the idea, and found it very logical. Camille had been deprived of the possibility of having her own home, her own children. And what else was there for a woman? She was more right than he had understood before. He had opportunities to make changes. She had nothing.

Not comfortable with that thought, Adrian excused himself and went upstairs. He had more to think about than whether Camille LeFebvre would ever have a life of her own. If he was not greatly mistaken, he had bedded a virgin last night. Somehow, he was going to have to find her.

He wasn't at all certain what he was going to do with her when he found her. Intellectually, he knew he had done wrong and that he must pay the price despite the fact that he had sworn never to marry or have children. Emotionally and physically, he didn't give a devil about what was proper. He wanted a repeat of the experience while he was sober enough to appreciate it.

The two needs warred within him, but for the first time in years, he felt truly alive again. He didn't give a damn about right or wrong. He just wanted to know that he would keep feeling this way. Riding out with Emile had been the right thing to do. He needed to get out more, learn more about the plantation, discover the best means of matching the plantation's resources with his own. And he needed to find the water nymph and thank her for bringing him to life again.

She was real. She had to be real and not some figment of his dreams. That hadn't been his own blood on his shirt. Why had she let him do it? Or had he forced her? It was too hazy to remember clearly, but he seemed to remember only willing eagerness. But then, he had heard men who thought a woman begged for it even when they were saying no, just because that was what they wanted to believe. Is that what he had done?

Nameless horror filled him at that notion. She had given him something more than life itself. He would have to make certain he had not harmed her irreparably. He would have to go back tonight and find her.

That thought both cheered and frightened him. He went down to dinner grave with apprehension. Marguerite's ebullient laughter greeted him, and Adrian tried not to stare at her in astonishment. She had always seemed so restrained, but tonight she was glittering.

She grabbed his hand and led him to the table. "My poor little one, you look dreadfully tired. Are you not sleeping well? See my niece? She is much the same. I tell her she must drink her auntie's tisanes, but she doesn't listen. She would rather wait for ghosts. Now you, what is your problem? Will you tell me, or shall I read your tea leaves and tell you?"

Appalled and fascinated, Adrian let himself be led to the place next to Camille's. Marguerite beamed approvingly and patted him on the shoulder. Even though she wore the stark black of mourning, she glittered with diamonds at her throat and ears, and her black hair had been arranged in soft dangling curls that danced provocatively when she moved. Tonight, she gave every sign of being a willing woman as she watched him through bright eyes and with a smile of hunger on ruby lips.

Now that his hungers were thoroughly aroused again, she offered an opportunity that he could easily ignore. She was a widow who would know way of these things. There would be no child of their coupling, only pleasure. She seemed to be offering it to him on a silver platter, just like the scallops she handed to him now.

Emile laughed and gently scolded this aunt, who was nearly his own age. It was obvious they had grown up together and treated each other with the familiarity of playmates. Camille, some years younger, sat silently moving food around her plate.

She had none of the other woman's vivaciousness, but Adrian found himself excruciatingly sensitive to the younger woman's presence. It was as if she vibrated with unspoken emotions. He had never thought such a thing about anyone in his life, and he didn't know what caused him to think it now. He just knew she was there, at his side, seething with words that never came out.

"The bread is delicious, Miss LeFebvre," he murmured for her ears alone, biting suggestively into a slice.

She glanced at him, flushed, and looked away. "Cook made it today."

"It was even better yesterday." Adrian smiled as she finally gave him a flashing look of anger. He was alive again, and he wanted her to notice it. He was tired of being ignored.

"You are welcome to try your hand at it any time," she informed him stonily.

"Lately, I have not felt the need to punch anything. I find that very curious."

She jerked nervously and didn't look at him. "I'm certain you do. Perhaps you would prefer shooting?"

That put him back where he belonged. Beneath all those soft golden tresses and wide violet-blue eyes, she had a sharp tongue and wielded it well. He didn't need to be reminded of what he meant to her. She would see him as little better than a murdering cut-throat, and rightly so.

"I have no more wish to surrender than you do. Can we not call a truce?" he whispered beneath the laughing flow of conversation across the table.

"I have never attacked you," Camille answered stiffly. "Now if you will excuse me, I have chores to do."

Her abrupt departure caused eyebrows to raise, and Emile sent his friend a questioning look. "Have you two had words?"

Marguerite patted Adrian's hand. "It is a woman's problem, I think. I will fix her something to make her feel better. You two gentlemen continue your meal."

Emile regarded Adrian thoughtfully. "The man to whom she was betrothed was killed while on leave. He was on his way home for their wedding. There is no certainty that he was killed by Yankees. It was late in the war, and there were deserters everywhere."

"Perhaps I should leave if I make her uncomfortable." Adrian played with his tableware. He found himself strangely reluctant to make this offer.

"She must learn to live in the real world. She was always an imaginative tyke, seeing ghosts in the night and hearing songs on the wind. It is good to see that she has come back to us enough to fight with you. Only a few weeks ago she would have looked right through you."

She had done that when he first arrived. Adrian wasn't at all certain that being a victim of her sharp tongue was any more pleasant, but speaking as one who had been there, he was glad she was returning from that deep sleep. He wasn't at all certain that he might not slip back into that living death himself. Perhaps they could spend their spare time antagonizing each other just to be certain they were alive.

But tonight he had other plans. Impatiently, he waited through the after-dinner routine in the parlor. Marguerite attempted a few tunes on the harpsichord, but the instrument was out of tune and she wasn't very talented. Camille embroidered lacy stitches on an infant nightgown while Emile read aloud to them from a book by Scott. Marguerite declared the hero a dashing bore, and Camille labeled the golden-haired heroine a ninny. The party broke up much earlier than was usual.

Sorry that some unseen frustration was eating at the friendly family scene he had first encountered here, Adrian didn't linger long to debate the cause of it. He took the steps two at a time and let himself out onto the gallery to watch the path again. This time, he would be sober enough to follow quickly.

He had spent the day wondering and looking for the real woman who had answered his dreams so willingly, but he couldn't settle on any one. He could rule out Marguerite as too experienced and Camille as too unlikely. He had seen very little of the nymph in the deep shadows of the bayou, but he had felt that she was more white than black, which ruled out Esther. That still left a wide range of females to choose from. It could even be one of the neighbors he had yet to meet. Emile had hinted that they might indulge in the voodoo rites occasionally. But why was she bathing in the pool and not with the others?

It made no sense at all. The only thing that made sense was that he'd had a drunken dream, but that didn't explain the stain on his shirt or the state of his clothes. Besides, he wanted to believe that she was real. He even had wild ideas that she needed saving from some pending disaster and that he could help her in some way. He wanted to feel a hero for a change.

But he had acted a cad. Impatiently, Adrian leaned against a post and waited for that flicker of motion again. He wanted a cheroot, but he was afraid the embers would be seen in the darkness and she would be frightened away.

The moon came up and the drums began again on schedule. This time, he didn't respond to their arousing beat. He didn't need the drums to stir his blood. The memory of his water nymph had already done a fine job of making his loins ache.

At last, he saw the movement of shadow across darkness, a glimpse of silver in the moonlight, and he was halfway down the stairs before he lost her. But she had disappeared at the path, and he followed without hesitation.

This time, he was close enough to catch occasional glimpses of her as she raced ahead of him. He could see little more than a piece of red caught in an unexpected patch of moonlight or a blur of white against the silhouettes of trees, but it was enough to keep him going. Neither of the women in the house ever wore red. His heart pounded with trepidation when they sped past the pool he had hoped was her destination.

Suddenly, he sensed that she was gone. The drums pounded from a distance to his right, but where he stood there was only the sleepy call of some bird and the hollow plunk of an animal diving into shallow water. He felt oddly out of place, and he swung around to determine if he could find his way out again.

This wasn't the same path he had followed earlier. He could take his chances and go forward and hope he found her, or turn back and wait for another night. He didn't want to wait.

Cautiously, Adrian followed what looked to be a trace of a path. The sound of the drums was at such a distance that he couldn't discern if he had gone past them or in a different direction. He was very much afraid that this particular ghost had led him astray to lose him in the swamps, but he didn't intend to indulge her. Two days ago it might have suited him to lose himself on a mad adventure. Tonight, he meant to change all that.

He almost missed the crumbling cottage set back off the path and covered in vines and moss. Had it been the clear light of day, he might have called it a shack and avoided it, but in the darkness he could only see that it was the perfect hiding place. Whoever he had been following must have run in here and hoped he would pass by.

That wasn't the way he wanted to look at it. He had hoped she would be running to him, not from him, but perhaps she had just been frightened at being followed. There were too many unexplained mysteries for him to ignore this opportunity. Somehow, he would have to show her he wouldn't harm her, but last night might not have been as reassuring for her as it had been for him.

Trusting that snakes slept somewhere under the ground at night, Adrian approached the gaping door to the cottage. He called softly to warn her, hoping not to frighten her further. He didn't expect a reply, but he wished he'd brought a lantern. He hadn't survived the war by walking into places where he couldn't see.

He pushed back the rotting door and a rustle of tiny feet on the floor told him all he needed to know. She wasn't here.

He leaned back against the door frame and tilted his head to search for the moon through the layers of foliage above. How could he have lost her? She had been right in front of him. He could swear to it. Or perhaps she was just a phantom who could disappear at will.

He rubbed his hand over the old scar and tried to decide what to do next, but all he could do was feel the immense disappointment building up inside of him. What had he thought he would accomplish by coming here tonight? Proving that dreams come true? He really was losing his mind if that was what he had thought.

Lost in self-flagellation, he almost didn't hear her. Her step was hesitant as she approached. A twig snapped, and he jumped to attention, and she froze where she was.

"I was afraid I'd frightened you away forever," he murmured. He didn't know how she had come up behind him like that, but he wasn't going to ask minor questions when the major ones went unspoken. He knew it was her, just from the silhouette against the darkness. He could see her silken hair streaming down her back, knew every curve and angle of that slender body as she took another step forward.

"I was afraid I owed you an apology. I was the worse for drink last night. If I forced you . . ."

She was in front of him now, and the musky night

air seemed suddenly sweeter, more pure. He couldn't even remember consciously opening his arms to her, but she was in them at once, cuddled close against his chest, their hearts beating in rhythm with the distant drums.

"Tell me who you are," he whispered against her hair, drinking in the heavenly fragrance of gardenias. "I want to take care of you."

He could feel her shaking her head against his chest. Her fingers dug fiercely into his waist and she lifted her head for his kiss. It didn't make sense, but he did, and once their lips met, he couldn't let go.

She was like a drug shooting through his veins. Her hands flew around his neck, and he was carrying her inside, seeking the bed he knew would be there. He didn't know how he knew, he just knew the magic of the night wouldn't disappoint him.

There wasn't any point in talking. He knew she wouldn't reply. All the words they needed to hear were said with the pounding of the drums and the brush of fingers against skin as they removed each other's clothes.

She was dressed in simple cotton without the hoops and petticoats of fashion, but they would have been worse than useless in this place. Adrian skimmed his fingers along her legs, sliding away her garters and stockings, bringing a low cry to her throat. She wasn't resisting was the phrase his heart pounded over and over again. She wasn't resisting. She wanted this. She wanted him. For whatever reason, she had chosen to give herself to him.

Adrian was well aware that what he was doing was quite mad, but he had become so accustomed to irrationality that it didn't matter anymore. He had found himself in the magic of the moonlight, in the arms of a water sprite, and he wasn't going to deny what had happened, what was happening. He meant to revel in it, to take what he was given without questioning, just for this one beautiful moment, just so he knew what it meant to live again.

She stretched out beneath him, all sinuous, slender woman with perfumed skin and seeking lips and arms that held him as if her life depended on it. He hadn't known what it was like to have a woman all his own, one he didn't need to buy, one who gave herself for his sake alone. It was a heady feeling, and his senses spun with it. He couldn't get enough of her.

She moaned as he suckled at her breasts, and he wanted to pour wine there and drink from the hollow between. Just that thought made him drink deeper, until she was writhing wildly beneath him, tearing at his hair, and raking her fingers down his back. She was as wild for this as he was. She filled him with the storm of her passions, healed every crack and hole in his soul until there was no escape for the emotions exploding through him. He had never wanted to feel again, but now he could not stop himself.

He cupped her buttocks in his hands and lifted her, and she gave a wild cry that echoed the call of the night birds outside as he entered her swiftly and sharply. She arched her back and brought herself up tight against him, taking all of him until he thought he could go no further. And then she moved away and came back again and he was in even deeper.

Moonlight trickled through the cabin roof, splintering against ivory skin, glimmering against gold, and mixing with the night fog rising from the damp floor. He couldn't see her, she was no more than a wraith in his hands, but she was real. She was flesh and blood and a woman's body that opened and granted him everything his heart desired.

He felt her break beneath his urgent strokes, felt her quake and cry out and drive against him until he couldn't stop, couldn't hold back, couldn't do what he ought to do. In one mighty spasm, he poured himself into her, and she wept against his shoulder.

He kissed her tears and caressed her back and pulled her closer until she was touching him and kissing him back and his hands grew bolder. It had been so long since he had felt like this that there was no means of practicing restraint, no desire to do so. She could do whatever she wanted with him and he would oblige, just so he could feel the smooth sheath of her over him again and give in to the life-giving burdens of pleasure.

Afterward, he had no recollection of how often they came together or who did what to whom. He remembered only the silky feeling of her beneath him, the glimmer of moonlight against shadowed skin, and a soft hand that stroked his scarred cheek. He thought he felt her shiver against him at that touch, but she didn't stop what she was doing. She rose even higher against him, until they were both pushing hungrily for release. When it came, she clutched him close, dug her fingers into his back, and wouldn't let go.

They must have slept after that. He must have slept like one deprived of sleep for eternity. That was all he could think later when he woke to find her gone. How could she have eluded his hold and dressed and disappeared without his knowing of it? He had held her tightly, not wanting her to go, but she had managed it anyway. And now he had it to do all over again.

But Adrian knew a little more than he had, and he savored those pieces carefully as the room filled with fog and ghost beams rippled through the dying moonlight. The musky scent of gardenias swirled around him, but when he rose and dressed, he discovered a bush just outside the door giving off a heady fragrance.

Perhaps he was moon-crazed. Maybe she didn't exist except in his mind. The pieces that he possessed didn't match the puzzle that he knew, but he had to make them fit somehow. If he wasn't mad, he soon would be if he didn't find this sprite who held him captive.

He could excuse what had happened as lust, but he knew it was more than that. He had been empty, and now he was full. He had been dead, and she had returned him to life. She had created hope where there had been none. He didn't know why or how she had done it, but he couldn't let her go. Had he wanted surcease from lust, he could have gone to that midnight orgy with the voodoo witch. It wasn't lust he sought, then, it was hope.

Hope carried him through the black bayou to the clear expanse of lawn, dark now that the moon had disappeared. Hope carried him up the stairs to his room. Hope almost had him knocking on bedroom doors, but he wanted to keep it to himself for just a little longer.

Only—he discovered a minute later—someone else shared the news with him. As Adrian entered his unlit chamber, he could hear the squeaking of the wooden rocker near the veranda window. Shutting the door quietly, he stared at the darkened corner where the rocker moved back and forth, back and forth, until he was nearly paralyzed with fear.

For in that rocker sat the ghostly shape of a woman ripe with child, calmly wielding her knitting needles as she made a blanket for a cradle.

She looked up at him, smiled warmly, and disappeared.

Chills went up and down his spine. He grasped the bedpost and stared as if staring would produce the illusion again. And he felt a wildly plummeting surge of pleasure in his midsection as his mind leapt from what he had just done in the bayou to the consequences of that act reflected in the rounding body of his ghostly visitor. He was losing his mind of a certainty, but this was a much better way to lose it. He wanted the dawn to arrive immediately so he didn't have to go to his lonely bed.

A shadow passed through her room, caressed her forehead, and disappeared into the night. Camille lay as one stunned, unnoticing.

She wasn't certain what she had done or why. The first time had been an accident—it had happened so fast. She had been trying to find relief and a phantom had appeared out of the night to give it to her. She shouldn't have drunk Esther's restorative. There must have been bourbon in it to make her behave so wantonly.

But it had been sheer bliss, and tonight, she had set out deliberately to find that same solace. It hadn't been the drums or the restorative. She had watched and waited and seen him enter the shrubbery, and she had followed.

And even when she had known who he was, she had allowed him to do those things to her. She had encouraged him. She could still feel the power of his body inside hers, his hands claiming her. She ought to be devastated with shame and horror.

Instead, she was lying here stunned, feeling the drums pounding through her veins, wondering how she could see him again tonight. She had this mindless, urgent need to be with him, to merge with him, to take his seed and bear his child.

Her eyes flew open at that thought, and her hand touched her bare abdomen. She could have a child.

How odd. How very odd. She closed her eyes and slept.

Adrian stood nervously on the gallery and glanced in the direction of Camille's windows. Was she still in there? If he slipped into her room, would he find a red robe beside her bed?

It seemed utterly unlikely. She was too fair to wear red. Marguerite or Esther was much more likely to wear bright colors.

But what had that to do with anything? He couldn't even be certain the person he had followed was the person who had come to him. He couldn't be certain of anything other than that he had spent the night in the arms of a woman who had made him come alive again, and he wanted her for his own.

And he wanted that woman to be Camille. Not Marguerite, not Esther, not some stranger, but Camille, who hated him.

Whoever she was, she knew him now. The scar on his face was scarcely unnoticeable, and she had felt it. Would he see the recognition in her eyes when he found her? Or would she continue to play the elusive nymph and keep him away?

Perhaps she was married. His shoulders slumped as he leaned against the post. That would explain why she met him only in the dark, but it wouldn't explain the stain on his shirt. Married women weren't virgins.

And even though he had been drunk, he could remember how tight she had been, how she had cried out when he first entered her. She had been an innocent. He might doubt many things, including his own senses, but he wouldn't doubt that.

By process of elimination, that left Camille. Except that she hated him. He glanced impatiently at her window, waiting for her to rise and show some sign that she was alive. He wouldn't abuse Emile's hospitality, but he dearly wanted to walk in on his sister right now. Perhaps if he saw her with her hair down and in dishabille, he could be certain of his suspicions.

But when he saw her next, it was in the garden, and she had the molten gold of her hair caught up in thick loops inside a net. Her gown was the usual gray, this one with black braiding down the fitted bodice and around the hem. His gaze rested on the full curve of her breasts, and he felt her stiffen beneath his stare. He was certain she was the right size, but the damned corset and petticoats hid everything.

Her eyes were dark and wary when he met them. He was almost certain that it was she, but the notion seemed so farfetched that he was reluctant to voice it. She was all that was stiff and proper and ladylike. It could be that he just very much wanted this woman to be the woman who could make him live again. She didn't necessarily return the favor.

"I suppose if I tell you that you are more beautiful

than the morning, you will be compelled to slap my face," he offered casually.

Her eyes were that of a wounded doe, and Adrian thought he saw a flicker of fear in them, but she didn't run, and she didn't turn her sharp tongue against him.

"I might be compelled to doubt your eyesight, but I'd thank you for the sentiment." Camille tried to walk briskly between the rows of lilies and away from him, but just that action reminded her vividly of what she had done the night before. There was a soreness there that told her how forcefully she had been loved. She still couldn't believe it. If it weren't for the physical evidence, she would think she had dreamed it. Could one dream oneself sore?

He followed her, and she was aware of his presence in any number of subtle ways. His shaving soap had a spicy scent to it that she found altogether too pleasing. His shadow fell over hers, reminding her of his greater size. And just the vibrations of his body seemed to touch her even when he did not. And she wanted him to touch her.

When the row widened, he took her basket and placed her hand over his arm. She looked at it as if she had never seen her hand on a man's arm before. Then she looked up at him.

She had this horrifying feeling that he knew. There were questions in the depth of his eyes that she couldn't answer. She wasn't ready for this. She couldn't possibly admit what she had done. Or might have done. It still seemed too unreal to believe.

"Do you have any idea what your maid puts into those tonics she keeps giving me?"

The question was so far from what Camille was thinking that her eyes widened in surprise, and then she almost smiled. He was having doubts, too. Perhaps they had both been dreaming.

"Whatever it is can't be any worse than the tisanes my aunt makes me drink. I should be astonishingly healthy by now. Should we trade brews do you think?"

He watched her thoughtfully for a minute before answering. "I think we should not drink them at all."

Remembering her thought earlier that Esther must have put bourbon in her drink, Camille stared at him in astonishment. As she realized what he was hinting at, she felt a flush creep into her cheeks. Surely he couldn't know? It had been dark. The only way she knew him was by the scar on his cheek. She floundered, not knowing what to say, not daring to admit what he wanted to know.

Her reaction raised Adrian's hopes. Sorry to have flustered her, he continued conversationally, "I saw one of your ghosts last night."

She looked relieved. "And you think your tonic is making you see things?"

"I had thought of that, actually. I don't usually see ghosts when I'm drunk."

He looked very handsome when he was serious. Now that she was forced to see him as a man, she could admit that. He was still a Yankee, but he wasn't personally responsible for destroying her life. If she could just look at him as a man, perhaps she could more easily accept what she had done. Only she couldn't believe she had done it with any man at all.

"Which ghost did you see? Did the general try to chase you away?" she answered lightly, trying not to show how disturbed she was.

"No, the lady came to see me. She was rocking

in the chair, just as you said. And she seemed quite content."

Camille gasped and her hand instinctively went to cover her abdomen. Stepping back from him, she lowered herself to a stone bench and stared blindly at the hedge in front of her. Not the lady. He was just saying that. It couldn't be true.

"Are you ill? Shall I fetch your aunt?" Concerned, Adrian took her hand. She felt cold, and he felt the same chill seep into his bones. He wanted her to be warm and happy. That was absurd, but the longing was strong to see her laughing. He wanted to see her turn dancing eyes up to him. He wanted to be able to take her in his arms.

"No. No. I am fine. It's just . . . Well, the lady is supposed to come only when a child is conceived in the family. That doesn't seem very likely right now, does it?" She turned her eyes up to him for reassurance.

They were pleading and not dancing. Adrian squeezed her fingers and wished he could take away the pain. He sat down beside her, still holding her hand. "It's odd, but I never gave thought to babies before the war. And during the war, I vowed I would never bring a child of mine into a world filled with hatred and violence. But now, I'm beginning to wonder if I wasn't wrong. Maybe children are the hope of the future. They are too young to know the hatred that divided this country. They can be taught to love and accept life and to reach out a helping hand. If we can teach enough children to love, wouldn't the world be a better place?"

Her hand was beginning to warm inside of his, and Camille stared at their linked fingers. His hands were strong and callused, a working man's hands, even though Emile said he was rich. They had touched her with exquisite gentleness. She had never been afraid with him. She was more afraid of herself.

She bit her lip and didn't look up. "I never thought about having babies until recently, not even when Phillipe was alive. It's just, these last few months . . ." She cast about desperately for words to explain these urges that had been obsessing her lately, but there was no polite way she could say it.

"While I was denying the need to reproduce, you were learning to crave it," he finished for her.

Startled, she stared up at him. There was almost a smile in his eyes as he looked at her. They were no longer empty, she saw now. The change was so astonishing, she almost didn't understand the significance of what he said, until he touched her cheek and the tingle went all the way to her toes. Then she knew.

She shook her head in denial. "You are saying that I am filled with the needs that you threw out. You do not truly believe there is any connection? I never knew you. You are mad." But the whole time she was denying it, she was remembering the months after the war ended, the heat of the summer, the restlessness that had overtaken her from out of nowhere, and what it had led to. And those would have been the months when he was denying that very real part of himself, the part he had given to her these last nights, and that they now shared.

"Of course it's impossible, but it's odd, isn't it? I was empty of life while you were filled with it. And then we met, and I'm alive again. Of course, if you're still unsatisfied, then my theory doesn't work, does it?"

What a damnably subtle way of putting it. She ought to smack him, just on general principles. No one should be that clever. "I think you are right," she answered decisively, before she had time to think about it. "I think we ought not to drink our tonics tonight."

He laughed and let her draw away her hand. "All right. Let us be ourselves. Will you walk in the garden in the moonlight with me?"

She stood up and waited for him to stand before her. He was a head taller, but she felt very tall herself right now. She met his gaze boldly. "I should like that very much."

Adrian let her walk away. She lifted her skirts as proudly as any princess, held her head high, and never looked back. He had all but accused her of being the wanton he had met in the woods, and she had neither denied nor affirmed his suspicions. Of course, if she wasn't the one, she must think he was crazed, but they had actually carried out an entire conversation without arguing.

It boded well for the future. Thinking of the ghostly lady and the omen she represented, he felt a surge of hope. He would very much like to have a future. He was quite certain he could make one here, if she would just let him.

He let that "she" remain anonymous, but in his heart he knew it had to be Camille. They had started out with enormous barriers between them, but something had happened, something so strange that he had no wish to classify it. He only knew those barriers were crumbling and he could see her for the woman she was. He only hoped she could see him for himself now, and not just where he came from. When she did not coat it with vinegar, Camille had a voice as soft as honey, and he could easily listen to her speak for the rest of his life. And she would be a joy to hold in his arms, whenever he could prove to her that he had that right.

Emile laughed at him when Adrian took out the stallion and rode it until they were both lathered and tired. Marguerite gave him one of her sly smiles when he came in dripping with sweat, and Esther offered to bring him a tonic while he bathed. Adrian refused the tonic, but she brought it to him anyway when the servants carried up the bathwater.

He stared at the red juice in the glass as he scrubbed himself. Hard liquor made people do things they would not do otherwise, but there wasn't enough juice in that glass to affect a head like his. Perhaps there was some way of distilling the liquor to a more potent form? But he hadn't felt the effects of alcohol the next day, even after he had consumed a bottle of bourbon along with the tonic. It couldn't be the drink. Somehow, he had just got caught up in some temporary madness. He could only pray that the outcome would be as he hoped and not end in disaster.

The tonic beckoned to him as he dressed, but a will that could deny the desire for life could deny a glass of tomato juice. He would go to Camille tonight in full possession of his senses. If the temporary madness was gone and they found they couldn't look each other in the face, he would have to think through the consequences. But for now, he couldn't believe that it would be any different between them, if Camille was the woman he had met in the woods.

Emile and Marguerite laughed and carried on a lively conversation over their meal while Camille and

Adrian cast each other furtive looks when they thought the other wasn't looking.

She was beautiful tonight, Adrian thought to himself as he watched the way the candlelight from the chandelier danced off her golden curls. She had arranged her hair in a twisted knot at the crown of her head from which several large curls dangled and danced. Her eyes were the wide violet-blue of pansies, and he could easily drown in them if he dared look long enough. Emile was casting him knowing looks, however, and he didn't dare offer more than a casual glance.

He was handsome and very masculine tonight, Camille decided as Adrian's low male voice replied to some quip of Marguerite's. His shoulders filled his coat to the straining point, although she could tell from the way it fit his waist loosely that he had lost weight since the coat had been made. The war did that to Yankees, too, she supposed. She could no longer see him in his blue uniform, swinging his sword against the man she had thought she loved. She could only see him as he had been in the pool in the moonlight, naked, with streams of water rolling down his broad chest. She didn't think she could ever think of Phillipe in that way.

Thank goodness Marguerite and Emile had other plans for the evening. She couldn't have borne sitting calmly in the parlor, sewing, waiting for them to go to bed so she could escape into the garden. As it was, she almost had nervous palpitations when Adrian caught her eye at the news they were to be left alone. She was shameless, but the desire he had taught her streaked through her in a sudden wave of heat.

She nearly ran from the room after the meal was

over. It was nearly dark outside already. She couldn't just walk out as if she were in the habit of prowling the grounds at night. For the sake of propriety, she had to retire to her room with a complaint about a headache. Marguerite frowned in concern and sent Esther for a tisane.

When the maid arrived and waited calmly for Camille to drink it, she almost panicked. Why had she used a headache as an excuse? She knew Marguerite's instant response to any complaint. She had been drinking this foul liquid for years. It had never made her crazed before. Surely it would be safe to drink tonight? Adrian had only been looking for an excuse for their strange behavior.

But she had to know. She couldn't spend the rest of her life wondering if she had given up her innocence in a fit of some kind of drunkenness. She took the cup from Esther and set it on the table.

"Thank you, Esther, I shall drink it later. The headache is almost gone."

The maid's dusky brow wrinkled in a frown. "You know your auntie wishes you to drink it all at once. The effect is not the same later."

Camille stared at the maid, wondering if she were part of this, too, if there was some insane conspiracy going on here to see her drugged and thrown into bed with the wealthy Yankee. That thought was a madness in itself. Marguerite would never do that to her.

She relaxed and smiled. "If the headache is gone, then I don't need the tisane. Thank you anyway, Esther."

Left with no other choice, the maid left. Camille could hear her talking to her aunt down the hall. With sudden decision, she barred her door, grabbed a cloak, and slipped out the window to the gallery. The tisane went untouched on the bedside table.

The drums were starting their nightly beat as she hurried along the gallery to the stairs. Excitement tripped through her veins as it had these past nights, but this time she knew what—and who—she was going to. Despite all the reservations she might hold in her mind, her heart sang as she raced down the stairs in the moonlight to meet her lover.

Her lover. How odd to think like that after a lifetime of being taught that a lady never gave away her favors. He might never marry her. He might go back north and leave her to grow big with child. She didn't care. She had an opportunity for a future again, and she was grabbing it with both hands. It had to be the moonlight that made her mad.

He was waiting for her. He stood tall and straight in the silver light between the rose beds. His dark hair brushed against his collar, and she longed to run her fingers through it. Instead, she halted uncertainly in front of him. What if he had been under the influence of too much liquor these last nights and no longer wanted her tonight?

The silver of moonlight caught on the gold of Camille's curls and the cream of her skin as she turned her face up to him. Adrian caught his breath at the beauty captured by that magic beam. His sprite had a face, then, and it was the face of the woman he loved. He reached out to wrap her in his arms, feeling how perfectly she fit into them.

"Do you believe in magic, my love?" he whispered against her hair as she pressed against his chest, her fingers curling into his coat. The scent of gardenias filled the air between them.

"Are you certain it's not madness?" She curled a little closer to him and turned haunted eyes to his strong face. "Tonight, I am terrified. I'm not certain what I'm doing here." The drums pounded, she could hear them, but she no longer had the confidence of before.

Adrian caressed her cheek with his finger. She was trembling, and he didn't want her to be frightened. He could think of only one good way to reassure her. Gently, he lowered his head to take her mouth with his.

It was magic, he was certain of it. He could feel himself fill with life just from the breath of her lips. He drank deeply, and she came more boldly into his arms, wrapping her hands behind his neck. Aware that they were visible for all to see, he carried her out of sight behind the garden wall, pressing her against the warm bricks with his body as their lips and tongues hungrily sought solace in their mixing. His hands slid inside her cloak and cupped her breasts through her bodice, and she yielded without protest, arching against him as she had these past nights, offering herself to his touch.

The drums pounded louder as he finally caught his breath and looked down at the pale oval of her face in the shadows. "Camille . . ." He didn't know how to go on. He wanted her so much that it hurt, but he didn't want to do anything to frighten her away. It was too soon. It was too strange. But he had to know that she was his. "What we have done . . ."

No that wasn't the way. He didn't want her to feel obligated. Taking a breath, he tried again. "What is between us is more beautiful than anything I have ever known. I want it to be like this always, my love.

Can you see now that it is right? We are meant for each other."

He was tall and frightening with a vivid scar on his face. He had the power to take her away from her family to a world of strangers, strangers who had destroyed the world as she knew it. He was asking the impossible. And she was touching his face, stroking his hair, and saying yes. She was insane.

But she could feel the root of him pressed against her, knew soon they would be between the sheets together, his body inside hers, and they would make babies and love in some natural order, and she could want nothing more than that this be the man who did this for her. She knew this with all the certainty of her heart as he lifted her into his arms to carry her from the garden.

And when he whispered "Marry me?" against her ear, she knew that feeling was justified.

"Please, yes," she managed to answer before his mouth swooped to take hers again.

And as the two entwining figures disappeared from the moonlight into the shadows of the house, a silvery laugh echoed from above.

Emile smiled and rubbed his hand down Marguerite's bare arm as he watched the two lovers disappear from his view in the upper story windows. "I cannot believe it. I did not think it would ever work. You must be a witch, my dear."

"You wished for a spell, did you not? You said it would take magic to save the plantation. Your friend will stay and help make this place what it was before. And Camille will be happy again. I think I have done very well."

She turned laughing eyes up to him for confirmation. Emile smiled into them, seeing the girl she had once been before the war. "You would have me believe you did this all yourself? You did not even know Adrian before he came here. I was the one who brought him here."

She laughed and smoothed his coat and her voice was as sultry as her eyes as she replied, "Men have such conceit. As if your proud friend would ever have asked for help without a little persuasion. Come darling, I am lonely, and they have made me hungry. You know your uncle would never wish me to do without."

Emile knew that as well as he knew that in the morning he would wake with aching head and smelling of smoke, but Marguerite's lips were spicy and hot and her hands worked a magic of their own, and he could deny her no more than his uncle ever could.

In a dark corner of the room, beside a puddle of red silk, a pair of eyes watched from a small doll dressed in frock coat and trousers and wearing a vivid scar down the side of its face. Beside that doll sat another with golden curls and garbed in familiar gray silk.

As Marguerite's laughter carried through the open window, the two dolls leaned together, until one entwined with the other.

In the silver beams of the moon, the resident ghosts nodded and sighed their approval, and the old house settled to the murmuring moans of midnight lovers.